Rock Bottom

Cate Masters

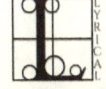

LYRICAL PRESS
Kensington Publishing Corp.
www.kensingtonbooks.com

Lyrical Press books are published by
Kensington Publishing Corp. 119 West 40th Street New York, NY 10018

All Kensington titles, imprints, and distributed lines are available at special
quantity discounts for bulk purchases for sales promotion, premiums, fund-
raising, and educational or institutional use.

Special book excerpts or customized printings can also be created to fit
specific needs. For details, write or phone the office of the Kensington
Special Sales Manager:
Kensington Publishing Corp.
119 West 40th Street
New York, NY 10018
Attn. Special Sales Department. Phone: 1-800-221-2647.

Kensington and the K logo Reg. U.S. Pat. & TM Off.
Lyrical Press and the L logo are trademarks of Kensington Publishing Corp.

First Electronic Edition: July 2011
eISBN-13: 978-1-61650-282-9
eISBN-10: 1-61650-282-7

First Print Edition: July 2011
ISBN-13: 978-1-61650-890-6
ISBN-10: 1-61650-890-6

Printed in the United States of America

Can success trap you at Rock Bottom?

For rocker Jet Trently, success means playing the same platinum-selling hits ad nauseum. Philly rock journalist Billie Prescott thrives on covering the latest music releases. When her editor sends her to Malibu to cover Jet's reality dating show, Rock Bottom, her blog's success keeps her trapped there. Her life's at Rock Bottom too, until she hears Jet's new songs. They touch her heart as his music did when she was fifteen. When Jet touches her heart as well, will the reality show ruin the real thing?

Books by Cate Masters

Rock Bottom
Twice in A Blue Moon
The Griffin's Secret

The Goddess Connection Series
Goddess Awakened

Published by Kensington Publishing Corporation

To Jerry, who showed us all how to aim for excellence.
Rock that heavenly choir!

Acknowledgements

As always, I'm indebted to my wonderful critique partners for your thoughtful and caring guidance and expertise.
To my hubby, Gary, I'd be lost without you. Blue skies ahead, babe.

Chapter 1

The laptop screen cast a pale blue-white light across the keyboard, enough to navigate the web. Billie Prescott clicked through the pages. "How perfect."

From the bedroom sounded a creak, then footsteps padded up. Strong arms encircled her waist, and a deep voice rumbled in her ear. "Porn surfing? Without me?"

Giggling, she leaned into him. "This is porn to me."

"Tree houses?" He rested his chin on her shoulder and then nudged his shirt away from her neck to nuzzle.

"For adults. Aren't they amazing?" Since reading *Robinson Crusoe* as a little girl, she'd harbored a dream to live in a life-sized house in the trees.

"Come back to bed. You're wrinkling my shirt."

His sexy growl trembled along her skin, made her yearn for what it promised. "But these are--"

He cupped her breast and squeezed.

Instinctively, she slid her hand up into his hair. "You're right. I can look at them some other time." Two years she'd waited for him. Two long years of flirting and innuendo, and a date here and there in various states of undress before finally landing him in her bed. As much as it had delighted her to awaken and see Everett sleeping beside her, she had difficulty imagining him in her dream house.

Still, she took his hand and let him lead her to the bedroom. He may or may not be her soul mate, but only a thorough investigation would reveal the truth. A long, deep, intensive investigation.

Everett excelled at intensive. For short intervals, at least.

* * * *

Billie bumped open the conference room door, dribbling coffee down her pant leg. "Ach." One reason her wardrobe consisted of black and chocolate: stains didn't show as well. Besides, her long dark hair and fair complexion never fit the summery light tones.

Around the small circular table, the staff of *Strung Out*, Philly's struggling music magazine, halted conversations to send haughty glares in her direction. Billie liked to joke *Strung Out* wanted to be *Rolling Stone* when it grew up. In her five years there, they'd lost a few staffers to the better-known and respected national competitor. More would follow if they could, if only to escape these cramped quarters and this grimy city to trendier New York, Chicago or LA. Not Billie. She liked staying closer to home. And Everett. Especially now that things had begun to get interesting.

Sliding onto a seat, she dabbed at the coffee spot. When her gaze landed on Zinta, Billie smiled and said hello. "Hey, I want to hear about that Incubus concert later. Next time they play in town, they're mine."

"Yeah. Later." Zinta's shoulder-length blond hair glinted in the morning sun, and she arched a brow. Not a good sign. Others found her a hard read, probably because of her striking features--rosebud mouth in ever-present rose-red lipstick, dark brows framing green eyes rimmed with thick lashes. But Billie picked up her friend's subtle cues: a lifted brow-flicked glance combo could spell real trouble.

Everett's glare hardened. "As I was saying…"

Billie would have to be on her best behavior. "Sorry. What'd I miss?"

He pursed his lips. "The assignments." His exaggerated diction left no doubt of his disapproval.

A knot formed in her stomach. Her editor had warned her about arriving late. Zinta had warned her about sleeping with her editor. She hadn't paid attention to either. Zin claimed his pointed dark eyebrows, onyx eyes and black hair set off by an impeccably trimmed goatee gave him a devilish appearance deserving of his reputation. Billie thought he could pass for Soundgarden's Chris Cornell in trendy business casual dress.

Rocking back in his chair, steepling his fingers to his lips, no one here would be able to guess those lips had explored every inch of her all weekend. She'd tell him later how brilliant he'd acted. Better yet, she'd demonstrate her awe. Lack of sleep may have diminished her looks, but not Everett's.

"All of the assignments?" she ventured.

"All but one." Sipping his coffee, he concentrated on his cup.

"Please tell me it's half-decent. My fact-checking call kept me, or I swear I'd have been on time." She grinned. "This time." Hopefully she could sweet-talk her way out of trouble and back into his good graces.

He drummed his fingers against the entertainment magazines strewn near his portfolio.

The top cover caught her eye. "Oh, geez. Look at him. How pathetic." She lifted it to study it.

Jet Trently, muscled arms crossed over his smooth, chiseled chest. A red bandanna wrapped across his unruly layers of sandy blond hair, the only clothing in view with the photo cropped at his hips. Scantily clad girls draped across his arms and shoulders, glistening pink lips parted as if panting.

Fifteen years ago, she'd have given anything to have been one of them. Then twenty, Jet had been one of the hottest guys on the planet. His rock ballads ruled the airwaves--and her CD player. The songs wound their way into her mind, her soul. She'd awakened singing them and fallen asleep humming them. But now, after hearing the same songs repeated ad nauseum on the radio, they grated her nerves. Though he continued to generate titillated energy among females wherever he went, Jet's attempt at a musical comeback fell flat until he'd agreed to star in a reality show tracking his revived attempt--and his love life, of all things.

Tilting the magazine to get a better view, she gave a *tsk*. "*Rock Bottom*--such an appropriate title. He needs a catapult to help him back from the depths. So is this the latest round of fawning women?" How could such an obviously popular guy have trouble finding love? He must get offers everywhere he traveled, but something about his cocky stance suggested little interest in the women pawing him. Her reporter's instincts went into overdrive as she wondered what sort of female might appeal to him, if not the contestants.

Zinta clicked her bloodred nails. A sign of nervousness. Possibly a warning sign. "They're last season's bevy of beauties."

Something about Zin's steadfast gaze unnerved Billie. She'd have to confer with her after the meeting to find out what was up. And to catch her up on the weekend. An entire weekend this time. A first for Everett. Things definitely had heated up between them. Well, until this morning.

Jet's clear blue eyes captured her attention again. "Panting over him? Or the spotlight?" Sure he looked great, but had they no self-respect? Over the years, stories of his bad boy behavior had overshadowed his music. Trashing hotel rooms, showing up late for concerts, bitter arguments with his band.

Everett leaned back, his signature cool in deep play. Very convincing how he avoided her gaze and affected a stern boss persona. "They're after both, probably."

"Ugh. When will he give up? Or at least ditch the nineties persona." The hair style, at minimum.

"When he finds true love, apparently." Wide-eyed, Zinta glanced at Everett.

Something definitely must be up. "Yeah, right." Her confidence waned.

Ryan Watts yawned. "Or another record deal. He's already gone through two wives, hasn't he?"

Francisco Perez sat forward. "One, actually, and two fiancées. And God knows how many supermodels." A tabloid addict, Frank updated the gossip blog daily, though he tended to post on trendier people than Jet.

Billie could care less about gossip, or a musician's celebrity. She lived for the music alone. "And he hasn't found true love? Shock. But no hit record for what, five years?" She let the magazine fall to the tabletop. "So all the covers--market research?"

Standing, Everett touched his fingertips to the tabletop. "And your new assignment."

"No." Fresh bands. Exciting concerts. She lived to share those with readers. Not recycled rock.

Stacking the magazines, he set them atop her blank notepad. "Yes." His emphasis lent sibilance to his response. A hiss of warning he'd stand firm in his decision.

A softer tactic seemed required. If only the others would leave, she could sway him. In more ways than one. "Please no. The guy's music sounded passable at best then, but now it's intolerable." Listening to it nonstop would be akin to music hell.

The rest of the staff made excuses about the time, their workload, anything apparently, to vacate the room. Zinta's look of pity as she exited did little to ease Billie's impending sense of doom.

Everett held the portfolio to his charcoal cotton shirt. "Anyone can write compelling stories about great music. Only you can infuse some life into this story."

As she stood, she flipped the magazine over so she wouldn't have to see Jet Trently's smug smile. "I don't think--"

"Look, Billie, I can't give you every good assignment. Besides--" He turned, his voice softening. "--if you truly despise his songs that much, this will provide just the challenge you've needed."

Challenge? "What do you mean?" She spoke slowly to convey the depth of her dismay. To dismiss her offhand posed one insult. Attacking her writing stretched the truth beyond believable.

Pausing, he tilted his head. "I didn't want to say anything in front of the others, but your writing's been a little stale lately."

"Never." Squaring her shoulders, her earlier sentimental feelings for him fell away. "I put my heart and soul into every article. Every paragraph and sentence."

His mouth turned down, the warmth faded from his eyes. His expression read: *bullshit*. Okay, so occasionally she rushed through an article to finish. Only because the magazine wouldn't hire any more staff, and Everett overloaded each reporter, trying to keep up with *Rolling Stone*.

Her mind raced. "But this is a TV series."

"Correct." He navigated past the chairs and made for the door.

Close on his heels, she followed. "Which means I can cover an episode and--"

Turning, he held open the door, all business now. "A few episodes. I want daily blog posts and a weekly article."

"Don't do this." She clutched his shirt. "You're sending me away. Why?" She spoke through rigid lips in case others watched. "Is it because of this weekend? We both had too much to drink. We can cool it for a while." The hell she would. She'd hung on for two years waiting for him. Things had finally gotten to a good point. Almost.

"Billie. C'mon. We're both professionals. This is about the magazine, not our personal lives." His overly casual tone harkened to the same one he used while escorting unwanted salespeople to the door.

Sure. Okay. Facts dropped into her brain from obscurity. She'd never actually watched the show, but… "Isn't this set on the West Coast?"

"Mmm hmm." His mouth appeared a grim line. Nothing like the soft, sensual, full lips that had kissed her and had unleashed his oh-so-talented tongue. No tongue, whatever its level of skill, had a chance in hell of escaping those tight lips.

"In California?" The smog. The traffic. The general lack of cultural amenities, sequined shows aside.

"Yep." He popped the *p*. It sounded so final.

Her throat thickened with dread. "You probably already bought my ticket, didn't you?" *Bastard*.

"No. You can do that. But make it quick. They start shooting season two the day after tomorrow. I want you there the day before."

Tomorrow, then. Mere hours to pack.

Damn. Damn damn damn. He intended to railroad her out of town. Or fly her. Inwardly cringing at the humiliation, she balled her fists and debated whether to pummel him.

Sidling closer, she played the siren card, walking her fingers up his button placket. "Are you sure--"

"Book the flight, Billie. And no five-star hotel. You'll be staying on site. Oh, and stop in to see me before you leave today." With a wink, he strode toward his office.

"Wonderful." Her life was ruined. And he couldn't be happier.

Life went from blissful to bleak in a blink.

* * * *

At her desk, she stared past the computer screen where the receipt was displayed for her flight. The one-way ticket to a hell occupied by Beautiful People. Tanned with absurdly white teeth and plastic smiles to go with their surgically enhanced bodies. Tomorrow, she'd arrive--and stand out like a crow among peacocks and cockatiels. That reminded her: she needed to check on The Black Crowes tour schedule. She seemed to recall them having an upcoming concert on the West Coast.

Zinta approached and perched on her desk. "What's up with you and Everett?"

Despite her objection, she'd act professional. Cool. Calm. "Nothing. Things are…fine." She'd reserve her bitter venom for later.

Zinta sucked air through her teeth. "Sorry."

"No, we actually reached a milestone this weekend. And I mean *all weekend*." She widened her eyes to punctuate.

"Really. But now he's sending you away?"

Ignoring her friend's incredulous look, she set her messenger bag atop her desk, wondering how much it would hold. How much her heart could hold. The situation called for positivity. "It's been casual up to this point, but I really thought we broke new barriers this weekend. So in this new relationship zone, it'll take a while to sort out the signals." If one weekend in bed counted as new. Or counted for anything. *Damn.* She'd been so sure it had.

"That mixed?" Zinta cocked her head in a way suggesting she'd nailed the problem. "He failed the litmus test?"

After unplugging the laptop, she coiled the wires. "I don't have a litmus test. Exactly."

"You showed him the tree houses, didn't you?"

Her flat tone suggested Billie didn't need to answer. Zinta already knew.

Billie stuffed the mouse into a carrier pocket. "Too much junk to pack." Evasive tactics might stall her friend.

Zinta craned down to peer her in the eye. "It's way too soon."

Billie slumped her shoulders. "I know. That should come much later. I rushed it. But he might come around." Sure, he was sending her away, but that didn't necessarily mean he didn't want a relationship. Maybe just not right now.

Standing, Zinta sighed. "Honestly, you need to revise your list of Lust Haves. Cross Everett off."

Lust Haves. Zin liked to quantify and qualify everything into lists, descriptions, categories, goals. Billie, on the other hand, accepted what came her way with gratitude. And much less organization.

"I have a feeling Everett just revised it for me." He'd topped her Lust Have list. But such incredible sex couldn't all come from lust, could it? He had to have thought about her, given her more consideration than his usual dates. Maybe even pined for her, a little.

"Aw, honey. Play it cool. Let him make the next move."

He'd forced her to, temporarily. From Philadelphia to Malibu. Talk about culture shock.

"I have no choice. He's actively avoiding me. Of course, now he won't have to." She sat and opened her desk drawer, removed her digital recorder and a few notepads and pens. Whatever she forgot, she'd buy on site and charge back to the magazine.

Zinta tapped her nails against her mug. "I can't believe he gave you that assignment. He mentioned it earlier, but I didn't think he was serious."

Zipping her laptop case, Billie tried to keep anxiety from her voice. "Yes, on an extended story. He must really want me gone." Maybe things hadn't gone as well as she'd thought.

"No." Zinta's whine matched her pout. "I need you here."

"You're the only one, apparently." Biting her lip, Billie realized the truth of the statement. Going away might provide a better perspective on her life. And what she needed to change.

* * * *

The desk appeared too neat. Freakishly so. As if she'd never again sit at it to dash off a review or interview an up-and-coming band. To remedy that, she crumpled a sheet of paper and tossed it onto the desktop. Too staged. When she removed it, her stomach clenched. Would she never occupy this place again?

After stopping by Zinta's desk for a hug, she went to Everett's office and stood in the doorway. "Guess I'm off."

"Come in. Shut the door."

Oh no. Here it came. The final kiss-off. She did as he said, and turned to face the music.

He pinned her against the door, his body all hard warmth, his tongue already probing hers. "God, you taste good." His lips curled against hers in a smile.

Ignoring the alarm bells screaming in her head, her body melded to his. "Why--"

"It'll be good for us. *Both* of us."

She let her fingers wander south of his belt buckle, and made her voice breathy and low. "Are you sure?"

Releasing a pent-up sigh, he groaned. "Yes."

Damn. So much for sexual persuasion. She could only imagine how ineffectual she'd be in California.

* * * *

Through the wispy clouds, Los Angeles sprawled below and the plane tilted into its descent. If lucky, she'd spend less than an hour in the airport, and another hour trekking south to Malibu, if the traffic gods smiled upon her. Then she could collapse on whatever cot in a closet they provided.

Now she could unequivocally state she knew how Jet Trently felt when his life began its downward trajectory. "Luck, be a lady and plummet my jet from the sky to save me from this torture."

The plane touched down with not even a bump, and Frank Sinatra crooned endlessly in her head.

No such lady. Not in California.

All for the best. Everett wouldn't have grieved at her memorial. More likely he'd have angled for solace in the arms of someone else. Someone younger. Less available. Despite his lust-filled goodbye, his eagerness for her departure shone through, leaving her more confused than ever.

After collecting her suitcase from the carousel, she wheeled it toward the exit. At least the promised heat had allowed her to pack light. A few basic black essentials she could dress up with accessories. Hope sprung eternal Everett would cut her stay short.

Outside, the sun sizzled up from the sidewalk. Even sunglasses couldn't cut the glare. The dark suit jacket had to come off. Everywhere she looked, sun, sun and more sun. Could people go mad from too much sunlight? Might be a good angle. Would account for a lot, actually.

Hailing a cab, she gave the driver the address provided by Jet's manager and spent the drive with closed eyes hidden by sunglasses. When he slowed, she cleared the haze from her brain to take in Malibu. Getting to the beachfront house required the driver to meander through a high-end neighborhood. They pulled up outside a mustard-colored plaster wall with a wrought-iron gate. The driver pressed the intercom button. A woman answered, asked them to wait while she checked for Billie's name on the list. The gate swung open.

The immense house echoed the honey-colored wall, but its Spanish-Mediterranean architecture set it apart from the other homes. A mixture of funk and class, not at all the soulless sleek beach home she'd imagined.

The driver set her luggage from the taxi's trunk on the sidewalk. "Will that be all?"

She caught the look as his gaze sidled up her thighs and rear. "Yes, definitely all." A thought struck her. "Hold on. I do need something else." Switching on the cell camera, she handed it to him. "Take a quick pic. Get as much of the house in there as possible." She waved her middle finger.

He held it at eye level, clicked, surveyed his handiwork and gave it back. "Nice."

"It'll do." All the proof she needed of her landing on the West Coast. Adding two words, *I'm here*, she forwarded it to Everett, though she still had trouble believing it herself.

Malibu. The Bu, to locals. Twenty-one miles of sand and surf and vacuous, self-absorbed celebrities like Jet Trently, looking for a *Baywatch* babe to even out the beauty quotient for photo ops.

On the upside, the stunning views would enhance her stay. The branches of the tall cypress trees behind the sprawling two-story house swayed in the breeze off the Pacific. The home's architecture invited closer inspection, though its honey-mustard plaster she could live without. Still, it would be easy to spot coming back from long walks on the beach… Yes, she might get used to coastal life.

Maybe the *L.A. Times* needed a good reporter. Hey, she could do entertainment news as well as anyone. *Isn't that why you're here?* Silencing the snide voice in her head, she shouldered her carryon bag and wheeled the other. Everett would pay for this.

She hoped it wouldn't take long to get situated. She needed to study her map and learn the lay of the land.

That brought a chuckle. She was about to meet him, wasn't she?

Well, one of them, at least.

* * * *

The guitar strings vibrated, rich with the chord Jet Trently strummed. God, he loved playing. If George Harrison made his guitar gently weep, Jet could make it scream with pleasure, sigh or talk badass. Probably why his name frequently listed with Eric Clapton and Eddie Van Halen as the world's best.

"Jet?" his manager called. "It's time."

Shit. Already? One of the dangers of playing. Music carried him to a beautiful place devoid of time where no stress existed. No reality.

And definitely no reality TV. Why the hell had he signed on for another season of torture? He was no actor. Yeah, so reality TV didn't require him to be, but dealing with those crazy women they lined up definitely did. He didn't know if he could muster the necessary enthusiasm for another few months. At the end of the last season, he'd been so relieved he could've gone on a real binge.

But no, he wasn't going there again. Jeff had taught him that much. He owed his brother for saving him twice: once from the crappy New Jersey town they'd grown up in, and from becoming a total cliché, living the supposed rock star high life. At thirty-five, he wanted more than a quick lay. Was he expecting to find it in any of the season two beauties? Hell no. This gig gave him a steady paycheck and put his face out in front of the public. Reminded them who he was. How great his music had been.

Been. Yeah. Could be again. The few tunes he'd worked up this past year were crap. But workable crap. Each needed that elusive something. The indefinable quality that grabbed listeners and wouldn't let go.

Every time he thought he almost had it, the melody eluded him again. He could practically hear his muse laughing. Like she'd taken off for Tijuana on a drunken binge and he couldn't bribe her to come back.

"Jet."

"Coming." Reluctantly, he propped his guitar against the sofa, stretched up to a standing position and closed his eyes. *You can do this. A few more months, then you're home free.*

Man, how good did that sound?

Descending the steps, he steeled himself. *There's no such thing.*

* * * *

Wheeling her luggage up the flagstone walkway, Billie halted at the glass-enclosed foyer and pressed the doorbell.

The grapevine wreath on the leaded glass front door didn't exactly scream rock star's house. Odd, since the long drive and walled property would discourage drive-bys and paparazzi. Anyone wanting to spy would first need to clear the spike-topped iron fence.

A short, frumpish figure appeared through the thick glass, and the door opened. A woman, probably close to Billie's age, peered through black-rimmed glasses perched on her nose, blond hair pulled back in a barrette. "Yes?" Her mouth puckered tight, the only indication of impatience on her otherwise blank face.

"Hi, I'm Billie Prescott from *Strung Out*. Here to see Stu Gilbert." According to Everett, the manager's goofball persona hid a shrewd businessman. *Don't anger Stu*, he'd warned. *He'll cut you loose before you know what's happened.* She'd sworn she'd be on her best behavior. If Stu cut her loose, Everett might be tempted to do the same. If he hadn't already.

"Right. He's expecting you. Follow me." Spinning on her heel, she glided noiselessly across the Spanish tile foyer. A feat, given the unevenness of the golden-red flooring, which continued into the hallway.

Hauling her case inside, she set it beside the golden wall, which had a mottled parchment-like finish. A faded gold chandelier hung regally over the wide space that opened to a spacious living room on the left and a large dining room to the right. In the center of the hall, a blond-wood staircase invited her gaze to the second floor landing, generously lit by the same floor-to-ceiling windows the first floor had. The embossed copper ceiling caught her eye as she walked. The house had character, if no one living in it did.

"I'll have someone move your luggage when we know where they're putting you. I'm Cindy, by the way. Stu's assistant. Check with me if you need anything. Your timing's good--Stu and Jet are meeting with the producer in the office. Go on in." She nodded toward a closed door at the end of the hall opposite a narrow desk where she took a seat.

Maybe she'd needed to come west after all, if only to adjust her timing. "Thanks."

The office--if it could be called one--continued the golden color scheme, highlighted by the same stunning copper ceiling. A white stone fireplace dominated the opposite wall, with a quilted English sofa to one side and a matching quilted daybed on the other, separated by twin coffee tables. Behind the daybed stood double French doors topped with arched windows to the ceiling and framed by billowing white floor-length curtains. The doors stood open to a view of the rocky bluff. Beyond, the endless Pacific Ocean glittered in the late-afternoon sun.

After slipping inside, she approached the cluster of men standing at its center.

Dressed in tight jeans and a snug black t-shirt, Jet Trently laughed as he spoke, his too-white teeth flashing. His presence injected an undeniable energy into the room. It sizzled along her nerve endings when he looked her way, electrified by his crystal blue eyes.

A man turned at her approach. "Miss, we're having a meeting. Check in with my executive assistant." Stu Gilbert. More like one of the Three

Stooges with his wiry hair and bulbous nose. A disco version with two gold chains revealed by his half-unbuttoned shirt, heavy man-rings decorating his pudgy fingers.

Impatience had edged his tone. He thought her an intruder.

Billie affected a sharp business tone. "Already did. I'm Billie Prescott from *Strung Out*. My editor spoke with Mr. Gilbert about covering the show?"

Jet's eyes widened. "*You're* Billie Prescott?"

Billie had a feeling she'd just made Jet's Lust Have list, though she had no doubt the list, if printed, would require reams of paper. If he licked his lips, she'd be out of there before he could retract his tongue. "You're expecting me, aren't you?"

"Billie Prescott, yes. You--no." His appreciative gaze wandered the length of her.

The trio chuckled in unison.

Like she didn't get that same response every freakin' time. Biting back a snide reply, she forced out, "Do you have an information packet for me? Something that will help me catch up on where season one ended?"

Stu glanced at Jet. "Cindy can put something together."

Jet tilted his head. "Not a fan, eh?"

If she didn't know better, she'd think he appeared pleased.

Wrinkling her nose, she grinned. Let that be answer enough.

"Pity you weren't a contestant." He arched a brow and turned to the third man. "Now there's an idea."

Shaking his head, the man winced. "No." He slid his hands in the back pockets of his khaki Dockers, wrinkled like his faded denim shirt. The producer, had to be.

"What?" She'd missed something.

"It's perfect--an insider's perspective." Again Jet's gaze meandered across her. "I could make it worth the magazine's while."

Ugh. Now she understood. "No. I'm a journalist, not a reality show contestant."

He hunched his shoulders, not quite a shrug. "It's a fresh angle."

"Not if I can't stay objective. Journalists can never allow ourselves to become part of the story. I'll get a much better, um, perspective from staying neutral."

Jet's grin widened. "Neutral's no fun."

Time to move this conversation along to a new topic. "It gives me the big picture, which is what I'm after." *All* I'm after, she stopped herself from adding. No way would she ever join a pack of feral females to compete for one guy. Especially a shallow has-been like Jet Trently. She had zero respect for an artist who let his talents go to waste.

Though he did have amazing eyes. She'd give him that. And an incendiary presence. He'd toned up since she'd last seen him in concert six years ago when he'd sported the beginnings of a paunch. It had gone along with the DUI charge or two, plus busting up a few hotel rooms. Had he checked into rehab after? She'd have to research it.

"So? What'd I miss?" The phrase would be her epitaph if she weren't careful. At least she'd caught them during their meeting.

Stu reached for a folder on the table and thrust it in her direction. "Here's a schedule. We start shooting tomorrow at one."

Jet groaned. "Couldn't we make it three? Or four?"

Adopting the condescending tone of a parent, Stu asked, "You don't have a concert tonight, do you?"

Hugging his arms to his chest, Jet widened his stance. The stubborn child. "No but--"

The third man heaved a sigh. "Your contract states--"

"My contract states the show's about me. And I'm not at my best at one." Though Jet smiled, the tone of authority in his voice warned against trifling with him.

Hmm. Maybe the show should've been named *Jet Trently: Center of the Universe*.

Narrowing his eyes, Stu smiled. "All right. Two thirty. I don't suppose it will hurt the girls to wait a while. Might make for some interesting onscreen tension. But you'd better be on set, ready to go, no later than that."

"Oh, I'll be ready. And I live 'on set,' remember?" Jet glared.

Speaking of tension... Fishing out a pen, she jotted some notes, hoping to appear inconspicuous, but feeling the group tense. As the outsider, she had to be careful not to alarm them, put them on guard. Or she'd miss all the good stuff.

She slid the notepad behind her. "So nothing going on tonight? No pre-show parties?"

Jet sidled near. "There's always a party. I'm looking forward to you joining us."

Shoving his hand between her and Jet, Stu effectively blocked him. "We haven't been formally introduced. Stu Gilbert, Jet's manager. No parties tonight. Tomorrow's the first shooting day. We want to be fresh, don't we, Jet?"

"We certainly do. Fresh as can be." His gaze crawled across her to punctuate the double entendre.

Billie's skin crawled, though not uncomfortably. She could almost imagine his hands caressing her instead of his gaze. Perhaps steroids had become part of his daily regimen. If only she weren't the sole female in the room, she'd escape his intense attention. It brought out some animal instinct against her will. As if his testosterone piqued her pheromones to life.

Shifting to relieve her discomfort, she focused on Stu. "Can I connect with any of the girls before tomorrow?"

"Not likely. Half haven't checked in yet. They'll arrive as a group tomorrow. Makes for a dramatic entrance." Rubbing his hands together, Stu's enthusiasm contrasted Jet's disinterest.

"How many--"

Pointedly, Stu glanced at the folder. "All in the packet." Turning, he slung his arm around Jet's shoulder and steered him toward the door, murmuring.

Smiling, Jet glanced back and winked.

She'd almost forgotten. "Wait--where can I bunk?"

Jet broke away from Stu. "With me, if you like."

His manager steered him to the hall. "Cindy'll take care of you."

Shuddering, alarm bells went off in Billie's head in realization of her instinct to take Jet up on the offer. She had enough problems without Jet Trently adding to them. And no matter how re-energized, his libido wouldn't impress her into sparkling reviews of praise.

Oh no. She'd developed an immunity to rock stars years ago.

Chapter 2

He couldn't stop staring. Rude, yeah, but something about her got to him. Like the second she'd walked in. Bam, straight to his core.

"Did you know about her?" he asked Stu.

His manager tugged him along the hallway. "What about her?"

"Being female. When you said Billie Prescott, she is not what I imagined." The best he'd hoped for was someone new, a fresh face. Someone to hang with, drink a beer, talk about music. Life. Women.

Forget that.

As they continued outside, Stu droned on about the schedule, other stuff Jet could care less about. Stu had a good head for details, but didn't work as hard as he pretended to.

Every so often, Jet interjected a grunt or nod so his manager would think he listened. Or gave a shit.

With Jeff gone, he hadn't talked to anyone about things that mattered. Issues. Opinions. He knew better than to bring his new songs to the band. They'd grown so lazy, they were fine with being pigeonholed as Jet, the once-great band.

No one gave him an honest opinion, anyway.

Stu's elbow connected with Jet's side. "Why the long face?"

"Ah. You know. All this."

"What, you're depressed because you'll have gorgeous girls hanging on your every word again?" He gave a false wince. "Come on."

"Yeah, it's great. Really. But it would be nice, just once, to find someone--" He shrugged. "--to talk to, all right? For once, it would be nice to feel the passion in my lyrics for a girl who's beautiful and intelligent."

"You want the package deal, eh? Forget it. You don't want someone who understands you. She'd blow your whole mystique."

He blew raspberries. "I'm just a guy, Stu. It's not impossible--look at McCartney. He's miserable without Linda. Or..." He cast about for another example of a successful long-term marriage.

"The public loves Jet Trently--rock star. Not Jerry Trently from New Jersey. Anyway, rock stars aren't supposed to find real love, or their muses become jealous and abandon them."

"Right." He should've known better than to broach this subject with Stu. Divorced three times himself, Stu had no idea how to talk to anyone without an angle. Blowing smoke up asses was Stu's specialty, his talent. He couldn't set it aside if he tried.

"Look, you made it into your thirties. You're healthy, and thanks to me, wealthy. You have millions of fans. Women throw themselves at you, would leave their husbands for you. What the fuck are you complaining about?" His mouth curled in disgust. Probably because he wished he could change places.

"Nothing. You're right." He blew out a breath and lied, "Just nervous about this next round, I guess." Especially after reading the contestants' bios. They might well have been the same as last time, for all he knew.

"No worries, bro. You'll knock 'em dead like always." Stu winked. "I have to check in, make sure everything's set up in the edit room. My work is never done."

"You're the man." Such phrases placated Stu. Got him off his back.

"Catch you later." Stu stepped inside and closed the door.

Jet stood there, a trickle of sweat reminding him to get out of the hot sun. But to where? His studio? He could practice, he guessed. Or work on the song that had been nagging at him.

Or go back in the house. Where Billie was.

Hit the studio, man. Yeah, probably should.

Having another woman around didn't raise his expectations for real conversation. Most women told him what they thought he wanted to hear. Season one gave him his fill. It was like falling into pheromone quicksand. Almost cozy at first, then it closed in tight, squeezed away his breath and left him nowhere to turn.

And now there was one more to deal with. Billie Prescott. A reporter, to boot--someone he could never speak to without selecting his words carefully. Guarding against misquotes or misconceptions. Mis-whatever.

He couldn't deny she made a hell of a first impression. Something in the way she looked at him contradicted her screw-you attitude. Ah, shit. With women, it was always the same. Some sort of con to gain a foothold. They all wanted something he couldn't give. Total devotion. He gave all to his music. Girls provided inspiration, for a while. None had ever gotten to him the way his songs made him think they should. He'd never fallen in love like that. Probably never would.

Still, maybe he should go check on Billie. Make sure she had everything she needed.

* * * *

At Cindy's summoning via walkie-talkie, a man in a polo bearing the *Rock Bottom* logo begrudgingly dragged Billie's luggage through the dining room to the spacious eat-in kitchen beyond. She followed him out the French doors to the patio. Between the doors stood an outdoor fireplace, its mustard-hued chimney flanked by tall concrete pineapple statuary. In front, cushioned seating around a low coffee table, then two oversized chaise lounges with matching umbrellas sat atop an outdoor rug.

"Because they can't decide whether to tan or not?" she joked to her unhappy valet.

"If they're anything like the last batch, it'll be the least of what they can't decide."

Foreboding words, if she'd ever heard them. She followed her guide down a wide stretch of patio leading to the ceramic-tiled pool. Beyond the pool, eight woven wicker chairs surrounded a teak oval table canopied by tree branches. She could only imagine what those gatherings must be like. Jet holding court over contestants, the glow of candlelight not softening their glares at one another through the overflowing flower centerpiece.

Past the cabana at the far end of the pool, the flagstone patio funneled into a walkway lined with shrubbery. At the back of the cabana, a door stood open, and two guys wearing identical polos worked at a long table loaded with equipment.

Slowing, she asked, "What's that?"

The guy glanced over. "An ad hoc editing room."

"Cool. Could I check that out later?"

"Check with Cindy." He veered off onto a side path leading to a small cottage. From there, the walkway wound around and out of sight.

Unlocking the door, he set her suitcase inside the door and handed her the key. "Cindy said to let her know if you needed anything else."

"Thanks." The way it sounded, Cindy could be her best friend here, or her worst stumbling block. The gatekeeper to Stu, who controlled access to Jet.

The cottage appeared tiny from the outside, but actually had two stories if the bedroom loft counted. A boomerang-shaped overstuffed sofa dominated the main floor, and cabinets topped with bookshelves lined either wall. In a small nook sat a ceramic-topped iron bistro table and two chairs.

As cozy as a beach getaway.

She swung her carryon bag atop the tufted ottoman. Turning to retrieve her suitcases, she stopped short.

Jet leaned against the doorway. If his presence had been palpable in the house, he overwhelmed this small space.

His lopsided smile appeared almost shy. "Need any help settling in?"

The personal touch. If he hoped to make it literal, he could forget it. Despite her resolve, she found him overwhelmingly distracting. She had trouble recalling what she'd planned to do.

Glancing around, she thought she'd be pretty pathetic if she claimed to need help. "Nope, I think I can find everything."

Stepping inside, he closed the door and moved toward her slowly. Purposefully.

Her pulse quickening, she tensed, but couldn't find her voice to ask what he wanted.

He touched the cabinet. "There's a small fridge under here. I'll have Cindy stock it for you."

Nodding, she tucked her hair behind her ear. "Great. Thanks." She felt sure he must hear her heart pounding. And think her an idiot. "It's an adorable little place. You're saving the magazine a bundle by letting me stay here."

When he moved closer, his crystal blue eyes felt like a laser piercing her own.

To clear her head, she turned away. "It's situated perfectly too. Right next to the house." Could she possibly sound any more brainless?

She sensed him directly behind her. His soft tone made her muscles go fluid. Her eyes drifted shut, imagining his famous voice singing to her alone.

"If you look out your bedroom window, you can see into mine. Right over there." His arm lifted beside her and pointed.

His warmth penetrated her skin. He smelled like ocean and musk. An impulse struck her to guide his arm around her, fit herself against him. Fill her senses with him.

Snapping to reality, she fumed at his flirting, but made her voice sweet as honey. "Oh, over there? I appreciate you telling me." Smiling, she turned. "I'll be sure to keep my curtains closed."

Tensing, he straightened, and his nostrils flared.

Her muscles drew taut in response. *You shouldn't have made him mad--not the first day.*

But his eyes crinkled at the corners, and he cocked his jaw and nodded. "Billie Prescott." He said her name with a kind of wonder.

Not quite knowing what to make of it, she gave a giddy laugh. And wanted to die. "Jet Trently. We finally meet." As though she'd been waiting. Or it had been prearranged. By whom? The universe?

To recover her composure, she went to her bag and pulled out her laptop. "Any internet connection in here?"

He flopped onto the sofa and extended his arms across the back. "Wireless, pretty much from everywhere." With a kind of amused curiosity, he watched her. "We need to talk."

Her mind blanked. The way he spoke sounded so intimate, as if he wanted to discuss their relationship. His gaze seared into her, and she had trouble remembering they had no relationship. "About what?"

His mouth curled into a smile. "The show. Don't you want to interview me?"

She felt her face flush. He played a cat and mouse game. And he'd trapped her already. "Yeah, absolutely. I need to review the materials to get some notes together first." And her head. She couldn't let him mess with her mind any further. She'd come to do a story. And she intended to make it great. Get it over with, so she could go home.

He leaned forward, elbows on his knees. "I could give you the grand tour."

"Yes, great." Damn, his intense focus wiped clean her slate of thought. She stepped away to retrieve some semblance of dignity. "But what about the cameras? I have to be invisible. I'm not part of any of this."

He rose slowly. "The show doesn't start until tomorrow."

"Right." She must be making one hell of an impression. Stu would regale Everett with her complete idiocy. Maybe the flight had dehydrated her. Or the time difference had thrown her off balance. "Could I see the kitchen first? I'm really thirsty. My day started at four thirty this morning Eastern."

"Sorry. Why didn't you say something? Did you come straight from the airport?"

"Yes, I didn't think the driver would want to stop along the way, even if I offered to buy him a drink." Ah. The return of the old Billie. The girl not impressed by rock stars. Not starstruck like some teenage fan.

He went to open the door and inclined his head toward the outside. "Let's go raid the fridge."

"Are you sure you have time?" What, like he needed to study a script? All he had to do tomorrow, it seemed, was roll out of bed on time.

"Absolutely."

Egotistical, but also a gentleman. Interesting combo.

Grabbing her messenger bag containing the essential digital camera and recorder, she followed him back the way she'd come. Much nicer walking beside Jet than following the *Rock Bottom* worker. Jet made eye contact when he spoke. Strolled along as if he enjoyed her company.

He kept the conversation going. "So you're from Philly?"

A true marketing pro, pretending interest in her life.

"Yes. Pennsylvania born and bred." God, she made herself sound like a crop of corn. "Where are you from?"

"Jersey, mostly. Though my dad lived in Philly, so we split our time with him."

"That must have been tough. Do you have brothers and sisters?" The instant she said it, regret snapped her attention to him.

"A sister. My brother, Jeff, died a few years ago." A catch in his voice, then he flashed a smile, though his pain still came through.

"That's right. I'm so sorry." The news came to mind then: the death of Jet's brother, the lead guitarist, had nearly destroyed the band, already almost lost in obscurity. Then Jet launched the group anew, though Chalmer Freeburn, Jeff's replacement, caused immediate friction within the band. The media couldn't get enough news about his wild partying. Onstage, Chalmer's presence loomed as strong as Jet's, and his searing guitar licks sometimes overshadowed Jet. With the public's interest renewed, Jet's musical career slid back on track. Or rather, back into the same tired old track. "That must have been terrible for you."

He paused at the door, his expression unreadable. Surprise? Wariness? Pushing open the door, he gestured. "To the right."

She knew when to drop a subject. Jet obviously drew the line at discussing his family. Surprising for someone who'd made every move of his personal life open for public discussion. Good for him. Some celebrities didn't know when to keep the public out of their lives.

On her earlier walk through, she hadn't noticed the state-of-the-art kitchen. "Do you cook?" Or did anyone, she wondered. Such a waste of sleek, overpriced appliances--for show only. Like everything in the place. Especially the people.

He shrugged. "I've been known to scramble a mean egg. Not much beyond that." Opening the refrigerator, he bent to look inside and named the contents. "Or I have these mini bottles of wine--a nice Riesling. Want to try one?"

"That sounds nice. To take the edge off my frazzled nerves."

He popped open two and clinked his bottle against hers. "Cheers." He leaned an elbow against the counter.

She didn't mind the unhurried nature of the tour. A nice contrast to her nonstop rush of a day.

When her phone buzzed, she slid it from her pocket. Everett texted: *Glad you arrived safe and sound. Looking forward to news from the West Coast.*

Erasing it, she could almost taste her bitterness. *Right. I miss you too.*

"Boyfriend?" Jet renewed his intense focus.

She dropped the phone in her bag where she'd be less likely to hear it. "No. My editor checking in. Sometimes I loathe the person who invented cell phones. Not a moment's peace."

"Part of the biz we're in, I guess."

"Speaking of which..." From her bag, she pulled the Canon Rebel. "Do you mind if I get some still shots for the blog?"

"Not at all. The house has been filmed so many times I'm surprised people aren't tired of it."

"Not at the start of a new season. People can't get enough." Other people, not her. She couldn't admit to the star of *Rock Bottom* she hated reality shows, thought them a total bore.

He made a noise of acknowledgment, the sound of a thought held back.

"That doesn't thrill you, huh?" Curiosity piqued her interest, and she leaned on the counter beside him.

"Oh yeah. I'm happy people want to watch the show." Straightening, he gestured. "Shall we?"

"Yes." Following him through the dining room, she let the subject drop. Whatever his thought, he obviously had no intention of sharing it. She'd have to make him feel at ease again. "Amazing house." Snapping random photos, she couldn't imagine wanting to purchase such a monstrosity, but he probably needed something this large to house his reportedly oversized ego.

"Isn't it? The architecture's 1930s, tweaked by a designer to modernize it. We'd planned to set the show in LA, but someone told me about this place."

"You bought this place specifically for *Rock Bottom*?" She aimed the camera at him.

He leaned against the back of a chair, legs crossed, and aimed those amazing blue eyes at her. Snapping a few shots, she thought his smoldering gaze might melt the lens, but had the odd sensation he looked beyond the camera--to her.

Strolling into the hallway, he continued, "Actually it's a rental. A little large for my taste, but the additional rooms come in handy for the girls to stay in."

Ah yes. The girls. His personal harem. A good reminder not to get too caught up in the Jet mystique.

To keep the casual conversation flowing, she asked, "What sort of house do you prefer, if not one like this?"

He flashed a wry smile. "Something cozier, less flashy. I always thought McCartney had the right idea, living in a small house where the entire family had to watch TV in the same room."

Her breath caught in her throat. "You have kids?" She hadn't heard that. Maybe he'd kept them secret. She gripped the camera more tightly, awaiting his response.

"Not yet. I hope to someday."

Whatever knot twisted inside her released. Instinctively, her palm went to her belly. What did she care if he had kids? "Ah, after you find your soul mate."

His voice thickened. "Ideally, yes."

Surprise made her turn. Her open mouth clamped shut when she realized the emotion he struggled to restrain seemed to be amusement, not yearning.

Grinning, he leaned in. "What about you?"

He had a way of zeroing in on her, catching her off guard. "Sorry?"

"Any kids?" His casual tone conflicted with his sharp gaze.

She turned away, pretending interest in the abstract painting hanging over the dining room credenza, red squares within other red squares, echoing like a tunnel. "No."

He moved behind her. "Don't want them?"

The space between them crackled to life like a science experiment. If she touched him, she felt sure the resulting zap would have damaging consequences to her psyche. She stepped away. "Yes. But not now."

Following, he asked softly, "When you find your soul mate?"

A blush burned her cheeks. "Let's stick with you, shall we?"

"You're more interesting."

Did he always pursue women so relentlessly? Probably her lack of interest made her seem more interesting to him.

"Can you turn it off, at least for the interview?" It came out more sharply than she'd intended, and she ducked her head.

"My charm? Sorry, it's natural." He smirked.

"Mmm." Her noncommittal grunt neither confirmed nor denied it. If pressed, she'd admit he had charm--but not to him, of course. For Billie, a man's charm diminished when overshadowed by ego. Someone should school Jet in the *less is more* concept. Though right now, she needed more space between them to clear her head.

* * * *

Following her, Jet chuckled to himself. Billie Prescott was not what he expected in any sense. Female. Smart. A little shy--cute, he hadn't run up against a shy girl in a while. Even cuter, she tried to hide it by acting tough. Despite the act, she had another quality he hadn't come across in too long. She was genuine. Grounded. She knew what she wanted, apparently, and wasn't easily impressed. Because of that, he found he could relax. It felt good. So good, he wanted to keep teasing her.

In the front hall, she touched the banister. "I think I've seen most of the first floor. Can we go upstairs?"

"I thought you'd never ask," he murmured near her ear. His hand grazed the small of her back.

She stiffened at his touch. Adjusting the strap of her bag, she ascended the steps.

Huh. Not the usual reaction. A contestant would have draped herself around him and pulled him down to the steps. "Would you like me to carry that? It looks heavy."

"I'm used to it. But thanks." Her look of surprise disappeared and she started upstairs again. "So all the contestants stay here while you're taping the show? How many to start?"

Okay. Strictly business. So be it. "Six. They stay in these three bedrooms." He jogged to the top of the steps and swung to the right.

This house fit the show. Each bedroom held two double beds, two vanities and had its own small bathroom. Less for the women to share, so presumably less to fuss about. Or so he'd thought.

As they strolled past, Billie shot some pics. "Nice. So where do you stay?"

He held back a grin at her formality. "On the other side." He walked past the stairway and opened the first door. "This is a getaway space. To read, whatever."

Her gaze took in the L-shaped overstuffed sofa facing the French door to the balcony to the staircase winding to the first floor.

"Read?" She bit her lip as if realizing her insult.

Too late. No retractions. He pursed his lips. "Yeah. Sometimes I even read *Strung Out*."

A faint blush tinged her cheeks. "Where does that lead?" She nodded toward the stairs.

"To the downstairs office, where we first met." He opened the door behind him. "Through here is my room."

Taking in the view, she caught her breath.

Almost the same reaction he'd first had at seeing the three sets of double French doors that opened to the balcony, framed by the branches of the towering Cypress trees. Beyond, a rocky bluff, where ocean waves crashed and exploded upward like a geyser.

"It's incredible. Almost like a tree house."

He turned to her. "Exactly. That's what I thought the first time I saw it." He eased past her. "Sometimes I spot dolphins playing in the waves, or a whale in the distance. It's really something."

"I can only imagine." Delight filled her face.

His gaze steadied on hers. Something in her look reached inside him, and unearthed a deep yearning in need of release. He could swear she felt it too.

Abruptly, she turned away. Faced with the four-poster bed, she stammered, "Nice… fireplace."

The mantle sat beside the bed. She strode past the loveseat and coffee table near the balcony, then turned toward the alcove. "What's down there?"

"Bathroom." He affected a bored tone.

After taking a few shots, she strolled through. At the entrance, she halted and laughed breathlessly. "Are you kidding? This is amazing too."

One of his favorite rooms. Golden-red Mexican tile spanned the floor. To one side, a walk-in shower, bordered by a wide picture window. Weathered white stone climbed half the adjoining walls, topped by a botanical print wallpaper.

To the left stood a double-sink vanity encrusted with seashells. She ran her fingers along their whorls and curves.

He leaned on the doorjamb. "Pretty cool, huh? According to the realtor, the former owner collected those shells."

"Nice touch."

"Yes." Nicer if he could give her a demonstration of the shower.

She stood at her full height, eye level with him. "So this concludes the tour, I guess?"

"It usually ends up here, yeah."

Her eyes glazed over. "Fascinating. But I should get back to my room and settle in. What time is it?"

He shrugged. "Six thirty? Seven?"

"No wonder I'm starving. Do any local places deliver here?"

Wincing, he straightened. "Takeout? No, I'll take you to dinner."

"No, I can't let you."

"Come on, there's a great sushi place not far from here. You need to re-energize and unwind."

After a beat, she agreed. "All right. But it's on me."

"No." He laid a hand on her arm.

She grasped his shirt. "Yes. *Strung Out* will pay."

Shifting his hips, he eased closer. "Since you put it that way. It's a date."

A fleeting look of horror crossed her face. Releasing him, she stepped back. "No. It's an interview, or the magazine won't cover it."

Pretending surrender, he clucked his tongue, but he was the one who'd won. "You drive a tough bargain." He wished more women would challenge him once in a while. For now, he'd enjoy the company of Ms. Billie Prescott.

* * * *

Billie let herself relax when the hostess seated them in the noisy front room. Her fears of Jet's public appearance causing a stir proved unfounded. At least three other major celebrities sat in the restaurant with a few minor stars forming a less impressive constellation. No one would bother them during dinner.

Ordering the sushi, Jet recommended it to Billie, and appeared pleased when she followed his recommendation. The waiter returned with the bottle of wine and poured.

Raising her glass, she toasted. "To *Rock Bottom*."

"Cheers."

Odd he didn't echo her toast. Had season one stripped the luster from his quest to find love?

"So what happened to the first set of contestants?"

His smile appeared forced. "They went on to lead their lives, relatively unscathed by their short association with me."

He probably intended for his self-deprecating humor to deflect her questions. "I didn't mean--"

"Cindy could tell you their last known contact info if you need it."

Actually, she hadn't thought of it, but not a bad idea. "Throughout the show, you put them through their paces, so to speak, and eliminate a girl every other week?"

"That's one way of putting it."

"The final contestant--what happened to her?"

With a shrug, he sat back.

The waiter delivered their food, refreshed their wine and left.

Jet's sudden coyness wouldn't deter her. Still, she inflected a casual tone to make it seem like conversation rather than an interrogation. "She apparently isn't your soul mate, but did you date for a while after the show ended?"

Averting his gaze, his mouth turned down. "A while, yes."

"What happened?"

"She moved on." He clammed up tighter than the sushi roll he put between his lips.

Nice lips, she noted. Not too full or too thin. Too bad so many other mouths had tasted them.

Again, her train of thought had veered off track and she struggled to regain it. "To where?"

"Another reality show. Tanya's a serial contestant. If a new show's proposed, Tanya will be in line ready to compete."

"So her interest centered on merely participating, and not in having a relationship with you?" At his noncommittal shrug, she probed further. "Don't you screen the contestants ahead of time?"

His chest swelled with a deep breath, and his nostrils flared. Oops. Must have touched a nerve.

She sat back. Body language for *I'm not here to cut you open*, even though she hoped to do exactly that. Metaphorically. "Sorry, I'm trying to get a feel for the mechanics of the show."

With a quick glance, his blue eyes appeared laser sharp. "We altered it for this season."

Ah, progress. An in, however vague. Nodding, she sipped her wine. "How will this year differ from last?"

"Throwing people together in a social setting doesn't allow them to get to know each other. Not in important ways."

Maybe her brain still circled waiting to land, but she couldn't follow. "So you didn't get to know the contestants by dating them?"

"To a degree, sure. But this year, we're including other... activities."

Besides making out? She forced a straight face. "Such as?"

"Things I like. It's the only way to know if I'm compatible with someone."

"But what sort of activities?"

His voice turned teasing. "You haven't read your packet, have you?"

"I haven't had a chance." *I've been with you*, she wanted to say. It now struck her as odd. They'd been together practically every minute since meeting. Talking as easily as friends.

Jet's gaze swept her face. "Mmm."

The grunt somehow had an underlying meaning.

"Stop doing that." The words slipped across her tongue before she could trap them.

His eyes crinkled in amusement.

So unprofessional. Shame crept over her. "Sorry. I--"

"--don't travel well, I know." He reached across the table and his hand enveloped hers.

His warmth sent a buzz of energy along her nerves. "Thanks for remembering." Captured in his gaze, she felt the bustling restaurant around them fall away.

Until the waiter reappeared and asked if they needed anything else.

Sliding her hand away, she fidgeted with her napkin. What the hell was wrong with her today?

"Dessert?" Jet sounded as casual as a business associate.

Sipping her wine, Billie declined. "I'm sorry, my nerves really are frazzled. I'm exhausted from the trip." Though saying it made her realize she felt fine. Good, in fact.

"We'll continue the interview some other time. Don't worry, I won't tell your boss."

Everett. She hadn't thought of him in hours. That felt good too.

"You're very generous."

He held her gaze. "Only with people I like."

Her insides tightened as if drawn up along a tether toward Jet. Compliments flowed freely, she reminded herself, because he had schooled himself in self-marketing. People in power extended grace. Every bit as much as flexing his muscles, it was a show of machismo. She'd have to be very careful around him. In many ways.

Forcing her focus out the window allowed her to clear her head. "What a shame the windows don't face the sunset."

"Contrary to popular belief, most of Malibu faces south, not west. I think that's why there are so many windows in my house. The colors of the sunset permeate the house, light up the walls. But next time, I'll take you to the Sunset Restaurant."

Her breath hitched in her chest. Next time?

He signaled the waiter, oblivious to her stare.

An offhand remark, obviously meaningless.

They drove back to the house, the sky a multicolored light show.

Driving down his street, he glanced over. "It's a shame you're so tired. It's a great night for a walk along the beach."

Unable to admit her inexplicable second wind, she shrugged. "I could handle a walk."

Arching his brows, he smiled. "Well, all right. We'll make a traveler out of you yet."

Unconsciously, her grip tightened around her bag. She hadn't intended to stay long enough for him to make anything of her.

He hit the gas and sped past the gate. "We have to go down a mile or so. The bluff behind the house is useful for keeping people out, but it's a little too high to climb down." He pulled off the road. "If you want, I can stash that bag. Unless you want to lug it around."

"That would be great." Before handing it over, she decided to bring the camera. Such a gorgeous sunset might make for a great shot, all the better if she could work Jet into it. The more photos she snapped for the blog the less she'd have to write. Tonight, her initial post would say something like: The Bu. Anything more might come out as gibberish.

He climbed out, lifted the locker lid behind the seat and stowed her bag.

She'd unlatched her seat belt and was reaching for the handle when the door opened.

Smiling, Jet waited.

They crossed a short expanse of brush to the sand. The warm, salty breeze wafted over her, filled her senses. Better than the Jersey shore, she had to admit.

"So how do you like living in Malibu?"

He wrinkled his nose, his aviator sunglasses hiding his eyes. "It's nice."

"So enthusiastic," she chided.

Chuckling, he jammed his hands in his pockets as he strolled. "It just doesn't feel like home. Occupational hazard, I guess. Not many places do."

"What about your sister? Did she settle anywhere, or is she a drifter too?"

He gazed to the horizon.

"Sorry, if family's off-limits, I won't write about them."

"I'd prefer if you didn't."

She nodded. "I won't."

"Off the record…it's another reason I wanted the show to be based here. She lives less than an hour away, so when there's any downtime, I'll be able to visit."

"Nice."

His protectiveness touched her. So many things about him surprised her. For a rocker, he seemed surprisingly down to earth. Authentic, like his earlier music.

"I remember going to see you play many years ago. Even then I was struck by the quality of your sound. Not overwhelming like some bands who crank up the speakers to blast the audience from their seats." An unusual attention to detail, signaling a perfectionist. An artist who cared about every level of the performance.

"No, our music never set out to deafen anyone. Unlike The Who. Did you know someone measured their decibel level at a concert, and it equaled the noise of an airplane takeoff only fifteen feet away?" He glanced over.

She'd read something like that, but forgotten it. "No kidding." She liked to hear him talk. Liked the way he leaned toward her as he spoke, the wind ruffling his hair. It made her want to run her fingers through it. Instead, she raised the camera, framed him against the orange-pink sky and bracketed several shots.

He chuckled. "Makes me wonder how many Boomers walk around with hearing aids now because of The Who."

Reviewing the pictures, she thought they'd be perfect for the first blog, along with the photo of him in the dining room. Something clenched inside her to think she had to share that shot with others. It felt so private. Intimate. *Don't be an ass. Do your damn job.* If she intended getting anything done tonight, she needed to settle in, make sure no technical issues reared their ugly heads.

Halting, she hugged her arms. "I should probably get back."

"Already?"

The disappointment in his tone came as another surprise.

Turning away, she dug her toe into the sand. "Yes, I have a lot of homework to do. I haven't even unpacked."

"Mmm." His mouth turned down. "Sorry."

She grinned. Another odd thing he remembered.

As slowly as they'd come, they strolled back to the Jeep. When Radiohead came on the radio, he uttered, "Oh!" and turned up the volume, drumming on the steering wheel.

When he glanced over, he caught her smile. "What?"

"Nothing. I see you're a Radiohead fan."

His voice was infused with enthusiasm, and his gestures became livelier. "Did you see them at the Grammies? He played this song with a marching band and it sounded fantastic." He shook his head, as if he'd never thought of such a thing.

"I did. It amazed me too. Really inventive." Music still moved him, made him come alive. The genius of other bands must inspire him, why didn't it move him to create new songs of his own? A question better left to another day, she thought as they reached the house. Discussions about music could last long into the night, and she still had work to do.

Shadows darkened the walkways, the light draining from the sky.

He walked her to the cottage, leaned on the jamb. "Anything else you need?"

She unlocked the door and gripped the knob. "Can't think of anything," she lied. If he were anyone but Jet Trently, she could think of plenty.

Easing away, he gazed down the path. "Guess I'll go find my guitar then."

"Good night." She stepped inside.

He stood, hands in his pockets. "Mmm." Dropping his chin to his chest, he walked on away from the house and disappeared around the bend.

After closing the door, she slid the deadbolt across. A key wouldn't get anyone inside.

With a sigh, she turned. Unpack, she told herself. Frowning at the suitcase, she instead sank into the overstuffed sofa, her muscles reminding her how many hours they'd put in.

"Better not get too comfy yet." Scooting to the edge, she dug out her laptop and powered up. Sure enough, the internet came up on the first try. She downloaded the photos and skimmed through them. The beach photo would be as big a hit as the dining room pic. She could almost hear the collective sigh of Jet fans across the globe.

He hadn't aimed that million-watt smile at them, though. Or taken them to dinner.

She shot off a text to Zinta. *Malibu better than expected.*

In a few minutes, her cell buzzed. Zinta's name showed in the display. "Spill."

The events of the day bubbled forth from Billie's mouth, somewhat incoherently. Zinta's silence unnerved her. "Hello?"

"You do know he's playing you." Zin's words stung sure as a slap.

"What?"

"Buttering you up. To get you on his side."

"He's not like that." Irritated at her for ruining a nice day--unexpectedly nice--Billie hadn't intended to snap her response, but felt no shame, either.

"Billie, my sweet. Don't fall for it."

Despair welled up. *But he likes tree houses.* Such a ridiculous thought, it snapped her to the realization she was heading for disaster. The kind of disaster she swore she'd never get into again. "God, you're right. It's like I landed in Oz instead of Malibu." Maybe the two were closer than she'd thought. "My brain got lost in the whirlwind, but it's on straight now. Thank you."

"I know you'd do the same for me."

And had several times, but she wouldn't rub it in. In this business, the buddy system proved critical for survival. "Listen, I have to get this blog up. I'll talk to you later." She clicked off, thankful for her best friend, the person who knew her intimate secrets.

Zin was right. Jet made a living from practiced charm. And she made a living from guarding against it. How careless could she be?

She downloaded the photos onto the laptop, and scrolled through. Not bad, considering she had no photography training other than on-the-job. The pictures captured the house in a warm light, and Jet's striking good looks. His ocean-blue eyes reached out from the screen and pierced hers as they had when she'd snapped the shot. Yes, the pic would get great reader reaction. But posting it on the blog felt almost like sharing something personal.

Drafting an accompanying entry proved more difficult. She typed a sentence, read it over and deleted it, sickened by its gushing. Did the Malibu breezes infect her brain? Disconnect her thought process? She came across as an empty-headed fool with stars in her eyes. True to her original thought, she left it at: The Bu.

Logging off, she yawned. The time difference had caught up to her, and her energy faded.

After rummaging some items from her suitcase, she changed in the bathroom and climbed the stairs to the loft.

Windows ringed the space, and she wound them open to let in the night air. Muted music sounded, and a light shone through the trees. Jet's studio? Another thing to investigate. Tomorrow.

The house stood in the opposite direction, a light on the far side silhouetting it, Jet's bedroom dark and empty.

Weariness washed over her. She laid her head on the pillow, and the soft strains of his guitar lulled her to sleep.

* * * *

Muted musical tones caused her eyes to flicker open. Much too bright sunlight stabbed them closed again. Instinctively, she reached for her cell phone. Unable to read the display in the morning glare, she flipped it open. "Billie Prescott."

"The one and only?" Everett teased.

At hearing his voice, she sat up. "Hey. What's up?"

The washed-out blue walls crowded the king-sized bed, which seemed suspended in space. Like one of her nightmares where she awakened naked in public. But she wore a tank top and shorts, and no one else was in sight. All seemed quiet. So where the hell was she?

"Apparently not you. But I'll let it slide, since you worked so hard yesterday."

"Oh." Cobwebs slowly dissipated from her brain. "Thanks." Rubbing her forehead, she couldn't think straight. The enthusiasm in his voice confused her more than her surroundings. "What are you talking about?"

"The blog--fifty-some comments already. Did I seriously wake you?"

"Uh, yeah. Like you said, yesterday went late." At the window, the sprawling mustard Mediterranean house reminded her: Jet Trently's house. And the curving walkway below beckoned her to follow it, though the soft music had long ended.

"I didn't say that."

Uh-oh. A hint of irritation in his tone.

"Jet kept you up late, huh?"

And maybe a touch of jealousy. California might be just what she needed to get back on Everett's Lust Have list. "A little. The time difference poses a challenge. After dinner--"

"He took you to dinner?"

"I hadn't eaten all day, Everett. We started an interview."

"But the walk on the beach and the house tour interrupted?"

"No." He wasn't letting her finish. "Look, the trip fried my brain. I have notes, but I'm not putting anything out there until I can make it coherent."

A sharp exhale came as his only response. Time to change subjects.

"So the blog's a hit already?" The pics of Jet--she knew viewers would love them.

"They're clamoring for more. Keep the camera handy and post as many shots as you can."

"I'd planned to." Why so stiff all of a sudden? Had she exhausted his patience already? That usually came later.

"If you plan to post any substantive text, run it by me first."

"That's not exactly blogging." Did he not trust her to post professional entries? His comment about her writing going stale stung anew. Had that only been two days ago? Already it seemed like forever.

"*Rock Bottom* isn't exactly reality, either. Everything needs polish and spin."

"Right."

"Okay, gotta go. Great job."

"So when can I come home?"

"You just landed yesterday, babe."

Babe. Now he turned on the charm, just before leaving. A pattern was taking shape... Irritation boiled up. "Everett..."

"I'm late. Talk to you soon."

Late? A glance at the clock showed nine twenty. Six twenty in Philly. "But how long do I have to stay? Everett?"

Holding the cell out, the display showed the call had ended. With an aggravated groan, she descended the stairs to the main floor and closed the blinds, though outside the walkway appeared deserted and the house quiet. Staying in the cottage would keep her out of the camera's range. Better than upstairs with the bimbos. And Jet.

It reminded her of what he said yesterday. Jogging upstairs again, she peeked out the window. His blinds stood closed. No seeing into his room this morning. Plopping on the bed, the events of yesterday replayed in her head. The interview with Jet had surprised her. What other surprises awaited, she now looked forward to finding out.

"Not so boring as I thought." Another interview--or more--would provide her better insight. It felt more like a conversation with an old friend than an interview. He had a way of putting her at ease and exciting her at the same time. Those blue, blue eyes seared into her. Standing next to him felt like standing next to a bonfire full of crackling heat and energy. Scorching her skin.

"Yeah, you and every other female." But every other female didn't have press credentials, and weren't living in his guest house.

Everett hadn't liked her spending time with Jet. Giggling, she lay back. "You sent me here, babe. All in the line of duty." Groaning, she sat up. "Speaking of which..."

After a shower, she powered up the laptop. A few emails cluttered her inbox, and the blog's comments now numbered more than eighty. She jotted down a few of the questions posed.

A commotion outside grabbed her attention. A squabble, so early? She peered through the blinds. Three women strutted down the walkway toward the house. All appeared high-maintenance, done up to the hilt. Right--the contestants. She'd managed to block them from consciousness, but now they'd occupy front and center whether she willed it or not. Their incessant high-pitched chatter, their preening and nudging to get closer to the camera. Her earlier dread returned. She'd spend lots of time with these females.

The *Rock Bottom* guy who'd helped her yesterday hauled their luggage. He caught her watching, rolled his eyes and shook his head. She didn't envy him.

The contestants' arrival prompted her into action. After dressing in black slacks and a silky tee, banging made her pause the blow-dryer.

"Hello?" called a woman outside.

Barefoot, Billie ran to the door.

Cindy shot her a tight smile. "Hope we're not interrupting. Just here with supplies."

A man stood behind her holding a plastic crate.

Opening the door wide, she stood aside. "Not at all. I appreciate it."

The assistant went straight to work unloading into the refrigerator. Cindy opened a cabinet and revealed a coffeemaker.

"Oh, bless you."

Static erupted on Cindy's walkie-talkie. "Anything else you need besides the basics?"

"Fruit yogurt would be great. And power bars." At Cindy's skeptical look, she added, "I work late a lot."

"Me too. I'll let you know when we're doing a takeout run."

Though Cindy appeared calm on the surface, a harried woman lurked beneath, Billie suspected. And she might be the only person to talk to. Jet's time would be occupied now by his Bimbo Brigade. At that thought, her insides gave a familiar twinge.

Cindy frowned. "Are you all right?"

A flush went through Billie's cheeks. "Yes, great. Hey, we'll have to have a drink by the pool some night." Her cell buzzed. Zinta's name appeared. "Excuse me, I should take this."

"Sure. I need to get back anyway." Cindy ushered her assistant out.

Billie flipped open her cell. "Hey, you're up early."

"I needed to check on you. Are you all right?"

Last night. She'd practically drooled into the phone. "Yes. I'm well rested, and my head's clear now." Especially now that the Bimbo Squad had invaded, bringing reality with them.

"Whew. You had me worried. You sounded...different."

She couldn't admit that yesterday, some naïve version of herself overwhelmed world-wise Billie. She reminded herself what she'd learned long ago: life didn't give anyone sunshine and roses. Not without taking something in return. "Thanks for worrying. I miss you."

"It's weird not having you here."

"Yeah, I'm hoping bad ratings will kill the show early so I can get the hell out of here. Hey, if you hear of any good bands playing out here, let me know, will you?" Already she felt starved for good music. New music.

Zinta promised to call.

After starting a pot of coffee, Billie settled on the sofa with the *Rock Bottom* packet of information. Last night hadn't left much time for actual work. An image of Jet leaning in the doorway, saying good night, returned vividly. Startled her from her thoughts. It seemed like a dream.

Or like a reality show, she reminded herself. Too unreal to be true. Oh, he was good--he must make every girl believe he wanted only her. His mesmerizing gaze probably convinced every female he only had eyes for her. Beautiful eyes, clear blue as the Caribbean.

Coffee. She needed coffee. The time lag must have gotten to her more than she realized.

Voices outside returned her to the window for a peek. The remaining divas had arrived.

Now the show would begin in earnest.

Chapter 3

Not even his guitar distracted Jet. He'd played for hours last night, into this morning, after leaving the cottage. Striking a hard chord, he stilled the strings with his palm and set down the guitar. Standing, he strolled to the window.

You're outta your head. It had been months since Carrie. She should have been enough to teach him he couldn't find love on a reality dating show. Ah, hell. He never expected to find The One. Not really. Stu set this up for the publicity. So far, so good. Except he'd rather play concerts, and now those presented a conflict.

Quite a predicament. Held back from doing the thing he loved most because he had to market himself.

The one woman who interested him for the first time in a long time held the key. He heard his brother saying *Tread very carefully*. If he fell through this thin ice, he might never be able to resurface.

It's the jitters, nothing more. Something about this new round of contestants put him on edge. Their video interviews either left him cold or grated his nerves. How the hell was he supposed to deal with that for months on end?

The response rang through his head in Stu's voice: *Like a pro, bro.*

Yes. If anything, he was a professional. He'd be careful around them all, but especially Ms. Prescott. The one who might pry open the door he'd closed long ago within himself--and then prop it open for the world to see.

No way could he let that happen. Music was the only thing he could depend on in life, and he had to protect it.

* * * *

Outside the cottage, Billie paused only moments. To stay in the sun any longer would invite heat stroke in these dark colors. Instead of heading left to the rear patio, she strolled the opposite way and followed the winding offshoot path veering off the main walkway where the edge of another outbuilding came in view. Surrounded by overgrown bushes, Billie guessed it might be Jet's studio. Silent now. Of course. Jet wouldn't be there at this time of day.

Stepping backward, she wished she could see inside. Hear him play. An image floated into her mind of Jet serenading her, and her alone. One of his songs sounded from near the house, so she followed it to the back of the pool house. One of the two guys from the previous day--the tall, wiry guy, kinda cute, she'd noted yesterday--entered the equipment-loaded workroom, and the door closed, muting the music.

"Ms. Prescott." Arms pumping, Stu Gilbert walked her way. "I'm glad I caught up with you."

"Hi, Mr. Gilbert." Thank goodness she'd worn sunglasses. The lime shirt he wore glowed in the sun like neon.

"Call me Stu."

His heavy-lidded gaze and ever-present grin grated her nerves. "Stu. I wondered if I might be able to get a look inside the editing room."

"Great idea. They're pre-editing the show now. Come in. I'll introduce you."

"Pre-editing?" What the hell could that mean? Hopefully repeating his lingo would entice an explanation.

She followed him inside. The cabana appeared deceptively smaller from the outside. Half had been partitioned off to allow an impromptu editing room complete with extra-wide flat screen monitors connected to the Macintosh computer.

"Danny, Justin, meet Billie Prescott. She's on board to follow the episodes for *Strung Out*."

The two men glanced back, mumbled hello. Justin's glance lingered longer, his brow arched as his gaze lowered.

Stu ran through the projected schedule for the day, then touched Billie's arm. "You do understand how critical it is for you to stay behind the cameras' line of vision, correct?"

"Oh yes--"

"Because I reviewed it repeatedly with Everett, and he assured me you'd be on board."

Affecting a serious expression, she nodded. "Completely."

As if she hadn't spoken, Stu continued. "Because Justin and Danny work very hard at shooting from the best possible angle and…"

Tuning him out, Billie folded her arms and struggled to keep her face a mask of seriousness as he droned on about maintaining the integrity of the videography.

Integrity! As if *Rock Bottom* might win an award of excellence.

"These two only get one chance at a shot--isn't that right, boys?" He winked at the cameramen.

The two grunted in bored acknowledgment.

Stu clasped his hands. "Wonderful. The girls are changing into their bikinis now."

The swimsuit competition? Billie fought to keep a straight face. "Their bikinis?"

"Yes, they'll be poolside when Jet arrives at two thirty."

His gaze wandered across her as if in comparison, and she stifled a shudder.

"Great photo op." Justin glanced back with a grin.

At Stu's throaty chuckling, Billie clenched her teeth.

After reminding them everything needed to be in place well in advance of two thirty, Stu exited.

The video onscreen caught Billie's attention. Jet and his band on some outdoor stage. "What's this?"

Danny's nasal reply came through the fist propped against his chin. "One of Jet's concerts a few years ago."

Before the show began then. "Where?"

Justin shrugged. "Lollapalooza? Farm Aid? Some days-long event." He winced at an off note, his puckered lips exaggerated for effect.

The camera panned to the audience--a huge crowd, but every woman was riveted to the stage. Jet played with little effort. Very little. If ever she'd seen a rote performance, she viewed one now. The women in the audience didn't seem to mind.

Danny increased the volume so they might have been in the audience themselves.

"Ugh. This used to be my favorite song." Years ago, but lately it stood out as one of the few she could still stand to listen to. No more.

"Yeah, kinda kills it for me too." Justin turned back to the computer, murmured something to Danny.

When he blocked her view, she angled closer. "Are you using that video in the show?"

Danny said, "Only a few seconds of it to splice into the opening collage."

At an off-key chord made worse by the out-of-synch keyboards and drums, Billie clenched her teeth. "Maybe Jet should work on tightening his sound instead of his abs."

Glancing back, Justin's eyes rounded, his face blanked.

Behind her the door slammed.

Billie whirled. "Who was that?"

Working the mouse, Danny said, "Jet must not have appreciated the joke."

Frozen, she wrestled with whether to go after him. He must be angry, and she couldn't blame him. Still, if she waited, explaining would be more difficult. She pushed open the door, but the walkway was deserted.

Justin laughed too emphatically. "Relax. I'm sure he's heard that before."

"More than he'd like," Danny deadpanned.

She sighed, wondering how she might make up for the insult to Jet. "Does Jet normally come in while you're working?"

Justin shrugged. "Once in a while."

She wished she'd known that earlier. "Does he have any editorial control?"

Danny maneuvered the mouse. "Nah, he just comes in to hang out mostly."

"He's cool about it. Lets us do our work, no hassles." Justin inclined his head. "I think he likes to get away from them."

"The contestants? Or his manager and assistant?"

They exchanged knowing glances, and Justin said, "All of the above."

"It must be exhausting, having people glomming onto him every waking moment." Filming his every move. Vying for his attention. Snatching little bits of him away, slowly. She no longer wondered how he'd lost himself, but wondered how he managed to retain any semblance of himself at all.

Snickering, Justin fiddled with the boom mic. "If he hated attention, he wouldn't have signed up for season two." Bitterness edged his tone.

Did Billie sound so acidic when her jaded side surfaced? "I'd better get back. Nice to meet you."

"See you soon," Justin crooned.

Back in the cottage, she drafted an initial blog post touching on Jet's pathetic concert performance as well as sympathy for his unenviable position. Having fallen from the heady heights of success, now vampires surrounded him, though he had precious little blood to spare. The Jet of today might appear fit and robust, but his music was neither. Both, she wrote, lacked the vibrant soul from their humble beginnings.

Re-reading it, she realized the post seemed overly harsh. Saving it as a draft on the blog site, she'd soften it later.

Damn. If she'd known he'd snuck in the editing room, she'd have curbed her comments. He'd gone out of his way yesterday to tend to her needs. Still, the magazine paid her to air the truth as she saw it. No matter how nice, Jet couldn't be an exception. If his band hadn't been so great in the beginning, their performance might not have seemed so terrible by contrast. And if he hadn't heard her say it here, he'd have read it elsewhere. No matter how much she wanted to, she could not hold back to spare his feelings.

Still, she wanted the blog to be more than a dig. Jet could be a great musician if he'd focus on his craft instead of other nonsense. Like reality television. Dare she write that? Maybe it would get her sent home in a hurry… No, she wouldn't taint her writing with any ulterior motive. If it inspired Jet, helped him realize his full potential, all the better.

With that thought, her burden of guilt lightened. She'd corner him later and apologize.

* * * *

After two hours of lurking on the fringes of the camera's view, Billie felt as persecuted as a soul in purgatory. And every bit as overheated. Even in the shade, her dark top and pants seemed to absorb sunlight. If the cameras weren't rolling, she'd love to dive in the pool.

Listening to the excited babble and chatter of the six contestants brought back torturous memories of high school: the girls' bathroom where the popular ones debated boys, fashion and makeup. The gym locker where cheerleaders rapturously described dates with jocks. At least then she could walk away when it grew too nauseating. Now, she had to stay. Worse, she had to regurgitate their babble in some coherent way.

Billie scanned the show's outline. Today, the contestants officially met Jet, though he'd greeted them earlier inside. To put them at ease, Stu explained to Billie--off the record, of course. The public had no need to know, he said. Billie conceded. She'd pick her battles.

When Jet finally put in an appearance just before three, Billie again flashed back to high school. Her stomach clenched, her senses pricked to alert at his every movement. She tensed, waiting for him to look her way, smile, speak to her.

He strode in scowling, head ducked purposefully, as if he were on his way to somewhere else. Or wanted to be.

One glance. As he approached the back patio, that's all he gave her. One piercing glance. It burned into her, the second expanding into infinity, throwing all time out of synch.

The producer swiveled at his approach, called, "Jet, good. Let's run through some notes before we start."

Staring into hers, something deadened in Jet's eyes, and then his frown intensified, his stride hastened.

Despite the heat, she shuddered with the unexpected chill. If only everyone else would take a break, leave them alone long enough so she could explain her earlier comment. Above all else, she wanted Jet to view her as a professional. Her opinions didn't play into her writing, but curbing her tongue wasn't her strong suit.

Still scowling, Jet scanned through the pages, the producer and Stu murmuring to him.

The producer stepped out of the camera's frame. "Ready?"

"In a minute." The pages fluttered as he flipped one, then another.

"Something wrong?" Stu asked.

"I can't find anything about the gig."

His sharp tone silenced the tittering women, snapped everyone's attention to him. Especially Billie's.

Only Stu seemed unaffected, and spoke with his usual snake oil smoothness. "It's not in this outline."

"When will it be?" Jet spoke more softly, but sounded no less threatening.

Riveted, Billie watched, hugging herself.

Obviously, Jet had been promised things. When would he realize: the show parodied real life. It didn't enrich it.

Stepping near, Stu murmured something inaudible, something sounding like an urging. Or a warning.

Jet threw down the pages. "Fine. Let's get this over with." He shot a sharp glance at Billie.

She slunk behind the nearest cameraman. Why focus on her? An innocent bystander? A neutral observer?

Well, not so neutral. Not after her remark.

A few minutes later, the producer said they couldn't hold up shooting any longer, and counted down from ten. Jet paced, his expression blanking more with each step. By the count of one, he smiled rather stiffly in the direction of the pool.

Season two had begun.

* * * *

All morning, Jet had given himself pep talks. It would just be another performance. A very long performance. *It has nothing to do with my music, no matter what Stu says.* He'd have to work it in somehow. And stick it out until the contract ran out. But after this, no more.

The alarm on his cell went off. Ah, hell. Time to get on set. Ironic how claustrophobic he'd become in such a big house. Literally nowhere to hide that the cameras couldn't follow, starting today. Already it chafed his nerves. Bad enough he had to endure the microscopic attention of the cameras, but now *her* too. Worse than a video, Billie Prescott would interpret. Opine. Slant. Her audience would listen--the very people who mattered. The ones who loved music.

At least he'd found out her true nature. Walking into the editing room at precisely the wrong--no, right--moment. He might not have believed she could be so cruel otherwise. Until he'd read the blog. Yeah, if anything drove home that she was just another leech, the blog post did it. Funny how she separated herself from those sucking his blood dry when she made her living from it.

He glanced over and the sting came back fresh. He had to remind himself again: just one more bitch to deal with. But one who had no stakes in any of this. His career rode on it.

"All right. Let's do this." He tossed the script aside and let the producer position him. On with the farce.

He plastered on a smile. The six contestants had endured a lot to get here, and they deserved his consideration. None appeared well-to-do, and he pegged all as high-maintenance, but each looked upon him with true excitement, eager to get a turn with him alone. Oh yeah, and a shot at a hundred grand.

They waited together, and their competitive electricity permeated the air. Competitive beauty. That brought a chuckle, and he relaxed as he called the first girl.

"Hello, Cat."

The mocha-skinned beauty whose father hailed from Cuba and mother from Malaysia. No age provided on the spec sheet, and impossible to tell from studying her. Tall and lithe, she walked with the grace of Cleopatra, dark almond-shaped eyes focused on Jet as she approached. She slunk toward him like her feline nickname, her sexual confidence sizzling. Sliding her arms around his neck, she drew him to her in a kiss much longer than any introduction.

Holding her waist, he gently moved her away with a grin. "Save some for next time." Might have to change the rating on the show for this one.

A glance at Billie heightened his attention. Arms folded, her nauseated expression appeared tainted with something more. Jealousy?

Couldn't be. She must want to get back in his good graces. Too bad.

Relieved when Cat sidled away, he turned to the waiting group. "Ashley."

The only blonde, surprisingly. Her pale blue eyes brightened when she approached, beaming. In her late twenties, the report said, but brittle hair and laugh lines made her appear older. Jet wondered what hard life she'd led. Sensing her fragility, Jet spoke softly as he welcomed her, but sent her off quickly too.

Next, he called Brianna, who might have been Ashley's brunette alter ego. Brianna mimicked Ashley's movements, her appearance, everything but her high-voltage eagerness. Oh, she smiled at Jet, but without the giggly exuberance. Or desperation.

Terry, another exotic beauty, had a full mouth graced with wide lips. Her smile filled her face. Dark brows arched into a peak above dark eyes. Like the others, long hair cascaded down her back.

If Jet had to describe Amber, he'd be hard pressed. Nothing set her apart from the others.

Of all the contestants, Julie baffled Jet the most. Fresh-faced and pretty, she appeared younger than twenty-four. Something about the way she carried herself suggested a better upbringing. When Jet spoke her name, she went to him without undue haste or excitement, as if the line had been for a restaurant table. What the hell was she doing here at all?

No matter. None of them interested him. To be fair, he'd try to dig beneath the surface of too much makeup, generous doses of perfume and hair product. Maybe a real person lurked, for one at least.

And he'd get a kick out of teasing Billie with the act. The way she fanned herself, his taunts already got to her, adding a little extra interest to this season. The best way to rid himself of leeches was to burn them.

* * * *

Watching Jet fawn over each woman, kiss her cheek as she said hello, grew more nauseating each moment. Billie scanned the handout, but it gave sparse biographical details for all the women. Intentionally glossing over their pasts? Or did no juicy details exist to fill in the blanks? Billie bet the former.

During the introductions, Billie fanned herself, wrote some notes, wondered how long she'd have to endure this crap. Wandering down the walkway, she texted Zin: *Rescue me.*

Zinta replied, *That bad, huh?*

The pits. If only the series would be cancelled. Slight chance if the ratings slipped any farther. *How's everything there?*

Oh fine, Zin messaged.

Right. And I'm Mick Jagger's love child. No, but she could have been his lover for an hour or two. Another mega-ego she'd neatly ignored. Scar tissue made for a strong protective barrier.

Billie hated texting, and called Zin. "Spill."

"You won't like it." Zin's voice cracked, and not from the bad connection.

"I thought Everett loved the blog?"

Airily, she said, "Oh, he did. It's difficult to elaborate at the moment."

"He's nearby?" Damn him. Always in the right spot at the wrong time.

"Exactly. It's along the lines of Jet's old song *Don't Know Where You Been.*"

Racking her brain, Billie ran through the lyrics in her head, but came up with sparse lines. "I remember the video better. One of Jet's best." Shot in black and white in a small club, the video showed Jet sidling up to the microphone. He shone with a mercurial glow in the spotlight, lips curled as his voice growled and grinded against the sexy backbeat of the drums. He stroked his guitar like a lover, and no one heard the lyrics.

Zin bubbled with curious enthusiasm. "Yeah, what's he like? Is he as hot in person?"

"As hot as a nearing-middle-age guy can be. Yeah, he's cute. But clueless."

"How so?"

Her frustration funneled into a rant on Jet's musical ambition. Or lack thereof. "He seems to think this show is really to showcase his musical talent. How thick can he be? The show's titled *Rock Bottom.* Did that escape his notice? Does he not get that they're setting him up for a full-on persecution?" The fine hairs on the back of her neck stood on end. She glanced over.

Jet stood a few feet away, mouth set in a grim line, narrowed eyes directed at her.

Surprise prickled her skin. *Damn.* She never meant for him to hear that, either, yet here she stood, foot squarely in her mouth again. She straightened. "Will do. Thanks for the info."

"Uh-oh. Within hearing range?"

"It's the way of it lately. Talk to you soon." She flipped shut the cell, pulled out her notepad and wrote nonsensical notations, willing the warmth crawling up her neck to disappear. Explaining one misspoken remark would have been hard enough, but how could she explain two?

In her peripheral vision, Jet stood still as a statue. The weight of his stare grew heavier each moment.

Around them, the sounds of the set echoed. Only the two of them remained unmoving, isolated within the bustle.

Finally his voice bridged the distance. "When the world doesn't give you opportunities, you take them."

"Pardon?" So he knew the real premise of the show? To stake him to the TV screen and let viewers rip him to shreds?

He moved closer, the gleam in his eyes sharpening. "Do you have to put other people down to feel good about yourself?"

"Of course not. I'm a professional." At the moment, she felt anything but. Her job didn't include unintentionally skewering people, and she obviously had.

"You write like a snotty high school girl. 'Jet doesn't want to acknowledge the series is a joke--that the network's made him the butt of it--because his music is laughable.'"

Heat pricked her cheeks. "How did you..." Realization struck. "Oh my God. The blog." She hadn't posted it accidently, had she? Of course he'd have read it sooner or later. She'd have preferred later. After she'd revised it, softened the edges so they weren't quite so cutting.

"Yeah. The blog."

"How did you read it?"

His furrowed brows intensified his gaze, hard and beautiful as ice blue diamonds. "Like everyone else. Online."

"I didn't... it wasn't..." *Stick to writing, Billie. Speaking is not your forte.* "I hadn't finished it."

With an incredulous chuckle, he sounded as if the wind had been knocked from him. "Oh, you had more? Wait." He patted his chest, his sides, then craned his neck to look behind him. "Oh yeah--here it is. The one place you didn't twist the knife."

Damn. He was taking this really hard. "You don't understand--"

"Obviously, I never will." He strode off down the walkway toward his studio.

The hurt in his voice stung her equally hard.

Halfheartedly, she said, "Jet." As much as she wanted to follow, she didn't. Couldn't. Until she came up with a plausible explanation, he'd never listen, anyway.

* * * *

Anger propelled him down the path. Other days, he'd smile at the sunshine, revel in his fortune at living the life he loved. *Rock Bottom* was an inconvenience, but one that would help him get his music noticed again. Eyes on the prize, as Stu said. Until yesterday, he was okay with that. Why did it now feel like not enough?

He hadn't met Billie Prescott before yesterday.

Bitch didn't describe her fully enough. She sure had him fooled. At first, she'd been a little cold, sure, but he'd chalked that up to professionalism and jet lag.

Yesterday the show hadn't begun.

Today, apparently, all bets were off. His opinion of her changed as radically as her attitude. "Work on my music instead of my abs. Clueless reporter."

The key word. He had to remember her purpose here. Cover the show, report to fans. If he didn't want to alienate those fans, he'd have to walk a thin line. Set his emotions aside.

Every time he spoke to her, the line blurred. Her warmth and caring--were those an act too? Turned on when she needed them, and off as easily?

From the patio, Stu called, "Jet."

He kept walking.

Huffing, his manager caught up to him. "Where are you going?"

"I'm taking five."

"We just started."

We. It rattled him how Stu insinuated himself into every aspect of Jet's work. His manager had put forth no effort today but wanted to take credit.

"I need to clear my head. Play some music."

"The girls are waiting."

"Fuck the girls."

"I'm hoping you will. Ratings will skyrocket."

He whirled to face Stu. "What about my music? When do we get some real gigs? You promised--"

"I said after the show."

He wanted to swipe that sickly grin off Stu's face. "You said you'd work at least one into the show. At least one. It's not too much to ask, Stu."

"I think--"

"I don't pay you to think. I pay you to promote me. Get me a gig, Stu. Or so help me, I'll walk." Jet's voice shook. He dragged a hand across his mouth and reeled in his anger.

"All right, all right. I'll get on it. In the meantime, I'll coordinate with the producer to film a studio session."

Jet blinked hard, wanting to swipe Stu from his sight. His mealy-mouthed arguments, disguised in soothing tones, used to convince Jet his manager had everything under control. Now he had to wonder whether it was himself he controlled. "A studio session would be good. But a concert is what I need." Not playing to a live audience made him jittery.

Stu raised his hands near Jet's chest, but didn't make contact. "For now, I need you to go back on set. All right? Stay focused, man. We all have obligations. This isn't forever."

"Good thing. Or I'd take the express to visit Cobain and Hendrix."

Stu inclined his head toward the patio. "They're waiting."

A sharp inhale fortified him. With a nod, he followed Stu. When Billie was nowhere in sight, relief washed over him. He couldn't take any more from her right now.

* * * *

Over the next week and a half, Billie did her best to remain invisible. While her blog posts enjoyed insane popularity with the public, no one in the compound shared the sentiment. Except Justin. Every morning, he'd say, "Excellent post," even if all she'd done was upload photos--a practice that seemed safest. In her cottage at night, she closed the blinds and bolted the door.

Jet appeared to actively avoid her. The few times their glances met by accident, he immediately frowned, as if the experience pained him, as if the reminder reopened the gash made by her cutting remarks. Shame burned deep, but she couldn't approach him.

Everett ignored her complaints, downplayed her worries about revenge. "You only imagine they're angry. They exist for drama, babe. Without the blog, the show might have tanked by now."

Her hopes sank as dread filled her. "Are you serious?"

"Absolutely."

Then she'd been perpetuating her own purgatory. Time to get back into real writing. "Maybe we should focus on articles instead. From Philly."

"No way. You have a huge following. You're hot."

How many times she'd longed to hear him exclaim those words with such enthusiasm, but face-to-face. "I don't want to be hot." Never had she imagined uttering those words. "I want to come home."

Issuing a noise meant to indicate he was thinking when all the while she knew he intended her to stay indefinitely, he said, finally, "Not yet."

"Where are my other assignments?" Concentrating solely on this bunch of loonies could prove contagious.

"For now, focus on *Rock Bottom*." Tapping noises. He must be either drumming his fingers, or his pen. Which meant his patience had nearly run out.

Well, so was hers. "You promised--"

"Gotta go, babe. Keep up the great work." Then silence.

Groaning, she flipped shut her cell. "Damn jerk."

"Whoa, careful. My ears."

Glancing up, she realized she'd wandered to the side of the pool house. Justin smiled as he stepped outside.

"Sorry." She held her head and blew through her teeth.

"Have you never heard sarcasm before?" Cocking his head, he arched a brow. "Hey, what's wrong?"

"Oh, my stupid boss." With a wave, she turned. No need to elaborate.

"Yeah, bosses can be a drag."

"I'm beginning to feel as if I checked into the Hotel California." Like the Eagles song, she'd checked in, apparently for good.

Bending to adjust a boom mic pole, Justin grinned up at her. "This place can get a little small."

"I really need to get out of here." She thought out loud. "Does any place rent scooters? Maybe I'll just call a cab."

"If you can wait until later, I'll take you."

Her heart leapt. She stepped closer. "Where?"

"Where do you want to go?"

His tantalizing tone inspired giddiness, made her feel lighter. She could escape this prison tonight. "Ooo. The Getty Villa's supposed to have wonderful ancient artifacts. Or Malibu Wines…"

Wincing, Justin clucked his tongue. "I'm talking *late* late. Like after midnight. We usually keep filming until then."

Her light feeling deflated. "Oh."

"You need to stop getting up so early. Stay up with the night owls."

No thanks. Their screeching kept her up some nights. "I'm hoping I'll be pulled from this assignment soon."

Disappointment showed in his frown. "Oh no. We'd miss you."

"You'd be the only one."

He bumped his shoulder against hers. "Hey, cheer up. The big day will be here soon."

"For?"

"One of them gets the ax." He mimed slitting his throat.

"One less bimbo." More than one would suit her. The quicker they went, the quicker she could leave.

Chapter 4

Shooting went smoothly the next few days. Billie kept to herself to relieve the awkwardness, but it magnified the feeling of being an outsider. One who didn't belong.

Maybe Jet would ease up on her a bit. After all those sweet things he said her first day here, all pretenses of innocence faded once the others had arrived. Like Zin had warned, he wanted to play her, to woo her most sympathetic writing in his favor. How could she have fooled herself into thinking he was a nice guy for real?

Still, while ostracized, the Jet compound had a military air. She was a prisoner of her own making. No--Everett's making.

In her cottage, she found the phone book and called a cab. Damn if she would spend another full day in this hormone-saturated prison.

When it whisked her away, the knot in her chest eased. She was free.

Nothing else in Malibu was.

Trying on a three-thousand-dollar sundress, Billie took a picture in the dressing room and sent it to Zin in a text message.

Within seconds, Zinta called. "Have you lost your mind?"

"No, but the danger looms ever closer." Not close enough to shell out three thousand, though. She unzipped it and slipped it off.

"Where are you?"

"The Malibu Country Mart. I need a bathing suit. Can you believe I forgot mine? I might even get some Malibu Rock Star jewelry. Isn't that a hoot?" The brand predated Jet's show, but the coincidence amused her.

"I'm worried about you."

That makes two of us. "I needed to get out of there. That place gets smaller every day. It's making me claustrophobic."

"You need a concert."

"Exactly. Tell Everett he promised." A shift in focus would ease the constricted feeling in her chest.

"I'm going to review Wilco next week and Kings of Leon the week after."

"Stop torturing me." She'd kill to take Zin's place. "Now I'm really depressed. All I have to look forward to is fishing."

"Fishing? Really?"

"And I can't even participate. I have to keep out of the camera's view, watch from a distance." Not that she had a great love of the sport, but it had to be better than being relegated to spectator.

"Well, make it sound even more boring and readers will lose interest."

"Not likely." Not after today's studio session. "Call me from the concert, let me listen in, will you?"

Zin promised, then said goodbye.

Going from store to store, Billie's depression grew. No bathing suits for less than two hundred dollars. She tried the adjacent shopping complex, the Malibu Lumber Yard. J. Crew offered the most affordable, if least impressive option.

Tonight, she'd dine out.

When she arrived at Geoffrey's, the hostess gave her the once-over and said, "Sorry, we're full."

Billie flashed her *Strung Out* ID. "I was hoping to eat here so I could include your place on our blog dedicated to--"

The woman's eyes practically flashed dollar signs. "You're *that* Billie Prescott? I've been following your posts."

"If I could get in, Geoffrey's would get some really great publicity."

"Joffrey's."

"Pardon?"

"It's pronounced Joffrey's. Let me take another look…" She scanned the reservation list, and beamed at Billie. "Oh, how could I have missed this? We had a cancellation, if you can wait a few minutes."

Time to make the hostess squirm instead. "Hmm. How long of a wait?"

Her tone turned apologetic. "A few minutes. We'll have a table ready in a jiff."

"Sounds great." Yes, a decent meal would make a nice change from takeout and power bars.

The hostess clip-clopped into the dining room and, as promised, returned within minutes to lead Billie to a table. "The lobster Cobb salad's excellent." With a wink, she strolled away, and a waiter appeared. From his eagerness, she guessed the hostess tipped him off.

Billie ordered the recommended salad and a glass of wine. "No, make that a margarita." What the hell, she wouldn't be driving.

After a leisurely meal, the hostess reappeared. "How is everything? Do you need anything else?"

"A cab? And would you mind?" She held up the digital camera. "I'd love to get a photo with you."

With a gushing sigh and psycho-bright eyes, the woman smiled. "For the blog? I'd love that too."

Billie would bet the hostess aspired to be an actress, or worse, a reality show contestant. Everyone craved the spotlight.

The photo op garnered Billie a complimentary slice of chocolate dessert, and a sendoff worthy of royalty. Waving, she climbed into the cab and gave the address.

At the gate, Billie got out. "I can walk from here, thanks." She pressed the intercom button. Cindy, ever-present at her desk, buzzed her in.

Stars pierced a thin veil of clouds overhead as she strolled down the solar-lit drive. Pausing at the cottage door, the strains of guitar licks clashed with screeching laughter and splashing from the pool.

Billie pushed inside. "Back to the unreal world of reality TV." These people needed real jobs, if only to allow her a decent night's rest. No matter. Tonight, she had a blog to post.

* * * *

Billie slipped onto the patio unnoticed in time for the shoot.

The producer clasped his hands. "All right, ladies. Everyone set for today's trip to the winery?" When they responded yes in unison, he turned to Stu. "Jet ready?"

"RWA. Ready, willing and able." Stu glanced nervously at the house.

He'd never win any originality awards. Jet had made himself scarce yesterday and today. Her cottage walls vibrated with muted music from the studio. Jet and his band practiced from midday to midnight, picking up again today.

"We're supposed to be live." Ashley smoothed her hair.

Cat popped a breath mint between her teeth. "Not these scenes, honey."

Stu made a show of checking his watch. "I'll go make sure he's RWA." He strode around the side of the house.

The producer cursed when the time lapsed. Muttering, he herded the women. "Let's go over here and we'll get some preliminary shots. Can't keep wasting time."

Fifteen minutes lapsed before Stu returned, Jet leading the way. He wore shorts and a tee from one of his tours, fitted to his contoured chest. A broad smile lit his face--a music high. Billie would know that look anywhere. His practice had obviously gone well. And he'd practiced because of her. An inexplicable bubble of happiness welled within.

"Excuse me." Jet gestured to the producer.

"Yes?" The response dripped with sarcasm.

Jet huddled with the stodgy man. "I'd love the girls to join me in the studio."

"What? Malibu Wines has cleared their schedule--"

"I appreciate that. Everyone's put a lot of work into this. We're on a roll, though, and it would be great to get the reaction of these girls on film, don't you think? The audience would eat it up." His voice surged with enthusiasm.

Maybe he'd supplemented the musical high with a little something extra, despite his touted health regimen. Whatever he'd taken, everyone and everything around him picked it up. Since he'd arrived, the air buzzed with energy.

Billie caught the buzz like a drug and wanted more.

"Jet, we're wasting time."

"Then let's go. The band's waiting." He turned to Danny and Justin. "You guys are mobile, right? That's the beauty of live television. You can go anywhere. So come on." His teeth flashed bright in a smile.

He sure could turn on the charm when he wanted. Even the camera guys couldn't resist. Without waiting for the producer's okay, they followed. The women, predictably, followed the cameras.

"It's more than just the cameras. It's lighting…" The producer's hands flew in the air, then flopped. "Fine. So today's not a total black hole."

Thankful for her low heels, Billie scooted to Justin's side.

Tall and lanky, he smiled down at her. "Unpredictable as ever."

"Really? Did he do this a lot last year?"

"Never." Danny pushed his glasses up his nose. "This is a first."

"Hmm." She needed to get her hands on more season one DVDs as a gauge, though it still wouldn't provide any insight behind the scenes.

Inside the studio, the other band members picked random notes, joked in low tones. The contestants arranged themselves in front of the main mic where Jet lifted his guitar to his chest.

Billie drifted to a corner to stay out of sight, but not miss anything.

"Should we have them come in again?" Jet asked Danny.

"Good idea. Let's have you all go out and when we're ready, we'll call you."

With pouted lips, the girls exchanged puzzled glances, hair swishing around their shoulders like a shampoo commercial. With Cat leading, they did as instructed.

The producer entered. "Now what?"

Danny moved opposite Justin's position. "Setting up. They'll be back in a sec."

Heaving a frustrated sigh, the producer went outside.

Jet signaled the band, and they launched into a song. But tonight, they played as one, their song a harmonious blend of pitch-perfect notes.

Billie's excitement rose. She couldn't wait to tell Zinta. She wouldn't say she couldn't keep her eyes off Jet. His blond hair shone in the lights, giving him an aura of radiance. His voice raw with emotion, his singing drew her in, made her want to go to him, somehow catch the energy he put into his song. Her heart raced like it had in high school, listening to him for the first time.

The band finished the song, and surprise overtook her when the girls clapped. When had they come in? How could she have missed it? But there they huddled like cheerleaders, a seething mass of sighs and lip gloss and overstyled hair.

Jet aimed his megawatt smile at them, and an unfamiliar twinge went through Billie. He conversed with each like an old friend. "Did you like it?"

Did he really need to ask? The band hadn't sounded this tight in years.

She gasped. Her recorder--she hadn't turned it on. Rummaging in her handbag, she pulled it out and clicked it on with the excitement of a high school girl sneaking into a concert.

* * * *

Holding a guitar was the most natural pose for Jet. Being nervous made no sense today. He'd played in this studio for months. Loved the acoustics in here. But now, standing in the center of the room with his band behind him and the six new contestants seated on chairs in a semicircle, sweat greased his palm.

Justin and Danny made final adjustments to the pole holding the boom mic above their heads. Thousands of people would watch their performance. His performance. He had to make it good. No, great.

The last to enter the studio, Billie hesitated in the doorway.

He glanced up and held her gaze a beat more than comfortable.

She looked around and moved a folding chair to the side of a large speaker. Good. An inconspicuous spot.

Danny nodded to the producer, who held up two fingers. Jet waved in acknowledgment. He'd have to ignore Ms. Prescott. Not think about what she might write.

Strumming idly, he flashed a smile at his adoring audience. "We have some songs in mind, but if you have any requests--"

Ashley's hand shot up, and she squirmed in her seat. "*Gotta Have Your Love.*"

"One of my favorites." His glance flicked to Billie, and a nerve in his jaw pulsed.

She sat straighter and leaned forward. He'd almost think she was excited to hear him play live.

With narrowed eyes, Cat glared in Billie's direction, her long-nailed hands clenched like claws.

After a nod to the band, Jet launched into the song as much to ease the tension as anything.

Amber and Julie watched with rapt attention. Terry examined her nails, glanced around the room, did everything but yawn. At Ashley's fifth request, Terry rolled her eyes. The band ended another song, and she excused herself.

When she passed Billie, the reporter wrote in her notebook. Probably predicting Terry would be cut first. Accurately.

Unless she critiqued his set. Though unplugged, he rendered each as a toned-down version of the recorded song. Words like "rehashed performance" flew through his head, and fear stiffened his fingers.

Yet when his gaze connected with hers, he knew his singing affected her too. The excitement in the room equaled any mega concert's. Billie may have sat farther away than the others, but her enthusiasm showed in her tapping foot, nodding head and intense focus. He couldn't help but stare as he sang as if to her alone.

Jutting out her chin, Ashley waved. "Play *Not Gonna Take It No More*, will you?" With narrowed eyes, she glanced back.

Uh-oh. Busted. Jet couldn't hold back a grin. "Sure, darlin'."

He launched into the hard beat with gusto, moved his whole body to the rhythm.

Ashley slithered upward, arms in the air. Head bobbing, hips swaying, she strutted toward him.

Whoa, when did she turn into an exotic dancer?

Cat pounced to Jet's other side, hips sliding so near his guitar he had to shift its neck forward, laughing. Yikes, crazy women. He used to love them that way. Lately, they proved a little too much work. But that was the name of this game. Anything for attention. Anything to come in first. Sometimes he wished he could find someone he could just hang with, hold her hand without having to say a word. Or if they did speak, it would be a meaningful conversation.

He'd felt it the first night with Billie. Too bad they'd probably never share such a night again.

* * * *

For the next hour, Billie wrote almost nonstop, adding whatever else transpired.

When she wasn't staring at Jet. His long layered hair fell across his face at the end of a sad ballad, his features hardened while singing a rebellious anthem, and practically glowed during a love song. Once they aired this segment, every woman alive would want to sleep with him again.

Billie had already found out--the hard way--what it was like to rank below the fans, always second to some demand of stardom. Or some other girl. She pitied anyone who lived through the same experience.

Jet spoke with the contestants, joked with them, asked insightful questions. When he flirted with Ashley, Billie's gut burned.

So predictable. The long-legged, long-haired blonde. A stream of vehement phrases flowed from her pen.

Most of the contestants appeared ready to throw themselves at Jet already. Of course, he must know the effect he had on women, and he knew how to work it. It might explain why he turned his gaze to her more often than the bimbos. So frequently Billie felt herself blush when Ashley and Cat glanced back, eyes glimmering bright with jealousy. She'd had to divert her attention, bend over her notepad to write something, anything. The resulting article would paint him in a positive light.

The others she'd reserve for a future blog. Maybe Ashley's moves appeared practiced because they were. Billie had made a note to check into her work history. And Cat--she'd be very careful around her. If Cat could have, she'd probably have hissed, or worse.

The lights dimmed, forcing her to pause. The group milled toward the door.

"Great sound, Jet." Danny tapped Jet's shoulder.

Jet glanced at Billie. "Thanks. I owe it all to Ms. Prescott."

Her spine snapped straight. "What?"

Justin furrowed his brows. "She is inspiring."

"Oh yeah." The glint in Jet's eyes conveyed triumph. "She thinks the band sucks. She made me want to prove her wrong."

Uh-oh. She couldn't become part of the story, but she relaxed a little when she realized Danny and Justin had their cameras off.

"You proved me wrong." If allowing him victory would get her back in his good graces, she'd concede.

To Danny, Jet said, "She thinks I'm a loser."

The urge to straighten out his twisted opinion propelled her from her seat. "I never said--"

"She thinks you're all vampires too. Should I worry about that? Start wearing a garlic necklace?"

Their laughter held an edge of discomfort. So did their glances.

Time to wrap it up. She had enough material. And she had no intention of inserting herself in the mix. Ducking her head in embarrassment, she headed for the door.

Jet called, "I hope I didn't insult you."

Pausing, she turned. "Likewise. But honestly, if that's the kind of catalyst you needed to break out of your slump, I'm glad I could be of assistance."

Instead of appeasing him as she hoped, his mouth hardened, and his eyes shone with anger. "Everyone hits a slump now and then. Even music journalists, I hear."

She bristled.

He went on. "For someone who despises others seeking fame by using another person, she seems to have overlooked herself. Ironic, isn't it? Your byline's featured prominently above those opening paragraphs beating me down."

Her jaw dropped only for a moment. "Excuse me." Her heels pounded against the stone walk. His words seared into her flesh like a branding iron.

Inside the cottage, she threw her handbag on the ottoman with a furious groan. She cursed and paced, paced and cursed. Then dragging out her laptop, her fingers flew across the keyboard, spewing venom.

Far too long for a blog entry. She read it back aloud to get a better handle on it. Pure crap. She'd lost her objectivity.

With a deep breath, she stood. Of course. That's exactly what he'd meant to happen. Engage her in the whole bloody mess so she couldn't write worth a damn.

If she lost this assignment, it would be like flunking kindergarten. Well, screw him. She'd keep her head--and everything else--out of his reach. Stay at a distance and report the truth, whether he cared to hear it or not.

Closing her eyes, she inhaled deeply, poised her fingers over the keyboard and cleared her head. From her past swirled a rush of feelings: excitement over Jet's latest single, singing along in the car, feeling as if his music documented her life. A spark of that earlier flame came through in his jam session. Too bad he expelled it playing the same old songs, performing as if by rote.

Reviewers once likened his earlier music to the honest optimism of Lennon, the searing intense guitar of Hendrix. Those artists no longer had the chance to compose new songs. Jet should respect his fans--and trust them--but more importantly, she wrote, trust himself. He still had that power within him to excite his fans. Why not give them what they really wanted: something new?

Reading it over, it felt right. She'd captured what she really wanted to say from a place of truth, not vengeance. Her prose had its own sparkle, connected to the music. The whole reason she'd become a music journalist.

Too good for the blog, but she couldn't allow Everett to edit this one. She posted it, then settled back against the pillow.

Next thing she knew, daylight streamed through the window. Voices sounded outside.

With a groan, she sat up. She hadn't even closed the blinds. Shielding her bleary eyes, she went to the window and caught Danny edging to the back patio, videocam at his shoulder. The girls swimming already? She glanced at the clock. Almost nine. Time to get moving.

After a quick shower, she checked her email. As expected, a message from Everett. *Your blog read more like an article. You posted before approval. Next time you post anything substantive, schedule it to post a few hours ahead and shoot me a text to review beforehand, like I asked. Nice work, though.*

Gee, thanks. Nice roundabout way of getting to the compliment. So personalized too. He must really miss her.

Funny, she hadn't thought about Everett in a while.

It felt good.

* * * *

The next morning seemed eerily quiet except for the rain dripping down the window. Rain always made Jet restless. Laughter sounded from downstairs. The girls wouldn't risk ruining their makeup by venturing out in this weather. The house grew too small very fast.

Hunched against the misty rain, he strode past the cottage.

that blue wash over and over her. The heat of his body made her hungry for more.

Don't go there! You already know how this story ends. She'd sung that sorry love song before.

"Are these your best moves? They're as stale as your music." Her words caught in her throat, but managed to hit their mark.

His features hardened. Searching her face, he froze, then eased away.

With a shuddering exhale, she steadied herself against the wall. Funny, she'd never been prone to vertigo before. But when he'd pulled away from her, he seemed to take some of her along.

He strode to the door. He touched the knob, hesitated a moment, then yanked it open and slammed it behind him.

Wow, she didn't know she could be such a bitch. *Pure self-defense. I can't afford to play his games.*

Or be another one of his playmates. He had enough already lined up for the sacrifice. Thinking about him spending time with them made her so angry. But after tonight, there would be one less.

Holding a hand to her belly, she took a moment to shake off the haze. Somehow, the moo shoo pork didn't seem as appetizing now.

* * * *

As if on cue, the rain subsided for the evening's taping. Thank God. If he'd been trapped inside one more hour, he might've been tempted to smash something. Instead, he did pushups and sit-ups until he ached.

Stale moves. He'd show her.

Stu's voice echoed up the stairwell. "Ready, Jet?"

"Coming." He jogged down, brushed past Stu who babbled about the schedule, and kept going until he hit the patio. A quick huddle with Stu and the producer, and Jet was ready.

He averted his gaze from the crew, knowing Billie would linger behind.

The producer called, "On three."

The speakers blared one of Jet's ballads. When it faded, the camera panned along the girls' faces, the epitome of hope and anguish. All but Cat. Her wickedly arched brow and smug smile conveyed her self-confidence. She'd stay. The perfect rocker girl, always wearing the skimpiest, clingiest outfits to show off her whiplash curves, set off by spiked heels. Plumped lips glistening, Cat waited third in line. She all but oozed sex.

Jet didn't relish the job ahead. "Brianna."

The girl squared her shoulders, tucked her chin and sauntered forth like a runway model.

He took her hands, pecked at her cheek. "We've had a good week." *A little more enthusiasm would sound more convincing.*

Brianna beamed. "Yes, we have." Her arms stiffened, and her grip tightened.

"I'm looking forward to getting to know more about you."

With a high-pitched sigh, she bounced to tiptoe. "Likewise, Jet." Her smile could have filled the room.

Winking, he leaned in. Before his lips touched her cheek, he glanced at Billie. He got the reaction he wanted.

She gasped, and her eyes blazed with fuming heat. Crossing her arms, she blanked her expression.

No beer could have given more of a lift. "Ashley," he crooned.

The second contestant sidled toward him, all but drooling.

He slid his hands into hers. "You've been so good to me this week."

"I tried." Batting her lashes, she swished her hips.

"Keep trying, darlin'."

Ashley swung her arms around his neck, her voluminous blonde hair obstructing his view.

Laughing, he pushed her shoulders back. "All right. Nice enthusiasm, Ashley. Mmm." His thumb and forefinger traced his mouth. "Terry."

Her smile tight, she approached with the nervousness of a first-time beauty pageant contestant.

Jet reached for both her hands. "You're a sweet girl, but I think we both know there's no connection. No spark." Not that he could claim to have one with any of them.

Terry jerked her head in what he assumed to be a nod.

"I appreciate you coming here, and wish you all the best in life."

"Goodbye." She leaned forward, kissed his cheek and then hurried through the French doors, making him wonder if her packed bags waited by the front entrance.

With the aim of a heat-seeking missile, Cat slunk toward him and draped an arm across his shoulder.

He hadn't even called her name. "Well, hello."

Cat silenced his greeting by pressing against him, her hips sliding in concert with her lips.

A gasp of shock, maybe frustration, came from the remaining women. Jet angled to see one cameraman cut to Ashley, standing openmouthed. Another camera zoomed close on the couple. He firmed his grip to ease her away, but Cat's locked arms signaled she intended to hold fast.

Why not? He had no reason not to enjoy this. He relaxed, and the barracuda in his arms renewed her attack.

When it grew a little hot for prime-time television, he broke away. "Easy now." His forced smile faded when he saw Billie retreat down the walkway.

Probably to slice him open on the blog again. She had no other reason to leave.

The thought sent a pang of regret through him.

* * * *

Ocean waves crashed against the bluff behind the house, sending sprays of water into the air. With pink, gold and orange streaking the sky, the water lit up like a light show.

Billie phoned Zinta. "I miss Philly."

"It's fifty and raining. Stop whining."

"Trade places with you," she offered. Its gritty gloom was part of Philly's signature charm.

"Not on your life."

Billie grunted. She'd suspected as much. "So how's Caleb?"

"I don't know." Zin's terse reply signaled trouble.

"Why? What's wrong?"

"We haven't been talking much. Or anything else."

"Zin..."

"Listen, I have to go. I'll talk to you tomorrow."

Billie frowned at her cell. She knew those avoidance tactics. She'd used them on Zinta. Something must be wrong.

Justin appeared at her side, and gazed out over the bluff. "Pretty cool."

"Yes, it's beautiful."

"You shouldn't let it get to you."

Had she been so obvious? "What?"

"Back there. It's all for show. We'll film commentary later and intercut it here. Probably Ashley will complain about Jet pushing her away, but allowing Cat to maul him onscreen. They all know the value of screen time."

"I get it. I needed a walk, that's all."

He nodded. "I'm leaving soon to shoot Ashley's date with Jet."

Billie chuckled. She'd like to shoot Jet too.

"I'd offer to give you a lift, but I have to ride in the limo."

"No, don't worry about me. I can live without witnessing the big date." So what if Everett squawked. She wrote about music, dammit. Not the dating habits of the semi-rich and used-to-be-famous.

"See you tomorrow." Justin backed away as if reluctant.

Did he think she'd leap off the bluff or something? "Goodnight."

Raising her camera, Billie captured a few shots. Enough for one day.

She'd spent the dawn hours on the Malibu Pier, famous for its *Baywatch* babes leaping into the ocean to save men floundering, hoping to be buoyed by Pamela Anderson's boobs. The Bimbo Squad could give Pam a run for her money in their skimpy tops and shorts, casting their fishing rods into the ocean. Except for Amber, who complained fishing bored her, and yawned frequently. Billie targeted her for Round Two's elimination.

Predictably, no one caught any fish. The bimbos had bigger fish to fry, anyway: hooking Jet. With his surly attitude, Billie wondered why anyone would want to. Fishing had a reputation for relaxing people, not making them uptight. The fishing industry wouldn't be asking Jet to be their spokesperson after he'd stomped off the pier an hour later muttering, the contestants scrambling to catch up.

On the beach, Billie stiffened as he neared. Glancing up, his eyes narrowed and he veered away from her. Cat and Ashley paraded by with a gleam of triumph.

Rock Bottom was four weeks into season two. Billie's body clock had adjusted after a few days to California time. The rest of her never would.

* * * *

Jet's fingers slid across the laptop's touch pad, scrolling the blog page. "Unbelievable." The best set they'd played in too long, and she ripped even that apart. "Vengeful bitch."

All the pride bolstering his ego fell away. What was wrong with her? They sounded great. *He'd* sounded great.

And he'd meant what he said about her inspiring him to be better. He'd needed someone to kick his ass into gear, but not to keep kicking it. Damn her. Privately, he could put up with her slams, but trying to turn his fans against him went too far.

A knock sounded. "Yeah."

Stu peered around the door. "Remember, the winery trip's on for today."

Great. Smile for the cameras. Make nice with the girls. Today he felt anything but nice. "What time again?"

"We leave in five minutes."

"Great." Some time away from here, at least. "Is Ms. Prescott attending?"

A frown flickered across Stu's face. "Of course. Why?"

He plopped back against the sofa. "Getting tired of her and her blog."

Stu pointed. "The blog is shit. But we need to keep Ms. Prescott happy."

"Right. Like that's even possible."

His manager shrugged. "Our ratings are higher every week. Like it or not, the blog's a big part of it."

Wincing, he stood. "Whatever. Let's go." He'd give her as wide a berth as possible.

"You look great." Stu's hand brushed his back. "It's all good."

What the hell did that mean? Ah, screw it. Maybe Jet should dumb himself down, lower his expectations so he could say it too. *It's all good.*

Repeating it like a mantra, he followed Stu down to the patio, but he couldn't get the words out of his head. When his gaze settled on Billie, his fists clenched and he stomped toward her. "Is this how it's going to be? You reaming me out every day online?"

His anger charged the atmosphere. He hadn't intended to broach this subject. Seeing her ignited all his senses.

"What?" She held up a hand toward Justin. "Stop filming." To him, she said, "This isn't the time--"

"It's the perfect time. I won't allow you to write this crap."

"My feelings aren't crap." Her brows furrowed, and hurt edged her voice.

"So now it's about your feelings, is it?" What about his feelings?

"Yes. As a fan. Aren't you interested in your fans' feelings?"

"Please. You're no fan. You're a disgruntled reporter. About what, I have no idea. Life in general, maybe?" His sneer softened when his gaze dropped to her mouth.

"I wrote the truth. If you can't handle it--"

"The truth according to Billie Prescott? What a joke." He stood so close, he could smell the coffee on her breath, feel her heat.

"Readers don't think so," she shot back.

Jet's nostrils flared, his fists clenched. He flinched at a hand on his shoulder.

Stu said, "Hey, shake it off. We can discuss this later. Right now, your contestants--and your public--await. Please don't keep them waiting any longer. Or the crew."

After an intense moment, Jet broke away with a nod. "Sorry. You're right. I shouldn't waste my time." His implied *on her* hung heavy in the air.

Give it up, he told himself. Somehow, he knew it was easier said than done.

* * * *

As Jet turned away, Billie released a ragged breath. Her senses had sharpened by his nearness. Every part of her snapped aware of every inch of him. At close range, the crystal blue of his eyes had pierced hers.

She silenced the voice within urging her to ask: Hadn't he read the comments following the blog? Some barbed, but the majority had been positive. Encouraging. Excited about the possibility of Jet recording something new.

She hadn't meant to wound him. Only to ignite some long-lost spark in his music. The flame in him now appeared more like hatred. Unbridled fury. All aimed at her.

His last cutting comment stuck in Billie's gut. Instinctively, she slid her palm across her stomach.

Appearing at her side, Justin winked. "Ignore the blowhard."

Attempting a smile, she stepped back, wishing she could disappear. "Yeah." Ignore the subject of her assignment. Good advice.

Not wanting to alienate Justin, she said nothing. Right now, he proved the only bright spot.

Jet consulted with Stu a moment, strode back down the stone path. When he emerged again, his smile could melt the panties off an ice queen.

Billie's insides twisted. The phony. The bimbos ate it up too. All giggly and cozy, Ashley stuck to him like a blonde barnacle, and the others close behind. Danny followed them all to the limo.

Justin tapped her arm. "Come on, I'll buy you a drink."

She tried not to smile. "They're free tonight."

"Then I'll buy you a few." Tilting his head, he urged her to follow and headed to the front.

True to his word, Justin kept her glass filled throughout the afternoon into the evening. She sipped, staying a distance from Jet, who kept a girl beneath each arm at all times. The moment one moved away, he coaxed another to his side. Jet's smile appeared conspiratorial. Intimate. As if he knew what each could do to him and couldn't wait for it. The way he flirted, he mistook the winery for a singles bar, though he'd go home with all of them tonight.

Disappointment pricked at her when he never glanced in her direction once. She wandered onto a side deck and leaned over the rail. Light edged the horizon, though the sky overhead darkened and stars emerged one by one.

"Are you all right?" Justin slipped out the door.

Damn. She'd hoped for a moment to gather herself. "Aren't you supposed to be working?"

"I'm taking five. You're shivering." He ran his hands up her arms to her shoulders.

Stiffening, she straightened, looked away. "No, I'm fine." Hopefully he'd get the hint.

His long legs straddled her. "I bet I could warm you up." He tilted his head, as if readying to kiss her.

"What? No." She moved to duck away.

He gripped her arms. "Oh, come on, Billie."

"No." Flailing, she jerked from his grasp.

"Everything all right?" Jet stepped through the doorway.

Sliding away to her side, Justin leaned against the rail. "It's cool, man."

Apparently unconvinced, Jet stared at Billie. "Is it?"

She hardly knew how to answer. Now, yes. But she didn't want to get Justin in trouble. Nodding, she whispered, "Yeah."

With narrowed eyes, Jet glanced from her to the videographer.

If Jet left, she'd have to deal with Justin again. Something she didn't quite feel up to. "Excuse me." She strode past Jet and into the hall.

Jet said something to Justin, she couldn't hear what. Footsteps sounded behind her, but she pushed through the door to the restroom.

At the mirror, two women froze to glare into the glass at her reflection.

Great. Just what she needed. A bimbo confrontation. "Hi, ladies." She hoped she sounded pleasant, but entered a stall before they could throw anything at her. Following an icy pause, they resumed discussing makeup, Jet and the wine.

Tomorrow, she planned to ask Stu about interviewing the contestants before Jet eliminated the next one. If Stu told them to do it, they'd agree. Maybe she could request all sharp objects be removed from the room ahead of time.

After a few minutes, the two exited, leaving Billie alone. Lately, she seemed to be alone too often, even in a crowd. For now, she welcomed it. Reveled in the blessed silence before she forced herself to go back to the group and face the endless chattering again. To appear busy, she shot a few photos for the blog.

"Psst." Lowering the videocam, Justin inclined his head.

With a wave, she moved away, ignoring the invitation. Instead, she strolled near the window and pretended to fiddle with the camera to eavesdrop on Stu's conversation with the winery host.

The man asked Stu how much longer they'd be staying. Stu shrugged. "It's reality TV, man."

The employee snapped, "Well, the reality is, we closed an hour ago."

With a practiced smile, Stu lowered his voice. "You want to say that louder for the cameras?"

The host's eyes narrowed, and he responded through clenched teeth, "You said you'd be gone by closing. You're costing us money."

Jet glanced over and seemed to assess the situation. "What time is it, darlin'?"

"Who cares?" With a sneering smile, Cat sipped her wine.

"It's eleven." Amber crossed an arm over her chest, swilling her drink, bored as could be.

Oh yeah, she'd be gone next.

"Eleven?" Jet feigned surprise. "Time to go, then."

Billie glanced at the winery host who slumped with relief. Jet must have realized they'd overstayed their welcome.

Over the whining cacophony, Jet's soothing voice rose. "We'll move the party to the pool. Doesn't that sound nice? And we'll buy a few bottles to go, and have a few cases shipped later." He winked at the employee.

Subversively classy. Making up for their mistake. But she wouldn't put any of this in tonight's post.

Cat whooped. "All right."

Outside, Billie forced herself to wait for the others to climb into the limo, Danny documenting even that.

Carrying his gear, Justin paused at her side. "Ready?"

"Oh yes." For once, she couldn't wait to get back to the cottage.

In the car, she added appropriate nods and smiles to Justin's banter. He went on, not seeming to notice the one-sided conversation.

She couldn't quite focus on what he said, anyway. In her mind, Jet's face appeared, scenes replaying vividly. She'd read about his gentlemanly charms, his professionalism in taking care of his band and crew.

"So what do you think?" Justin steered the van into the long driveway and parked behind the limo.

"About what?" Whatever he'd said, she'd missed it.

He knit his brows. "Am I boring you?"

"Sorry, I'm preoccupied. Things going on back at the magazine…"

He shifted to face her. "What things?"

Wishing she hadn't encouraged more conversation, her mind raced. "Oh, you know. Issues with the editor. Worried he'll fire me now," she lied. At least, she hoped it was a lie.

He slid an arm behind her seat. "I'd hate for that to happen."

Damn. She didn't feel up to fending him off again. "Thanks for the ride. See you tomorrow."

"You're not leaving already?" he teased.

"I'm exhausted. 'Night." Before he could say or do anything else, she climbed out.

In the limo ahead, Jet held the door open, watching Billie. Ashley slithered out, shot her a look of sheer poison.

Hearing Justin's door shut, Billie ducked her head and headed down the sidewalk to her cottage.

The two-room place constricted her. Even her laptop couldn't release the emotions roiling inside. Worse, she couldn't quite label them. Surprise, yes. Annoyance, maybe. But something else too. Indefinable but undeniable. Every time she forced herself to think of something else, Jet's face popped into her head. Angry. Sweet. Yearning…

Having to post photos of him online only reinforced the images. To relieve her brain of overdosing on Jet, she took a novel from her handbag and sprawled in bed. Even that couldn't distract her for long. After about an hour of reading the same passages and not absorbing anything, she set the book aside and turned off the light.

No matter what position she lay in, she could not get comfortable. "Damn pillow." She punched it, but the marshmallowy stuffing returned to picture-perfect shape again and again. She slammed it against the headboard. The air even seemed stifling. She rose to open a window. A breeze, even a hot one, would at least stir things up.

The strumming of a guitar captivated her. Such a gorgeous melody. Slipping into flip-flops and a shirt over her tank top, she crept outside and followed the tune to the studio, scattered solar lights along the path leading her way.

* * * *

A candle provided a warm glow. Sitting on the stoop, Jet bent over his guitar, completely lost in his song. Like he had in the earliest days, he gave himself over to the melody, played with his entire body, head keeping time with the beat, shoulders fluid as a dancer. His fingers flew along the frets, strings squeaking. With a final downward thrust, he strummed the last chord. Its harmony hung in the night air like fireflies.

The sound of scuffing caught his attention. Glancing up, he scowled. "Who's there?"

Waiting, his chest tightened with something like hope.

"Just me." With hesitating steps, Billie moved forward.

Delight gave way to wariness. He frowned. "What are you doing here?"

"I heard you playing. It was nice." She hastened to add, "Really good."

"Ple--ase." Wincing, he tuned one string, then another. Anything to divert his attention.

She moved closer. "No, I mean it."

"You're trying to save your ass," he mumbled.

"What?" She froze, eyes wide.

"Your job. It won't work. My manager's dead set on having you sacked." Sipping bottled water, he glanced up. His machismo faded when he saw the fear in her eyes.

"Sacked?"

"You're counterproductive to the show, he says. To me." He gave a bitter laugh. "Though I tend to disagree with him on that point." Whether she meant to or not, she'd inspired him to be better. He set the guitar aside. "You were right. You have been a catalyst in a lot of ways."

"I didn't come here to be your friend. I'm a journalist. Not an ego massager like the rest of them." She bit her lip.

Stretching out a leg, he taunted, "But you said it was nice. Really liked it."

"And I meant it. You played like you used to, full of passion, putting yourself into the song. I haven't seen you do that in a long time." She closed the distance between them, and now stood by the stoop. The glow of the candlelight softened her fair skin, her face framed by dark hair flowing in long waves.

Studying her, he pressed his lips together. "No. Maybe not." Pausing his fingers along the strings, he laid the guitar atop his lap.

"Is it new? I don't remember it."

Standing, he pulled the studio door shut. "It's late. Tomorrow's a busy day." Shouldering the guitar strap, he trudged down the walkway. He had to get away from her. Get her out of his head. She drove him crazy, stirred up too many emotions at once.

She followed him down the path. "For you. For me, it could be the first day of unemployment."

He clamped his jaw tight. She wouldn't taunt him into an argument.

"You can't fault me for doing my job." Desperation edged her tone.

His open shirt riffled in the breeze as he walked. "I don't. Like I said, Stu's rethinking the arrangement. For a reporter, you assume an awful lot about people. Maybe you should dig a little deeper than the surface next time."

"I can't believe it."

He shot her a sharp glance. Just long enough to send shockwaves down his spine. "It's best if you go, anyway."

Her pace increased. "Why?"

He whirled to face her. She bumped into him, and her hands flew up and landed on his chest. He stood riveted, the only movement his gaze, his quick breaths beneath her fingers.

She tensed, searching his face.

The soft solar lights enhanced the blaze in her eyes. The emotion clouding her face wasn't fury. That much he knew.

Careful, he told himself. *She's a reporter.*

Easing away, he softened his voice. "You're a distraction."

Her lips parted. He recognized something rising within her, reaching for him.

Something he wanted. With the slightest twitch in his eyes, he steeled himself. Stiffly, he stepped back. "Good night."

Clutching the guitar strap, he turned and walked.

"Jet," she whispered.

Her coarse tone alighted his nerves faster than a match to gasoline.

Uttering a curse, he ducked his head and strode faster, letting the darkness separate them.

* * * *

Banging startled her awake. An assistant called, "Meeting in Stu's office in five."

Rushing to the door, she yanked it open. "Five minutes? I'm not even dressed."

Arching a brow, he tilted his head. "Better hurry then." Pursing his lips, he scuffled away.

Geez, even the guys here were bitchy. Slamming the door, she stripped off her tank top as she walked to the bathroom. She groaned at her image and quickly applied some mascara and concealer to little effect. Late nights always left their mark. Sleepless nights compounded the damage. And last night she'd gotten very little sleep.

She reached in the closet and pulled out a black sundress. Might as well dress for the morbid occasion. Yep, like flunking kindergarten. Could she fail any more miserably?

Nothing to do with her hair except pull it back in a barrette. An oversized mother-of-pearl necklace would draw attention from her raccoon eyes, so she clasped it around her neck, grabbed her bag and rushed to the house.

So she'd taken ten minutes. Everyone else kept Stu waiting. Why shouldn't she?

Holding a hand to her cell phone, Cindy nodded at the door. "Go on in."

Nodding her thanks, she knocked once and pushed open the door.

Stu smiled, hands jammed in his khaki Dockers. "Ah, there she is."

Jet turned. And the man next to him. Everett. Smiling at her.

Surprise pricked her alert. Struggling to comprehend, she stammered, "What are you doing here?" Had they really assembled to crucify her?

Smiling, Everett linked arms and tugged her to the others. "Billie. We were just talking about the effects of your coverage."

Her hand splayed across her stomach to quell its flip-flops. "Effects?" So far, they'd been positive, hadn't they? Or had Everett exaggerated to keep her here longer? All this, and no coffee yet.

Jet's chin dropped to his chest, and he hunched his shoulders. Bracing himself.

So here it came: the public flogging. Her firing. A wonder Stu didn't have the cameras rolling for his big triumph. And Jet couldn't even face her.

With a clownish grin, Stu rocked back on his heels. "Yes, the show's ratings are through the roof. All because of you."

"Oh?" That sounded positive. Why the hell had they called Everett in?

Everett's pleasant expression mirrored Stu's--a scary thought. "It's a mutual success."

She couldn't follow any of this. "I need coffee."

Boisterous as a circus performer, Stu bounded to the credenza. "Will an espresso do the trick?" He poured and held out the cup.

Everett clinked his cup against hers. "Here's to continued success."

Her heart sank. *Continued.* "So I'm staying?" Overnight, she'd almost gotten used to the notion of being fired. It would at least have gotten her out of here.

Stu's laughter sounded like a barking seal. "Of course you're staying."

A glance at Jet arrested her. He watched her with the intensity of a laser.

Her fingers ached to touch him again. She reminded herself to breathe.

Jet broke away his gaze. "I have some things to wrap up. I'll leave you to work out the details. Everett, thanks for coming. Talk to you later," he said to his manager.

She waited for him to acknowledge her, but he left without looking back.

Stu's phone rang. "Excuse me."

Glancing after Jet, Everett stepped close. "Everything all right?"

Ignoring her basic emotions--same old Everett. But she'd save that conversation for another time. "You know how it is, rock stars' egos easily bruise. But I really hoped this would be over soon."

He threw an arm around her shoulder and tugged her close. "We're just getting started."

"Everett…" Seeing him didn't excite her the way she'd imagined. This morning, standing next to Jet, he appeared a diminished version of the man she'd left in Philadelphia.

His arm encircled her waist. "Listen, I can't stay long or I'd take you to lunch. When you get back, maybe we could go out and celebrate."

"Yeah. Maybe." Forcing a wan smile, she couldn't imagine that lunch date.

"Can I look forward to a blog post today?"

"Of course." She knew exactly what she wanted to say.

* * * *

Date night. Jet tried to muster some enthusiasm, but he couldn't. Cat gave him the jitters, and not in a good way. Feral as a jaguar, he sensed she'd go for the jugular if given a chance.

He trudged downstairs, and his wariness shot through the roof.

Her dress, if he could call it that, skimmed her thighs, its tiny silver circles like liquid as she moved. "There you are," she cooed.

"Yep. Here I am." Not exactly RWA. He glanced at Stu who winked, a lascivious gleam in his eye.

Cat's hips sent her dress in motion. When her glistening lips brushed his cheek, he subdued the urge to wipe it away. "You look amazing."

"Don't I always?" She tittered.

"Yes," he lied. In truth, if he'd seen her out somewhere, he'd never have given her a second glance. Amazing? Sure, but also high-maintenance. Devious. He bet himself a beer he would have nothing in common with her. Not a single damn thing.

In the limo, she wasted no time. Her hands wandered down his buttons, and his shirt fell open.

In the seat opposite, Justin adjusted the camera lens. Zooming in, no doubt, so as not to miss a detail.

He covered her hand with his and sent her a look of warning. "Why don't you tell me more about yourself?"

With a whine, she cozied closer. "Not now." Her tongue circled inside his ear.

He tightened his hand over hers, and whispered in her ear. "Exactly. Not now."

Bad enough having this captured for an audience. Somehow, he only imagined one person watching: Billie. He didn't want her to see this. She had to understand he wasn't some washed-up, clueless dude. He aimed for excellence, in music and in life. He hoped she'd convey that to her readers.

And realize it herself.

* * * *

In the isolated containment of the cottage, Billie nestled on the bed, laptop on a pillow.

She couldn't deny she'd had preconceived notions about the show, about him--how could she not? His music had been part of her life for fifteen years. His constant persona made him seem as familiar as any guy she attended high school with. His face appeared everywhere: on MTV, in the trade and entertainment magazines. She'd never considered he might want more of himself too. That he'd grown tired of playing at being himself.

She had no trouble writing about how he'd tightened his sound. In the studio, his soulful renditions captivated Billie as much as the others. Ditto about how amazing he looked. To praise his appearance would not only sink her to the level of gossip columnist, but pump up his already overinflated ego.

Jet Trently, she wrote, is an artist, but also a lost soul. She painted him as someone who wanted more from himself, but perhaps didn't know how to extract it from within. Perhaps, she wrote, he'd been discouraged from expanding his music by those around him.

Wincing, she hesitated. She had to be careful to make no blatant accusations. Something about Stu always made her cringe, and not only his balding pate, his thinning hair pulled back into a ponytail and excessive jewelry. His new pinkie ring came to mind: platinum, and a square chunk of onyx with a diamond set in the center. A self-given bonus?

Research might bear it out. Her investigative journalism skills might prove a little rusty, but something niggled at her to find out. Stu seemed to be the one pushing for the "sure thing," who didn't want Jet taking chances. Or ruining Stu's good thing. Even if Jet drowned in frustration in the meantime.

Despite the fact too many years passed since Jet recorded anything new, she suspected he yearned for it most of all. If he allowed himself to open to it, he'd find it.

If she could guide him in that direction, so much the better.

Chapter 5

In the morning, Billie cornered Stu in the kitchen. "Hey, I'd love to interview the contestants."

"Sure. Set it up with Cindy." Opening a Perrier, he strode toward his office.

Great, easier than she thought. The actual interview, probably not so easy. Cindy flipped through the schedule. "How about five o'clock?"

Craning to see the date, she asked, "Today?"

"Too soon?"

Cindy rivaled the Sphinx for inscrutability. Gazing up, blank-faced as ever, she might have hated Billie's guts at that moment. More likely, she had no expression because she simply didn't care.

"No, five is perfect. But...no cameras, right?" Just to be clear.

"Right." Cindy promised to alert the girls.

Walking through the hallway, Billie texted Zin: *So is Everett screwing someone else?*

Immediately, Zin called. "How did you know?"

Okay, so the shot in the dark was a bulls-eye. One that ricocheted to strike her in the gut. Not hard to guess when he flew across country and didn't even take the time to pretend to miss her. The goodbye kiss he offered felt more like a peck. He always saved his best moves for the current girl. She should know--he'd left her swooning, even as she packed to leave.

"I didn't. In spite of his warm send-off, he's been a bit...professional since I arrived here." Her insides churned. Of course it was why he sent her to California. The bastard!

"Sorry."

"Don't be. He's my editor. Like you said, I should have known better." Foresight seemed an unnecessary virtue at the time. Hindsight proved more damaging.

"You and dozens of others."

"Ouch." Her friend's barb struck deep.

"You knew that going in, right?"

"I suppose. Hope springs eternal, and all that bull." Though she knew, deep down, Everett wouldn't commit. Like the Radiohead song, he admitted up-front to being an unworthy creep.

"Guys like Everett don't change."

"I don't know what made me think he was the best of both worlds-- rock star enough to feed my bad girl addiction, and normal enough to be boyfriend material." Time to stop wishing on the moon. Every guy in the rock and roll business, apparently, made awful boyfriend material.

Justin rounded the corner of the pool house as she headed down the path. "Hey there."

Pointing to the phone, she shrugged an apology, though relief flooded through her. After last night, she wanted to give Justin a wide berth.

"What's the emergency, Zin?"

"Have you gone mad? There's no emer-- Ah. Someone's there?"

Feigning concern, she walked on. "Extremely."

The door to the editing room opened, and she turned to see him disappear inside. Chuckling, she walked on. "You saved me again."

"What the hell is going on in that little aspiring-to-be-reality show?"

"I now know how Alice felt when she fell through the rabbit hole. Everything's growing curioser and curioser."

"Don't sample any bottles labeled 'drink me'. And don't keep me in suspense. What's up?"

"Weirdness. Justin, the camera guy."

"But Justin's a diversion?"

"He's kinda cute in a British-hangdog kind of way, but a little overbearing." She relayed the events of the previous night.

"Sounds like a creep."

Billie feared the same, though he also represented her only friend here. "So tell me about you and Caleb." She needed some good news for a change.

"Not much to tell. I've been busy, he's been busy, neither the twain have met." Frustration crackled through the phone.

So much for happy news. "You'll get your groove back."

"Maybe."

Or maybe not, if Zinta's abrupt change of subject provided any insight. Seemed like more than a mere slump.

Billie found herself outside the path to Jet's studio. "I understand." More than Zin knew. She'd wrestled thoughts of Jet away since last night.

"Right. Well, what's on your happy little agenda today?"

Billie sighed. "Interviewing the Bimbo Babes."

Zin chuckled. "A mindless exercise."

"A few might surprise me. Julie, for instance. She doesn't fit the profile. And Cat, though interviewing her might require a little self-defense."

"Sharp claws?"

"Very." The way she looked at Billie, she wanted to use those claws on her.

"If she attacks, squirt hairspray into her eyes."

"I'll keep a can handy." Though she'd have to borrow one. She'd long ago abandoned attempts to keep her long layers in check. They flowed as they wished without restraint. One less thing to pack, anyway. "What about you?"

"Lucky me, I'll be speaking with Justin Timberlake." She spoke with the enthusiasm of the condemned.

"Hey, he makes a hilarious Gibb brother."

"I'll ask him to do an impression for me."

After Zin said goodbye, Billie retraced her steps to the cottage. Research had turned up little on any of the contestants except Julie, a college student working toward a degree in communications, making her the biggest puzzle. Still, if any of the others had a shady past, Billie hoped to coax some clues from them. If Ashley had been a dancer, she probably used a stage name to keep her true identity a secret.

At ten minutes to five, she opened her messenger bag and tossed in the digital recorder, camera, a fresh steno pad and pen. Slipping a white blouse over her silky tank top and slacks, she pulled her hair back loosely into a barrette. Maybe it would help put them at ease if she appeared more frumpish.

Except for Cindy speaking on her cell at the back of the hall, the house seemed deserted. Ascending the stairs, Billie steeled herself.

Behind the last door, the women shrieked and squabbled. With a steadying breath, she went inside.

Three vanities lined the walls, lit with megawatt bulbs forcing the air conditioner to strain. Cat, Ashley and Brianna sat at the vanities applying makeup.

"Jet looked so hot last night." "My makeup's smeared already." "Do you think Stu would mind if I had a wardrobe malfunction?"

No one responded to any comment, making Billie wonder if they all babbled rhetorically. The only voice not in the cacophony was Julie's. She sat on the bed bent over a book.

With the camera off, maybe they'd allow their true selves to speak rather than their personas. Some, like Ashley, appeared so malleable, so willing to adapt to whatever the producers and Jet wanted, it made Billie wonder if they'd ever truly defined themselves. Or if they knew the true cost to themselves of adapting so easily.

Billie forced a smile. "So, ladies. How's it going?"

In the mirror, Cat's gaze met hers. "Look who it is. The *Strung Out* bitch." She stroked the makeup brush across her cheek.

Definite frost in the room, and not just the air conditioner. "Got a few minutes? For some girl talk?" Hopefully that sounded sincere. Girl talk never held much appeal, but she'd have to feign an interest.

"Why?" Brianna gripped the back of her padded slipper chair. "So you can write awful things about us too?" With the regal harrumph of a princess, she turned back to the mirror.

Uh-oh. They'd aligned themselves against her, on the Jet Team. "'Course not. I'd love to hear what you think about the show. About Jet. About each other." In saying the last, she tensed, ready to duck if necessary. Tensions on the set ebbed and flowed, always with an undercurrent that made it seem as if it could turn on a dime to sheer nastiness. To have the full force of it aimed at her might prove fatal.

Ashley lifted her chin, stared at her image. "Jet is a sweetheart. He deserves better treatment."

Pen poised, Billie asked, "From the producer?"

Brianna whirled. "No. Duh--you!"

"I treat him well." She had to turn this conversation around quick.

Glaring, Cat paused her makeup application. "You called him a has-been."

"A washout," Ashley said.

"A joke." Cat's glare held an icy gleam.

"Help me see another side of him. What do you think of him?" Billie drew her digital recorder and clicked it on. "Ashley, you're from North Carolina, correct? What brings you to the show?"

Her blue eyes wide, Ashley's face blanked. "Jet, of course. I've loved his music for years."

Billie moved closer, hoping they'd open up more. "It's the same music from years ago. How do you feel about that?"

Blinking, Ashley shrugged. "It's still good."

"It rocks," Brianna interjected.

"Brianna, you're from New Jersey?" Billie sat on the edge of the bed.

Chin tilted up, lips pursed, she stroked mascara on her lashes. "Yes."

"You left the Garden State for this?" Partly a joke. Most Jerseyites Billie knew left for any reason possible.

"No, I left years ago to study acting. I've been waitressing to pay the bills. Until now."

"So the show's lucrative for you?" The winner would gain a hundred grand, but what did each contestant receive?

"More than waitressing," Amber said.

"Not much," Julie muttered.

Definite disappointment surfacing there. And a conversational in with the quiet one. "Julie, you're from Montana?"

The girl slouched farther on the bed. "Yes."

"A college grad. Impressive. What major?"

Fingering her bookmark, she glanced up. "Communications."

"Really? A journalist in the making."

Julie turned back to her book. "We'll see."

"Why are you here?" Obviously, she could do much better for herself pursuing an actual career rather than a virtual one.

Pinning her smooth hair behind her ear, she shrugged. "I tried out and got the call. Seemed like a good experience."

"So you're not into Jet? Or his music?"

"I didn't say that. I tried out for the same reasons as everyone else."

Sirens went off in Billie's head. This girl didn't belong here. To regain a conversational foothold, she made her voice casual. "Longtime fan? You want to sleep with him?"

"I do." Ashley's enthusiasm nearly choked her. "He's hotter now than ever."

"You don't mind he's at 'rock bottom'?" Billie's fingers arced quotation marks.

Cat slammed her brush atop the vanity. "It's just the name of the show. Not a description of Jet."

Now she'd have to tread softly. "True, but didn't they name it that because Jet's there now? To help him up from the bottom?"

Ashley stood. "No. He sounds great. He works really hard at his music."

Billie shrugged. "Most musicians do. It doesn't mean they all deserve air play."

"And he really loves it." Brianna pouted. "He pours his heart out into every song."

Clasping her hands, Ashley sighed. "I know. When he's at the microphone, every emotion's right there on his face. It makes me want to rush up and grab him."

Billie'd said the same things to her girlfriends--in high school. She wouldn't be trading doe-eyed comments over cocktails with these women anytime soon. "So is that part of the show's premise?"

The women exchanged confused, if overly made up, glances.

Time for a different approach. "When you're on a date, what happens when the cameras stop rolling? Is it anything goes?"

The glances they exchanged seemed filled with suspicion.

"Are you not allowed to discuss it?" Billie prompted.

"Oh, we're allowed." Ashley flipped her hair behind her shoulder.

Cat arched a brow. "We just don't."

"So you have a code of honor for when the camera stops filming?" Billie hoped she didn't sound condescending.

Cat crossed her legs. "Not exactly." Her cutting tone sounded as dangerous as her long spiked heels appeared.

Now Billie understood. "Oh. You're holding out on each other. Why?"

Ashley appeared moony. "It would become hurtful."

"Vicious," Amber added, her tone hinting she wouldn't mind being the first to try it.

"Julie? What about you?"

"Exactly. What they said." Shoving the book inside the backpack, she stood. "Excuse me."

"Me too." Cat rose, still primping her hair.

"Yes, we have to dress now," Ashley said with the snideness of a teenager.

Brianna glanced up as she followed the others.

"Maybe we can continue some other…time."

The door closed, and laughter erupted outside.

Interview over. But not the intrigue. Julie stood out among this group, her natural beauty enhanced with little makeup, her clothes well-fitting but not skin-tight, her quiet intelligence a definite juxtaposition to the loud shallow-minded girls. Definitely not trying as hard as the others.

Billie would have to do a little more digging. On all of them.

* * * *

Jet emerged from the office, Stu in tow, droning on, he had no clue about what. He hesitated when the contestants' voices drifted down the stairs. They swarmed into the kitchen, and he grasped the railing and turned to Stu. "Sounds great, but right now, I have to catch up on some things."

Hearing the door open upstairs, he readied to flee but stilled at the sight of Billie descending.

"Your interview with the girls go well?" Stu folded his arms across his chest.

Pausing at the bottom of the steps, she dropped the recorder into her bag. "Yes, very well." Her gaze flicked up to his.

Something electric zipped across his skin. "Don't I get to finish our interview?"

Surprise showed in her parted lips, her steady gaze. She recovered quickly. "Absolutely. Whenever you have time."

"I always have time for a one-on-one." His attempt to lighten the air between them fell flat.

She gave a thin smile. "Whenever you're ready, let me know."

"Tonight. I'll take you to dinner." And straighten things out once and for all.

"No need. Anywhere away from the cameras will be fine." She glanced at Stu.

Stu shrugged. "It's a reality show. They follow wherever."

"You have a show to do. And I need an exclusive." She appeared confused about his change of heart.

He hoped to clear the confusion. Approaching with arms wide, he grinned. "I'm exclusively yours."

Stu followed. "Jet--"

"Stu, a few hours away won't make a damn bit of difference. You have plenty of drama right here to keep the cameramen busy."

She hastily said, "No dinner. Please. A restaurant might prove too distracting, what with all your fans asking for autographs."

He shifted closer. "I know a little place where no one will disturb us. And a band's playing tonight I've been wanting to see."

"It'll be too noisy." Eyeing him, she tilted her head. "What band?"

"You'll love them." He didn't need to name them. He had her. She was as eager to ditch this place as he was.

Defeat weighed her voice. "All right."

"All right," he repeated. "Nine o'clock. I promise I won't keep you up too late."

"Okay." Confusion clouded her face, and she hesitated before moving away.

Of course he'd remembered. He thought of it every night when he played in his studio, and the light in her cottage winked out.

* * * *

"I must be crazy." Searching through her meager wardrobe, Billie waited for Zinta to argue otherwise.

"Let me get this straight. You're going out with him?"

She held up a white top, and discarded it. Too plain. "No. I'm interviewing him, and he's taking me to hear a band."

"Sounds like he's taking you out. Is he driving you there?"

Oh, geez. She hadn't thought about that. "I guess."

"What time are you leaving?"

"Nine." She laid a silky black top on the bed. Too sexy.

"Sounds like a date to me."

"No. It's an interview." She was ninety-nine percent certain of it. Why else would he take her away from here if not to glom onto the blog spotlight?

"At a club? Billie, please."

"I'll start it on the way there. It'll be good to see him away from here. This place is so…oppressive. Everyone's always so guarded." Or over the top, in a staged way. Every move calculated ahead of time. It irked her. While the cameras rolled, no one voiced a sincere off-the-cuff comment.

"So you're observing him in various environments? Now you're a cultural anthropologist?"

"It's part of what we do, isn't it? He got so excited about this band, I couldn't say no."

"What band?"

She checked her notes. It couldn't be. "Uhhh…"

"You have no idea, do you?"

"He mentioned the name. It didn't ring a bell." Why lie? To Zin? She always came clean with her friend.

Skepticism edged Zin's tone. "Someone new, I'm sure."

"Must be." This was not a date.

"Well, have fun. But be careful."

"It's not a social thing. It's an interview. Careful of what?"

"The situation. Him."

"I told you, it's an interview."

"Yeah. So was my interview with Jakob Dylan."

"Oh, I envy you. How'd that go?" Had she still been in Philadelphia, she'd have fought for that one, even against Zinta.

"He plied me with tequila."

Billie froze. She knew what tequila did to Zin. "And?"

"And now I can confirm the rumors about his sexual prowess are all true. I hope Caleb never finds out. Or maybe I do."

"No! But you love Caleb."

"That's the hell of it. My point is: I never intended for it to happen. And I want you to be careful."

"Yeah." She wouldn't contradict Zin when she was obviously hurt. "I'll talk to you tomorrow."

Her earlier sense of foreboding returned. She shook it off. Tonight, she'd get away from here, dressed in work casual clothes so he wouldn't misunderstand.

* * * *

Quarter to nine. She'd be here any moment. Jet stood at the kitchen island and flipped through the newspaper, not registering a word of it.

What the hell was he doing? Stu reamed him out, but he could give no good excuse. Something snapped. He had to set things straight. He had to know whether he'd been wrong about her.

When she entered the backdoor, he straightened slowly and gulped hard. "Ready?"

"Yes. But are you sure this won't rock the *Rock Bottom* boat?"

His hand at the small of her back, he guided her to the front door. "A little healthy competition will make it all the more interesting."

"I'm not competition--"

"Come on, before they see you." He grabbed his keys with one hand, and her with the other.

"I'm just going to interview you."

Laughing, he pulled her along the walkway. "Don't you ever have fun?"

"Of course, but I'm here to work."

Swirling to a stop outside the garage, he caught her in his arms. "Work, fun--it should be the same, shouldn't it?"

Hands at her narrow waist, her scent filled her nostrils. To his surprise, she splayed her hands against his chest.

"If you love what you do."

"I do." His chest expanded with a breath and he released her.

"I can tell."

Surprise again. "Mmm." He backed away until he reached the side of a vehicle, then opened the door.

Following, she climbed in. "A Wrangler?"

"This disappoints you?" He tugged the seat belt down and pulled it across her to fasten it.

"No, surprised is more like it."

His hand lingered on the seat. "I like what I like. My needs are simple." His gaze dropped to her lips. No, he'd pushed it too far already. He shut the door.

"I bet." She chuckled.

Climbing in, he froze. "What?" Was she playing him?

"Nothing. I'm having fun, that's all."

Sounded genuine enough. He started the engine. "It's about time." Revving it, he peeled out of the garage and down the curling driveway.

She grasped her bag bouncing across her lap and giggled.

He loved the sound. Found it contagious, and he laughed.

The gates swung open, and he pulled through and stopped. Drumming on the steering wheel, he hummed a song he'd been composing.

"That would make a great reggae tune."

Exactly what he already had in mind. To demonstrate, he sang, "I like what I like, ain't no rhyme or reason." Words had stumped him, until now.

She continued singing, "I do what I do, no matter what the season."

"Hey, not bad." Nodding his head in time, he sang on, "I like what I do, baby, because of you." Shifting, he reached farther to nudge his knuckles into her leg. "I think we should collaborate." That was beginning to have a nice ring to it.

She arched a brow. "If we did, would you record it?"

Clucking his tongue, he wagged his finger. "Ah-ah-ah."

"Would you?" Her tone grew urgent. She wasn't kidding.

Unable to commit, he shrugged. "Maybe."

Frustration escaped in a part-groan, part-sigh. "I'll believe that when I see it."

Sometimes she pushed too hard. He set his jaw. "Why does it matter so much?"

"The question is, why doesn't it matter to you?" She seemed to want to make him angry.

Instead, he clammed up tight, stared straight ahead and fumed silently.

Softly, she sang, "I like what I like, ain't no rhyme or reason."

Hiding his surprise, he glanced over. "It is pretty catchy." And sounded better when she sang it.

"It would even be great as a hard rock song with a driving guitar sound."

His voice gritty, he tried the new beat with the few lyrics, and nodded. "Mmm."

She settled back in her seat, visibly relaxed. "So what band are we going to see?"

"Does it make a difference?"

Biting back a smile, she shrugged. "So tell me, Mr. Trently, which musicians influenced you most?"

Shaking his head, he looked away. "You can't just relax? It must suck to be you."

"The Beatles? Stones? Hendrix?"

"All of the above. Everyone from Donovan to Dylan to U2."

Her smile faded, and she gazed away into the night. "So how would you categorize your music? Who would you say it's a mix of?"

He hated this question. "Why does it have to be a mix of anyone else? Can't it be my own?"

"Absolutely. And I've heard people describe other bands as sounding like yours. But I've also heard definite influences of other musicians in your songs."

Ouch. He took pride in crafting original music. "Such as?"

"Springsteen's slice-of-life scenes, his searing lyrics that spoke counter to the hard-driving rhythms. Like your early hit, *Nobody Home*. I remember people singing along to that like a rebel anthem when really it spoke of the disappearance of small town America, the loss of downtown businesses contributing to the growth of Walmarts and urban sprawl." She glanced over.

Mouth agape, he stared.

She tensed. "What? Am I completely wrong on that one?"

"That's exactly it. Most people miss it." Turning away, his mood sobered.

After a moment, she asked, "Are you able to get away from the show often?"

"No." Downshifting, he steered into a parking lot and found a space.

"What about last season? How many times did you leave the cameras behind?" Her hand paused on the door handle.

Pursing his lips, he stared ahead. "Never." Why hadn't he? No wonder he'd been so miserable.

"Never?"

Did she never let anything go? "Do you want to go in?" He leaned close and eased closer. Another few inches, and...

"Yes, let's go." She scrambled out and walked.

Slowly, he stepped out and followed. At the door, she waited for him to catch up. The bouncer nodded at Jet, and his palm on the small of her back guided her in. The music shook the walls.

When he put his mouth to her ear, his hand slid around her waist. "Where do you want to sit?" If he was lucky, she'd say the Wrangler. Now that he had hold of her, he didn't want to let go.

* * * *

Intoxicated by the moment, Billie closed her eyes, then took a steadying breath. "Anywhere's fine." Her lips brushed his hair, softer than she'd imagined. It made her want to twine her fingers in it. Smooth it from his cheek. Afraid of the crazy thoughts coursing through her mind, she turned away.

Scanning the room, he nodded toward an empty booth, his hand sliding higher up her side, making her tense and flush warm.

A few heads turned as they passed, women and men sizing Billie up. Most people ignored celebrities, but all it would take would be one cell phone shot, one digital camera, and their faces would be splashed all over the entertainment news.

Sliding into the booth first, she had to keep moving over when he followed close behind.

He nudged her. "A little more. We'll have a better view of the band."

She inched over, and his shoulder bumped hers as he settled. "Yeah, there."

"Would you rather sit here?" Not wanting to trust her messenger bag so close to the outside, she hugged it to her.

"No, this is good. Don't you think?" He grinned, glanced down and grabbed her bag. "Let me take that."

"No, I'll--"

"It'll be safe beside me, don't worry." His eyes glittered in the darkness with a youthful wildness.

"But I--" How could she interview him without her recorder? Or at least a notepad?

A blonde in a low-cut tank top smiled at Jet.

Jet touched Billie's arm. "Margarita?"

Not after Zin's fateful tequila episode. "Riesling?" she asked.

The blonde nodded and leaned over the table as Jet ordered a beer.

Over the loud music, she asked, "What time is the band starting?"

He tilted his head toward her as she spoke. "Uh... soon?" His mouth shrugged down, but his eyes twinkled with mischief.

Had there even been a band scheduled to play? Why drag her out here then? "Who is it again?"

The waitress returned with their drinks, and he dug his wallet from his back pocket.

Sipping, she tamped down the paranoia setting in. Zin's words haunted her. If he wanted an excuse to get away, wouldn't he have gone with one of the Bimbo Brigade? At least it would have made fodder for the show.

The piped-in music faded, and a man bound onto the small platform where a drum kit sat behind a few microphones. As the announcer welcomed the crowd, she glanced at Jet. He strained to see, and excitement erased decades from his face. Engrossed in him, she forgot to listen for the name of the band. They took the stage and slammed into a driving song that had Jet banging his head, bouncing his knee.

With a wicked grin, he asked, "Aren't they great?"

She had to admit they were good. Worthy of a blog post. Maybe she could talk to them afterward, get a few photos.

The group launched into a rousing song, and Billie couldn't help tapping her fingers, nodding her head in time. If she had come with anyone else, she'd be out in the writhing crowd, letting the music move her to its rhythm.

Jet nudged her. "Let's go."

Confused, she glanced back. "What?"

"We have to dance. This song's too good to sit still to."

"But my bag--"

He slid it beneath the table. "No one will touch it. Come on."

When he pressed close on the dance floor, she felt his energy. Contagious--and dangerous. The music got to her, and she let it slide through her limbs. His fluid movements got to her even more. Matching his moves came easily. Naturally.

Rather than making her tense, his intense focus loosened her tight muscles. Or maybe it was the wine. Bodies swayed all around them. Here, they could be anonymous. Just two people dancing. One incredibly sexy guy dancing with her.

Raising her arms, she let the slow, heavy music command her. Its rhythm mesmerized her.

Jet's legs grazed hers. His hands slid along her waist and back.

When the song ended abruptly, her breath hitched in her chest, and her heart pounded. They stood, Jet's gaze locked on hers.

It felt like waking up from a dream. A really good dream. Or the morning after. When Zinta's warning echoed in her mind, she blocked it.

"Should we…" She gestured to the table.

The singer announced the next song dedicated to his girl.

"No." Jet entwined his fingers in hers and pulled her close, swaying.

Closing her eyes, she gave herself over to the searing guitar. She tried to ignore how well her body fit against his, how his hips circled invitingly, how his mouth brushed her neck as he nuzzled into her. *Don't be stupid, Willamina.*

She broke away, broke whatever spell she'd been under. "I should be going."

Furrowing his brow, he searched her face, his embrace firm. "Now?"

Now or never. She nodded. "You could stay. I could take a cab."

"No, I don't want to stay if you're leaving."

"Oh, right. You'd be alone." Not for long, she bet. *Shut up before he thinks you're a complete idiot.* She pushed through the crowd to the table and grabbed her bag.

"It's fine. We can go. If you really want to."

"Yes, I should." Even if he now thought her behavior irrational, rushing away like the place was on fire. *No, not the club. Just me.*

Walking to the car, a warm breeze did little to cool her down.

She glanced over. "Thanks for bringing me. Good band."

"Yeah. Thanks for going with me." Sarcasm edged his voice. Or confusion. He pointed the clicker at the Jeep and the doors unlocked.

"Does this top come down?"

In the dim light, his eyes sparkled with a devilish light. "You want to go topless?"

Ugh. The Jet she knew and disliked had returned. *Thank you.* "It's such a nice night."

"I'd have suggested it, but I knew it would mess up your hair."

Digging in her bag, she held up a scrunchy hair tie. "No problem."

"Give me one minute." Opening the door, he unsnapped the levers and grunted as he worked.

"Can I help? I didn't realize the process was so involved."

"Nope. Got it." Pushing the soft top back, he secured it in place, then got behind the wheel and shifted into first. "Much better."

"The wind's a bit loud. I mean, for an interview."

He pressed his lips together. "I know where we could go." In minutes, he turned off onto an overlook and parked. "Nice, huh?"

Below, the ocean swelled toward shore, light pooling in a trail from the rising moon.

"It's spectacular."

"Yeah." His chuckle faded as he studied her.

"What?" She eased closer to the door.

Smirking, he leaned his elbow against the window frame. "Nothing." Moonlight made his features even more striking. Dangerously sexy, the way those blue shadows made him seem mysterious.

Talk. About anything. "What does your family think of the show?"

With a shrug, he gazed off across the Pacific. "They probably don't watch it."

Right. Steer away from family questions. "Do you?"

"No, I don't watch much television. PBS, sometimes BBC America. Movies, CNN."

"No kidding."

"My mom discouraged us at a young age from TV. It's why I picked up a guitar."

"Interesting. At what age?"

"Twelve. My brother and I played together."

"And you kept it up." The conversation had segued into an interview, but she wanted to hear more about him.

"Yeah, it got in my blood. Even when I didn't have my guitar in my hands, my fingers would move to chords I heard in my head." He smiled at the memory.

"Did you ever try any other instruments?"

"Sure--keyboards, bongos, banjo, zephyr. I used to experiment a lot."

"I remember some of your earliest songs had some interesting sounds."

"Yeah, and those received some critical acclaim, but didn't make the charts, so…" Absently, he drummed his fingers on the steering wheel.

"So you stopped experimenting. That's a shame."

He shrugged.

Openness on her part might make him open up again. "You never know what you'll discover. What new things might open up."

Jet stared ahead with a glazed look.

To fill the silence, she lapsed back into interview mode. "So your first hit. How old were you?"

"Ha. Nineteen." He shook his head, like the thought amazed him too.

"So young for stardom. Were you ready for it?"

"No one's ever really ready. I did my best to run with it."

"But sometimes you were caught beneath the wave instead of riding on top?" The question came from her own curiosity, though she could always use the material.

"Sometimes. Mistakes are part of the learning process. I've learned from mine. I'm a better person now."

The conviction in his tone made it sound important she believe him.

"Musically? Or personally?"

"Both. I like to think so, at least."

"In what ways?"

"Musically, I've perfected my sound. It's now my personal brand. People identify my sound with me."

"And you're not tempted to stretch the brand? Add a little lemon to the cola?"

His mouth puckered as if in distaste. "Sometimes."

"But?" Her instinct told her this story went deeper.

Impatience edged his voice. "But now's not the time."

She softened hers. "If not now, then when?" If making him angry would help him out of his stagnation, she'd do that too. Her comment seemed to have had the opposite reaction, but the blaze in his eyes told her she'd hit the intended mark.

A nerve pulsed in his cheek. "I don't know."

Time for a change of tack. "So, personally, do you think you're different now?"

"Absolutely. My head's on straight. I have no filters now. I see people as they are." He said it like a challenge.

"Filters--you mean drugs?"

"Right. I'm health conscious. I take care of myself in every aspect."

Sounded ominous. "Such as…you're protective of your interests? Musically?"

"I'm careful who I let in."

"Seems a funny thing to say, considering you have so many strangers in your home."

"Everyone's been thoroughly screened. Including you."

Duly noted. "What about those people already on the inside?"

His brows twitched together. "What?"

"Do you ever re-evaluate old relationships based on your current perspective?" Naming Stu outright would raise an outcry from both camps. Something about the guy didn't sit right, and users like Stu ran rampant throughout the music business.

"No. I trust the people in my life."

"But you set the rules, right? Rather than follow them?" She knew she'd tested the limits with that one.

He studied her. "You like to push, don't you? Push every button until the buzzer rings, the lights go off and--jackpot."

He thought she meant to ensnare him in some trap. "You're wrong." How could she make him see what she saw? Feel the threat she felt on his behalf? She'd bet a paycheck Stu siphoned profits away, and would keep on doing so until the well ran empty, then leave Jet high and dry. She'd seen it too many times before.

"I'm pretty tolerant, but I don't like to be pushed too far."

Bluntness seemed the best approach. She clicked off the recorder so he'd know she spoke from the heart. "I'm worried about you."

He spat a laugh. "I'm touched by your concern. But there's no need."

Her cell buzzed, and Everett's name showed in the display. "Damn. Excuse me, I have to take this. Hello?"

"Where the hell have you been?" Tension ratcheted up her editor's voice.

None of his damn business. "What's wrong?"

"I called you six times, and texted you at least that many. Where the hell are you?"

"I'm out, all right?" *Asshole.*

"No, it's not all right. Someone's hacked into the blog, and I have a feeling it's someone there."

Dread chilled her. "How? What did they do?" Oh God. The laptop. Someone must have broken into the cottage, and she must have still been logged on.

Jet touched her leg, concern sharpened his features. She bit her lip and fought the urge to slip her hand in his.

Everett described the erotic photos of the contestants. "I deleted the post, then more reappeared. I suggest you head back now."

"We will."

His voice rose. "We?"

"I'll call you when I get there." She closed her cell. "Sorry, I really need to get back."

Starting the engine, he shifted into reverse. "What's up?"

Relaying what Everett told her, she cursed herself anew for leaving. She should have known nothing good would come of this.

* * * *

"Shit." Slamming into high gear, his foot punched the accelerator. When she'd joked earlier about not wanting to rock the boat, he'd thought her too cautious. He should have known something like this could happen.

He sped along the highway and side streets until reaching the gate. Clicking the remote, he pulled in, barely making it through the opening. He opened the door at the same time he stopped. They rushed down the path.

The cottage door stood locked, and she fumbled with the key. "Maybe Everett was wrong…" She flipped the lights on and gasped.

"Son of a bitch." No. He'd been absolutely right.

The laptop lay on the floor, along with all her things. "Who would do this?"

Jet eased beside her. "The window--they came in that way. Goddammit. Give me your camera." He'd document it all. Retribution required proof.

Appearing dazed, she reached in her bag and held it out.

He switched it on and took photos from every angle, then ran upstairs. "Man." He'd hoped they'd spared one room, at least. Raising the camera, he snapped away. Sheets lay in strips on the floor, her underwear, tank tops and shorts hung from open dresser drawers, shredded.

"Up there too?" She hurried up the steps, and halted abruptly, eyes wide. She flung open the closet and moaned. "No."

The same had been done to the few outfits she had.

Restrained anger shook his voice. "Whoever did this will pay. And the show will reimburse you for whatever you lost."

"Why would someone do this?"

"I intend to find out. I'll be back. Don't touch anything." After jogging downstairs, he strode out the door.

Within minutes, he rounded them all up. "Get over to the cottage. Now. Every single one of you."

Most exchanged questioning glances. A few grumbled but showed no surprise.

He glared before rushing back. He could see her head as she sat slumped on the bed. "They're on their way."

A moment later, Cindy came in. "Oh my God."

No faking that surprise. But he hadn't suspected her.

Stu followed, and murmured something to Cindy, who nodded and left.

"Miss Prescott? Are you all right?" Stu called.

"A little shaken, but fine." She halted on the steps when Cat, Ashley, Brianna and Julie entered.

Just after came Justin and Danny. "Holy shit," said one of them.

Jet moved to the side, blocking the stairs. "Anyone have any idea how this happened?"

Ashley and Brianna shifted their hips, folded their arms. Julie stared, alarm in her wide eyes.

Cat arched a brow and folded her arms. "You brought us here for this?"

Nostrils flared, Jet paced. "Someone hacked into the *Strung Out* blog site. I don't suppose anyone knows anything about that either?"

Cat primped her hair. "I'm sure it was an improvement over the usual crap."

Brianna tittered.

Rising to his full height, Jet glared. "You think this is funny? Destroying personal property? Do you want the magazine to sue us? Do any of you want the public to know about this?"

Cat pointed a long red fingernail at Billie. "She should never have come here."

Jet spoke softly but pointedly. "You don't decide who comes and goes. I do."

"And you're supposed to spend time with us, not her." Cat jerked her head in Billie's direction.

"It's none of your damn business who I spend time with. Any of you."

"Jet," Ashley gasped, tears welling.

"Someone better apologize, or I'll have to call the police. It's a federal crime to hack into a website."

He exaggerated for effect, and it seemed to be working. Cat, Ashley and Brianna exchanged nervous glances. Ashley nudged Cat and whispered.

Jet shuffled his feet. "It's getting late. Maybe I should just call nine-one-one."

Brianna glared at Cat. "This is all your fault."

"My fault?" she shrieked. "If that bitch hadn't stolen Jet--"

Billie gripped the rail. "I didn't steal anyone."

The contestants argued, accusing one another.

"Enough!" Jet threw his hands in the air. "Get out. Just go. And so help me, if anything remotely like this happens again, someone--or all of you--will be hauled off."

Billie slumped to the step as they left.

Stu paused in the doorway. "Sorry about all this."

Jet shooed him with a wave, and with a skeptical glance, Stu closed the door behind him. Crouching, Jet set the laptop on the sofa and gathered up the papers.

"Hey, don't worry about this. I'll take care of it." She slipped the papers from him.

Rising, he raked a hand through his hair and heaved a sigh. "You can sleep in the house tonight."

"Oh no."

"But your bed…"

"Right here's fine. I am not sleeping under the same roof with them."

He couldn't blame her. She was probably afraid she'd awake to a neat slit across her throat. "I'm so sorry about this."

She sat on the sofa. "It's not your fault."

"This is not how I thought this evening would end."

Tensing, she stared at the folder in her hand.

He sat beside her. "I meant, I enjoyed talking to you about music. The craft. It's been a long time since I've done that, or since anyone's asked. It felt good to be taken seriously as an artist. Thank you."

She met his gaze. "You're welcome. I enjoyed it too. You have so much talent. I'm expecting great things from you in the future."

He searched her face. "You are, huh?"

"Yes."

She said it with such confidence, he almost believed it himself.

"Maybe we could talk more sometime."

"I'd like that." The words slipped out softly, and with enthusiasm.

Jet stilled, watching her intently.

A knock sounded. Stu called, "Jet? Can I speak with you?"

Wincing, Jet sat there. "In a minute." Heaving a long breath, he went to each window and locked them. "Tomorrow, you can take the corporate credit card and go shopping. Anything you need."

"No, I--"

Jet reached for the door handle. "No arguments." First time he had to argue with a woman to convince her to shop.

She blurted, "I had fun. You know, until all this. Thanks."

He had too. More than he'd realized. Wishing he could stay, he said, "Goodnight."

* * * *

With a wave, she sank back onto the sofa. If Stu hadn't come back… Such a tight leash. Stu didn't like her being alone with his client, she knew. But why? What didn't he want her to find out?

Or did Stu not approve of them spending time together? If he'd violated some part of his contract by leaving, she'd suffer the repercussions too.

Such a surreal night. The jealous bimbos ransacking her cottage. Dancing with Jet Trently. She wished she could relive that dance. Curling a pillow to her chest, she closed her eyes and imagined herself in his arms.

Coziness wrapped around her like Jet's embrace and eased the tension from her body.

She awoke with a start to banging on the door. Squinting against the sunlight, she clutched the pillow and listened. Had the bimbos returned?

"Billie? It's Cindy."

With a sigh of relief, she rose and opened the door. "Hi. What's up?"

Cindy held up a hangered dry cleaning bag and a plastic shopping bag. "I brought you some things. Sorry if I woke you."

She waved her inside. "No problem. I normally don't sleep late, but I had a restless night." She wouldn't elaborate she'd been unable to sleep because her head swirled with thoughts of Jet. Something about him last night, alone at the club, had stayed with her long into the night. How he looked at her with no pretense, just sheer desire while they danced. How he spoke so openly, revealing bits of himself he might not have to another reporter.

How could she be so naïve? He either wanted to get her into bed as another conquest, or to sway her writing in his favor as Zin warned. Probably the latter.

Cindy set the bag on the ottoman and laid the dry cleaning across the sofa. "I can imagine. What a nightmare to come back to. But I brought you an outfit from wardrobe, new sheets and pillows, and someone will be by with breakfast soon."

Did the woman never sleep? "How nice. An outfit too?" Billie had worried she'd have to wear the same clothes as yesterday.

"A sundress, I figured that was safest size-wise. We'll restock your fridge today too. If there's anything special you want--anything at all, Stu says--just say so."

"Thanks, but the usual is fine."

"You should take advantage. Stu doesn't make these offers lightly, or often. Hey, I'll send you a case of the wine Jet had delivered." She nodded decisively and pulled a card from her pocket. "Oh, and here's the corporate card. Go crazy." Pausing at the door, Cindy winked before closing it.

Billie held a hand to her head. "I think I already have."

Showering, she couldn't help but wonder whether he still slept. Had he slept with any of the *Rock Bottom* girls? An image flashed in her mind of Jet, dripping with rain. Of her sliding her hands beneath his clinging tee shirt, pushing it up over his head. His arms tugging her close, wet skin sliding along hers.

As always, lines of appropriate songs crept into her head: *Better keep your head, little girl.* If this job had taught her anything, she knew better than to become starstruck. A rookie mistake taught her not to let the job--or the rockers--seduce her.

But she couldn't claim to be starstruck. Jet's fame had nothing to do with the deep feelings churning inside. When she'd danced with him, she'd felt more herself than she had in a long time. Free, as if she could reveal her true self and he'd accept her. A heady feeling.

Coffee would help. Wrapped in a towel, she went to the cabinet and scowled into the half full bag of grounds. They wouldn't have dared taint it. Would they? She dropped it into the waste can. Better not tempt fate. Her laptop had survived. She wanted to too.

Untying the bottom of the dry cleaning bag, she slipped out a silky purple sundress and slipped it on. The neckline plunged low, and the hemline skimmed past her thighs, showing her absurdly white legs. "Not bad otherwise."

Shouldering her bag, she headed for the patio and through the backdoor.

Standing at the kitchen sink, washing his cup, stood Jet. Wet with sweat, his tee shirt and shorts clung to his contours.

Her heart fluttered against her ribs as she approached.

Glancing over, he set the cup in the sink and dried his hands on the kitchen towel. "Morning. Did you sleep well?"

"Yes, very." No point telling him otherwise. But why did he seem disappointed at her answer? "You're up early."

"I couldn't sleep, so I went out for a run. Thought some coffee would revive me."

"My thought exactly."

He pulled a cup from the cabinet and handed it to her.

"Thanks." She poured, acutely aware he stood within inches.

"I kept thinking of things I should have said last night." At her surprised glance, he added, "Clarified. I don't want any misunderstanding."

Any hopes he'd raised, he'd quashed with that announcement. "When I get my notes together, I'd be happy to go over them with you. *Strung Out* takes pride in accuracy." If he wished to be formal today, she'd be every bit the professional.

He gave a lazy shrug. "Or we could talk some more."

The expectancy in his face took her aback. "All right, sure. I don't have my recorder with me, but I could resort to pen and paper if you have any."

Julie strolled in. "Hi."

Billie clutched her cup. "Hi."

"Morning." Jet moved to the French doors. "I'll be outside for a while. Billie's interviewing me, so if you could tell the others not to interrupt…"

Julie tilted her head. "I thought you did the interview last night?"

"We started it." Billie's neck prickled with warmth. How could she explain dancing took precedence over the interview?

Jet opened the door. "Yeah, but it got cut short. And with all the confusion last night…" He gestured her through.

Billie glanced at Julie. "Right. I need to get my notes straight. Don't forget that pen and pad," she reminded Jet.

"Yes--thanks. I meant to get that for you." He rummaged in a kitchen drawer and drew out a pencil and rumpled sheets, grabbed his sunglasses from the countertop, then hurried to the door. Putting on his sunglasses, he gave a tight smile and steered her to the shaded table and chairs. "Sorry."

"Don't be." She had to face the Bimbo Brigade at some point. Sitting, she set down her cup.

The wicker chair scraped as Jet pulled it closer to hers, then placed the paper and pencil on the table.

Smoothing the paper did little. She shot him a smile. "Guess it'll do. So what did you want to add?"

He drew in an audible breath. "I feel terrible about what happened."

"Not at all. It's fine." Yes, that should reassure him. Fine.

His aviator sunglasses hid his beautiful eyes as he stared at her. If only she could see his face, she might have a clue what he thought. "I don't understand. Did you want me to ask more questions, or did you want to add something to what you said last night…"

He propped his elbow on the chair arm, his chin resting between his thumb and forefinger. "It's important you understand how seriously I take my music."

She blinked back her disappointment. "You made that clear last night."

"Did I?"

"Look, if you have any question about the facts you gave me, I'm happy to clear them up, but--"

"No, not the facts."

"Then what?"

"You're wrong about me. I'm not…" He leaned back with a frustrated sigh. "See, I can't say the things I want to say to you because then you'll print them." Leaning close, he grabbed her chair. "I need to know you won't print them."

"So this isn't an interview?" What did he want then?

"Give me some slack, Billie."

Afraid to voice the question, she remained silent. She wanted to rip those glasses away to see his eyes. Maybe then she might have a clue what he was up to.

Still as a jaguar ready to pounce, he hovered close. His tone softened. "What about you? What do you want?"

"Me? Nothing," she lied. Yeah, her life was perfect.

He turned away. "Never mind then."

"What?" Now it was her turn for her stare to bore into him.

"It can't be all one way. You can't expect me to bare my soul to you when you reveal nothing." In a rush, he pushed himself up, his sandals scraping the pavers as he headed to the house.

Why did it matter to him? And it must, or he wouldn't act so disappointed. She blurted the first thing that popped into her head. "Poetry."

Halting, he turned. "Really? Since when?"

"Always." She'd never revealed that to anyone.

Strolling back, he sat. "Why not pursue it?"

"I made a half-assed attempt in high school. A teacher actually discouraged me." The sting of his criticism came back vividly.

"A teacher? How?"

"He read it in class, tore it to pieces, called it crap. I've never wanted to die so badly." Except for now.

"And you let him shame you without ripping his head off?" He sounded incredulous, yet teasing too.

A sharp breath escaped her. So that was what this was about? To level the playing field between them somehow?

"No, I'm serious. Why didn't you fight back?"

"I was a kid. He was a teacher."

"Probably had a thing for you."

"Does everything have to come down to that? No."

"I know how guys think. They see a hot chick--"

"I am not a hot chick. And I certainly wasn't at sixteen."

More slowly, he repeated, "They see a hot chick, and will use any means available to get closer."

She pursed her lips. "So embarrassing me in front of the class was supposed to...do what exactly?"

"Make you come to him for guidance. A shoulder to cry on. But really, I'm surprised at you. You let him get to you, let his judgment prevail."

Why *had* she surrendered so easily? She loved writing about music, but writing articles was far from lyrical.

"Did you love the poem?" he asked.

"Yes, of course, but that didn't make it any good. In fact, in retrospect, he probably did me a favor. It probably sucked."

"So?"

"So...it probably sucked." How much clearer could she make it?

"Everyone sucks when they're just starting out. But you keep at it until you don't suck. Until you feel yourself breaking through to a new level."

She had to turn this around. Away from her. "Is that how you feel when you create music?"

"Absolutely. It's life-sustaining. It gives me vibrant energy having my songs resonate out in the world. That's what it's all about--putting yourself out there, trusting the world to accept it."

"Or knock you on your ass."

"Sometimes. But you keep trying. Believing in yourself. Because if you don't believe, who else will?"

"Is that what happened? You stopped believing in yourself?"

He jerked away. "What?"

"I'm not asking as a journalist." She pushed away the paper and pencil, unused though it was. "I'd like to know why you're not trying any longer."

His mouth agape in a breathless laugh, he turned away.

She had to make him understand. "You could revive that vibrancy. Put new music out there for others to catch that vibe."

Slowly, he faced her. If only she could remove those sunglasses and reveal his eyes. Did he hate her for saying it? She obviously struck a nerve. He sat statuelike. What the hell was he thinking right now? She gripped her chair, waiting.

Leaning in, he traced a finger up her forearm.

She held very still. She shouldn't encourage this. But she couldn't stop it.

He opened his mouth and took a breath. "I--"

From beyond the pool, Stu's coarse voice sounded. "Jet. There you are." He shuffled toward them, holding a clipboard.

Billie sat back, pulled her hands onto her lap. Damn that man. He had the instinct of a tracker. Always showing up at the wrong moment.

Jet leaned back. "Jesus," he muttered. "What is it?"

Stu peered over his sunglasses. "What's the matter?"

"We're in the middle of an interview." Disgust sounded in Jet's voice.

"Again?" Stu glanced at the blank paper atop the table. "Yes, I see how involved the interview is. But I need your approval on this."

Billie gathered the paper, her coffee cup. "I need to get going, anyway."

"See you."

The sun blazed against the light stone, blinding her. She felt the weight of his stare as she walked. Felt its pull. Stumbling in the door, she slammed it.

Brianna and Ashley stared from the table.

Her quick smile only served to intensify their already cool glares.

"I'm just bringing back my cup." As if she needed to apologize to them for her presence. They should apologize to her. One of them was guilty as hell.

Or maybe she should thank them. The incident opened a new side of Jet. Made her see the good in him. Hearing he took his music seriously excited her. He wanted to take it to the next level. She wouldn't give up hope.

Dumping the tepid contents of her cup down the drain, she realized she hadn't drunk any of it. Or called a cab. Pulling out her cell, she headed to the door. "Have a good day."

Their stony faces answered.

Or not. Following the walkway to the front, she gave the cab company the address, and halted at the Wrangler still parked out front. Her finger trailed the driver side door. *Oh, Willamina. Tread carefully.*

* * * *

Leaning back, Jet stretched out his legs to appear relaxed. He felt anything but. He wanted Stu out of his face, but if he didn't let his manager speak his peace now, he'd dog him until he could.

After sitting down with a heavy sigh, Stu slurped his coffee. "You and Ms. Prescott are spending a lot of time together."

"So?"

Stu shrugged. "So you're supposed to be spending time with the contestants. Not the reporter."

"You're right." He rose.

Stu's tone grew harsh. "Sit down, Jet."

He paused. "Excuse me?"

"Please." His manager flashed a thin smile.

Condescending bastard. Jet perched on the edge of the chair. He'd put up with his manager because he believed in him. At first. After Jeff died, Stu acted as a touchstone when Jet went into a tailspin. Forced him back on his feet. Unsteady feet, and Jet had drifted along through life, not caring. Until he met Billie, he didn't realize how stagnant his life had become. So stagnant it stunk. He wanted to change that. But now Stu seemed more of an obstacle than a support system.

With a lighter air, Stu continued. "The producer isn't happy. The girls aren't happy. I'm not happy."

"Neither am I." That was the problem.

"You appear to be. So does Ms. Prescott."

Get to the freaking point. "What are you driving at?"

"You're putting us in a bad place, Jet."

Could the man never speak in anything but roundabout clichés? "I don't see it, frankly."

"Because you have your head up your ass. Get with the program."

The only way to shut Stu up was to agree. "All right."

Suspicion edged his tone. "All right?"

"Yeah. Fine. We done?" *Better say yes.*

Studying him, Stu leaned back. "Yeah."

With a grunt, Jet stood. Man, he needed to get away from here.

Chapter 6

Shopping never appealed much to Billie. Today, using someone else's credit card to pay for her purchases lessened the usual stress. Buying clothes more suited to California helped too. Dark colors worked in Philly where buildings blocked the sun. At the outlets, she found plenty of things she liked in creamy fabrics and colors. In the dressing room, she snapped a photo with her cell and sent it to Zin with a message saying: *The new me.*

I like the old you, Zin texted.

She wouldn't argue. Instead, she called her mom. In answering her mother's simple *How's it going?* the conversation veered quickly south.

Her mother cut to the quick. "Get out of there, Willamina. Those women aren't to be trusted."

Billie needed no reminder. "It'll be over in a few more months." Not soon enough.

"Then will you visit?"

"As soon as I can. Love you." Ending the call, a powerful homesickness washed over her. She hadn't seen Mom in months, and season two didn't end for another six weeks. *I miss you,* she texted Zin.

Her cell buzzed. "Are you all right?" Zin asked.

"So far. If the bimbos don't go bonkers again, I might survive this craziness."

"Don't let it get to you. One of them will get the prize and they'll all move on."

"Right." She should too. Before things with Jet went any further.

* * * *

The producer directed Jet toward the pool. "Show the audience you want to get to know these girls."

"I'm not so sure I do," he muttered.

"What?" Stu snapped.

"It's a little hard to warm up to them after what happened."

Like a wasp, Stu hovered in Jet's face. "Last night *didn't* happen. It's off the *Rock Bottom* radar. Leave it there."

"Yeah, sure." He assessed the girls, posing on the chaises. Brianna, Cat and Ashley coolly preening, adjusting their bathing suits, hair, whatever. Empty shells of people, all of them. Except for Julie, who read a book. The only one who had no hand in it, if his gut steered him right. And it usually did.

At that moment, he decided the process of elimination. Julie would be the last girl standing.

A weight lifted from him. "All right then. Let's get this party started." The sooner it started, the sooner this gig would end. And the sooner he could concentrate on Billie. See if his gut was right about her too. He smiled as he approached the contestants. It usually was.

* * * *

Sipping the wine Cindy had sent, Billie silently thanked her, then set her feet on the ottoman and propped the laptop on a pillow atop her legs. Tonight, she'd stay in, answer emails, maybe write a little. When someone knocked at the door, she felt tempted to ignore it, but the lights would give her away.

When she pulled open the door, Justin smiled and stepped inside. "Hi."

"Justin. What are you doing here?" Still holding the door open, she hoped he'd get the hint.

He plopped onto the sofa. "I wanted to make sure you're all right. You've been scarce all day."

Not one to take subtle cues, apparently. "I had other things to do. I was going to turn in early. I'm kind of tired."

Extending his arms across the back of the sofa, he mock-frowned. "You're not even going to offer me a drink?"

She shouldn't be rude, and she couldn't afford to lose one of the few friendly faces here. Closing the door, she went to the fridge. "Sorry. What would you like?"

"The wine looks tasty."

"It is, actually." She poured a glass, handed it to him, then settled on the sofa.

"Cheers." He touched his glass to hers. "So are you all right, really? You're not leaving or anything?"

"No." Only if she could convince Everett to replace her. Threaten to sue for cruel and unusual methods of breaking up.

"Good." His voice softened. "I'd hate to see you go."

Tensing, she shrank back. "That's very nice."

Another knock sounded.

Justin pursed his lips. "Wow, you're popular."

"Unless Cat's come to finish me off." Grinning, she went to the door.

From the doorway, Jet glanced from her, to Justin, to the wine she held. "Hey."

"Jet. Hi." She tensed, wishing she could block Justin from his view.

He cocked his jaw. "I wanted to see if you needed anything. But I see you have everything you need."

An ache surprised her, an invisible tether drawing her to him. He could give her what she really needed. *Stop. Keep your distance.* "I'm good, thanks." Saying it felt like a betrayal.

With a nod, he stepped back. "Goodnight."

"Night." Closing the door, guilt twisted her insides.

Downing his wine, Justin winced. "That dude's a pain in the ass."

She forced a smile. Then why did she feel so terrible?

Justin prattled on about the events of the day, and Billie did her best to focus on what he said, but the image of Jet haunted her.

When he slid closer on the sofa, she stood. "I'm sorry, but my head is splitting. I need to hit the sack."

"I could keep you company." He looked up, his face a mask of sincerity.

Not the company she wanted. "That's sweet, but I'm not fit to be with tonight. I really need to rest."

Frowning at his glass, he finished it off and rose. "Thanks for the drink." He bent to kiss her cheek.

She froze, not wanting to encourage him. "Thanks for checking on me."

"Maybe when you're feeling better you can invite me back."

Or not. "Good night, Justin."

When he opened the door, the soaring strains of a guitar echoed from Jet's studio. "He's at it again. You might think he had a tour coming up." Justin shut the door, and so muted the music.

She closed her eyes and stood there a moment. *Keep your distance. Keep your head.* "Think Philadelphia." Home. She'd be there in a few more months, and all this would be a surreal memory.

* * * *

Running had grown into a daily necessity. The only way Jet could escape and try to clear his head.

Try being the operative word. No matter how many scenarios he assembled, he couldn't figure Billie out. Why so warm and open one night, and so guarded the next? Except with the camera guy, apparently.

For the second time today, his running shoes pounded on the pavement, now hot from the late afternoon sun.

Fool. He'd been ready to open his heart and take a chance. He hadn't realized it until the chance had been snatched away. Hadn't realized how much he wanted it, either.

Sweat pooled on his forehead and trickled down. Wiping it away, he cursed Danny, whose camera pointed out the van window. It was a wonder he could take a piss alone.

A few more months, he reminded himself.

Then what? Everything seemed turned upside down. Until he learned the truth, he couldn't decide. Life had a way of screwing up whatever plans he made, anyway.

Might as well head back. He could use some water.

In the spacious kitchen, the crew worked behind the markers. Danny had arrived back first, and the two cameramen filmed at cross angles as the contestants nibbled their dinner salads.

Jet forced a smile as he entered. "Hello, ladies." A generous description.

Near the French doors, Billie visibly cringed. Maybe she didn't appreciate him lavishing attention on the contestants. Ironic when her charm proved so fickle.

Ashley wrinkled her nose. "Ew, you need a shower."

Cat slunk closer. "I'd be happy to scrub your back. And your front." She bit into a celery stalk.

"Thanks, darlin'. You girls know I exercise every day. I'd want my partner to support that." That should dampen their enthusiasm.

He dragged his arm across his forehead. "So tomorrow we're hiking into the Santa Monicas."

"The mountains?" Brianna whined.

Amusement buoyed his spirits. "Don't worry, darlin'. We'll take the beginner trails. But you'll need better shoes."

Cat shifted her shoulders. "I have brand new running shoes I've been hoping to break in."

Approaching, Ashley blocked the camera's view of Cat. "We all do. Hiking will be great."

Danny shifted to bring Cat back into view, and signaled Justin to circle around.

Her lower lip jutted out, Brianna held a hand to her hip. "What about us? Don't you care what we like?"

Jet pulled a bottle of water from the fridge. "Of course. It's not all about me. We have other things planned. A trip to the Getty Villa--"

Billie gasped. Audibly. Shrinking back, she held up a hand and backed away.

Brianna and Ashley glanced over, daggers in their gazes. Cat, as always, never shifted her attention from Jet.

"What's the Getty Villa?" Brianna asked.

"Oh, a really cool museum." To keep from rolling his eyes, he tilted the bottle to his lips.

"Museum?" Brianna and Ashley whined in unison.

"Yes, it has amazing artifacts from thousands of years ago." According to his contract, this season aimed to find common interests. If none of them shared his interests, the show served its purpose.

Wincing, Brianna gave a *tsk*. "What about LA? I want to go clubbing."

Cat pointed a sharp fingernail. "Ooo, dinner on the rooftop patio at The Kress."

Brianna's eyes widened. "Or that restaurant where Wolfgang Puck cooks."

Billie covered her mouth with her hand, but Jet could see her chuckle. Yeah, if Puck merely cooked other chefs made mud pies.

Jiggling like a five-year-old, Ashley gasped. "Universal Studios! Come on, Jet--you can't say no to Hard Rock Café, can you?"

With a sigh, Jet glanced up at Stu, whose eyes gleamed. Jet could see the cogs in Stu's brain chugging to life with dollar signs, scheming potential gimmicks to make a buck. Majority ruled.

"Yeah, sure. We'll go." His tone sounded heavy with defeat.

Cat sashayed toward him, hips swaying. "Ooh, I'd love to merengue with you at The Rumba Room."

Holding up his hands, Jet backed away. "I don't know if that'll happen." Ever.

Cat slid her hand into his and slithered downward, then up. Apparently either not caring or unaware he had no interest in dancing, she continued twisting and shaking her head from side to side, using him as a human pole.

His gaze met Billie's in a silent plea. He'd never wanted someone to rescue him from his own sorry life so badly.

Sorrow filled her face. Silently, she slipped outside.

He closed his eyes for a moment. *Focus. Camera's rolling.* When he opened them, he smiled and opened his arms. He'd never open his heart. Not to them.

* * * *

Billie could take no more. Gathering her things, she slipped out the door. Fresh air didn't ease the queasiness building up. She needed a walk. A break from this place.

To her surprise, Everett picked up his cell. Before he could ply her with lies, she blurted, "I want to come home."

"Babe, the ratings spiked after the Cat episode. Viewers are totally invested in the outcome. Things are just heating up."

A laugh escaped. "You said it." If she had to watch the contestants maul Jet one more night, she might puke.

"What do you mean?"

Pinching the bridge of her nose, she told herself not to bother. If anyone was invested in her being there, it was Everett. "Nothing. I'm sick of the heat. Sick of the bimbos. Sick of this assignment." Sick of Jet looking at her as if she might throw him a lifeline. Didn't he know those were his decisions to make? He'd put himself here. If anyone needed rescuing, Billie would like to go first.

"It's not like you." Everett sounded like a scolding father.

His patronizing tone galled her. "Of course it is. I didn't become a journalist to write about a Bimbo Squad chasing a loser. I write about music, the culture--"

"Reality shows are today's culture. Like it or not." Professionalism stripped his sincerity.

"But--"

"Our readers love the show. And they love reading your reaction. Our single copy sales rose along with the show's ratings."

Clenching her teeth, she had a sudden urge to spit. "So you're not letting me come home."

"Not yet." Two more decisive words he'd never spoken.

Try a different tack. "Maybe you need a fresh voice on this piece."

Through the phone, she heard him shuffle papers, then the click of the keyboard. "Readers like your voice, babe."

You used to like more than my voice. She ushered that thought away. It seemed ludicrous now. "Only because they can't hear me say how much I hate the damn show. Tell them I have Jet lag." If thinking about him too often could be called that. Never had she met anyone more infuriating. Frustrating. Enticing.

"Billie…"

Don't beg. "Hanging up now." *Before you can hang up on me. Creep.*

Pressing the *off* key, she slumped into a wicker chair and stared through the leafy canopy overhead. Not even a star to cheer her tonight. How long had it been since she'd had a day off? Any free time? With no way to mark off her hours, she felt as if she had to be present each spare moment, or risk missing something. What was the worst that would happen? Everett would replace her with someone who actually cared? He obviously didn't.

Instinctively, she called Zin. Her voice of reason and sanity.

Music blared through the cell. "Hello! Billie, my wild girl, what are you doing calling on a Friday night? You should be out in LA with some hot man."

"You're my voice of reason and sanity?" Billie was in deeper than she thought, though a hot man wasn't a bad idea.

"What? Speak up, love, I can't hear you very well."

"I said, is it really Friday night? I've lost track."

"Oh, my poor sweets. Can I come rescue you?"

"Would you?" Though she wouldn't ask Zin to travel in an inebriated state.

"You might wish you'd stayed if I did."

A warning if she ever heard one. "Tell me, I can take it. What's Everett doing now? Or should I ask who?"

"He spends hours behind closed doors with some girl. He takes long lunches and leaves early."

"Sounds serious." She could care less, she realized.

"He's boinking her in his office, apparently."

"A new low. I must have been insane." She still felt slightly crazy where he was concerned, but the time away had lent clarity to her perspective. Everett was officially a lost cause. Her favorite mistake, as Sheryl Crow cawed.

"Sorry to break the news so abruptly, but I had to."

"Yes. Shock treatment's good therapy. Thanks." Just what she'd needed, a good jolt to her psyche. Yet somehow it had little effect. Let Everett boink whomever he wanted.

"So have some fun yourself. Go do something. Don't stay in blogging at all hours. And don't tell me you haven't. You're spoiling the frenzied masses, making them eager for more. They love you as much as Jet, you know."

"No, they envy me. Want to be here instead of me." If only. With a sigh, Billie stood. "Hey, have fun at the party and I'll talk to you later, all right?"

A thundering beat drowned out Zin's response, then the phone display went dark.

Lights inside the house lit the patio. The backdoor creaked open, then shut. Jet strolled past the outdoor fireplace and chaises to the open patio, threw his head back and sighed up at the sky.

Funny he should be so alone too in the middle of the noisy crowd.

So she didn't alarm him, Billie softly said, "Hey."

Approaching slowly, he might have been facing a snake pit for all his caution.

She couldn't blame him.

* * * *

Jet closed his eyes for a moment before he turned. If he'd known she'd lingered out here, he might have stayed inside. So many unanswered questions bottled inside him, threatening to explode. He couldn't afford for any to repeat in the media. "Hey."

"Nice night," she said. "Quiet out here."

"Yep." Still holding back on him. "So are you waiting for someone?"

Her brows furrowed. "Who would I be waiting for?"

He pursed his lips. "A certain cameraman maybe."

She frowned at the cell she still held. "I didn't invite him to the cottage. He just showed up. To check on me--like you."

"Mmm." But she hadn't invited Jet in for wine. Unable to stop himself, he strolled over. "So are you working?

Standing, she walked to the back edge of the stone lined with bushes, and ripped off a leaf. "No. I'm done working. Lately, all I do is work."

"I understand." Work had taken over his life. Some reality.

Ripping a leaf apart, she tossed bits to the ground. "Yeah, we're stuck in the same weird little bubble."

She seemed none too happy about it, either. If he had to be stuck in a bubble with anyone, he'd select her. What did she want from him? Anything? Or did she open to him sometimes simply because he was there?

She turned. "It's safe to speak, you know. I'm off the clock, off the record."

"Are you?" He eased closer.

"Yes."

What did being off the clock entail? Leaving her guardedness behind too? At the creak of the backdoor, he swung his head. "Dammit."

Videocam poised to shoot, Danny came into view.

"Dammit is right." With a sharp breath, she moved closer to the darkness of the hedge.

Probably to avoid being on camera with him. Still, it gave him an idea. He lifted a finger to his lips, grasped her arm and nudged her through.

She stumbled into a wedge of space near a wall.

Still holding her, he stumbled behind, pinning her against it. "You okay?" He placed his hands on the wall beside her, and liked the way she fit. Liked the way light and shadows played across her features. The space was just big enough for both of them, but he didn't mind. She didn't seem to, either.

She nodded, and whispered, "Where are we?"

"Outside the garage." An idea lit his brain like a floodlight. "Where I keep the Wrangler." Maybe they could kidnap each other.

Whatever spark he'd felt seemed to condense in her eyes. "They say if you don't run your car every so often it ruins the engine. How long has it been?"

"Before the other night?" He withheld a smile. "Too long. Maybe I should take it for a spin."

Her voice fell flat, all enthusiasm gone. "Yes. You should."

Disappointment coursed through him. But maybe she thought he didn't want her to come along? They had argued, after all. "To give it a fair run, the weight should be evenly distributed." Easing away, he skimmed his gaze down her body, imagining his weight distributed across it.

"I'm a few pounds lighter than you, but--"

"It doesn't need to be exact." He tugged her to the corner and paused, glancing left, then right. "Let's go."

Halting, she winced. "Wait. My bag."

"Leave it." What was with women and their purses?

"I can't. It has my cell phone, the recorder, the camera... I have to go get it." Quietly, she whirled in the opposite direction.

His hand on her arm halted her. "Where is it?"

"On the table."

"I'll get it." He grazed past, but stopped when she clutched at his shirt. "No--what if Danny sees you? I'll go."

She had a point. He glanced toward the hedge. "Okay, but hurry."

Her expression lightened with something like delight. "You'll wait?"

His gaze locked on hers, and his chest tightened. "Of course."

"Be right back." Creeping along the hedge, she found the spot where the branches thinned, and stepped through.

"Who's there?" called Danny.

Shit. No.

"Just me." Her voice wavered.

The cameraman neared. "Where did you come from?"

"I've been sitting here a while."

Jet parted the branches, and leaves rustled. Maybe if he reached through and pulled her back, Danny would disappear too.

Slipping her arms behind her back, she waved him away.

"But I checked and no one seemed to be here."

"I didn't notice you either, though I was texting my editor and he demands my full attention."

Glancing around, Danny seemed to lose interest in interrogating her. "Any idea where Jet is?"

"Haven't seen him. Have you tried his studio?"

"Yeah, Stu's looking there."

Oh, man. The whole world hunted him down.

"Why, what's up?" she asked.

Danny shrugged. "He disappeared."

Billie moved closer to the cameraman. "Can't he have a little time to himself?"

Might as well surrender. He'd catch up to Billie later. He'd make sure of it.

His runner's feet took him silently around the garage to the front of the house, and he emerged on the opposite walkway.

Brows furrowed, Danny turned. "Jet."

"Danny." *Jerkwad.* Jet continued toward the backdoors.

"Jet," Stu called from the walkway, and Jet turned to wait. "Where the hell have you been?" With one wave at Danny, the videographer shuffled off.

"Nowhere." Jet couldn't keep irritation from his tone.

Stu came at him, scolding. Yammering on.

Jet stared at Billie. "Yeah, yeah," he responded to whatever Stu had said. His chest expanded with a breath, and he strode away. Fuck it all. He still had to play the *Rock Bottom* himbo--male counterpart to the bimbos inside.

Opening the backdoor, music and laughter drifted out. Surreal. Maybe they should've called it a surreality show. More fitting. Not a reality he wanted to experience, but for now, he had to endure it.

* * * *

The door closed, muffling the noise.

Billie crept onto the patio. Inside, Cat still danced, now with Ashley and Brittany, Julie on a stool by the breakfast bar drinking a glass of wine. All turned when Jet entered, and they surrounded him. He joined their dance, even Julie now, facing each in turn, their hands on his chest, waist, thighs, ass…Justin and Danny crouching for the zoom shots.

Sudden tears blurred her vision. "What the hell."

A few minutes ago, Jet had made her feel as if she was the only woman alive. When their gazes met across the patio, it felt like being caught in a *Star Trek* tractor beam, dragging her in toward Jet's blue-ray eyes. When he'd captured her against the garage wall, she'd even congratulated Everett for finally getting something right: things had heated up. Their plan to escape made her sure they'd definitely heated up.

Now this.

Swiping at her cheek, she stomped away, then remembered and went back for her bag. Another Friday night wasted.

Slamming the door to the cottage, Billie dropped her bag to the sofa and paced. "Tomorrow I'm getting out of here. I don't care where." Screw Everett. Screw *Strung Out*. After grabbing an iced tea from the mini fridge, she sat cross-legged on the sofa and Googled visitor guides for Malibu and LA, then remembered. The Bimbo Brigade would be hiking the Santa Monicas tomorrow, and then possibly hauling Jet off to a club. If she didn't tag along and get pictures for at least part of it, she'd never hear the end of it.

With a groan, she lay back and scanned the schedule. At ten in the morning, they'd leave in the limo. Only in Malibu would anyone take a limo to go hiking.

She checked the camera. Not even one photo to upload to the blog. She had to go tomorrow.

"Guess I'll be the tagalong bimbo." But Sunday, she would disappear somewhere. Anywhere. Before she disappeared even to herself.

* * * *

Whining had its merits, Billie learned, especially when conducted in harmony with nearby whiners. When she climbed into the van with Danny, he glanced at her sandals. "Good thing we're not going to the mountains today. You'd be in trouble in those things."

"We're not? Where are we going then?"

He pulled out behind the limo. "Point Dume State Preserve. Easier walking. We may never get past the tide pool."

True to Danny's prediction, the women insisted on inspecting the tide pool at great length. When Ashley bent to tickle a sea star, Billie had to pause her picture taking and speak up. "Those are protected."

Frowning, Danny snapped his head toward her. She'd ruined his shot.

Billie glanced at Jet. "Sorry, but this is national television. Someone will report you and it's a hefty fine--California law gives its highest protection to this area."

"She's right." Julie stepped forward. "If *Rock Bottom* doesn't want to pay through its teeth, you'll erase that."

"Let's go, girls. We should move on." Jet walked close by. "Thanks."

Nodding, she folded her arms to keep from touching him, pulling him aside. *You're no better than the others*, she told herself. The memory of last night crawled across her skin like fire ants. What might have happened if she'd escaped with him? More importantly, what happened with Jet and the Bimbo Squad after she'd left?

Bending to take a few close-ups of the colorful anemones and sea stars, she hastened to catch up.

Brianna's arms swung as she picked her way through the high grass. "Can we just go back to the house and...Ahh!" She jumped out of the way of a long-legged bird running across her path.

Jet laughed. "It's a roadrunner."

"Like the Wile E. Coyote road runner?" Ashley asked.

With a wince, he turned away. "More authentic."

Cat clucked her tongue. "Even I knew that, Ashley."

A feeling of doom hovered over Billie. If she had to listen to their nonsensical babbling any longer...she paused to look out over the ocean, and zoomed her lens in on a brown pelican that swooped down and landed on the bluff. Not far away, two sea lions sunbathed on a rock. Out to sea, a dolphin leapt up, then disappeared under the surface. Great shots for the blog.

Walking toward the limo, a few butterflies settled on the giant coreopsis. Billie crouched low to capture it digitally.

"Oh, let me get in the shot." Ashley crept close to the flower and smiled.

Billie obliged. The readers would eat it up. And so would Everett.

Justin shot Brianna at close range. She struck several poses, then giggled and ran to Jet. "Can we go back and shower? You're taking us to dinner, right, Jet?"

"Yeah, if I don't go dancing tonight, I'll just die." It might have been Ashley speaking, or maybe Amber. They'd all become indistinguishable from one another.

If Billie had to go, she might die too. Even a night alone in the cottage topped spending more time with these women.

Later, when the limo pulled away, something tugged at her. Maybe she should have gone, if only for the sake of leaving here. Each day in this place made her more claustrophobic.

After she called a cab, she went inside the house. "Cindy?"

"Yes?" came the reply from the back of the hall.

Did the girl never stop working? "I'm heading out for a bite to eat. Want to come along?"

"Can't, I have paperwork to catch up on." Sure enough, there she sat, papers scattered across her desktop.

"Can I bring you anything?" Her heart went out to this woman who apparently had less of a life than Billie.

Cindy shrugged. "I have a salad."

So much for conversation. "All right. Just thought I'd check."

A buzz sounded, and Cindy said, "Your taxi's at the gate."

"Thanks." Billie hurried to the front and gave the driver the address of a small café she'd found online. In the small, casual eatery, she read *The Malibu Times*. When loneliness engulfed her, she reminded herself the assignment had to end sometime, preferably sooner rather than later, but she'd endure it like a professional. She refused to call Zinta again to complain.

Instead, she called a cab to take her back to the gate, and walked up the long drive. Music caught her ear, and she followed it to the back of the house, which sat dark and quiet.

* * * *

Sitting on the edge of the pool, Jet strummed his guitar. Where had Billie gone? He'd been just as disappointed not to get away last night. She had to understand. He had to make her.

As if on cue, she wandered onto the patio. "Hey. A new song?"

To hide his excitement, he picked a few notes. "It's nothing. An old one."

"I thought you were out clubbing." She glanced around warily.

Chuckling, he swigged his beer. "The rest of them are. It's not really my scene. Where did you go? Off with your boyfriend?"

Scowling, she folded her arms. "I don't have a boyfriend. I went to some little café. Takeout's getting old."

"You could have come to dinner with us."

Grinning, she said, "No stomach for it."

He understood. He'd much rather have been with her.

"I'd love to hear more."

Flamenco-style, his fingers flew across the frets in a powerful riff. "Put that on your blog."

"Amazing. I can't remember hearing it before. Or in that way. What album was it from?"

He paused, the beer bottle and a smile, at his lips. "If I told you the name, would you know it?" Her articles seemed well researched.

"Of course. I have some of your albums." She slipped off her sandals, sat on the edge of the pool and dipped in her toes.

"Some. Ooh." He tuned the strings to ease the sting of disappointment.

"I can't afford to buy every CD I like." She raised her feet from the water and wiggled her toes.

"You're that passionate about music?"

"Why do you think I'm in this business?"

He shrugged. "A groupie with a permanent backstage pass?"

With a frown, she said, "I'm no groupie. My judgment's subjective, not obsessive."

"Obsessions can be fun." He'd like to show her how much.

"Until they bite you in the ass."

"A bite in the ass can be fun too," he growled.

Her breath left her in a huff. "Do you ever relax? Just be yourself?"

Leaning his elbows atop the guitar, he eyed her warily. "What do you mean?"

"Seriously? I mean, turn it off. Turn off the Jet stream and relax."

"Jet stream." He chuckled. "Unfortunately, darlin'--"

"Billie. Please."

Good for her, not wanting him to relegate her to that level, a nameless bimbo in a fawning crowd. "An unusual name. What's it stand for?"

She pressed her lips together. "My dad thought it would be a good joke. Toughen me up. He couldn't be there to raise me, being in prison."

Listening, Jet set his jaw. Was she serious?

"Of course, when I finally found him, I went up and introduced myself. 'How do you do? My name is…Billie.'" She stifled a smile.

Cute. An impromptu rewrite of Johnny Cash's *My Name Is Sue* lyrics. He couldn't help but laugh. "Fine. Tell me some bullshit Johnny Cash story instead of the real thing."

"Ah. A fan, are you?" She gripped the edge of the pool and grinned.

Was that what it took to impress her? He lived, breathed, ate and shat music. Mostly shat, these days. "Of course. Cash was a masterful musician. An artistic songwriter. A genius at adaptation. Just look at the Nine Inch Nails song. Pure inspiration." He heaved a breath. "Wish I had it." His fingers moved nimbly across the strings.

"You do. You should record these. Put out a new release."

He hesitated, but kept his focus on the strings. "No."

"Why not? It would be great. Fans would love--"

"I said no."

"But why?" she persisted.

Furrowing his brows, he launched into one of his first singles.

"I've definitely heard that one already."

His gaze flicked up. Was she goading him?

"You won't even discuss it? You can't let your guard down for two seconds? What a horrible existence you lead." After standing, she grabbed the strap of her bag and headed for the path.

"You're a journalist." The retort explained everything.

Whirling, she paused. "So?"

The interior pool lights lit her face better than a stage spotlight. Outlined her figure with its stark beam. Made her seem surreal too.

He tilted the bottle to his mouth and sipped. *Careful, man. She might knock you off the proverbial wagon.* He'd been there, and didn't ever want to go back.

Strolling in his direction, she prompted, "All you have to do is say the three magic words."

"I love you?" he managed to croon. He hadn't said that to a woman in many years.

She enunciated clearly. "Off the record."

He concentrated on his guitar and said wistfully, "Not quite as magic as the other three."

Shifting her stance, she folded her arms. "Oh, you're such a romantic."

"I am, actually. I believe my soul mate's out there somewhere." Watching her intently, he swigged his beer.

"Just one?"

Her caustic tone froze his fingers. "So jaded for one so young."

"Being jaded keeps it real. And I'm not so young."

He studied her, confused what to make of her.

"What?" she asked.

He set his guitar on the chaise beside his. "Is Justin treating you so badly?"

She opened her mouth as if to speak, then closed it with a look of belligerence.

He stood slowly. "Danny worked alone tonight."

Confusion clouded her features. "Where was Justin?"

Was she kidding? "You weren't with him?"

"I told you...never mind. I should go." Anger replaced confusion.

"Then who was it?" Slowly, he walked toward her.

She averted her gaze. "Who was what?"

Hiding something. "Who hurt you so badly?"

"I never said--"

"Were you married?" The softness of his voice contradicted his urgency.

"No."

"Someone you trusted, though." He walked closer. "Your boss."

Squeezing shut her eyes, she murmured, "Damn."

Bingo. But something in her soft voice got to him. "It's okay. I feel better now."

"Why? Because you're not the only one who's screwed up?"

"We're all screwed up. No, it's a kind of leverage. Now I can relax." He grinned. "A little."

Her intense scrutiny made him acutely aware of every movement, every body part. "So spill. Do you really believe in true love? For a lifetime?"

He leveled his gaze at her. "Yes."

A laugh burst forth. "I almost believed you."

"I'm completely serious."

"Somehow your actions don't quite match your ideology."

"You disappoint me."

"Me?" Her tone signaled a challenge, as if she could say the same thing. If she had any expectations of him.

"You've been around this business long enough to know better."

"Than what? This is all a put-on? A façade to protect your sensitive side?" She blew raspberries.

"I'm more interested in you." He circled her, wishing she would match his steps, writhe against him. "What made you fall for him?" If he knew, he'd have the tools to win her.

"He's very...attentive."

"Mmm." He moved behind her. Not hard to be attentive to her. Though he sensed disappointment, as if she'd lavished in the guy's limelight, but now the anticipation seemed more delicious than the attainment.

"And sensitive. He knows what I like."

He gave a bitter laugh, then leaned close to her ear. "Oh, well then." Had she really been taken in so easily?

Blinking hard, she folded her arms. "Now who's jaded?"

He backed away slowly, taking her all in. "Come on. It's so easy for a guy to generalize and make it seem tailored to you alone."

Throwing her head back, she gazed up at the dark, hazy sky. "That's cruel." Her hesitation shone through.

"It's what I do on the show. One look at a girl tells me whether she's into sports or indoor activities, whether she's a mall addict or if the waters run a little deeper."

"Really. One look."

"Absolutely."

Tilting her head, she taunted, "Fine. What about me?"

"You?" As hard as he'd studied her, he couldn't say he knew her. Much as he wanted to.

"Yes, read me. Go ahead." Hardness glittered in her eyes.

"I already have," he lied. She was too difficult to read.

She shifted under his scrutiny. "And?"

Speaking as if from authority, he listed the things he hoped she liked. "You prefer intimate talks to groups. Discussing everything--food, movies, life." He walked toward her as if walking across hot coals.

She rubbed her arms as if she'd caught a chill, though the night was warm.

Good. He was getting to her. "You're in great shape, but not because you work out. Because you're busy. You get bored lying out in the sun, doing nothing. You like to be engaged in what you're doing."

Her slow smile sizzled hotter than bare feet on an LA sidewalk. "Go on."

Sidling nearer, he softened his voice. Her shirt felt like a whisper on his arm, beckoning to him. He'd put everything on the line, and tell her what he hoped she wanted. "You want to find a man who respects you equally, but can crack you open like a lobster. Break that hard shell to get to the soft flesh inside. Someone who's not frightened of the fierce front you put up, because they know underneath you want to be held, loved as if you were the only woman in the world. Kissed as if your lips are the sustenance of life." His gaze drifted across her lips.

Her mouth parted. "Yes," she whispered.

His eyes half closed, he eased close.

She evaded his embrace at the last second. "Oh no. No, you don't. You son of a bitch."

"What?" Had he blown it? He held out his arms as if waiting to fill them with her, his entire body begging silently.

Tensing as if in restraint, she bit her lip. "You pretend to be Mr. Sincerity. But it's all a game, isn't it? Some reality show. Nothing's real to you." Her voice broke. It seemed to startle her into flight toward the cottage.

"Billie, wait." She couldn't be more wrong. He'd never felt anything so real.

* * * *

Hearing him say her name made her pause. Such a powerful way to ensnare her. Make a girl believe he wanted only her. She struggled against whatever he'd used to get inside her. Damn, he was good. She wouldn't tell him that.

She could not afford this kind of mistake. "You made your point. Now leave me alone."

In an instant, he stood beside her, holding her arm. "What's wrong?"

Good question. She couldn't reveal her earlier mistake. One she wouldn't repeat, even with him.

"Nothing. I have to go." God, she sounded like a brazen teenager. Ducking her head, she froze, afraid if she moved at all she'd throw her arms around his neck. But why had she revealed herself to him? He'd asked a question, and she willingly bared her wounds for him to sprinkle salt onto.

His grip relaxed, and his fingers trailed down her arm. "Please don't."

The deep timbre of his voice roiled through her head, clouding her thoughts. Searching his face, she asked, "Don't what?" Was he asking her to stay?

A thumping beat signaled the approach of the limo down the drive.

He opened his mouth, clamped it shut. "Never mind." Releasing her, he stepped back.

Reality slapped her to her senses. Something inside twinged, resonated along her skin. Trembling, she rubbed her arms. She couldn't get back to the cottage fast enough.

Chapter 7

"I'm dying out here." Just standing by the bedroom window, Billie was engulfed by heat. It was almost eleven thirty and she couldn't decide whether to stay or leave. The sleepless night clouded her mind more than the confusion over what had happened with Jet. She hoped the sound of Zinta's voice would ground her again, though she couldn't mention their strange encounter. "What's going on in Philly? I'm missing everything, aren't I?"

Zin's voice sounded small, as if she were a million miles away. Or wanted to be. "Not much."

"You're a terrible liar."

"Only with people I care about."

She gasped. That could only mean one thing. "Everett's moved on again? To someone new? Already?"

"You are good. How did you get that from--"

"Reporter's intuition. Who? Spill." Now she'd have an outlet for her frustration.

"I honestly don't know who she is. She's very young, just graduated journalism school."

"Oh no." Her insides churned. He'd replaced her with a Millennium girl. Would the girl take her job too?

"He's not interviewing, if that's your worry." Zin had read her mind.

"Then how did they connect?"

"Friend of a friend, I heard." Zin yawned.

"I hate those." Nebulous connections could prove the most difficult to sever. They had a way of resurfacing. Unexpectedly. No matter--if not the graduate, it would be someone else.

Her voice scratchy with sleep, she made no attempt to hide her disgust. "You're not still hung up on him, are you?"

"No. Just morbid curiosity." She'd hoped he wallowed in misery like her. Apparently no wallowing for Everett.

"Ah, Billie, my girl." Her friend's tone indicated her total disbelief.

"I do need to get out of here, though."

"Maybe Jet will elope with one of them. End the series." Zin cackled.

"No." The protest escaped before she could stifle it.

"Why? Do you have a vested interest? Other than the story?"

"I meant...never mind. I have to go. Shooting's about to start. See you." Flipping shut her cell, she heaved a breath. Why did such suggestions elicit visceral reactions? Like her teenage self had taken over, raging hormones and all?

Switching on the radio, Jet's smooth voice arrested her. *Be My Girl*, one of his first hits. The one that ignited her teenage lust for him. She sat on the bed, let the melody sink in. Let images of a younger, leaner Jet wash over her consciousness. Oh, the things she used to imagine him doing to her.

She'd imagined them again last night. All night. Only this time, the possibility seemed all too real.

"That's it, I'm gone." If she saw him today, she'd be all moony-eyed, and he'd think she wanted him. Some sort of mass hysteria must have set in, or beyond brainwashing, every woman's pheromones within a ten-mile radius aligned to Jet, and all lusted after him equally. All except Cindy.

"It's temporary insanity, that's all. Brought on by unnatural confinement. I need perspective. New scenery. I need to get the hell out of here." And someone to talk to besides herself.

After a shower, she powered up the laptop. Malibu wouldn't do today. She'd expect to see Jet at every turn. No--today, she'd go to LA.

Googling the Los Angeles Convention and Visitors Bureau site, she sifted through the museum listings. The California Science Center, the Getty Center, the Autry National Center... LA had a surprising number of interesting museums. Ah! The Grammy Museum at LA Live. Absolutely first on her agenda. Perfect.

Slipping on a sundress and sandals, she packed the camera and laptop in her messenger bag. There had to be somewhere with a wireless connection. She could update the blog on the fly.

Her breath untangled in her chest. She could forget *Rock Bottom* and all its crazy celebrities and wannabes for a day. Especially Jet.

* * * *

The Grammy Museum felt like home. Billie wandered through, reliving each Grammy moment. A photo of Jet halted her. Of course. He'd won three early on. So young, he looked. And wild, his smile more of a smirk, his layered hair untamed beneath the signature red bandanna. And blonder. He kept it a little shorter now, but had abandoned the bandanna. A step in the right direction.

Two middle-aged women approached, stopping behind Billie. "Jet Trently. I just love him."

"Me too. Alan took me to a concert in ninety-five."

"Lucky bitch."

The matronly woman tittered. "I threw my panties onstage."

Billie couldn't hold back a laugh. "Sorry. Safe to say you're fans? Even now?"

"Oh yes," they said in unison.

"What about his music? Do you still love his songs? Or would you like to see him put out a new CD?"

"Are you with the museum?" one asked.

"No." Billie flashed a smile. "I'm a music journalist. Just curious." A little too curious sometimes.

"Oh, you're randomly polling people? Well, I have all of Jet's CDs, but a new one would be terribly exciting. Is he recording something new?"

"I'm not sure. I'm hoping."

The other chimed in. "Me too. That would be wonderful, wouldn't it, Barb?"

The woman clutched her arm. "I'd be first in line to buy it."

"Thanks. You've been very helpful." Satisfied, Billie strolled on, then stopped. "Would you mind if I took your photo by his display? I write a blog for *Rock Bottom* and--"

Barb's face lit up. "You write that blog? I check it every day."

"Seriously?" Didn't anyone have better things to do?

"We both do. It's wonderful. Yes, please take our picture. Come here, Sue." She linked arms with her friend, cheeks touching with wide smiles.

Billie snapped three shots. "Thanks. It'll be up today."

Sue squealed, "Oh, you're so lucky. What's Jet like, really?"

Good question. "I don't know." She wished she did.

A frown tinged Barb's smile. "But you must, you're with him every day, aren't you?"

"Not really. Sorry." Each time she thought she had a handle on him, a new facet emerged. It felt like looking into a prism, light refracting everywhere. All an illusion.

"Oh, right. You can't talk about it. That's all right." Nodding, Sue pressed her lips together and nodded at Barb knowingly. "But tell him we're his biggest fans."

"I'll be sure to." How could she explain--she only knew what he projected to others. They might know him better than she did. She said goodbye and walked on.

Her stomach grumbled, reminding her she'd only had a coffee and yogurt all day. Three thirty. The Hard Rock Café might not be overcrowded at this hour. Stepping back into the heat, she hailed a cab and arrived there in twenty minutes.

* * * *

Jet knocked on the cottage door and shifted nervously. If any of the girls saw him, they'd raise a fuss. He had no handy excuse. Other than he needed to see her. It took everything he had not to follow her last night.

Except that she'd seemed to want him not to. Her mixed signals drove him crazy. He knocked again, but no sound came from within. Shielding his eyes, he peered in the window. No sign of movement.

Maybe Cindy knew something. He shoved his hands into his shorts' pockets and strode inside.

As always, Cindy sat at her desk. "Hey, Jet."

"Hey. Any idea where Billie is?"

A knowing look flicked across her face. "I believe she went out."

He gripped the edge of the desk. "When? She didn't have suitcases with her, did she?"

"I didn't actually see her, but it seems unlikely. She's not the type to leave without saying goodbye."

"Yeah. You're right. Thanks."

The office doors opened and Julie emerged, followed closely by Stu. "Jet. What time are you going today?"

"Going where?"

Julie tilted her head. "LA. You promised the other night."

"Weren't they just there?" They could go back by themselves. And when did Julie convert to bimboism?

"Look, Jet," Stu droned. "The producer's been at me. You're not getting in enough camera time." He ended with that falsetto enthusiasm that turned Jet's stomach.

He could care less. His heart wasn't in the show. "Fine. We'll go to LA."

Stu gave a sickly smile. "Great."

For you. Jet would need Herculean strength to get through this day.

* * * *

Inside the Hard Rock Café lobby, a sequined Elvis outfit dominated the display case. Albums, photos, jackets, jeans and scarves, lyrics scrawled on scraps of paper or whatever had been handy, guitars and other instruments lined the walls. The hostess greeted Billie and led her to a semicircular booth. Sliding in, Jet smiled at her from the display behind her seat.

Billie gave an exasperated sigh. "Great."

The hostess handed her a menu. "You don't like him?"

"Oh, sure." More than she cared to admit. When she didn't want to strangle him, that was.

Gazing at the photo, the hostess hugged a menu to her chest. "This is my favorite booth. Those lyrics make me want to cry every time. Sometimes I sit here after the place closes and read them."

"Lyrics?" Sure enough, his scrawling handwritten draft of *Need Your Love*. "Do you mind if I photograph them?"

"So you are a fan."

"A music journalist. I write the *Rock Bottom* blog, and--"

She gasped. "Omigod. You're Billie Prescott!"

At nearby tables, patrons turned with curious stares.

Lowering her voice, Billie held up a hand to tone down the hostess' excitement. "Yes. I'd love to have a photo for the blog."

"Could you take one of me by it?" Leaning close, she confided, "I lost my virginity because of that song. I imagined he was Jet and--"

Not what Billie wanted to hear. "Sure. After I eat, though? I'm starving, and I don't want to cause a scene." Not before she could beat a hasty retreat if necessary.

"Yes, thank you. I'll send your waiter right over."

She might need more than one glass of wine to get through this meal. Feeling conspicuously alone, she took out her laptop and drafted the blog post in between bites. The hostess checked back twice, and Billie surrendered and took out her camera so the girl could pose at the display. After jotting down the hostess's name, Billie asked for the check.

Only five thirty, too early to return. Grauman's Chinese Theater might have some photo ops, and she could stroll around the city from there. In the cab, she passed a familiar white stretch limo parked outside a designer boutique, unnaturally brightened by spotlights. Sure enough, Danny stood inside, camera pointed at Ashley and Brianna.

Billie groaned. She'd come to LA to escape Jet and his entourage, but she ran into reminders at every turn.

Not that she'd needed any. The image of Jet seemed to have been tattooed on her mind. His ice blue eyes piercing hers. Bending to kiss her.

Her pulse surged and her cheeks burned, sure passersby knew what she'd thought. How foolish could she be? Getting caught up in a reality show. Nothing could be further from reality than that.

Wandering aimlessly grew tiresome. She might as well be back in the cottage, posting the blog and responding to emails. Reluctantly, she called another cab. When it dropped her off at the gate, she hurried down the walkway without seeing anyone. Music sounded from Jet's studio, so he must be there. The bimbos must still be out shopping, and with them, the camera crew. With a sigh of relief, she shut the door to the cottage behind her.

Glancing at her watch, Billie calculated. Everett would be finishing his dinner about now. Should be a safe time to call.

Counting down the seconds after dialing, she figured about one more and his voice mail would kick in. She didn't want to leave a message, and readied to press *off*.

Breathless, Everett answered. "Billie. What's up?"

"Checking in. Did I catch you at a bad time?" Had he taken up working out? Not likely. Everett's only indoor sport seemed to be chasing women.

"No." His voice strained.

The liar. To prove it, a girl giggled in the background. One of those breathy giggles that said *Come back to bed.*

"Are you sure?" she deadpanned.

"I'm finishing up a late meeting. What's going on?"

Late meeting her ass. "Not much. We haven't spoken in a while, and I wanted to get an update." She needed something to take her mind off Jet. No matter what she did, he intruded on her thoughts. What would have happened if she'd kissed him last night? *Get real, Willamina. He'd have kicked you to the curb the next morning.*

Everett said something, but she'd missed the first part.

"Uh-huh. But isn't it time to wrap things up here? Readers must be tired of the same old story." She sure was.

"Not at all. Our readership's gained steadily since this series started. We're on the right track."

Soft murmurs sounded. Urgings. He whispered something inaudible to…who, the journalist? Could he be serious about someone so young? Somehow, she no longer cared. Maybe if she told him that, he'd let her come home. "No, Everett--"

"Listen, we'll talk more on Monday. Keep up the good work."

Her phone display darkened. He'd hung up.

"Right. While you merely keep it up for your latest conquest."

The best she could do, she thought, was keep herself together. The Bimbo Brigade lessened one by one, bringing her closer, theoretically, to returning to Philadelphia.

The sooner the better, she thought with little conviction. Sure, she wanted to go home. But facing Everett would prove a challenge, though he'd long ago moved on. And on.

And on, according to Zinta, who called the next day. "Should I tell you? Or don't you want to hear?" Zin's tone left little doubt as to the topic.

Billie gasped. "Again? Seriously?" Had her absence left him in such a frenzy he couldn't deal any other way except by sleeping with someone, anyone? Yeah, right.

"Closer to his age this time. And IQ, surprisingly."

Sounded serious. Curiosity prompted her to ask. "A writer? Performer?"

"Singer."

"Get out." He'd always said he'd never get involved with one.

"He had me go to her concert. Write a feature on her." She spat *feature* as if it left a bitter taste.

"Ugh. Bad form." The worst kind of nepotism.

"Judge for yourself when it's released."

"I'll be among the first to read it. So…you and Caleb doing better?"

A pause, then a sigh. "He moved out."

"No! Zin, why?" Not the quintessential couple. If Zin and Caleb couldn't make it, no hope remained for anyone else.

"I confessed to the indiscretion, and he screamed at me, called me a bitch and said he couldn't stay with someone who placed so little value on his feelings." She gave a bitter laugh. "Ironic it doesn't work both ways."

That didn't sound like the sweet Caleb she knew. But then, maybe she didn't know him as well as she thought. Or maybe his emotions overtook his sanity. Seemed to be a lot of that going around. "He loves you. He'll be back."

"I don't know. I can't think about it." Zin's voice crumbled.

Billie wished she could say something to lessen Zin's pain, but only Caleb could do that. She had no idea who could lessen hers.

* * * *

Billie puttered around the cottage on Monday morning, procrastinating as long as she could. When she read Everett's email, anger obliterated all else. He praised the reader response to yesterday's LA outing, then wrote: *But keep it focused on Rock Bottom from now on, will you?*

Her fingers flew over the keyboard. *I could have just taken the day off as I'd planned. If you want someone to work 24/7, hire a damn robot.*

Shutting down the laptop, she packed her messenger bag and set out to find Cindy.

In the hallway, Justin stood by Cindy's desk. "Hey, why didn't you tag along with us yesterday?"

"Thanks, but I didn't want to get in your way. Besides, the contestants didn't seem interested in seeing the same sights."

Justin nudged her. "No, but I'd have loved to have seen you in some of those outfits."

A nervous laugh escaped. "Ah, well. I'm guessing they were out of my price range, anyway." She moved toward Cindy. "Hey, do you have this week's schedule?"

Cindy handed her a folder. "You'll be happy with it, I think."

"Yeah?" She opened it. "Oh, the Getty!"

"This afternoon." Justin sidled uncomfortably close. "I'll be in the limo, but Danny'll give you a lift."

"Great." After his comment, especially great she didn't have to ride with him. She wandered through the kitchen, grabbed a bottle of water from the fridge, then headed outside. Cindy had included background info on the museum and J. Paul Getty, though she'd have to double-check it, it would simplify her post.

"Hey."

Billie froze at Jet's voice coming from the table near the hedge where they'd nearly made an escape from *Rock Bottom*. She couldn't ignore him. Turning, she waved. "Hey." Aviator sunglasses made it impossible to tell whether he stared at her or something else.

* * * *

Legs splayed, Jet leaned back in the wicker chair. "Interesting blog yesterday." He'd cursed himself when he read it. In LA at the same time, almost the same place.

"Thanks," she said uncertainly.

"It's kind of weird, being stalked remotely." Heat pricked at his neck.

Shielding her eyes against the sun, she moved closer. "I'd hardly have to go to LA to stalk you."

"Your day might have been more informative if you'd had inside information." His day would have vastly improved.

After a beat, she nodded, then flashed a smile. "Maybe next time."

"Mmm." Clenching his teeth, he suppressed a growl. If she meant to tease, she was doing a good job of it.

"Well. Guess I should be--"

"I'm looking forward to the Getty today." After rising, he stepped onto the patio.

"Yes. Me too. I've been wanting to go."

Ducking his head, he grinned, remembering her outburst on set. "So I gathered."

Her cheeks tinged. "Sorry about the other night. I didn't mean to interrupt taping."

"Oh. That other night." Standing within arm's reach, he suppressed a surge of something indefinable rising in him.

She stepped closer. "Yes. What I wanted to--"

Stu barged through the backdoor. "Jet? Oh, there you are. Morning, Miss Prescott. Can you excuse us?" Guiding Jet by the elbow, he steered him away.

"Sure."

Damn. Every time he and Billie seemed about to have an actual conversation, someone interrupted. Everyone wanted a piece of him. *Because you're the star of* Rock Bottom. He didn't feel like a star. Hell, didn't even want to be one. He played rock, and it was all he wanted to do.

My world's become too small. Everything's distorted. A feeling of isolation washed over him.

Glancing back, he broke from Stu's grasp. "You're coming today, right?"

"Yes." She seemed surprised he'd asked. And pleased.

Something released inside him. "Good."

* * * *

The van sped down the Pacific Coast Highway to the Pacific Palisades just outside LA where the J. Paul Getty Museum sat. Billie's excitement rose as she gathered her bag, and reminded herself to follow, not race ahead into camera range.

The group entered the museum, open to the outside and scented with fresh eucalyptus and pine. When a woman greeted Jet's party and announced she'd be their private tour guide, Billie pressed as close as she could. The woman spoke too softly to hear clearly, and only Jet and Julie paid attention and asked questions. The only discussions Billie could hear were Ashley, Brianna, Amber and Cat's, who remarked on the anatomy of the oversized statue of Lansdowne Heracles and the statues of Orpheus and the Sirens. They seemed unimpressed that the pieces came from Italy in 1790, or with their detailed craftsmanship. Billie snapped photo after photo. Getty himself had most treasured these items, after admitting, "I buy the things I like, and I like the things I buy. I never like to follow the crowd." Billie's kind of guy. Classy and intelligent, interested in the world beyond himself.

I like what I like. The improvised reggae tune flashed through her mind. So Jet and J. Paul Getty had some things in common.

Passing the perfectly proportioned Getty Bronze, Cat leered. "Now there's an athlete I'd like to meet."

"And mighty Aphrodite," Amber added.

Billie seethed. These bimbos shouldn't have been allowed entrance.

The guide led the group to the second floor, which held some of the world's most expensive paintings by masters such as Van Gogh, Manet and Renoir. Billie caught her breath standing before them, the colors and textures bringing the images to life. She was nearly left behind when the rest went to the upper floor where several galleries displayed French tapestries, clocks and furniture.

The guide led them down to the gardens. As described in the brochure, the bronze statues lining the long reflecting pool caught the sunlight. Billie remembered to take some photos of the *Rock Bottom* cast.

As they were leaving, she paused to capture the museum exterior, a gorgeous reconstruction of a Roman country manor.

Justin approached. "Ready?"

Surprised, she noticed the limo pulling away. "Isn't Danny driving the van?"

"Nope, I am."

She followed, exhilaration still coursing through her as they headed back. "Wasn't that amazing? To be in the same room with a painting by a great artist. I'd forgotten what a jolt that is."

"A jolt?" He pulled onto the Pacific Coast Highway and jammed his foot onto the gas pedal.

"Yeah, didn't you feel it? Like the energy reached out and zapped you?"

"Um, no…"

"You were probably too busy filming. But I have to come back here sometime."

"Why? We saw everything in the place."

If he didn't appreciate the rare antiquities, she couldn't explain it. "So what's the rush?"

"Still on the clock. One of them gets the boot tonight."

"Right." She'd almost forgotten. One less, and if she had to guess, it would be Amber. Jet's graciousness ebbed when she complained and whined, though he'd said little.

Justin gunned it and they passed the limo. Its tinted windows left her to guess what went on inside. Girls must flank him, Ashley and Cat, if she were a betting woman. The two most aggressive contestants.

He pulled into the driveway beyond the house, and jumped out to film the limo's arrival. Julie and Amber climbed out, followed by Ashley, then Cat and Jet. After they walked en masse down the walkway to the rear, Danny followed. By the time Billie snuck onto the patio, Jet stood by the pool, holding Julie's hands, speaking softly.

The unexpectedly tender scene caused something inside Billie to roil up. Jet could certainly turn it on for the cameras. *And for you--or whomever suited the moment.*

So confusing. His mirrored sunglasses reflected her distorted image, but she'd sensed his yearning. If only she could have seen his eyes. Seen what he was thinking.

He'd appeared so eager for her to come along today, even though they spent zero time together. *Because he's the star of* Rock Bottom, *Willamina. Get real.*

She missed Zin, missed her mom--everyone she cared about. But they were across the country, and Zin had enough of her own problems.

At least she'd gotten the hell out of here today, but she now had to endure watching him fawn over other women.

* * * *

What a nasty job. Let some other guy have it. Every day became more difficult to spend time with these women. He'd like to tell them all to hit the highway. His life wouldn't be his own again until this reality nightmare ended.

After Julie kissed his cheek and moved away, he called Cat. Then Brianna. By the time he called Amber, everyone knew the obvious outcome, and a tear streaked her cheek.

Amber had to have seen it coming. Maybe even wanted it, until now. The moment of truth. She'd allowed herself to be relegated to the shadow of the others. With a sad smile, she kissed Jet goodbye and went inside. Camera rolling, Justin followed, no doubt for commentary. Her final minute of the allotted fifteen.

One down, four to go.

* * * *

Billie couldn't stand watching one more second. *And you have work to do.* According to her agreement, she couldn't inform viewers of Jet's decision before the episode aired. But she could provide clues. Select telling photos of Amber on the fringes of the entourage, frowning or wincing, leaving no doubt as to the latest loser.

Still, her elimination only made Julie's staying more of a puzzle.

Enough. People with no lives ruminated on such trivialities. *People like you.*

Lying in bed, Billie kicked at the covers, glanced at the clock again and again.

None of these girls seemed a good match for Jet. The only one smart enough seemed to be Julie, but Billie saw no spark between the two. He spoke to her with exaggerated politeness, almost on a professional level. She treated him respectfully, not like an adoring fan. *How do you know what goes on in that house?* He might be in her bed every night, or she in his. The image that flashed through her head forced her upward.

Billie paced to the window. Sleep would elude her until she worked off some of the buzz in her nerves. A walk, maybe. Better yet, a swim. Glancing at the clock, she wondered if anyone else might be awake at two forty-five. Probably never a better time to have the pool to herself. This way, no one would have the chance to mock her modest two-piece bathing suit.

Outside, a balmy breeze swirled. The solar lights around the pool still gave off a soft glow, and the light below the water stayed on all night, apparently. A safety precaution, she guessed, so any floating bodies could be skimmed away before prying paparazzi found them.

Kicking off her flip-flops, she dropped her towel on a lounge chaise and went to the steps. Dipping in a toe, she found the water pleasantly warm, so she descended and pushed off midway down. Relaxing as a bath. Her even strokes wouldn't win any medals, but they helped unwind her tight nerves. At the other end, she swirled underwater and thrust away from the wall, emerging midway. Something caught her eye, made her slow and surface.

Jet sat on the edge of the pool, beer bottle in hand. "I thought you weren't a night owl."

Smoothing back her hair, she treaded water. "I'm not usually."

"You miss the best part of the day, you know."

Seeing him sitting there, something tugged at her heart. As surrounded as he normally was by too many people, he seemed so alone.

After submerging, she emerged at the side and leaned her elbows on the tile. "When it's quiet?"

He tilted the bottle to his lips. "The only time it's cool all day. And the stars." Looking up, he leaned back. "If the city lights don't drown them out. There's a few tonight."

She pushed up and sat beside him. "Nothing like back home."

He swung toward her easily. "Where's that?"

She tried to ignore the warmth of his shoulder permeating hers. "My mom's farm. More stars there than you could imagine."

"Sounds nice."

"It is." A new wave of homesickness made her wish she was there.

"I'd love to see it sometime." He said it with complete earnestness, a wistfulness in his voice.

She laughed. "If you're ever in central Pennsylvania, knock on her door. She'll make you a nice pot roast too."

He clutched his stomach. "Oh, you're killing me. I might have to go now."

"It's probably a little too much reality for you. The farm odors alone can overwhelm you on humid days."

"I bet you get used to it. And I'd put up with a few minor downsides to heaven." His steady gaze and teasing grin unnerved her, made her catch her breath. Made her wish for things she knew were impossible. "I should say goodnight." After standing, she retrieved her towel and wrapped it around her waist.

"I've been thinking," he blurted.

She paused.

"About our interview."

"Oh?" She could think of nothing more meaningful, but knew she didn't have to. He wanted to keep the conversation going, to keep her there. It must get lonely in that crowd of people with no one to talk to. She'd lend a sympathetic ear. No other body parts, no matter how his open shirt ruffled in the breeze to reveal his chiseled chest and six-pack abs. No matter how ocean blue his eyes appeared.

She took her place beside him. "Pick up whatever thread you want."

* * * *

Jet fingered the edge of her towel and cast her a mischievous grin.

Pulling away the towel, she said pointedly, "Thread of conversation."

He clucked his tongue. "All right." After jumping up, he jogged to the pool house. "Hold that thought." He ran inside and grabbed two bottles. Handing her one, he plunked down again.

"Thanks." She scanned the patio, the house. "Are you sure we're okay here? No one filming from the bushes?"

Biting his lip, he stood. "You're right. Might be a good idea to get out of sight." An excellent idea, in fact. He grabbed her arm and tugged her up. "Let's take a walk. If any bushes move, signal me."

"Okay."

When she squeezed his hand, it both energized him and stole his breath away.

He led her behind the pool house and across an expanse of grass to a walkway. "There's a really nice garden over this way. So I'm told." He headed across the driveway.

"You've never seen it?" Stumbling, she hissed through her teeth and halted abruptly.

His arm around her waist steadied her. "You all right?" Warmth surged through him.

Wincing, she held her foot and inspected it. "I should've worn my flip-flops."

"Here." He bent, looped his arm behind her knee and lifted.

Gasping, her arm around his neck. "What are you doing?"

"I don't often get the opportunity to show my chivalrous side. Don't argue." He tried to ignore the feel of her soft flesh pressing into his muscles, how her body fit his contours.

"So what did you want to talk about?"

"Music, of course." He'd ease into other subjects. "I'm curious. Why are you pushing so hard for me to record something new?"

"Because that's why you're in this business, isn't it? Because you love music so much you have to create more?"

He stared ahead, concentrated on carrying her. Her question dredged up too many unanswered questions of his own. Frustrations.

She curled the bottle to her chest. "Your first album excited me more than any other musician's. And when you released your second, I thought, oh, the sophomore album, the letdown. I'll excuse him this one. But when I heard it, your music was even better. And you kept evolving, album after album, and each one made me more excited than the last. But then you just stopped. You went stagnant. I was so frustrated. I knew you had more in you, but you're not letting it out. Now I find out you've been creating new music, but you won't record it. I just don't understand what you're afraid of."

His body grew rigid. "I'm not afraid." How could she know how terrifying failure could be? He loved the new songs he wrote, but his fans might not. Stu would call them "outside the box," if Jet allowed him to hear.

"What's holding you back then?"

Irritation flared. "You really think I'm nothing but a fake. That this is all a put-on."

"Isn't it?" Her tone carried a challenge.

He set her down on the grass.

She straightened. "You can't seriously think you'll find a soul mate on a reality show?"

He clutched the bottle tighter, but gave a nonchalant shrug. "Who's to say? Fate determines where. If it's here, then I'm not going to fight it."

"So you think one of them might be...the one?"

"I didn't say that." And wouldn't.

She stood so near, his skin felt abuzz with her warmth. Lights lining the driveway muted her face.

A nervous chuckle bubbled from her.

He flinched. "What?"

Ducking her head, she gave a wry smile. "I just flashed back to high school. Senior prom. I slow danced with Bob Myers to your song."

"Lucky Bob." The words rumbled from his throat.

"I wanted him to be you so badly." She looked off into the darkness.

Why the hell was she telling him this? "You did?" *You do?*

"Me and every other girl there."

"So you were in love with me?" He teased. A little too smugly, he realized, when her smile faded.

"Like I said, me and every other teeny-bopper in America. And you don't feel loved enough?"

"No." Seriousness settled over him as he studied her. "So what are your thoughts on finding a soul mate?"

"Maybe not everyone does." Her soft voice was thick with yearning.

He *tsk*ed. "You're such a cynic. Come on, really--you're not hoping to find 'the one'?"

A wistful sadness crept across her. "Hoping and finding are two different things."

"Not necessarily."

She stood so near, every pore of his body came alive, seemed to reach for her.

When her only answer was to furrow her brow, he went on. *Now or never.*

"Sometimes the universe doesn't give you what you want when you want it." He added more softly, "Sometimes, it gives it to you when you're ready for it." He reached up to brush a strand of hair past her shoulder.

At his touch, she drew in a soft breath as she faced him. Studied him.

Being here with her now felt very right. Very good. Almost too good to be real. He waited for some signal from her, some sign she felt the same.

Her words caught in her throat. "I have to go." Abruptly, she strode off.

"Wait." What the hell just happened?

"No. I'm not listening to any more of your spin. You should have been a reporter."

"You want to hear what I have to say," he called.

"What an ego! Every female's waiting to hear you proposition them."

"I only meant--"

"Save your breath."

When he caught up to her, she seemed to have trouble catching her own. Her breaths came so fast, she might be hyperventilating.

"Listen to me." He gripped her arm.

She jerked her arm. "Stop it."

Stifling a smile, he held fast. "Stop you from going the wrong way?"

"Yes, just stop…" She glanced over his shoulder to where the driveway lights shone.

Grinning, he softened his hold. "The house is over there." He inclined his head in the opposite direction.

"Dammit." Angry, she met his gaze.

His intense focus only wavered when his gaze drifted to her lips. He delved his fingers into her soft hair and hovered close enough to feel her breath, but held back.

She slipped her arms around his neck and drew him to her.

The fuses in his brain exploded, sending a wave of energy through his nerves. All he wanted was to hold her close, stay enclosed in her embrace.

From a distance, a man called, "Jet?"

The roaring in his ears made it impossible to tell who spoke. When she eased away, he felt stripped of his senses, unbalanced. Reaching for her, he whispered, "Ignore him."

"Jet?" Stu called again.

Always Stu, always at the wrong moment.

"He must have radar or something." Her joke wasn't so funny. "I have to go."

"Billie, no." He held tight.

Her voice shook. "Please, Jet. I have to go." Hugging herself, she picked her way through the shadows away from him, taking with her the only real moment he'd had in much too long.

Chapter 8

Morning intruded on the little sleep Billie finally had. She felt so out of sorts, she imagined herself a Picasso painting--her mouth twisted, eyes jagged in her head. A shower provided absolutely no aid in restoring her former self.

From now on, Billie told herself, she would keep to herself. If Jet spoke to her, she'd respond politely. If she found him alone, she'd turn the other way. Last night, she'd made the mistake of kissing him. And broke her vow never to get involved with a rock star again. Yes, she'd built up immunity to rockers, but that immunity had been hard-won after one broke her heart. A rookie mistake, and she was no rookie now.

I wish I could talk to Zin about this. Her lack of self-control humiliated her, and Zin wouldn't hesitate to point out the folly and futility of getting involved with Jet.

Getting involved with anyone right now would be a mistake. Not that she'd been madly in love with Everett. If she'd laid out his traits on a chart beside hers, the majority would have come up as compatible. Plain and simple, he fit well. He said the right things, made the right moves. Not earth-shattering, can't-live-without-you stuff, but sturdy, reliable in the long haul stuff.

Who was she kidding? His philandering after her departure had not only been expected, but a relief. Part of Everett's allure was the mystique of who would finally snag him. Like Jet. That thought stung worse than any of Everett with another girl.

Focus on the contestants. Learn more about the behind-the-scenes stuff from Justin.

By two o'clock, she'd answered every email, drafted a few articles and put off going outside as long as she could. Peering out the window, she saw no sign of anyone, so she grabbed her bag and hurried out.

Voices came from down the walkway. Jet and Stu. *Damn.*

Head down, she pretended to text as she aimed for the house.

"Billie," Jet said.

Hearing him call her name felt like a Taser to her heart. Stiffly, she turned. "Oh, hi."

He jogged toward her. "I was hoping to see you."

"I have to, uh, go…" She raised her arm to gesture, but had no idea what direction to indicate.

"Where?" Hands on his hips, he leaned close.

She said the first thing that popped into her head. "The editing room."

"You just passed it." He cocked his jaw.

"Right. I knew that. I was going to stop in and talk to Cindy first." What an awful liar.

Grasping her arm, he tugged her to the side of the pool house.

Oh, if she let herself be alone with him now, she'd be in trouble. Big trouble. "I really can't."

"Billie." The urgency in his whisper made her blood boil.

"No. Please." She made the mistake of glancing up.

Hurt intensified his eyes to a storm of blue, flashing bright, erasing her thoughts. It sent an uncontrollable reaction through her, made her long to fall into his arms. Touch him. His kiss had ignited something powerful, and it grew stronger. Hungrier.

"What's wrong?" He loosened his grasp.

Only everything. *Don't look at him.* "I can't. That's all. I have to go." Stumbling away, she wrenched open the editing room door and went inside.

Justin and Danny turned, and their faces blanked when the door opened again and Jet entered. "Hey. Sorry to barge in." Stepping in front of her, he murmured, "Can you spare a minute, please?"

She focused on Justin, who glanced from her to Jet. "Sorry, no." Slipping from his side, she shakily moved toward Justin. "So did you get those shots? It would be great to have them for the blog."

The door slammed, and her heart lurched.

Justin looked from her to the closed door. "Am I missing something?"

Frowning, she covered with, "Didn't we talk about that? I meant to ask you the other day."

His brow furrowed. "Is everything okay?"

"Sure. It's great. I'm getting a little claustrophobic here, but otherwise, wonderful."

"Don't let this place get to you. A few more weeks, and it'll all be over."

"Right." Good reminder, though technically, it was only midseason. "Thanks."

"Until then, stop by anytime. I'm happy to provide a diversion. Or whatever."

Smiling, she wasn't sure she wanted the kind of diversion he offered, and especially not a "whatever," but she nodded.

"So did you really need still shots?"

No sense in keeping up the pretense. "Forget it."

"No problem." Justin turned back to his work.

The tension ebbed away. Hanging out here seemed safer for now. Justin was easy enough to talk to. "So tell me more about the editing process."

He launched into a detailed explanation, most of which she missed, but she kept him talking by prompting with nods and an occasional "interesting." Jet interested her more. Why pursue her? He had women after him everywhere. He couldn't stand the fact she didn't want him? *Liar, Willamina. There's no good ending to this story, so get a grip.* Easier said than done when he looked at her that way.

With the excuse she had to check in with her editor, she left the editing room, unsure where to go. In the house, she might blend in behind the scenes, but she couldn't face him just yet. Walking seemed out of the question, out in the open where he could see her. The cottage, for now, represented the best option.

Man, I really need to widen my horizons. When she'd snuck inside and locked the door behind her, she let out a sigh, went to the sofa and powered up her laptop. "I'll work, and mark off the days like a prisoner. And when I get back, I'll torture Everett for every day of this madness."

A knock sounded. She sat unmoving, hoping whoever it was would go away.

The door muffled Jet's voice. "Billie, open up."

She fought the wild instinct to let him in. "Go away."

"Will you please talk to me?"

Did he have to sound so pathetic? Why couldn't he play with his Bimbo Squad and leave her alone? "There's nothing to talk about."

The handle jiggled. "Come on."

A female, possibly Ashley, called his name.

Inaudible, his response might have been either *leave me alone* or *give me a minute.* Whichever, it ratcheted up the woman's tone to a shriek. "You're more interested in *her* than any of us."

Jet spoke in a clear and steady voice. "I need to finish discussing something with Ms. Prescott."

Billie peered through the peephole. In a bikini and spiked heels, Ashley stood, hands on hips, grim-faced, leaning forward as if fighting the force of nature. Or ready to unleash it.

Cat, never one to be outdone, strutted in their direction. "She's right. This is getting ridiculous. If it doesn't stop, I'm going to the media."

Idiot. I am the media. But Billie had no doubt Cat would make good on her threat. Maybe it would end the show, get her out of here. *Like a nuclear blast.* Not the way she wanted to go.

Brianna joined the melee, and Danny closed in with the videocam. Jet held up his hand, yelling for him to stop filming. Danny lowered the camera, and Stu approached, his usual silly grin absent for once.

Jet held his hands to his head. "What is with you people?"

Billie thrust open the door. "Stop! Everyone just stop."

Cat, Ashley and Brianna surged in a mass of jiggling boobs and pointing painted fingernails, ready to gouge her eyes out.

Arms outstretched, Jet blocked their way.

"Do you see? This is craziness. I can't deal with it. Go away, all of you." Billie slammed the door and waited. Blessed silence.

Within seconds, the cacophony erupted again, even louder.

She grabbed her camera and threw open the door. "This is your last warning. I'll give you five seconds, and then I shoot. And it'll be all over the blog within minutes. Five."

Cat threw back her head. "She's bluffing. She'd expose herself more than us."

"Four." Billie framed them in the display.

Glancing at Jet, Ashley stepped back. "I think we should go."

"Three." Billie forced a more decisive tone. The power felt heady.

Stu's clownish grin filled the frame, blocking her view. "Let's go, everyone. Sorry for the disturbance, Miss Prescott."

Bickering bitterly, the women moved off en masse. Billie lowered the camera.

For a moment, Jet stared.

"Go. Your harem's waiting." It hurt her to say it, but from his grimace, it hurt him equally to hear it.

His chest expanded with a breath, and he stepped back, then strode off.

She inhaled sharply, wanting to call him back, but held it in. When he turned the corner, she closed the door and rested her head against it. "Damn."

* * * *

Scanning the schedule the next morning, Jet felt a little relief. Today, they'd go sport climbing. At least if the girls were tethered to a cliff, none could attack Billie. He dressed in a tank tee and bike shorts. A little too snug, he realized, when Cat and Brianna eyed him like a male dancer. Julie, thankfully, displayed little interest.

With his arms folded across his chest and one foot crossed atop the other, he waited at the limo. The sight of Billie approaching arrested him. Not dressed for climbing, he noted. From behind aviator sunglasses, he watched her. Everything had grown so tangled between them. If they could spend some time alone, he could straighten it out. Not likely to happen today, though.

Billie moved to the van where Justin and Danny finished loading their equipment. Danny shot her a wary glance, but Justin had a ready smile.

"Riding with us?" he asked.

"If you don't mind." She glanced over.

Danny frowned as he went to the driver's side.

Justin held the passenger door wide. "We'd love to have you. Front or back?"

Recognizing the double entendre, Jet tensed. *Asshole.*

Powerless to offer her a ride, he could only climb inside the limo after the contestants and let it whisk him to the site. Cat and Brianna chattered away, but his thoughts swirled with Billie. Having to deal with the tension of living here had really gotten to her, and he feared it would drive her away.

Propping an elbow against the door, he held a hand to his mouth. The confusion between them must only add to the tension. He had to find a way to show her his feelings went beyond the masquerade of *Rock Bottom.*

A soft hand brushed his neck. "Nervous about today?" Cat purred.

"No. Looking forward to it." Soon he could eliminate another contestant. That alone was worth celebrating.

* * * *

When they stopped, Billie climbed from the van. The craggy mountain towered high above. "They're climbing that? Is it safe?" The women might be crazy, but they didn't deserve to be put through this gauntlet.

Justin shouldered his gear. "Absolutely. Some of the girls have climbed before."

"You're kidding." She couldn't imagine any tackling this monstrous cliff face.

He shrugged. "An instructor will give them a how-to, and they'll only go up as far as they're comfortable."

Right. "And the farther they go, the more points they'll score with Jet."

Standing a few feet away, Stu turned, his grin slightly surly. "We're not keeping score."

Billie lightened her tone. "Not technically, but that's the general idea, isn't it?"

With a wink, Stu moved away. "Let's join the others, shall we?"

Scoping out the area, she identified an instructor and a man wearing a Malibu Creek State Park tee shirt and cap. After shooting, she could speak with the girls about their experiences, but couldn't risk being in any of the shots. At least the videographers would capture this segment on tape, and could edit her out if necessary. During taping, she'd take notes, send updates from her phone to Twitter and Facebook.

Justin halted next to her, video camera poised on his shoulder. "Welcome to Planet of the Apes Wall."

"Feels pretty Neanderthal." If sport climbing equaled beating on hairy chests, this wall would be an eight-hundred-pound gorilla. Intimidating as all hell.

"You know they filmed the original movie nearby."

Her research last night had told her that much. "Yes, and the opening scene of *M*A*S*H* shows this wall, I read. Interesting."

"You did your homework."

"I try to keep up."

"You gonna give it a go?"

She laughed. "What, the wall? No way. I'm the reporter, not a participant."

"Don't you want to challenge yourself? It'd be awesome."

Falling wouldn't be. She'd impale herself on one of the spiky outcroppings. "I prefer to watch with both feet on solid ground."

Blowing through his lips, Justin strode toward the producer, who called for Jet and the contestants.

Staying toward the outside edge of the group, Billie edged close enough to hear, but out of any bimbo's reach. When the producer finished his spiel, he introduced the instructor, who tutored them in the basics.

First up: Jet and the instructor. Then the girls, one by one.

While the two men readied their gear, Billie readied her own, thankful her job didn't throw her into harm's way. She paid little attention until the instructor scaled upward, Jet watching from the ground.

"I'm set," the instructor called. "Climb when ready."

Billie bit her lip and hoped Jet wouldn't go up too far. A rope seemed too fragile a thing to trust his life to. She hugged herself, then remembered she should take photos. Raising the camera, she never felt more like a paparazzi vulture preying on a celebrity.

The rope holding him stretched and creaked. Billie's nerves tightened in tandem.

* * * *

After chalking his hands, Jet reached and toed up the steep mountain facade. His laborious climb brought every muscle and vein into sharp relief beneath his skin. His shoe slipped on a loose rock, and he flattened against the wall. *Concentrate.*

A gasp went up from below, Billie's among them. He thought he heard her ask, "Is this really a good idea? What if he falls?"

Against his better judgment, he glanced down. She cared. At least a little.

Closer to the wall, Justin and Danny alternated shooting video of Jet and the contestants who stood watching. Ashley and Brianna grasped each other's arms, Julie bit her nail. Cat seemed turned on by the primal ritual, watching with an arched brow over lowered eyelids and a smoldering smile. Something definitely not right about her.

Her face a mask of concern, Billie shifted closer.

Buoyed by her worry, Jet scaled the rock slowly, passing the instructor. It made for better drama, and so far, he'd proven himself the least dramatic person on *Rock Bottom*. This would get Stu off his back for a while.

They continued climbing past each other until they reached a height some found sickening. Jet found it exhilarating.

He wanted Billie to feel it too. Every nerve-shaking sensation. The high of conquering the wall.

The instructor signaled, then walked down the rock face. Jet followed. He touched ground, then called to the instructor, whose grimace and grunts showed more strain.

People gathered around Jet, asked how it felt.

"Incredible. It's a real rush."

Billie scowled. "Ridiculously dangerous. Not worth the extra ratings."

Hearing her say that sent his pulse racing faster. A laugh burst from him.

The producer glared at her, and she shrank back. Her gaze connected with his and sent a zip of lightning through him. The most powerful rush of all.

* * * *

Billie knew she shouldn't have spoken, but no one else would speak up for Jet.

Yeah, her pulse had rushed all right. Now that he'd safely landed, she sought out the park employee to verify some facts.

"Yes, about two thousand sport climbers come to Malibu Creek State Park each year--here to Apes Wall and Echo Cliffs. Lots of LA residents are regulars."

"And the climbs reach as high as three hundred and fifty feet?"

"Yes, more than four rope lengths, with ocean views."

She preferred ocean views with sand between her toes, or from a hotel window. "You called it sport climbing?"

He explained how the preplaced bolts along the rock face allowed climbers to latch on securely, but still provided a challenge.

Billie felt as if she were back in journalism school. Dutifully, she jotted down the facts. Some readers would care if the Santa Monicas boasted hundreds of climbing opportunities, but she'd never make use of one.

The guide caught her interest by asking if she knew the movies filmed in Malibu Creek State Park. "Most recently, *Iron Man* used the Point Dume cliff as the site for the mansion. Of course, they didn't build one there, just superimposed the image atop the cliff, but still, it was pretty cool." He widened his stance. "And everyone knows about *Tarzan Escapes* and *Butch Cassidy*."

She stifled a chuckle. In Malibu, even climbing walls were celebrities. Thanking the man, she ambled back to the group, finishing her notes.

The instructor set up the contestants to climb while he stayed on the ground, tightening or slackening the rope as required.

Julie climbed half as high as Jet, and signaled to come down. Brianna's foot slipped at about twenty-five feet up, and she screamed when her knee slammed into the wall.

Billie sucked air through her teeth. "That had to hurt."

"Get me off this fucking rock!" Kicking, Brianna caused the rope to sway.

The instructor called, "Hold still. Place your feet against the wall and walk down. And if you feel yourself fall, alert those around you by calling out *falling*."

"What are you, blind? You can't see I'm falling? Lower me now!"

"Put your feet against the rock," he said.

"Get me down!" She shrieked again when her shoulder slammed into stone.

Danny and Justin zoomed their cameras in. Yes, viewers would love this.

Letting out the rope bit by bit, his lesson fell on deaf ears. Brianna plopped to the ground and whimpered as she dusted off her hands. "I'm getting blisters."

No, you're getting busted. Adios, bimbette.

Next came Ashley, who frequently glanced at Jet. Her fingers peeled from hold after hold, and she nervously announced she'd finished at about thirty feet up.

Ashley descended delicately. Cat edged closer, clipping the rope to her harness as soon as Ashley unfastened it. Despite the instructor's urging to take it slow, Cat scaled upward as if imitating Spiderman. The muscles in her back, arms and legs rippled beneath the tight top and shorts. She slowed at about the height Jet had reached, then turned to pump a fist in the air. Her foot slipped, and the rope whizzed through the ring.

"Falling!" Grabbing the rope, she winced but held tight, dangling fifty feet up.

The instructor halted the rope. "You all right?"

"Yes." Defeat sounded in her voice, and she looked up as if weighing whether to reclimb or not.

"Walk your way down, nice and slow," the instructor called.

Cat hesitated, but did as he said. Once on the ground, she flexed her hands. "I could have gone twice as high."

"You did great." Jet stood beside her, aiming his smile at her, then the cameras.

The viewers would love that too, and Jet knew it. A master of playing to the audience, he'd lived half his life in the public eye. He wouldn't know how to have a regular life. Why did she let herself think otherwise? To remind herself, Billie snapped a photo of Cat draping an arm around Jet, pressing her cheek to his.

Time to fade into the background. They'd be packing up now, anyway. The thought of returning to the cottage held little appeal, even if it secluded her from this insane bunch. She sat on the open side of the van, kicking at a stone.

Justin carried his camera, tripod and boom mic over. "Someone's bored."

She forced a smile. "Never."

"Ha. I bet you'd--"

"Billie," Jet called and jogged toward her.

"What's wrong?"

"Nothing." He held his hands to his hips and jerked his head toward the cliff. "I thought you might want to give it a try."

"Me? Climb?" A nervous chuckle escaped. "Not likely." She hadn't climbed anything but steps since she was a tree-climbing tomboy.

Watching, Justin's movements imitated slow-mo.

"How can you effectively write about something if you haven't experienced it? Try it. You'll love it."

"Have you met me? No. Thank you." Why push her to do this? At his frown, she pointed. "The crew's leaving, anyway. The instructor's gone, probably."

"I'll be with you." He shifted closer, his feet planted next to hers as if in challenge.

"What?" She glanced up, but the damn sunglasses made it impossible to tell what he might be up to.

His voice held the hint of a challenge. "You and me. Come on."

He hadn't climbed with any of the bimbos. Grasping for any excuse, she blurted, "I don't want to waste your valuable time."

"Well, if that's all...my time is my least valuable asset." His features softened as he smiled.

It would take more than a smile to get her into a climbing harness. "I'm not exactly dressed for it." There. No way around that one.

His assessing gaze skimmed her head to toe. "What size shoe do you wear?"

"Seven, why?"

He turned and called, "Julie, what size shoe are you?"

Pausing a bottle of water in front of her lips, she said, "Seven."

Smiling, he turned to Billie. "Perfect. Can you lend them to Billie?"

Panic threatened. "I still don't have clothes."

"I brought an extra outfit," Julie offered, approaching.

"Thanks." Billie winced. Now the bimbos became helpful when she least wanted it.

"You can change in the limo. No one can see past the tinted windows."

Billie glanced over. Ashley, Brianna and Cat watched beside the limo, glossed lips tight, heavily mascara'd eyes glinting like daggers. The boobs might booby-trap the vehicle.

He rested a hand on the van door. "It's more than an athletic exercise."

"Right. It's an exercise in futility." She had no problem refusing a challenge. A bruised ego was better than a bruised body.

"No. It's an exercise in trust." He pushed his sunglasses atop his head and his eyes glinted. "Do you trust me?"

Justin made a strangling noise in his throat.

Jet's gaze pierced Billie's. "Do you?"

Something in his eyes drew her in, made her forget everything else. "Yes."

His mouth opened in a smile. Julie moved away, saying something about getting the clothes.

Billie bit her lip. "I must be crazy."

Jet extended his hand. "The best kind of crazy."

She slid her hand in his. Her step lightened, buoyed by inexplicable happiness. The image of him standing there, smiling down at her, his hand warm around hers, obliterated any other thought while she changed.

Until she stood at the base of the rock and leaned her head back, the wall towering over her. "I can't do this."

"Sure you can. One step at a time." He demonstrated how to clip onto the rings. "I'll have you the whole way."

Fear froze her in place. "Aren't you going up?"

"No, I'll act as belayer from the ground. Better leverage."

Going numb, she looked up, then back at him.

"Trust," he repeated.

"Trust." She blew through her lips and chalked her hands. "I'm not going far."

"Only as far as you want."

"Ha. Right." As if she hadn't heard that one before.

Gripping a small rock outcropping, she grimaced. This would likely be the shortest climb in history. Gulping back her nervousness, she focused on the next toehold, the next ledge to grab. The surface didn't appear gritty from below, but pebbles tumbled down as she scaled upward. The rope stayed taut with Jet reeling the line just enough.

"This isn't so harrrrrd," she squealed when stone crumbled beneath her shoe and she lost her hold. The rope tightened, fibers splitting away in the sunlight as she stretched its length and evened out, bumping against the wall. Heart pounding, she barely heard Jet below.

"You're okay. Take your time." He seemed so small, but she felt his pull on the rope. True to his word, he held it, watching her every move. He had her back.

"Probably wants your front too. Belayer." She giggled. "He's the biggest belayer of them all."

She channeled her focus and scanned the rock above for crevices and nooks. The cliff face smoothed out, leaving fewer choices.

Studying the few available, she debated going back. "I'm going to do this, dammit." Someone had written that the wall seemed like an eight-story slab of Swiss cheese. A fair description. She'd have to look up the type of igneous rock again. Basaltic something, sounded more like a vinaigrette than stone.

Stretching high, her fingers found a pocket.

"That's it, you got it," Jet called.

Billie wasn't so sure as she reached for the next hold and her fingers peeled away. Her toehold gave way, and she fell a few feet before the rope went taut, jerking the harness into her waist.

Jet held it tight. "You're doing great."

Seriously? It didn't feel that way. Swinging from shadow into sunlight, she dangled like a spider with vertigo, but somehow, it was fine. Jet wouldn't let her fall. Oh yeah, she was supposed to yell that. "Falling," she sing-songed, but not in the way others meant it. No, she was falling in a much more dangerous way.

She should feel defeated, but exhilaration pumped through her. Waving, she stopped herself from spinning. "I'm coming down." Planting her feet on the wall, she walked backward. Yeah, down was much easier.

He gripped her waist as she neared the ground and whirled her, his laughter mixing with hers. Lights flashed as Justin crouched with her camera.

Her feet finally touching solid earth, she beamed up at him. "That was incredible. I never thought I could do it."

"I told you you'd do great." He uncinched the ring from her harness.

Justin held the camera display toward her. "Look how high up you went."

She leaned over the image. "That's not me, is it?" Her knees shook. Against Apes Wall, she appeared miniscule.

Jet flashed a smile. "You conquered it."

"Because of you." She'd treated him so badly. Why couldn't he be nasty instead of supportive? And adorable?

"No. You did that yourself." His smile faded.

Stu clasped his shoulder. "Can we go now? The crew's on the clock."

"Yeah. We should go." Frowning, he wiped his hands and let Stu guide him toward the limo.

Tripod on his shoulder, Justin walked past, and imitated Stu's cheesy grin. "Let's go. On the clock."

"Yeah, sorry." Not a bit, she thought. Today she'd conquered Apes Wall. Okay, not the entire wall, but more than she'd ever thought possible.

The entire ride back, she relived each moment. The connection she'd felt with Jet today went deeper than the harness and rope linking them.

When Justin pulled up the driveway, she grabbed her bag.

He laid a hand on her leg. "Hey, come by the editing room later."

"Thanks, but I'm exhausted." His touch made her shudder, and not in a good way. "I have to finish up the blog and then…" She shrugged.

Slouching, he shoved open the door. "Yeah. Maybe some other time."

You really know how to leave 'em laughing. "Maybe tomorrow night?"

He brightened. "Yeah. Sounds great." The words curled from his throat, and his brow twitched upward as if in anticipation.

Oh, why did I open my mouth? She'd think of an excuse tomorrow. Tonight, she had work to do. On the walkway, she concocted complimentary captions for the photos. Maybe that would appease the bimbos.

Opening the door, the cottage seemed so tiny now. Confining.

The laptop powered up at her touch, and she downloaded the digital pictures. Seeing them from the cocoon of the cottage sent a shudder over her. She'd climbed Apes Wall. Exuberance buoyed her all over again. Exhilarated, she first posted the photos of Jet with some links back to park history. Movie buffs would love the cinematic connection. Others would drool over Jet's bulging muscles in his tight tank and exercise shorts. The entry ran long with so many photos. *Maybe I should leave out mine. After all, I'm not part of the show.* She couldn't stop staring at the photo of her and Jet, smiling, leaning heads together, victory in both expressions, but body language conveying something else too. Clinging to one another, yet also balancing each other. Mutual dependence--that's what she needed in a relationship. She knew Jet could never be that other half, the one to hold her up when she most needed it, for whom she could do the same without hesitation. Not really. This photo represented only a moment in time with him. Though it was a nice dream. A really nice dream.

Yes, she'd post it. If only to remind herself. From now on, she wouldn't settle for any less.

Not long after she'd uploaded it online, her cell buzzed, and Zinta's name displayed.

"Zin, I'm so glad you called. I've had such an amazing day."

"Are you out of your freaking head? Why would you do such a thing?"

"Oh. You've seen the blog I take it." Smug satisfaction filled her as she settled back on the sofa.

"Are you addle-brained?"

Hmm. Possibly. She wouldn't alarm Zin with that admission. "For the same reason everyone else does it. To conquer my fears."

"Seems like living with fear is a saner alternative."

"It was incredible. I've never felt that…powerful." The rush of victory came back to her anew.

"I have to get you out of there. The sun is bleaching your brain cells. You haven't gone blonde, have you?"

"Do I look blonde in the photos?" A giggle buoyed her up, and nervous energy made her pace.

"You're sounding somewhat blondish."

"It's not as if I'm taking it up as a hobby. I did it once, and now I can move on, feet firmly on the ground." She wouldn't mention her head, still up in the clouds.

"I'm glad to hear it."

Something about the way Zin sounded focused her attention on her friend. "You sound tired. Everything all right?" Some friend she was, so high on her climb she'd forgotten Zin's troubles.

"I suppose. Everything's weird. You're away, Caleb's gone, work's not even fun anymore." Zin sighed.

"Tell me about it." Her work consisted of following a bunch of bimbos and reporting on their scintillating activities. Like shopping.

"Sorry. I keep forgetting you have the worst of it."

After today, Billie could no longer make that claim. Guilt returned for her worsening friendship skills. "So you and Caleb still aren't speaking?"

"No. He hates me, as well he should. I will never allow myself to be in that position again. Let that be a lesson to you."

"Mmm." Although she could think of a few positions she'd like to be in with Jet, Zin's warning came as a timely reminder. "Hey, my nervous system's about to crash. I should head to bed."

"No more cliff climbing," she admonished.

"No, none." Unfortunately.

* * * *

Climbing had exhausted the contestants. As Jet had hoped.

Restlessness kept him awake. The house closed in on him, so he strolled to the cottage. Was she still wired from the high like him?

He stood on the doorstep, deciding whether to knock. Without her, it would have been just another climb. Meaningless. She made everything worthwhile. Made him yearn to share every detail with her.

Talk to her. Find out how she feels. He raised his hand to knock, and the light winked out.

Footsteps sounded, sending him down the walkway in a hurry. He'd play a while. Work on some songs. Prove she was wrong about him.

The studio echoed when he flipped the light switch. From the guitars lining the wall, he selected the vintage Martin D-45 acoustic. One of only ninety-one in the world. Some paid as much as $135,000, but he'd won his from Clapton in a blackjack game. It had seen him through the early years, and he valued it for its memories as much as its quality sound. Under his touch, it practically came alive.

Tonight, he only drew the sound of a sickly wailing animal from it. Unable to play worth a damn, he went back to the house.

Television couldn't hold his interest either, so he pressed the *off* button on the remote and let the sound of the waves lull him.

Chapter 9

Billie opened the bag of coffee grounds and found less than a scoop. She'd have to venture to the house. If Jet hadn't haunted her thoughts all night, she wouldn't need caffeine so badly. Taking the biggest mug in the cabinet, she crept outside. Women's laughter sounded near the pool. They might be swimming. She'd go around front.

When she went inside, Stu and Cindy's voices echoed down the hall, so she tiptoed through the dining room to the kitchen and breathed a sigh of relief. Empty. Despite rehearsing in her head how she'd flash a curt smile and make a hasty exit, she knew if she ran into Jet, he'd look at her with those baby blues and…

"Billie."

Hearing his voice, she stiffened, but kept moving. *Get coffee and go.*

Footsteps padded behind her. "I'm glad I ran into you. How are you feeling today?"

"Fine." *Keep your head down.*

"No sore muscles?"

In her peripheral vision, she saw him lean across the counter. "Oh. A little, yeah." *Don't look at him.* Sipping, she nodded.

"At least you kept your balance and didn't slam into the wall." He smiled.

Damn. She looked at his eyes. "Or fall to my death." Shucking her resolve, she smiled. Why did he always have to look so good?

His voice nearly a whisper, he said, "I've been thinking--"

"Billie. Hey." Justin strode in the backdoor and poured a cup of coffee. "Don't forget about tonight. I have a special treat planned for you." He winked.

Tonight! She hadn't had time to make up an excuse. "Uh…"

Jet glanced from Billie to Justin and back.

"I should be finished by nine thirty. Danny'll take over from there."

"Oh, uh…" *Think of something!*

"Just knock." With a sly grin, he strode out.

Straightening, Jet scratched his chin. "Guess I'll…" He lifted a hand and pivoted toward the hall.

"Jet…"

Halting, he turned, expectancy in his eyes.

Her breath stilled. *Let him go.*

Her cell buzzed. *Damn.* Couldn't anyone leave them alone? She blurted, "Thanks. For yesterday."

Frowning, he blinked hard, then gave a single nod and turned, his gait slower but somehow more determined.

Yes, she'd just made sure he'd leave her alone now. *It's what you wanted.*

She opened her cell without checking. Everett asked, "What the hell is going on there?"

"'Hell' encompasses about everything going on here."

"Are you so desperate to leave you've gone suicidal?"

The climb. "No. Just trying new things."

His laugh sounded incredulous. "I never would have guessed. I'm proud of you. But if you try anything crazier, I'll bring you home."

"No." The coffee tasted bitter, so she dumped it into the sink. "I mean, you said readers liked my posts, and sales are up. I should stay and see this through."

"Babe. Is something else going on I should know about?"

I'm not your babe. "Yeah. I'm still waiting for you to assign me a local concert. I need new music. So help me God, Everett, if you don't come up with something soon, I'll go insane." Had she covered well enough? His silence made it difficult to tell.

"I'll see what I can do."

"Bye." She switched off her cell, distracted by Ashley emerging from the corner of the pool to sit on the side. She squealed, so Billie moved to the French doors to see what was going on.

* * * *

Jet sat on a chaise in the shade, playing his guitar. One of the songs he'd been working on. The middle had eluded him before, but it flowed now. He had to imprint the tune in his memory, so he played it again and again until it felt right. The guitar hummed with life, and the song came together.

Yeah, how much better could life get? The bitter thought drew a sharp chord.

Danny pointed his videocamera at him, but he knew better than to expect this scene to make it on air. Likely it'd never leave the editing room.

Justin trained his camera at the girls. The money shots, Stu called them.

What the hell did she see in Justin? The guy boasted about women like possessions. He'd make a better rock star than videographer.

Billie's presence intensified his playing, as it intensified everything else for him. She took a seat at the table in the alcove, her gaze searing into him. She loved music. If he could win her with his songs, he'd play all day.

Stu walked to where she sat and frowned in his direction, and said something to Billie. The next time Jet glanced up, Stu's frown had deepened. It must have dawned on him Jet played something new. Obviously, he didn't like it.

Fuck him. *Rock Bottom* was his show not Stu's. Jet played with greater intensity, immersed in the music, fingers squeaking along the strings until the finish. Oh yeah. It felt good. He'd captured the essence of what he aimed for, and now had the song down.

As he fingered the strings in a ditty, Stu waved Brianna in his direction. She slid out of the pool and sashayed toward him, dripping. He murmured in her ear, and her eyes grew wide. Smiling, she flitted back to the pool and jumped in. The splash arced in Jet's direction. Without missing a beat, he played on as he stood to move to a chaise farther away from the pool.

Stu's nostrils flared. He signaled to Brianna. Reaching behind her back, she unhooked her top and swung it over her head with a whoop. Justin crouched, camera zoomed at her boobs.

Glancing at Billie, her look of disgust suggested she had no part in this. Unless that too was part of it. These days, he had no clue what was real and what wasn't.

Standing, Jet held his guitar and raked his fingers through his hair. "What the hell?"

When they laughed and splashed at him, he strode to Stu. "This is complete bullshit."

Stu chuckled. "Viewers will eat it up." From his tone, Stu wanted to be in on the feast.

Backing away, Jet shrugged. "The FCC will yank the show. Not that I'd mind."

Saddened at the betrayal, his gaze met Billie's before he turned away. In seconds, he was at his studio. His only sanctuary.

* * * *

"What a stupid bimbo." Billie clucked her tongue in disgust, then realized Stu had wanted her to do it. Asked her, in fact, to interrupt Jet's playing. If he debuted his new material on *Rock Bottom*, his career wouldn't stay at rock bottom for long.

"You ass," she hissed at him.

He glared. "Careful, Miss Prescott." Not so clownish now, Stu looked downright menacing, his lip curled in a snarl.

"Why are you holding him back? He needs to evolve--"

Stu stiffened. "Jet's none of your business. You better remember that."

"Maybe you better remember he's no good to you unless he's doing what makes him happy."

A gleam lit his eyes. "Don't worry about me, either."

She held herself in check. Later, she'd look into what Stu might be up to. Whatever it was, she'd bet money it wouldn't be to Jet's benefit.

When Jet left, a flash of acknowledgment lit Stu's face. These antics went beyond wardrobe malfunctions. Sliding his finger across his neck, he approached Danny. "Psst. Cut it."

Billie grabbed her camera and got in a few shots that managed to escape Stu's notice. So what if he raised a fuss? He'd initiated this mess.

Lying low for the rest of the day, Billie kept to the fringes out of harm's way. And the bimbos. Justin, however, presented another matter. No matter where she went, she ran into him.

It's a small environment. Of course there's no avoiding him.

Retreating to the table, she pulled up a wicker chair and texted Zinta she almost felt as if Justin stalked her. *Ridiculous, right? I mean, we're all stuck here together in this waking nightmare.*

Zin replied almost immediately. *Maybe not. If your instincts send up a red flag, pay attention. If he's bothering you, tell him to back off.*

No, a little too flirty, but harmless.

Ah ha. That's it. He's out to bed you, my dear.

No more than any other guy. And like I said, we're stuck here. He's probably as bored as me. Though he never appeared bored, zooming in on the bimbos' boobs. He especially seemed to like to film Brianna, and she, of course, always played to the camera.

Still, Zinta's blind observation niggled at the heart of what bothered her about him. In this microcommunity, Justin was the only one who'd lend a willing ear. Sure, he might want to lend other willing body parts, but she'd let him know she needed a friend most of all.

The contestants toweled off and went inside to change. Justin jogged over. "Hey, Jet's taking the girls to LA."

"Really? He made a quick recovery."

"Come along, it'll be fun." Leaning his elbows on the table, he nudged his shoulder into hers, his head angled close.

Jet walked onto the patio, and stiffened at seeing them.

Tensing, she pushed away from the table--and Justin. "Not today. I have other work to catch up on," she lied. Anything would be better than spending a day watching the bimbos fawn all over Jet.

"Okay, but don't forget about tonight." Rushing off, he pointed at her.

Did he have to say it so loud? Jet grimaced and walked inside the house. When he emerged again, his arms encompassed all four women, attached to him like barnacles. Smiling, he swept them toward the waiting limo at the end of the stone path.

Oh yeah, he'd recovered all right.

Billie snatched up her bag and stomped to the cottage to change. Today, she'd lie on the beach, and relax, maybe read. Jet would be the furthest thing from her mind.

* * * *

By eight thirty, Billie actually anticipated seeing Justin. The day had been long and boring, and not thinking of Jet had been akin to ignoring the three-ton elephant in the room. She couldn't do it. His sad eyes made her want to enfold him in her arms. His outrageous flirting with the bimbos made her want to strangle him.

Nine o'clock passed, and Justin hadn't returned. She knocked on the editing room door to no avail. In the house, she paged through *Cosmopolitan* and *People*, but threw the magazine when she came across a photo of Jet with some other woman. Who the hell was that? Not even one of the bimbos.

"Any idea when they'll be back?" she asked when Cindy ambled to the refrigerator.

"I wouldn't wait up." She popped open a can of diet soda and returned to her desk.

Good advice. Just go to bed. Put this day behind her.

"Goodnight," she called, and headed for the back door. As she passed the pool house, a light shone from the back, and the door to the editing room stood open.

"Hey, there you are." Justin came out of the shadows. "I just knocked on your door."

"I was in the house. Trying not to go insane from boredom."

"I might have an antidote." Grasping her wrist, he tugged her to the editing room, closed the door and removed a stash of pot from the desk drawer. He rolled a joint, took a long hit and offered it to her.

"No thanks." She had enough disillusions without getting high.

"I know what you'll like." He opened the mini fridge and held up a bottle of wine. When she smiled, he filled two paper cups and handed her one.

"Is this from the winery? It's very good."

After refilling her cup, Justin took another long hit. "Not as good as this," he rasped. "Sure you don't want some?"

"No, really. So where did you all go today?" Not knowing had been part of what drove her to distraction. And what they were doing.

Billie focused on Jet while Justin described in detail their shopping, "Jet looked bored," and eating out, "he signed some autographs, and got pissed when Cat insisted on posing in his pictures." In general, he portrayed Jet as unhappy. She certainly hadn't helped matters.

Justin's speech grew more mellow, and he stretched out his legs and patted them. "Come here."

The tiny room became a little stuffy. The musky scent made her claustrophobic. She should go find him and explain. "I need some air." She stepped outside and tripped.

Stumbling, Justin's arms snaked around her waist. "Hey, careful."

She giggled. "I think your pot made me high." Wooziness filled her head, her muscles felt fluid, disconnected.

Justin's legs wrapped around her like an octopus.

Thinking he meant to help her walk, she lifted her head to thank him. His smoky breath choked her.

"You're hot." His lips mashed into hers.

Her hands slipped against his shoulders. As hard as she tried, she couldn't disentangle herself. A "no" managed to escape.

"Yes," he hissed, and awkwardly wrapped a leg behind hers.

Her knee gave out as he pushed against it, and she tumbled to the grass, him atop her, his hands everywhere.

"Get off me!" Panic erased any sensation of being high. When he reached between her legs, she flailed. Somehow her elbow connected with his jaw. Dazed, he drifted to one side.

Some force thrust him upward. "You son of a bitch!" a man's thick voice cried. Thudding sounded, his fists pounding.

Justin groaned and slumped to the ground again.

Scrambling up, her heart pounded. Terrified, she could only stand by as the man bent over Justin, punches flying.

She realized then who that man was. "Jet?" He had to stop, or this could ruin everything for him. "Jet!"

* * * *

At hearing her scream, Jet halted, stepped over Justin and rushed to her. "Are you all right?"

She clutched his shirt. "Are you?"

"Don't worry about me." He held her shoulders and tightened his grip. "You're shaking."

"I have to get out of here."

Steadying her, he pulled her against him. "I'll help you inside."

Shuddering, she grasped his arms. "No, I have to get away. I can't stay in that cottage."

"You'll stay with me." He'd make sure no one would get to her.

Nodding, she leaned into him.

Behind them, Justin groaned, lifted a knee from the ground.

"Let's go." His arm around her waist, Jet tugged her toward the house. "I'll deal with him later."

"But the show…" She stumbled, and she tightened her grip around him.

"You're in bad shape."

"Ha. Sure, kick a girl when she's down."

"No, I meant…you're crazy." Scooping an arm behind her legs, he lifted her, and tension melted away when she nestled against him.

After opening the front door, he went down the hallway, through the office and up the backstairs. He bumped the door closed, turned on the light and strode to the bedroom. Laying her on the bed, he leaned over her, scanning for injuries.

After pulling the coverlet from the end of the bed, he tucked it around her. "I'll get you some water."

He wet a washcloth and filled a glass, then sat on the bed and pressed the washcloth to her face. "How's that?"

"Good," she whispered.

How could he have let this happen? All the *Rock Bottom* employees had been screened. Or so he'd thought.

If Stu had any part in this, he'd kill him for putting Billie at risk.

He sat on the edge of the bed studying her. "Did he hurt you?"

"I'm all right. Just an idiot."

"You shouldn't smoke pot." What a hypocrite, lecturing her.

Urgently, she said, "I didn't. I don't."

Arching a brow, he kept his gaze on hers. "You reek of it."

"We were in the editing room. Justin had a stash there. I only drank a little wine."

He drew in a long breath. "I'm sorry I went off like that." The producer wouldn't be happy. Fuck him too.

"No, don't apologize. I'm grateful. He might have…" She bit her lip and fell silent, the unspoken horror of what might have been plain in her face.

"Hey, you're safe here." Smoothing her hair, he whispered, "Shh."

Crying, she rolled onto the pillow and hugged it.

He rubbed her back and shoulders. He'd stay here as long as she needed him.

First, he needed to see to a few things. "I should go talk to Stu. If word gets out--"

"Don't leave," she blubbered, grasping his shirt. "Please."

Unsure of her meaning, he stiffened. With a breath, he opened his mouth, but didn't speak until she'd calmed. "I better go. Maybe I can straighten this out before it goes any further." He handed her a tissue.

She blew her nose. "I'm so sorry. I never would have gone there if I thought--"

He smoothed her hair. "It's okay."

"But I don't want this to come back on you."

She was right, of course. Justin could sue him, use the media to garner public support, and turn fans away from him.

"It won't." He stood and slowly slid her sandals from her feet and then lifted the coverlet from the bottom of the bed and tucked it around her. "I'll lock you in, all right?"

Practically tiptoeing to the door so he wouldn't upset her, he reached for the handle.

"Jet."

His hand on the doorknob, he paused.

"Thanks."

Pressing his lips together, he nodded and went out. The lock clicked into place.

* * * *

The sound reassured her only for seconds. In the darkness, every little noise became a danger. Out of her mind with fright, Billie couldn't even cry. Clutching the pillow, she sat up against the headboard. If she had to stay awake all night, she would. Not even the sound of the waves crashing against the bluff could soothe her tonight.

The door handle jiggled. Fear shot ice through her veins as the door opened and a tall figure stepped inside. Desperately glancing around, she slipped from the bed and grabbed the lamp. Never again would she let any guy do to her what Justin tried to do.

"Billie?"

Could it be? "Jet?"

The light blinded her. She snapped her arm straight to aim the lamp away.

"What are you doing?" Slowly, he approached.

"I didn't know…" She heaved a ragged breath. He must think her a fool. Or worse. She wanted to explain: she never wanted Justin to touch her. Nothing else seemed so important as for Jet to understand. But how could she deny any culpability? She'd gone to the editing room. Drank with him while he got high. She'd never wanted any more than company.

Bending warily, he slipped the lamp from her hand. "Didn't you want me to come back?"

"Yes." Her lip jutted out, trembling.

Sliding his arms around her, he pulled her close. "It's okay. You're safe. I promise."

She murmured into his shirt, "I kept hearing noises and thinking..."

"You need to sleep." He pressed her toward the bed.

"I can't. What if he--"

Crouching eye-to-eye, his palms cupped her head. "He's gone."

So quickly? Could it be true? "Are you sure?"

"I made sure, yes. Stu drove him." Studying her, he frowned. "Do you need anything? A drink?"

"No," she blurted, and gripped his shirt. If he left again, she'd collapse into a useless heap.

"Come on then. Into bed with you."

Somehow it didn't sound the way she'd imagined him saying it.

Holding her, he turned and released her atop the sheets. Sinking down, she pulled her legs up. He straightened the bedcovers and tucked the sheet around her.

With a nearly inaudible whisper, she asked, "You're staying, aren't you?"

Leaning against the bed, he studied her. "If you want me to."

"Yes."

After switching off the light, he sat on the edge of the bed and pulled off one shoe, then the other.

When he slid the belt from his jeans, she froze, wanting to tell him no, that wasn't why she wanted him to stay. But he lay beside her fully clothed.

"Sure you don't need anything?"

"I do, but you'll laugh." If she hadn't scared him away before, she would now.

"No, tell me."

"Would you hold me?" Her vision adjusted to the darkness enough to see him staring at her, wide-eyed. *Great going, Billie. Another foot-in-mouth situation.*

"Yes."

His hoarse whisper sent shivers across her skin. Was she crazy? Had she completely...

Sliding nearer, he eased an arm around her waist. She nestled into his neck, wanting to block out the world. His skin smelled of sweat and himself and a hint of ocean, making her want to float out to sea with him as her life ring.

His mouth grazed her forehead whispering, "Are you comfortable?"

Comfortable completely failed to describe her bliss. Every muscle immediately relaxed in his embrace, and her eyelids grew too heavy to keep open. "Yes. You?"

"Surprisingly." Amusement edged his voice.

"Right. I'm probably the last person you expected to be with tonight."

Inhaling, he stilled.

Great, now she'd frightened him. The last thing he needed was a whiny journalist ruining his reality show. Why did she always say the wrong thing to him? Lifting her head to glimpse him in the dark, she wanted to apologize, but didn't know where to start. She'd offended him so many times. His soft kiss on her forehead surprised and soothed her.

"Goodnight."

He'd forgiven her, without her even asking. Her body went fluid with the sound of the waves. She managed to say "goodnight" before floating off to sleep, safe in Jet's arms.

* * * *

Banging at the door interrupted his dream. A really nice dream about Billie. He could still feel her warm against him, their bodies spooning.

"Jet," Stu called. "I need to speak with you."

She turned toward him. Groaning, he pulled her closer, not wanting to leave this dream just yet.

The banging came louder.

"Jet," she whispered, shaking him.

Grunting, his embrace tightened. A thumb stroked his cheek, and her breath warmed his cheek. "Jet, wake up."

His eyes slitted open, and he smiled lazily. "Morning."

"You have to--"

Rolling atop her, his mouth enveloped hers. Much better than anything he could've dreamed up. Warm and luscious, she tasted sweeter than he remembered. When she stiffened, he pressed harder against her. His lips caressed hers, his hands caressed her waist to shoulder, and she clasped his head as if his breath were the only oxygen that could keep her alive.

The distant sound of banging broke through the haze. Stu called, "I'm not leaving until I talk to you. Open up."

Their tongues stopped wrestling, frozen like the rest of their bodies. Eyes wide, Jet eased away with the realization that this was no dream. "I..."

He glanced down. Her arms and legs gripped him in place. He raised his brows in question. Maybe he should forget Stu.

She released him. "Sorry."

"No, I am." He stared, incredulous, but stayed atop her. He'd been waiting months for this, and almost missed it.

"Well, I am in your bed." She smiled in a self-deprecating way.

"That's no excuse."

A loud, even rapping reminded them of Stu, still on the other side of the door.

Shit. As much as he wanted to continue, now was not the time.

His face inches from hers, he whispered, "Can we talk about this later?"

"Sure."

With a grin, he gazed at her lips, his chest expanding with a held breath.

"Jet Trently. It's your manager. Open up." Stu's singsong voice sounded more annoying than usual.

Jet hoisted up to sitting and reached for his shoes. "Tell him I slept in the studio." Standing, he leaned a hand on the bed and straightened his shoe, then paused, gazing at her. He cocked his jaw with a groan, and stood. "See you," he whispered, and crept to the door to the hallway.

She lifted a hand in a wave, but instead reached out for him.

Holding the knob, he straightened, nostrils flared, heat coursing through him. He'd definitely get back to her on that. With a slow grin, he slipped silently out the door.

* * * *

For a moment, Billie thought he might come back.

Unfair that guys should look so good first thing in the morning. Such long lashes--the bimbos would kill for naturally full lashes. His long hair fell across his forehead and cheek, bristled with whiskers. And his lips...

Stu knocked the image from her head.

Climbing out of bed, Billie hated Stu more than anyone in the world. At the door, she mussed her hair further and pulled open the door, rubbing her eyes. "What's going on?"

Stu's eyes narrowed as he peered at her, then past her to the bed. "Where is he?"

"Who?" She infused a sleepiness in her voice, quite convincingly.

Rooster-like, he craned his neck toward her. "Jet."

Had he made it safely there yet? "He brought me here last night. I told him I was too afraid to sleep in the cottage--"

"Where is he?"

Shaking her head, she frowned. "Um..." In her best performance of a bimbo to date, she pouted and held a hand to her temple. "I--"

"Miss Prescott." His teeth clenched, he turned uncertainly.

Jet had to be there by now. Pretending to suddenly remember, she blanked her face and shoved her hair back. "He said he was going to sleep in the studio."

Stu shuffled his feet, his gaze sliding to the floor. "The studio."

Following his stare, she saw Jet's belt on the floor. "Right. That's what he said."

He pursed his lips. "Mmm hmm."

All innocence, she shrugged.

His eyes twitched and he clucked his tongue. "Sure. The studio." Turning, he glanced back. "Tell him thank you."

"You'll see him before I will," she called.

With a wave, he walked downstairs.

Billie shut the door and leaned against it. All that work for nothing. Stu knew. Touching her cheek, warmth flushed through her thinking of his kiss. Hurrying to the bathroom, she skidded to a stop at the mirror.

No wonder Stu guessed, with her chin and cheeks rubbed red from his whiskers. Her fingers featherlight on her face, she couldn't pass off what happened as a dream, though it seemed like one. Too good to be real.

So it probably is.

The thought sobered her. Time to get back to her cottage. Returning to the bedroom, the sight of the bed halted her--covers mussed, pillows atop one another. Like she and Jet had been. She went to the bed and hugged his pillow to her, inhaling his scent.

He mistook you for one of the bimbos, that's all. Until he woke up and realized who you were. He probably shared his bed with each--maybe all--of them by now. It would explain why he hadn't tried anything with her last night.

Sadness slowed her movements as she made the bed. Sitting on it, she smoothed the duvet one last time. With a sigh, she rose and gathered her things, making sure no trace of her remained when she slowly closed the door behind her.

Trudging downstairs, a noise hastened her steps onto the first floor, through the dining room and out onto the back patio. Rounding the corner of the cabana, she tensed as a man entered the editing room.

Glancing back, Danny's features hardened as he saw her.

Another enemy to contend with now.

Ducking her head, she continued down the walk and inserted her key in the cottage door, pausing at approaching voices. Jet and Stu. Pulling out the key, she fumbled it to gain time.

They quieted when they turned the corner.

Jet slowed his pace. "Hey." Jamming a hand into his pocket, he strolled to her. "Guess you found everything?"

Did he mean her things? "Yes, thanks." Tucking her hair behind her ear, her mind blanked. "Thanks for everything."

Toeing the edge of the walkway, he looked up. "Everything?"

Her cheeks burned, and she fiddled with her key. "Well, you know…" A nervous chuckle escaped. "With everything last night," she mumbled. "If anyone asks, I'll tell the others…" she caught herself. The others, the competitors. Rivals.

Staring at her key, she forced her thoughts back on track. "I'll tell them it was Stu's idea that I stay in your room."

"Oh. Good thinking."

"So they wouldn't think you wanted me there." Her voice trailed off. Had he? She'd begged him to stay. Practically forced him. As she'd proclaimed, Jet was a gentleman if nothing else.

"Right. Well." He eased backward, glancing toward the house. "I should probably…" He jerked his thumb behind him.

"Me too. Lots of work to do."

He froze. "You won't write about it, will you?"

"Last night? No." Of course she wouldn't embarrass him. Sleeping with a journalist. And only sleeping. She couldn't even seduce the guy who slept with every girl in the universe. A bitter laugh escaped.

His brows furrowed. "Good. Okay then." His gaze held some tentative accusation, but what? Suspicion? Betrayal? "See you." He strode off.

Helpless as she'd ever felt, she stammered, searching for something to say. *Sorry if I kept you awake* didn't sound right, nor did *thanks for holding me while I wept like a baby.* How humiliating. Such a fool she'd acted, and today only made things worse. He really was kind not to mention how stupid she was. She'd remind herself, repeatedly, and maybe prevent future occurrences.

She fumbled the key in earnest, pushing blindly at the door to get inside. Humiliated and confused, she paced. She couldn't claim sleeplessness. Last night, she'd slept soundly, Jet's body warm against hers, a snug, comfortable fit.

Stop! Scooping grounds into the coffeemaker, not even the deep aroma distracted her. The machine's burbling didn't bring the usual anticipation of coffee, usually one of life's necessities.

Zin. She'd provide some much-needed perspective. Powering up her laptop, she typed as soon as the email program opened, detailing the events of last night. Pouring out her heart, Billie finished with: *Tell me straight. Am I crazy?*

Finger poised over the mouse, cursor poised over the *send* button, she froze. What the hell was she doing? Quickly she highlighted all the text and hit *delete.* Electronic messages had a way of reaching the wrong hands. Zin, she'd trust with her life, but to put any of this in writing would be to invite disaster. People had methods of watching others' personal accounts, and she couldn't jeopardize Jet's career. If anything leaked to the public, Justin might come forward and accuse Jet of assault. No. She'd have to be very careful. Discreet, even with Zin. Anyway, Billie already knew what her friend's response would be: *Yes, you're out of your mind.*

Of course she was. Blowing it all out of proportion. He'd have done the same for anyone. Except he might have done more than sleep. *That in itself should be a huge clue, moron. He has zero interest in you.* Why should she care? Jet was the last person she wanted to become involved with. It went against her professional ethics, as well as personal. Until the season ended, she'd maintain complete integrity.

Chapter 10

At Stu's insistence, everyone gathered in the kitchen. The day had been boring until now, with the bimbos apparently hung over, which made for less than riveting reality.

Danny explored the inside of his cheek with his tongue, apparently unsure what to do with himself with no camera in his hands. As soon as Danny had arrived, Stu mimed slicing his own throat, and Danny switched off the videocam.

Jet poured coffee, avoiding Billie's gaze, though he couldn't help glancing up. Last night solidified what he'd felt, melted away the confusion. He had to shift his stance when he remembered how good she felt beneath him. He couldn't wait to be alone with her again.

Tapping his fingers on the counter, Stu winced. "Where is she?"

Brianna clomped downstairs, suitcase in hand and set it in the hallway.

"What's up with you?" Cat paused her nail file.

Straightening, Brianna wobbled on her spiked heels. "I'm leaving."

The other contestants gasped in unison. "What?"

Her nose in the air, she sniffed. "I love Justin. I'm leaving to be with him."

Billie looked up in time to receive Brianna's glare.

"Jet, I'm sorry." Throwing her long scarf behind her shoulder, she reached for her bag.

He shot her a cursory glance. "Guess that'll save me the trouble of eliminating you tonight." Two left. Tom Petty had it right. The waiting was the hardest part.

With a gasp, Brianna whirled, grabbed her suitcase and hurled herself toward the door.

Stu snapped his fingers in the air. "Hold on. All right, listen up. Everyone." Scanning the room, his gaze found Billie. "Including you.

Especially you." Turning back to the group, he continued. "None of this leaves this room. Capiche?"

The contestants exchanged confused glances.

Brianna lifted her chin. "I don't care what you--"

Stu's voice shook. "You will care if I leak your history to the press, sweetheart." His finger shot toward Billie. "And that's no invitation for you to poke around."

She shrugged. "I write for a music magazine, not a gossip rag."

With a bitter laugh, his head bobbed. "Nonetheless. Cindy?"

His assistant stepped from the hallway.

"Get everyone to sign off on this. This is what the public will learn about today. Justin unexpectedly left the show. No details are to be shared other than that single fact. Brianna left to be with Justin. End of story. Got it?" Meeting each person's gaze, he waited until she nodded before moving on to the next. When he got to Billie, he repeated emphatically, "Got it?"

"Yes. Like I said..."

Jet set his cup on the counter. "You don't need to worry about Billie."

Stu narrowed his eyes. "We need to talk. In my office, now."

"Don't you mean my office?" The reminder was less than gentle.

Bowing with a sickly smile, Stu gestured toward the hall.

"Goodbye, Jet." Brianna's attempt at drama fell flat. Jet waved her out the door as he strode inside.

* * * *

When Jet and Stu left, Billie's gut clenched. Her reporter's instinct should kick in, ready for the fallout. Instead, she'd rather be anywhere but alone with the remaining contestants and crew. She buried her face in a magazine.

"What's going on with them?" Ashley sunk onto a stool.

Cat glared at Billie. "The bitch knows. Don't you?"

What the hell kind of lies had Justin told Brianna? "I don't know what you're talking about."

"You've been walking around all day with a stupid grin on your face." Cat slunk toward her.

"You're crazy." *Whoa, watch what you say.* The mob mentality might kick in, and feral bimbos could prove the fiercest predators.

Ashley stood. "And you slept in his room last night. Why?"

"The...pipes leaked in the cottage." Their faces clouded with confusion. "Stu suggested it, actually. Jet only agreed to sleep in his studio because he's a gentleman." Stu would back her up. He'd have to.

Cat crept closer. "Oh, so now he's a gentleman? I thought you couldn't stand him."

"I never said that." Tempted to fuel their jealousy by saying she slept in Jet's tee shirt, she stilled her tongue.

Ashley's tone turned shrill. "You didn't have to. You're nothing but a two-faced--"

"Ladies."

At Cindy's sharp tone, everyone turned to gawk.

Arms folded, she sounded as matronly as she appeared. "Shouldn't you be getting ready for your closeup? With Brianna gone, you'll have more air time. The pressure's on. You're down to three."

Ashley and Cat turned their sharp glances upon one another, then sashayed upstairs. Julie followed.

Billie sighed with relief. "Thanks. I owe you one." She repressed the urge to ask if Cindy could make Danny stop glaring. He adjusted the boom mic, fiddled with the camera, sending daggers in his glance every minute or so.

"No sweat. Yogurt?" Cindy opened the fridge.

"I'm good, thanks." If only she could say that with conviction. "So is everything all right?"

Cindy stirred her yogurt. "Yeah. Jet had Justin sign a waiver before he left. Jet promised he wouldn't press charges if Justin left quietly. And immediately."

"No worries he'll change his mind?" Or that Danny would talk?

"Not if he wants to keep working his plush new gig. He swapped jobs with a VH1 video guy. Should be here tomorrow. Danny'll break him in, right, Danny?"

He grunted and bent to straighten a cord.

"Danny understands the sensitivities of working on a reality show. And so do you, right?" Her clear-eyed gaze made no bones about the seriousness of the subject.

If Cindy turned against her, she'd have no one watching out for her. "Absolutely."

Watching Cindy walk back to her desk, Billie thought she had an excellent future in politics.

Another evil stare from Danny drove her to her feet and outside. Her cell buzzed, and Everett's name showed in the display. Not up to another argument, she let it go to voice mail.

Jet and Stu reappeared in the kitchen, so Billie slipped back inside. Cat, Ashley and Julie joined them, and Stu explained that Cindy was preparing a fact sheet for them to review before they began taping again. "Stick to these facts, and everything will be fine. If you decide to embellish in the least, let me assure you, you will follow Brianna out the door." His smile faded. "No exceptions." Turning to Billie, he aimed for her like a missile, guided her by the elbow to the doors. "If you have a minute, I'd like to speak with you."

"Sure." Not that she had a choice. She shot a questioning glance at Jet, who followed.

"You understand how important it is to *Rock Bottom* that none of these unusual events are made public. Don't you?"

Jet stepped outside behind them.

Damn, Jet must be worried she'd go behind his back after all.

Extracting her arm from Stu's grip, she straightened. "Of course." Journalistic integrity. Personal integrity. One and the same. "*Strung Out* is not a gossip rag." Though lately, she had trouble saying that convincingly. She hadn't written any music reviews in months.

Stu's smile appeared less than sweet. "I'm sure that's true, but I have to be sure everyone's on the same page."

Straightening, she spoke clearly and emphatically. "My reputation is every bit as important as yours."

Easing closer, he leered at her chest. "I'm sure that's true as well, but unless--"

"Stu." Jet stepped closer. "Give it a rest."

Holding up his hands, Stu backed away and went inside.

Frowning, Jet blocked the door. "Sorry about that."

"I told you I wouldn't write about this." She couldn't keep the hurt from her voice.

"I know."

"Well, don't sic your pit bull on me to keep me quiet." *And why didn't you make love to me last night?*

He frowned. "I didn't sic Stu on you. He's worried about everyone, not just you."

"Himself most of all," she grumbled.

"What do you mean?"

Keep out of it, Willamina. "Just be careful of him, will you?"

The French doors opened and Stu leaned out. "Can you two join us please? We're going to review the fact sheet point by point. I'd hate for you to miss anything." His syrupy tone fooled no one.

Jet exhaled. "Yeah."

His palm warmed the small of her back. Instantly, her nerves unwound. She turned to him. "I'm so sorry about all this."

For the first time that night, his face relaxed into a smile. "Don't be." His arm slid around her waist. "We better go in. If Stu comes out again, I'll be tempted to punch him."

Relaxing, she nestled into him, then caught Ashley and Cat's glare and pulled away. So much for integrity.

* * * *

Jet's gaze glazed over listening to Stu recite the "facts." Not in any position to argue or bargain, he couldn't do more. The show already lined up a replacement for Justin, which should be seamless for viewers, but incidents like this had a nasty habit of making their way to the public.

Leaning his elbows against his knees, he pretended to read the sheet, but he found reading the people around him more interesting.

Despite his complaints, Stu obviously got a kick out of bossing everyone around. They'd been through some tough times together, and sometimes his manager acted more like a brother. The past few years, they hadn't been as close, but Jet blamed himself. He'd be the first to admit he hadn't been pleasant to be around. He couldn't even stand himself.

That all changed. His pride wanted to be able to claim responsibility himself, but if he hadn't met Billie, he'd be in the same rut. She was just the kick in the ass he needed. His stubbornness prevented him from seeing it at first. He'd also be the first to admit what an ass he could be.

"Something funny, Jet?" Stu stared down at him like a haughty teacher.

"No, nothing funny about this. Thinking of something else. Carry on."

Stu wasted no time falling back into his speech. Jet wasted no time getting back to studying Billie.

Prettier than any of the *Rock Bottom* contestants, she knew her music. Her professional ethics guided her writing. He knew he could count on her not to write a word about any of this.

* * * *

Finishing the blog entry, Billie gave a frustrated sigh. It provided sparse details. Justin left, and Brianna left to be with him. Photos filled in what words could not. *Rock Bottom*'s remaining contestants appeared haggard, embattled. Desperate.

If only she'd set her camera to video Jet playing guitar. Even a few seconds, to give people a glimpse... Stupid Stu had ruined it all for him.

A soft knock sounded, and Billie jumped up, knowing it would be Jet.

The dim light softened his features, glinted in his eyes. "Hey. Can I come in a minute?"

"Yes." When he stepped inside, her nerves tightened in expectancy, but he walked past.

Don't be a fool. He's just being polite and checking in. Or checking up.
"Can I get you anything to drink?"

"No, I just wanted to make sure you're okay."

"Fine. Are you?"

He gave a wan smile. "I don't know what I am anymore."

"This place is getting to you worse than me." That didn't come out right. She didn't dare hope she'd gotten to him.

"Yeah. It'd be nice to get away from it, even for a day."

"Why don't you?" To keep from touching him, she jammed her hands in her back pockets.

He leaned against the credenza. "I meant without an entourage. Spend a day in private."

"Why don't you?" she repeated. "Surely you can have at least a day to yourself?"

"Not until the season's over."

Unsure what to say, she kept silent. He must have come here for a reason. She'd let him take his time. When quiet stretched too long, she blurted, "The song you played earlier sounded great."

"Mmm." He frowned at the floor as if the memory pained him, then peered into her eyes.

Her brain blanked, thoughts replaced with a feverish need to touch him. Slowly, she moved toward him.

Another knock at the door startled her. "Who now?"

"Jet?" Stu called.

Her shoulders slumped. "Damn him."

"At the very least." Touching her arm, he went to the door.

Stu smiled. "Ah. I thought I might find you here." His gaze slid to Billie.

Ugh. She felt slimed, and folded her arms.

Stu jerked his head. "We have some unfinished business we should wrap up tonight."

"Yeah, let's get this over with." Glancing back, Jet paused.

Billie's pulse fluttered, then fell when he followed his manager outside. Her gut twisted. Something felt wrong. She went to the window, but she couldn't see anything, so she slipped outside. Still no sign. She crept around the side walkway and halted as she rounded the corner.

Jet stood near the French doors speaking to Stu. Scowling, his words inaudible but sharp. Wincing, Stu shook his head as Jet spoke. Stu's expressions went through acrobatics as Jet gestured, his voice slightly louder but still not audible.

With no way to get any nearer without attracting notice, she retreated. Instinct told her Jet wanted his guitar segment to be aired, but Stu wouldn't allow it. Bastard.

Somehow, she had to make Jet see how dangerous Stu really was.

* * * *

"Five minutes," the producer called.

Tonight, Jet would select whom to eliminate. Which one? Billie's stomach churned.

In the kitchen foyer, Ashley sipped a glass of wine, her wide eyes glazed over. Cat had draped herself across a chair, one finger unconsciously twirling her hair. Julie stood behind the kitchen island, gripping its edges, her darting gaze indicating her nervousness.

"Let's go face the music." Cat threw her head back and strutted to the patio, Ashley and Julie in tow.

The contestants reassembled in a loose huddle on the other side of the pool, but Jet continued to argue with Stu by the door.

Careful to stay out of the camera's line of sight, Billie crept around the opposite way and stood behind a cameraman. Must be the new guy, blissfully ignorant of her existence. His dark skin contrasted with the white tee shirt.

The producer frowned when Stu waved him over. "We're on the clock."

"What's going on?" she whispered.

"Temperamental star." The new guy rolled his eyes, then crouched to straighten a cord and moved away.

She backed against the stone wall and sat.

Jet's argument expanded to the producer, apparently. The three of them spoke at once, until Jet raised both hands, said something she couldn't catch and stalked inside.

Stu murmured to the other man.

The producer raked a hand through his hair. "This better be the last time." Turning, he called, "Girls, we're going with something a little different tonight."

"Where's Jet?" Ashley whined, and they all took up the cry.

"He's not well," Stu said.

"He looked fine," Julie said.

Ashley smoothed her short skirt. "He looked great."

The producer held up a hand. "We're shooting without him."

Cat stepped forward. "But how? Jet's supposed to be here."

Billie sighed. Where was natural selection when it was needed most desperately? She slipped toward the door.

Cat pointed. "Where's she going?"

Like a feral pack, they glared in unison.

"Bathroom," Billie lied.

"Yeah, right." Cat shot back. "You're going to meet him, aren't you?"

Ashley's cold gaze scanned her. "That's not what the show's about. We're supposed to spend time with him. Not her."

Uh-oh. A bimbo riot in the making--the most dangerous kind. "I'm only headed to the restroom."

Ashley's lower lip jutted. "I have to go too." She stomped toward her.

"Me too." With feline speed, Cat slunk ahead.

"I'm not missing this." Julie followed.

"Are you kidding?" Stu's face twisted with apparent nausea.

The producer cursed. "All right. Take ten. But be ready to shoot, ladies."

They clamored behind Billie as she scooted inside, but not fast enough to lose them. Dread filled her as they surrounded her like a lynch mob. Did bimbos know how to lynch? Maybe not, but they could strangle her with their scarves, or pound a spiked heel into her skull to the same effect. Encircling her, they moved up the stairs to their dressing room.

Cat slammed the door behind them. "Get this straight, Billie bitch. You keep your hands off Jet."

She summoned up the old Billie. The Philly Billie who took crap from no one. "I haven't laid a hand on Jet." She wouldn't admit he had touched her.

Ashley inched nearer. "Yet, maybe. But you want to."

"We can tell," Cat sneered.

As if they thought with one mind. Probably the sum of their minds didn't equal a complete one between them. "I'll tell you the same thing I told him: I'm here to do a story. Not to do him."

Their responses swirled anonymously. "What do you mean, you told him?"

"Did he come on to you?"

Before she could answer, Cat replied for her. "He comes on to every girl. He can't help it."

They seemed to take strength from this.

Ashley held a hand to her hip. "Yeah, don't think you're something special."

Cat lifted her chin. "I slept with him twice since we started shooting."

Billie's insides lurched. Something close to her heart--the valves kinked up, not letting blood through. She slumped to the bed.

Ashley whirled to face Cat. "Liar!"

The other laughed. "You wish. He's totally picking me."

A melee broke out, a cacophony of shrieks, a chorus of drama as they fell upon the closest, yanking hair, shoving shoulders.

The journalist inside said this was great fodder. If only she had her digital camera. Or at least her cell phone. A few seconds of this video would be great.

Yet she felt an unfamiliar alliance with them. No--empathy.

The catfight raged. An opportune time to get the hell out.

Downstairs, Stu barged inside. "Where are they?"

She pointed. "You might want to bring some pepper spray."

He blanched as the shrieks echoed in the hallway. "Oh, man."

Billie heaved a breath. No good going out the backdoor. The front proved much safer. Closing it behind her, she glanced around. Now where? A bang from upstairs reminded her: anywhere. Without aim, she walked.

Strains of a guitar sounded from the studio. She snuck close. Through the window, she saw Jet on a stool, arched over a guitar, eyes squeezed shut. The tune made her forget everything else. Such a gorgeous song. Like his older songs, but indefinably beyond that sound. Like the one she'd heard him play earlier.

Footsteps clacked behind her along the walk. Awkward if someone found her snooping. From her purse, she grabbed her pad and pen and scribbled as if preparing for another interview.

A crew man approached. "Are you going in? Give him this, will you?" He shoved a folded paper at her.

"Sure."

As he made his way back, she wondered whether she could shove it under the door. She bent, but the door opened.

* * * *

"Hey." He leaned against the jamb. "What are you doing?" Hopefully coming to see him. She was just the person he wanted to see.

"Nothing. I was out walking and heard your music. It sounded amazing."

Her voice sounded strained and breathy at once. He shifted against the doorway and studied her.

She held out a paper. "Oh, and someone asked me to give you this. I was about to leave it under your door. I didn't want to interrupt."

"Interrupt anytime." He pushed the door open wide. "Come in."

"No, not if you were in the flow. And it really sounded like you were. It sounded great."

At her shyness, he cocked his jaw in a half smile. "I thought you weren't an ego massager."

Her response came straightforward. "I'm not. Unless it deserves to be."

He smirked. "So you only give your honest opinion?"

"Always."

Voices came from beyond the gate.

He grasped her arm. "Come in. Quick."

Closing the door, he slid the bolt across, then drew the blinds shut. "They know better than to bother me when these are closed." He held her gaze. In the dim light, her dark eyes mesmerized him, and he eased closer.

She stepped away and said uncertainly, "We could always continue our interview."

"If you want." If that's what it took to keep her here. Erase the awkwardness between them.

Strolling inside, she glanced around. "I love your studio." Retrieving her recorder from her purse, she switched it on.

"Me too. It's the only place I feel at home. Nothing in the house is mine, so I tell myself not to get too attached." Part of the reason his life was so unsettled. He had no real home.

"Isn't that the point of the show? To become attached?"

Her snide remark hit him as sharply as if she'd punched him, and he expelled a sharp breath. "You're right."

Picking up his guitar, he hugged it to him and sat. His fingers caressed the strings. "This studio used to be a guest house. I've grown partial to it."

"So what was that new music you played? For a new CD?"

Not ready to go there. He focused on the guitar. "Just jamming."

"Play it again," she urged.

Laughing, he scratched his head.

"Please?" She switched off the recorder. "Off the record. I'd really love to hear it."

He eyed her warily. "I don't want any reviews, bad or otherwise. No blogs, no articles."

"No reviews, nothing. I swear. It stays in this room." She perched on the stool next to his.

With a deep breath, he launched into the song. His fingers flew along the frets, made the strings squeal with pleasure at his touch. The song captivated him, made time stand still, made him forget life and all its troubles. The best kind of music. A little rough, but it sounded like a hit waiting to happen--sheer raw emotion, not preprocessed into a formula.

As he finished, he froze in place, the strings resonating.

From her blissful expression, she'd caught the same vibe.

After the tune faded to silence, she exhaled. "Incredible."

He set the guitar down gently in its stand. "Come on." If he wanted someone to tell him how great it was, he'd play for his sister. He needed someone to push him to make it better.

"I mean it. It's good. I won't say it's perfect. I can tell you'll be tweaking it."

"Ha. Tweaking. Yeah." Exactly. He rested his hands on his knees, watching her.

"The rough spots are easily fixed."

"Easily? You think so?" He jutted his lower lip, teasing. Not one to craft his songs with formulas, he did have a routine for writing songs.

"For you. You're a pro."

He inclined his head. "It's never easy."

"No, I suppose not. Not when you care so much, when you've invested so much of yourself in it. But that only makes it worth it in the end. Doesn't it?"

He studied her silently.

She laid her hand on his arm. "This could be the turnaround you've been looking for."

Up like a shot, he paced. "Don't say that." Too much pressure too soon.

She rose and followed close. "How can you doubt it?"

He whirled to face her. "It's one song."

"There'll be others." She bit her lip.

"There already are, but--"

"That's great! You must know how good they are. You must *feel* it."

He stepped toward her with an intensity that made her gasp. Hands clenched, he struggled to hold himself back. When he no longer could, he took hold of her arms.

"This is what I feel." His lips enveloped hers, and immediately brought back the warmth and passion of their earlier kiss. His breath caught in his throat. He couldn't breathe, couldn't think. When her arms encircled him, holding tight, he pinned her to the wall. Her mouth pressed against his with equal force. His hands moved along her back, lips sliding against hers with a slow, powerful rhythm that made him hunger for more.

Banging on the door roused them. "Jet? Why's the door bolted? Open up." Stu. He pounded again on the door, then rattled the windows. "Jet, I need to talk to you. Let's go, open up."

Loosening his embrace, he muttered, "Fuck." He'd grown tired of people intruding on his life.

* * * *

Her thought exactly, but not likely now.

"I, uh… I should go."

"No, don't."

The urgency in his tone drew her lips to his again, but reluctantly paused when Stu knocked again.

With a sigh of defeat, he moved away.

Tucking her hair behind her ear, she strained to recall what she'd brought. Seeing her handbag on the floor, she lifted it. "Thanks…for the interview. And the song. I loved it. All of it." Her stomach churned. *Shut up. Now.* "Goodnight."

"Billie, please."

"I have to go, Jet." Twisting the doorknob, she yanked, but the door didn't budge.

"Here." He reached around her to the bolt.

"Oh, right. The lock." *Please don't kiss me again.* She couldn't be responsible for what happened if he did.

"Goodnight," he whispered, his lips brushing her cheek.

"Night." *You said that already.*

He slid the bolt and opened the door.

Blindly, she brushed past Stu and almost ran down the walk.

Whatever Stu had intended to say came out in a blurt. "What? Again?" Jet's voice faded. "An interview, Stu. Relax. What's up?"

Stu's argument was lost to the screeching coming from beyond. How could the bimbos still be at it?

As she stepped inside, Ashley cried, "There she is."

"I knew she went to meet him." Cat's pace increased.

With a gasp, Billie froze. She had nowhere to go except back inside-- but she couldn't go there either.

"Now girls…" Stu glanced back. "We have a riot on our hands. Call security."

Emerging, Jet pushed past Stu. "I'll handle this." His voice smooth as heated rum, he held up his hands. "Whoa, whoa. Let's all calm down."

Cat led the charge. "Let me at her."

Ashley followed.

Jet grabbed her arm. "I said hold on." His rougher tone halted them. "You're upset about nothing. Billie and I were--"

Cat broke in, "We know what went on."

"You have no idea." Jet glared. "Billie's a professional. A journalist. Any time I spend with her is necessary for promotion." He softened. "Without promotion, the show's dead in the water. Is that what you ladies want?"

"No." Ashley glanced uncertainly at Cat.

"We want you. That's why we're here." Cat stroked his chest.

He threw his arms around Cat and Ashley, steering them back down the path.

Disgusted, Billie couldn't turn away. The line between reality and the reality show had become a blur. One moment, he looked at her with more feeling than any guy ever had, and the next, he strolled off with his harem.

"Ah, the lucky bastard." Stu grinned.

Shooting him a glare, she stalked to her cottage.

He got the bastard part right.

Fury blinded her to the words on her laptop screen as she entered her blog post. She described the pure joy of hearing Jet play beautiful new melodies, songs to make anyone's heart ache to hear more. Why, she wondered in print, couldn't he let his public decide whether the songs were good enough? Why keep them to himself? Her rant continued about the quality of music, how artists thrived by stretching their boundaries or withered within self-imposed ones.

How Jet continued to allow himself to be distracted by reality show nonsense instead of concentrating on his true love: music.

Submitting it, she shut down the laptop and slept from sheer exhaustion.

In the morning, she awoke with a start. "Oh God. What did I do?" She'd promised not to reveal his new songs. And broken that promise.

He'd surely hate her for this.

Fearful of his hate surfacing where others could see, she sequestered herself in the cabin. Voices sounded outside the walls, but passed.

Late in the afternoon, she had to find something to eat after exhausting her supply of crackers. Takeout might be a possibility, but then again, she'd rarely seen a delivery person past the gate.

She'd have to go out.

Peering out the door, the heat blasted in her face. Ugh. Why did people live here? The stone pavers burned through her soles. The pool water stood calm, undisturbed. No one else wanted to be out in the heat either, apparently.

Luckily, the kitchen stood empty. Maybe the bimbos had taken a spa day or shopping spree. Peering in the fridge, she rummaged for something nutritious but portable. Small prepackaged cheese rounds beckoned. Grabbing two, she closed the door. "Oh!" And wanted to die.

* * * *

Jet glanced at the package in her hand. "Cheese? How appropriate." How he managed to keep his cool, he couldn't say. Maybe he hoped beyond hope her blog post had been a ploy to appease her editor. Or maybe her kiss had been a ploy.

"I…" Her shoulders slumped, defeat deflating her.

Right. No explanation would satisfy him. Best not to try. "Does *Strung Out* practice the new journalism, then? All ethics aside?"

She straightened. "It was a great piece."

"Oh yeah. Very insightful. No personal feelings involved. How could I not see through you? Your false flattery? You only did it to get close. What would have come next, Billie?" Drifting closer, he watched her lips, wanting to know their touch again.

"Don't flatter yourself." Somehow her comeback lacked conviction.

"Oh, believe me. I've been in this business long enough to know I can't trust anyone. No matter how sweet they appear. If you'd been the girl I thought you were, then that review would have been on your blog the next day." He turned away, and muttered, "I should have listened to Cat from the beginning."

"Cat? What did she say?" Horror and anger mixed in her face as she slid in front of him.

Jet knew Cat would say anything to get in his good graces. But he had to know. "She told me you were in bed with your editor. Literally." Jaw clenched, he glared, waiting. Hoping she'd deny it.

Lifting her chin, she turned, her expression giving nothing away.

He moved in front of her. "Well? Is it true?"

Her nostrils flared. "No."

His stomach churned. He knew a lie when he saw one. "Come on, Billie. I know when I've been set up."

"It's not like that." She blew through her lips. "All right, yes. Everett and I…had a thing. It's over."

But before or after she came here? "He always was a schmuck."

"I swear, Jet. We never colluded to set you up. He sent me here, I think, to get rid of me."

"Then he's a bigger schmuck than I imagined."

Confusion crossed her face. Dropping her chin, she stepped back. "You're right. I should never have let my personal life--my feelings-- interfere with my work. It's completely unprofessional. I apologize."

A bitter laugh escaped. "So that's the only reason you're sorry? It's unprofessional?" Didn't she give a fuck about him?

"What do you want from me? You have an entire harem out there."

He kept his voice in check, but glared. "Tell me the truth. Is that the only reason you're sorry?" So gorgeous. *So dangerous.* If he weren't careful, she could do serious damage--internally.

Gulping hard, her features hardened. "No. I'm sorry I ever took this job. I should never have come here."

Deep sadness roiled through him. He couldn't spend another second with her.

* * * *

Watching Jet slam the door behind him, Billie stopped herself from calling him back. Her head swirled, unable to think straight. Did he hate her, or want her? Maybe both? The concern in his face couldn't have been for her. All those questions about the blog--self-protection, that's all he cared about. The sting of Everett's underhanded breakup felt mild compared to this.

You're giving yourself away too easily again.

Whatever had been building between them had to end. Now. Her heart couldn't recover from another break, not so soon. As much as she ached to ask him to trust her, she couldn't quite trust herself.

Rushing back to the cabin, she grabbed her cell phone from its charger and dialed.

Laughing, Everett answered. "Well, hello."

"Get me out of here." Her voice shook.

"Why? What's wrong?"

Holding her temple, she calmed herself. Forced a laugh. "I'm bored out of my skull." She wished. Boredom would be a welcome emotion at the moment.

"Babe. We need you there. Audience buzz is way up. Something's about to break. I can feel it."

Yeah. Me. "Your gut's wrong half the time."

"Not this time." His singsong tone made her want to reach through the line and strangle him.

"Give me something, Everett. I'm going insane here. At least let me cover another band while I'm here. There must be someone playing in this godforsaken town."

"Nothing going on there today?"

"The Bimbo Squad are out for a wax or something. You're killing me, Everett. I need new music. I'm in this business because I love bands. Not bimbos."

Papers rustled, his keyboard clicked. "Hmm. You might have a point. Let me look around."

"Hurry." Silence. "Hello?"

The call had ended. With a growl, she flipped her cell shut. "You better come up with something good," she said to it.

Knowing Everett, it would be days before she heard from him. And he'd likely claim he forgot.

Unwrapping her cheese, she plotted her revenge. She'd go out, get a newspaper. Better yet, just go to a club. But who would she go with? One of these days, she'd talk Zinta into an overnight visit.

Her cell buzzed. Everett's name displayed. "Hello?"

"There's a band I want you to cover--tomorrow night. Supposed to be influenced by Jet, actually."

Groaning, she bit her lip. Only a pseudo-escape. A cheap imitation of Jet. "Nothing else?"

"Hey, you asked for a side assignment. Take it or leave it."

At least it would get her away from here for a night. "Fine. Give me the details." Jotting the information, she sighed. "Okay. I'll file a story afterward."

If she still had a brain left.

Chapter 11

No matter how many times he played through it in his head, Jet couldn't believe Billie had set out to play him. He'd kissed other women who had, and they put all their efforts into kissing him, but none had gotten to him like Billie.

Hell, even if she was playing him, he wanted her. She made him feel good, and it had been too long since anyone had done that. If she were the devil, he'd dance with her, anyway.

In the morning, he skipped his run to stalk her. If he went inside the guest house, he knew how it would end. In bed. But he might not get the answers he wanted. He had to talk to her on neutral ground.

His heart skipped a beat when she emerged. In a hurry.

Jogging to her side, he fell into step. "Hey, I've been thinking about what you said yesterday. Are you busy?"

She kept her gaze ahead. "Yeah, actually. I have to go get a new digital recorder. Mine crapped out."

"I'll take you." What was he saying? He couldn't leave.

Her pace grew brisk. "No, thank you. The taxi's here."

Grasping her arm, he tugged her to a halt. "What's wrong?" *Wrong question, shithead.* What *went* wrong?

She slipped from his hold, and concentrated on the driveway. "Nothing. I have work to do. And you have three women to keep happy, so all's right with the world."

"Are you seriously mad about the other night?" Incredulousness replaced feigned pleasantness. Everything had gone to crap after he kissed her. Or after Stu showed up. Fucking Stu.

With a haughty laugh, she tossed her hair. "No. No, the other night was great. I almost throw myself at you, and you throw yourself at three crazy bimbos. Happy ending for everyone."

He lurched ahead. "Did you want me to step aside? Let them scratch your eyes out? I'm pretty sure that's what might have happened."

"I have to go. I need a new recorder for tonight." She winced as if in regret.

His senses pricked to alert. "What's tonight?"

"I'm…going somewhere." From her attitude, anywhere but here was great.

"Where?" Another assignment? To see another guy? His blood sizzled.

She blurted, "Just out. To see a band." With a groan, she fast-forwarded her gait to a sprint to the end of the driveway.

Excitement made it easy for him to keep pace. "Great. I'd love to see a band." Especially with her.

Halting, she whirled to face him. "No, you can't go. Isn't this your date night with Julie?"

"So? We'll all go." He couldn't give a shit about Julie.

"I'd rather go alone. I'll be working." She pressed the button for the gate. Repeatedly.

Stepping in front of her, he set his hands on his hips. "I'll go there anyway then. But wouldn't the magazine prefer you to tag along? It would save a taxi expense."

When she bit her lip, he could almost see her manufacture excuses in her mind.

Her chin jutted out. "I don't want to upset Julie." She sidestepped around him.

To block her path, he thrust out his arm. "She'd love for you to come along." He could be every damn bit as stubborn.

Her jaw clenched. "Perfect."

He couldn't hold back a smile. "Perfect. See you tonight."

After yanking the cab door open, she slammed it so hard the driver yelled, "Hey."

With a chuckle, he watched her sink into the seat. The taxi roared off.

When she glanced back, Jet's grip tightened on the gate.

Tonight.

He finally had something to look forward to.

* * * *

Billie cursed herself. How could she be so idiotic? So many verbal fumbles in so little time. *No wonder you're not a TV anchor. You say all the wrong things. To the wrong people.* Lack of sleep made her extremely witty too.

Could Jet be any more of a presumptuous jerk? Oh yeah, she'd love to go on his date with Julie. Because her dream had always been to be part of a threesome with him. She needed no further reminder of her place in his world--her nonexistent place.

His smugness tweaked her annoyance to high pitch. Her intention in going out was to get away from him, not spend more time with him.

She stifled a tortured groan.

Tonight would be a perfect hell, like the last few months had been. Destined to repeat, apparently, until she'd suffered sufficiently for her sins--whatever awful sins she'd committed to merit this sort of punishment, she had no clue.

Paying the driver, she climbed out in relief, glad to get away from the Jet asylum for a day. But still reliving his kiss like a recurring nightmare.

One she'd love to relive in reality. The feel of his weight atop her in his bed. She dreamed of wrapping her legs around his and…

"Watch it." A boy whizzed by on his skateboard.

With no time to react, she halted. "Sorry." *Wake up, Willamina.*

Browsing through the electronics store, she expected to see Jet at every turn. He must have waited for her today. Seemed so damn eager to talk to her.

Guilt plagued her. Of course he'd diverted the Bimbo Trio to save her. Her angry self retorted: *What else did he do to divert them?* Her hurt self whined: *Why would he leave with them and not me?* None of her selves wanted to face him tonight, so she stayed away until the last possible moment.

When the taxi dropped her off again outside the gate, she considered changing her clothes quickly and calling for another ride before Jet spied her. The walkway was deserted, the house quiet. If she hurried, she might be able to pull it off.

After a quick shower, she threw on the purple sundress, remembering how Jet couldn't keep his eyes from wandering down her curves last time she wore it. If she had to be in hell, she'd drag him along. This time, she had strappy silver sandals to go with it. Hastily adding a silver necklace, bracelet and earrings, she grabbed her bag and threw open the door.

Standing on her doorstep, Jet's mouth dropped open. As his gaze slid downward, his voice thickened. "I just wanted to let you know we're ready."

"Oh. Great. Me too." She slammed sunglasses onto her face. Grrr. A few seconds earlier, she could have dodged him. Bastard. Gorgeous too, dammit. Probably knew his light blue shirt made his eyes stand out even more.

Grinning, he cocked his head.

Two could play at the sweetness and light game. Hesitating as they walked, she put her best polite self forward. "Are you sure this is a good idea? I really hate to impose."

His hand at the small of her back guided her toward the limo. "No imposition. You may as well ride in the limo with us. Danny will follow in the van."

"Right." She had no desire to ride with Danny. His glares had long ago grown old, and she hadn't even introduced herself to Justin's replacement. He too acted as if she was poison and avoided her.

Once in the limo, she seated herself behind the driver. Julie took a place by the window, and Jet sat opposite. His knee relaxed in Julie's direction. Billie tensed. Would she have to witness their small talk? What if Julie flirted with him? Kissed him? Why had Billie agreed to this? She should have taken a cab. Hopefully the ride would be mercifully short.

To busy herself, she pulled out her cell and texted Zinta. *Off to my assignment. Same music, different location.*

Her phone buzzed. Zinta replied: *Got you out of the house and away from Jet. Have fun. Do something I'd do.*

Billie's fingers flew. *Only one out of two. I'm with him.*

The reply came swiftly: *What? Why? I take it back, don't do anything I'd do.*

She chuckled. *No worries. Talk to you later.*

Glancing up, Julie stared out the window.

Jet stared at Billie. "Working already?"

She couldn't hold in a haughty huff. "I have a life. Or I used to, before I came here."

She caught his arched brows, though hidden by sunglasses and bangs, and hoped she'd deterred him.

He leaned an elbow against the door and touched a finger to his lips. "Heard good buzz about this band?"

"Some, yeah." She didn't have the heart to say they were a Jet wannabe band.

"The venue's nice, anyway. The acoustics are great because it's small."

The limo began to feel very small with him directing his conversation at her instead of Julie. A nod was Billie's only response.

Julie turned to him. "Could I have a drink?"

Jet leaned forward. "Sure. What would you like?"

"Do you have any wine?" Julie raked her fingers through her long hair.

Why hadn't she raised a fuss at Billie's presence? The only contestant who couldn't be classified a bimbo, she should be smart enough to find ways around Billie to get to Jet. If that's what she really wanted.

Jet pulled out two glasses. "Billie?"

"Yes, thanks." One would help release the tension.

After pouring, he held up his. "To great music."

They touched together with a clink. Billie gulped and prayed the ride would end soon.

Julie made small talk about the band, the magazine. Jet extended his leg, his foot within inches of Billie's.

When the limo rounded a turn and came to a halt, she released a breath. She needed air.

* * * *

Jet waited for Billie and Julie to exit the limo, and followed them inside. The doorman greeted them with a smile. "Mr. Trently. Your table's ready, sir."

A petite woman led them up dark stairs and onto a balcony, then asked for their orders.

Tonight he'd splurge. "Bring us a bottle of your best champagne."

"Water for me, please." Billie moved to a seat near the rail.

Danny would probably stand in the doorway, taping Jet and Julie, and catching video of the band playing on the stage beyond. Unfortunately, it meant Billie would have to stay out of sight. No matter. Jet's chair sat less than a foot from hers.

The girl returned with a bucket and stand. After popping the cork, she poured.

Jet urged the flute at Billie. "Come on, we need to toast."

Despite her look of surprise, she accepted it.

Holding his glass aloft, he said, "To finding our soul mates."

Flashing a wry smile, Billie sipped.

Jet downed his drink and refilled it. "I can't wait to hear these guys play. I haven't heard another band in much too long."

Billie took out her new recorder and fiddled with the buttons.

"Relax." Jet refilled her flute to the rim, though she sipped slowly. He wanted to celebrate. With Billie. He'd have to pretend with Julie, though as usual, she acted reserved and seemed more interested in the people around them.

The house lights dimmed and the audience applauded. The band took the stage, and the spotlights came up, framing each.

The lead singer thanked them. "I understand we have a special guest tonight. Someone whose music inspired our own. Mr. Jet Trently." He gestured toward the balcony, and the spotlight swung on him.

"What the..." Jet stood and waved, bowed his head and took his seat. Nice of them to acknowledge him. Excitement shone in Billie's face, but Julie excused herself. Be nice if she'd just disappear.

On cue, the spotlight dimmed and the band launched into their first set.

From the first beat, the song captured his attention. The music riveted him. Excited him. Reminded him why he worked in this fickle industry. Great music gave him a high like no other.

True, their sound mimicked Jet's, only updated and revitalized. Obviously, he'd been a heavy influence. It both excited and saddened him. These guys carried on his work. The work he should be doing himself.

After each song, Jet clapped and whistled. After the third song, Jet leaned back. "They're great, aren't they?"

"Yeah, pretty good," Billie said. "Not as good as you."

Surprise made him blow through his lips. "Here, have more champagne." He realized Julie's seat remained empty. Good. Maybe she'd fulfill his wish.

The lead singer leaned away from the mic to talk to the guitar player, and then the keyboard player. Each nodded. The singer grabbed the mic. "Thanks so much. Many of you know we wouldn't be here tonight if it weren't for Jet Trently. Jet, we'd be honored if you'd join us onstage."

Delight buoyed him, but he held his hands to his chest in question.

The singer waved him down. Jet needed no further invitation. Playing with this band would be a thrill.

The hostess appeared in the doorway. "Follow me, Mr. Trently."

Glancing at Billie, he hesitated.

"Well, go on." She smiled. "Go cut loose."

"Yeah. You're right." Thank God she understood. He almost sprinted down the steps. The spotlight engulfed him when he jogged onto the stage. A cheer went up from the audience. One of the best sounds in life. He gave a casual wave.

The singer clasped his shoulder. "Thanks, man."

Jet nodded. "Hey, thank you."

When the band exploded in one of Jet's songs, he sang along as if they'd spent months rehearsing. The harmonies sounded tight, and his performance rocketed to the level of his early days. The band segued into another Jet tune, and he picked it up without flaw.

* * * *

Billie couldn't tear away her gaze. Jet came alive on stage like she'd never seen him. The music's raw energy sizzled along her nerve endings. Enthralled her, made her want to move, get inside it, get lost in it.

At the end of the set, the audience thundered its applause, standing. Jet bowed and exited gracefully, returning command of the stage to the band. Their next song sounded lackluster in comparison.

Julie slipped in just before the hostess appeared in the doorway and Jet entered, fists clenched in victory. When he smiled at Billie, the balcony buzzed with revitalized energy.

He caught the employee before she left. "Another bottle of champagne." He turned to Billie. "Did I sound all right?"

"Are you kidding? You made them sound a hundred times better." Imitations never outshone the original.

"No, they're incredible. So much better than me."

"That's not true." How could he doubt himself after the standing ovation?

The hostess returned with the champagne and popped the cork.

Jet instructed her to pour three, and emptied his glass. "Oh, man, it feels great to make music. This is reality. Bringing the songs alive in front of an audience. Getting them excited. Connecting with their energy." Staring at Billie, his eyes blazed with heat.

Aware of Danny's camera aimed at him, she drew back.

He glanced back. "Hey, turn that thing off. Call it a day, will you?"

The light dimmed. Danny lowered the video. "If you say so. I'm outta here."

Julie shifted in her seat. "Maybe I should go too."

Startled, Billie blurted, "What? No. I should. I'm intruding on your date--"

Jet's voice rose. "It's not a date."

Julie slid her handbag from the table. "I'm really tired. Wait up, Danny."

Jet tugged Billie's chair closer. "Don't make me feel like a total loser. Sit up here with me."

After hesitating, she pulled the chair up, her resistance against his cheerful mood fading.

He leaned an arm around the back of her seat. "Let me see what you wrote." Lifting her notepad, he read, then smiled. "Yes!"

Unable to recall the little bit she'd written, she scanned it. *Jet Trently obviously lives to make music*, she'd scrawled. Her only note for the entire night.

"You understand." He refilled their glasses and slurped. "But they are the future. My music's the past." He slugged down another glass and leaned back.

"Don't say that."

He slurred, "Come on, Billie. You said it yourself. My songs are stale. I'm a has-been."

"The audience went crazy when you appeared. They love you. They want more of you." She wished she could say she didn't want the same. But with his face so close, she could smell the champagne--wanted to taste it--her steely resolve wavered.

"Everyone does. But I don't have enough to give them anymore." Sadness filled his face.

"Yes, you do. I heard those songs. They're great. You just have to get them out there for other people to hear. They'll love them too." Too late, she realized she'd grabbed his wrist.

Hovering close, he glanced down, gave a slow blink and met her gaze. "We should go." Standing, the chair tipped behind him as his shoulder hit the doorway.

She scrambled to gather her things. "Wait." Afraid he might fall, she hooked her arm in his. When he weaved into her, she grabbed his waist and chest going down the stairs. Thankfully the steps were few. The hostess called for the car and held the door as Billie helped him in.

* * * *

Forlorn, Jet slumped against the seat. Everything he wanted, all around him yet so fucking far out of reach.

Billie sat beside him. "Are you feeling all right?"

"No." He slid down the seat and laid his head in her lap.

"Jet, this isn't--"

He stared at the limo ceiling. "They sounded a hundred times better than me." If they imitated him, how could they outdo him?

"Hey, they're a cheap imitation. If they do sound like you, then it's a great tribute. It's the highest compliment anyone could pay you. Who knows how many other musicians your music has inspired?"

"No. The best compliment would be for people to buy my records. But clearly, they're making better music." Of course she couldn't imagine having someone copy his life's work and make a profit. Still, he gave her a slow smile.

A hard gleam came into her eyes. "Your new songs would blow them out of the water."

"Those are…" He shrugged, then lifted an arm above his head, clasping her elbow, wanting to connect with her every way possible. Somehow each time their limbs entwined, it felt so natural. "Those are nothing." Mainly because he had so much trouble finishing them. They could be amazing.

She stroked his hair. "Bull. I heard them. They have real potential."

"No. Stu says people wouldn't respond." Talking to her like this was better than sex. Almost.

Indignance plain in her tone, she said, "That's bull too. I say they would."

"Stu says they expect me to stick with my brand. The tried and true. That's what drives sales." He repeated the words lifelessly. Why had he listened to Stu for so long?

She clutched Jet's head. "Forget Stu. What do you want?"

He met her gaze, grateful she cared enough not to let him wallow in his own self-pity. Eventually he'd drown. "Same as always. To make great music."

"Then do what you love."

Was that an invitation? He'd love to take her, right here. So beautiful, the way she looked at him with such intense frustration. It made him afraid to move for fear she'd try to bolt again.

"Look, it's like Dylan in reverse."

"Huh?" Blinking, he focused on her.

"Dylan started out a folk singer. But then he went electric, and it pissed people off. But it also brought him an entirely new audience, a bigger audience. So you changing your music would be--"

"--like Dylan in reverse. Except I'd just lose a lot of fans." Maybe Stu was right.

"Or make a lot of new ones," she countered.

In his dreams. If he could take her certainty to the bank, he'd be set.

"It's the mark of a true artist to experiment."

He couldn't ignore the challenge. More fierce than he intended, he said, "I do. I just don't put it out there."

She relaxed, seeming pleased with his reaction. "Well, until you do, you'll never know. It could change everything."

"That's what I'm afraid of." He settled against her lap. "Why are you in this business?"

"The same reason as you. The music."

Searching her face, he asked, "What makes you fall in love with a song?" Maybe if he knew, he could write it.

Her brows arched and for a moment she seemed lost in thought. "A great song has huge emotional impact. It reaches inside me, lifts me up off the floor, dances my soul in the air, sometimes slams me back down. I connect life events with songs. Songs can define a moment."

The truth of what she said blazed in his mind. Exactly what he needed to hear. "What moment?" He caressed her elbow to forearm.

"Anything. A date--"

"Like your prom?" he teased.

She neatly ignored the comment. "Or it can evoke a whole new moment."

"Like what?" He gave her his full attention.

Shaking her head, she narrowed her eyes. "A sunrise. The beginning of U2's *A Street with No Name* always makes me imagine a beautiful sunrise, orange and pink clouds spreading across the sky, bursting to life with sunlight. As the music swells stronger, the sunrise glows brighter." She gave a laugh. "I actually described it that way in a review and the editor winced, and asked me to change it. But every time I hear that song, the same sunrise bursts vividly to life in my head."

He could almost see it in her eyes. "That's beautiful." He ran his hand up her arm. "Why are you here?"

"What?" Confusion faded her smile.

"You should be out at concerts, hearing new bands. Why are you writing about this stupid show?" If he were her, he'd hate every part of *Rock Bottom*.

With a sigh, she said, "Good question."

"Everett's an ass." Underutilizing a great reporter like Billie. "He should be printing more about the music, not covering other media."

"You're preaching to the choir, baby."

It sounded so right for her to call him baby, though he knew she teased. "It's absurd. The media covering the media. It's some conspiracy to muddy our brains with nonsense instead of real news."

She pressed her lips together. "Right--the morning TV anchors promoting the late night TV hosts. It *is* absurd."

Finally, someone else noticed too. "You do get it."

"Absolutely. It's ridiculous. We're journalists, professionals who can sway public opinion."

"Then tell Everett."

"I have. He says the readers drive the stories. They respond to this crap more than music reviews."

He squeezed her arm. "But they like hearing about new bands."

Something registered in her face, some realization. Maybe she felt his energy return. She sobered. "Sometimes." She glanced out the window.

He had to put her at ease again. Searching her face, his thumbs caressed her arm. "When you write about the band we saw tonight, readers will respond. New groups need the exposure. It's too hard these days to get a band going."

"Maybe." She pressed her knees together.

A signal for him to get up. No way. He shifted his head but kept it in her lap. "You're a good writer. You can help them."

"Why do you want them to succeed?"

Good, he'd drawn her back in. Back from whatever argument she had with herself about keeping him on the outside. "It's only right. Other bands gave me a shot at the start. You have to keep the positive flow going, Billie."

"But what if they..." She winced, as if wanting to spare him pain.

He chuckled. "What if they displace my band? Eclipse us into oblivion?"

She scowled. "That won't happen."

"If it does, it's the laws of nature. Survival of the fittest, right? The newest? The best?"

"Your music's better than theirs."

He loved her enthusiasm, but didn't agree. "In its day, maybe it was."

Anger surged in her voice. "Stop saying that as if you don't have anything new to offer."

"It's not what the fans want."

"Screw the fans. Oops, sorry. You probably already have." She rolled her eyes. "You're letting Stu hold you back."

"Like Everett's holding you back," he countered, baiting her. He understood their employee-employer situations were reversed, but it was no excuse for her to capitulate.

"Don't change the subject. You're afraid to put those songs out there."

She had him there. "Maybe."

"Why? They're amazing."

He grinned. "Why do I feel as if you're trying to set me up?"

Her voice thick with angst, she said, "The longer you talk, your excuses only get worse."

The limo pulled up to the house.

She reached for the door handle. "Let me up. Get one of your bouncers to help you inside. Or a bimbo. Hell, make it two."

No fucking way was he losing her now. They were so close.

He flipped over and shut the door. "No." When he tapped on the shield behind the driver, it lowered. "Henry, drive--anywhere. Just keep going until I tell you to stop." The window raised and the limo peeled ahead.

* * * *

With a gasp, she clutched the seat as they roared away. "What do you think you're doing? Let me out, you asshole."

He knelt in front of her and slid his hands up her thighs. "You called me 'baby'."

She hoped he'd missed that. He definitely seemed too clear-eyed now.

Through clenched teeth, her voice shook. "It's an expression. I am not one of the Bimbo Brigade."

Clasping her neck, he drew her close. "Thank God." His lips brushed hers.

Anger melted into confusion, surged with passion. "Stop," she whispered.

"I can't." He leaned between her legs, gripped her ass and slid her against him. Tender yet fierce, his lips sought hers, his tongue probed.

White static filled her brain. How could he feel so good when he was all wrong?

"No." She broke away.

He sank onto his feet, the deepest yearning in his eyes. "Billie." His urgent whisper sounded like a fervent prayer.

His plea awakened something fierce and tender within her. "Dammit." Her urgent whisper matched his.

His face lit with hope.

"Jet." An overwhelming urge hijacked her reasoning. She fought to regain it but lost ground.

He drew a ragged breath and touched her cheek.

"Don't." She couldn't finish her thought. *Don't toy with me. Don't break my heart.*

"Shh." His finger traced her lips. He eased in slowly.

Although she had every opportunity to stop him, instead she clutched his shirt. "You won't remember this tomorrow, anyway." She pressed her lips to his, wrapped her legs behind his.

His embrace engulfed her as he pulled her to the floor. "Oh yes, I will." With soft, purposeful kisses, he kept his eyes open, watching as if to imprint her in his memory.

Yes, he'd remember.

And so would she. Dammit.

* * * *

"Hey, why's Everett squawking about you?" Zinta's voice grated through the cell the next morning.

Billie held a hand to her forehead. "Who knows? Why does he ever--" She gasped. "Oh, damn. I never filed my story."

"Which? About the concert?"

"Yes." The air left her lungs surely as if she'd entered a vacuum.

"Are you sick?"

Billie whimpered. "You might say that." Mental illness counted, didn't it? She could come up with no other plausible explanation for last night.

"Tell me."

"I…" What euphemism might fit the situation?

"Sweetie, no. Please tell me you didn't."

Tired of hiding her feelings from her best friend, she closed her eyes. "Zin, I couldn't help it. He's amazing."

Zinta's gasp extended for seconds. "I'm coming to get you."

"Stop. I'm fine. Feet firmly on the ground." All too well, she knew the challenges she faced.

"You've got him out of your system now, right? No more foolishness?"

Her voice cracked. "Yeah." *Way to sound convincing.*

"I don't want to see you get hurt again."

"Neither do I, believe me." But it seemed inevitable now.

"Remind yourself: He's just the rebound guy. And call me if you feel a sin coming on."

Despite herself, she grinned. "Thanks."

"For what?"

"The laugh. And understanding."

"All too well, as you know."

Maybe, Billie thought. But Zin's indiscretion had been one night. Billie knew if Jet came to her again, she wouldn't hesitate to let him in.

* * * *

The view from the office blew him away. How had Jet not appreciated it before?

Today, he saw everything with new eyes. He'd awakened excited to start the day. Man, that hadn't happened in probably a decade.

All because of Billie. Last night more than fulfilled his fantasies about her. It made him yearn for more. He couldn't think of anything else. It had nearly killed him to leave her at the guest house. Though he'd lain awake most of the night, he could run a marathon. Jazzed. Wired. Call it whatever, he had it bad.

Stu shuffled in. "What's with the shit-eating grin?"

His cynicism made Jet grin all the more. "It's a beautiful day, Stu. Open your eyes. We're in fucking Malibu."

Disgust tinged his expression. "And you're just realizing this now?" He narrowed his eyes. "Are you diddling with that reporter?"

Jet rolled off the couch with laughter. "Diddling?"

"You stupid ass. You are. What did I tell you? She's trouble with a capital *T.*"

And that rhymes with me. "You don't know what you're saying."

His manager squared off in front of him. "Look. The producer's up my ass day in and day out. I'm not going to fend him off so you can screw around with...her. You had six women to choose from. Six. Gorgeous. Women."

"You know what?"

"What?"

"I love you, Stu." He threw open the door. "You too, Cindy."

"Me too, what?"

"I love you."

"Great. Love you too, Jet."

Today, he loved everybody. Even himself.

* * * *

Billie emailed Everett, said she hadn't had a chance to interview the band yet but would submit her article as soon as she caught up with them.

Cindy could probably get a phone number. She knew every contact in town. Billie hurried to the house, hoping not to run into anyone else.

Walking down the hallway, she said, "Hey, Cindy, can you do me a favor?"

"Sure. What is it?"

"The band we saw last night--any way you could get a number for them? I couldn't get an interview last night and..."

Her heart fluttered when Jet leaned out the doorway, stiff as a statue. And every bit as cold.

"I thought that was you. Got a minute?"

Oh God, here it comes. "Sure."

No smile. No good morning. He'd apologize for last night, tell her it was all a mistake.

"I'll find that number for you." Cindy turned away, farther than she needed to.

Billie steeled herself, held her head high and walked in.

He closed the door behind her.

Don't look at him. Just tell him and leave. "I know what you're going to say. You had too much to drink. So did I."

The lock clicked.

Surprise forced her to glance over.

* * * *

With a sly smile, he gathered her in his arms, his mouth soft and warm on hers. White heat exploded in his brain as his pulse raced to the speed of light. When she slid her fingers through his hair, something like helium rose up inside, made him feel light enough to float away.

Tightening his embrace, he moved them away from the door and pressed her down on the sofa. His weight atop her grounded him again. Especially when she wrapped her legs behind his, her arms encircling him.

The door handle jiggled. Stu called, "Jet, why's the door locked? Jet."

They froze, lips and tongues entangled.

Billie rested her head back. "How does he know? Every single freaking time!"

"I'm going to fire him." He grinned, gave her a quick kiss and helped her up. "Let's make him wait." He pressed her to him, tongue probing hers.

"You better let him in."

His manager's knocking became louder, along with his voice.

The thought of Stu peering through the keyhole creeped him out too. He touched his lips to hers, eased away, and came back for a longer kiss. "Only so I can fire him."

She giggled. "Stop."

"Stop?" He jutted his lower lip in a pout.

She grabbed his head, pulled him to her. "Mmm, no, not that."

He could kiss her all day. If only Stu weren't ready to break down the door.

Jet heaved a sigh. "I'm not done with you." His teeth grazed her neck, and she clutched him close.

Definitely not done. Not even close.

Exasperation edged Stu's tone. "I swear if you don't open up now, I'm calling nine-one-one."

Restraining a groan, Jet pulled open the door. "Stu. Come on in."

Mouth agape, he looked from Jet to Billie. "Miss Prescott. Good morning."

"Yes, it is."

Raking a hand through his hair, Jet smiled. It would have been a great morning if Stu hadn't interrupted.

* * * *

Dazed by hormonal happiness, Billie drifted out into the hall.

Cindy's wide-eyed stare made her glance down. Her blouse had rumpled, buttons askew, hem half out of her wrinkled cotton pants. Walking away, she scrambled to fix it.

Inside the office, Jet and Stu argued loudly. She could guess about what. Or whom.

"I have that number." Cindy waved a piece of paper.

"You do? Thank you. Thanks so much." *Rambling again.* Taking the slip, she tucked it in her bag. "I think I need coffee. Can I get you anything?"

"I'm fine."

"Good." She wished she could say the same. Or at least give a rational appearance. Entering the kitchen, she tensed as Cat looked up from the table.

Head lowered, Billie aimed for the coffeemaker and poured herself a cup.

Cat angled toward her. "Why are your nose and mouth so red?"

She glanced up at Jet who came toward her. "I don't know. I must be coming down with something."

Cat turned to Jet. "I suppose you're coming down with the same thing?"

He leaned across the counter, smiling. "I think I am."

Practically hissing, Cat leaped from her chair and hurled herself out the door. "This is utter bullshit."

Billie moved along the counter. "I better go before she begins throwing knives."

His hand grazed her arm as she passed. "Don't go far."

Her cell buzzed, barely penetrating her consciousness. "I won't."

Ashley entered, hastening Billie's pace to the door. Outside, she checked her cell. Everett. When she wanted to reach him, he never had time. Now, he called too often. She'd call him back, after she'd at least set up an interview.

From the cottage, she changed into shorts, then made several calls, taking notes on the laptop as they spoke. The more she spoke to the band members, the greater the rush of writing about music returned. Oh, she'd missed it. Needed it. Music, she could write about forever.

After the last call, she wrote like her fingers were on fire, and only the words pouring from the keys could quench it. She emailed her story to Everett.

Her cell buzzed minutes later, and a knock sounded on her door. She opened her cell and the door at the same time.

Everett said, "Finally. Where have you been?"

Jet slipped inside, shut and locked the door, and took her in his arms. His mouth worked up her neck and along her jaw.

Billie's breath rushed from her. She managed to get out one thought before a tidal wave of energy wiped clean the slate of her brain. "Working. Where do you think?"

Jet's lips closed over hers, and a powerful surge took away her reasoning. She kissed him with all the force of her being.

"What's going on?" Everett said, sounding very far away. "Billie? Billie."

She dropped the phone, slid her arms around Jet's neck and abandoned herself to his kiss.

* * * *

Jet scooped his arm behind her legs and carried her up the steps.

Nuzzling against his neck, her tongue explored its contours, the throbbing vein that led to his earlobe. When her tongue teased his ear, he groaned and laid her on the bed, easing on top of her. His hands slid everywhere, his mouth tasting every inch, stripping her of her shirt and shorts. A wild frenzy filled him. Her fingers worked his shirt buttons, pausing only to clutch him closer as he suckled her nipple, and teased his tongue down her stomach. He had to have her. Now.

He tugged her shorts down.

She froze. "Oh God."

Worried he'd hurt her, he lifted his head. "Are you all right?"

Heaving a whimpering breath, she held her forehead. "I stopped taking birth control when I came here. I..."

Oh, she of little faith. Reaching into the heap of clothes, he held up a square packet and arched a brow. Not the best method, but she hadn't minded last night. Maybe she thought it their first and only time. He'd known better.

"Will this do?"

One quick glance was all it took. "Yes."

Smoothing hair from her face, he tenderly pressed his lips to hers, lifting away to gaze at her every few seconds. He kept his movements slow and deliberate until she guided him into her. When she locked her legs behind his, his breaths shuddered with the strain. No way could he hold back now. Arching her back, she rocked her hips, taking him as deep as she could. Every pore ached for her, needed her skin slick and warm against his. Her fingers dug into his back and he thrust harder, every muscle working to get inside her deeper. Tremors shook his body and his arms tightened around her. A climax reverberated from his core outward, sending shockwaves over him again and again.

Even after he'd softened inside her, he moved against her, riding the crest, not wanting to stop. He sensed another climax rising in her, and made sure she got there. She gripped him until it subsided, then collapsed her limbs with a laugh.

"Are you all right?" he asked.

Breathless, she fell back against the sheet. "Oh yes. How about you?"

"Better than ever." Rolling to his side, he pulled her close and inhaled deeply. His finger trailed lazily across her spine. "I couldn't stop thinking about you all night. I almost climbed the tree outside your bedroom window."

"You did? No one ever climbed a tree for me before."

"Since the day you came here, I've been thinking about you. You tortured me, kept me awake. When you stayed in my room, it was the first night I could actually sleep." Admitting it made him tense. He never put his feelings out there for other girls. With Billie, he wanted to share everything. It poured from him without thought.

"Me too. I felt so safe in your arms."

Closing his eyes, he said a silent thank you, and trailed his fingers along her waist.

She tilted her head back. "Aren't you supposed to be filming soon?"

Kissing her forehead, he grunted a noise of acknowledgment. He didn't want to think about it. Not now.

"You should go. Before Stu comes looking for you."

He gave a growl in answer. He rolled above her, studying her for some time. Amazing how someone so natural could appear so beautiful. But did she think this only a game? Did she find him half as interesting as he found her?

Smiling, she lifted her lips to his. "Go on." She pushed at his shoulders until he turned over and sat up.

Staring out the window, he wondered why she didn't seem to want him to make any promises. Other girls begged for him to say I love you. Ask when they'd see him again. Not Billie. She pushed him out of bed.

Maybe she still had a thing for Everett.

After pulling a tank top over her head and stepping into her underwear, she gathered his clothes and clucked her tongue. "These are so wrinkled." Smoothing them, she made him hold up his arms while she slid the shirt on. She bent down and opened his boxers. "Step in." When he did, she tugged them to his knees. "You're going to have to help."

Stifling the urge to ask why, he stood and pulled them over his hips.

She put his jeans into his hands, and slowly he put them on.

Running his hands along her arms, he asked, "I'll see you later?"

"Yeah, I'll be out there." Pain flickered across her face. "Don't forget your shoes."

His lips brushed hers, and he bent to retrieve one worn loafer from beside the bed and the other at the top of the steps. He padded downstairs to the door where he slipped them on his feet, still watching her. Waiting for some signal.

Standing at the rail, she waved.

Guess that's it. He opened the door a crack, then slipped out into the blinding sun, already wanting to go back to her.

Chapter 12

Facing the Bimbo Brigade--even the three remaining--required fortification. Billie picked up her cell, her finger hesitating over Zinta's number. She could hear her scolding tone already: *You must be crazy. Keep away from him. He'll break your heart. Ruin your life.* No, she couldn't confide even in Zin. Billie already knew she couldn't count on Jet, knew he'd leave her, so he couldn't break her heart. She only knew that for now, she wanted to be here with him, for however long. Then the show would end, and she'd go home, and he'd go--where? Probably somewhere to gear up for the third season. More bimbos. There would always be more bimbos to follow.

Staving off Everett's curiosity proved more difficult. He'd sent text after text after she dropped the phone. When Jet left, she remembered her cell and retrieved it from the floor. *Must have been a grid overload*, she messaged. *Or sunspots.* Or the Jet stream.

She wanted to get caught in it again. Moving atop her, he'd looked so gorgeous, blond hair rumpled, clear blue eyes sparkling with pure lust.

She giggled and fell back on the sofa. "If you go out there like this, the bimbos will know. Wipe the smile from your face." It would reappear, she knew, without her being conscious of it. She'd have to cover somehow.

With that quasi-formed plan, she dressed in plain black pants and a black sleeveless top, with a white scarf belt. Clouds skidded across the late afternoon sun, and soon would drop below the horizon.

Making her way into the house, she slipped behind the tangle of cords of the two cameramen.

Ashley and Cat stood by the kitchen island, half-filled wineglasses and an open bottle on the counter. Ashley shot her a stabbing glance, then emptied her glass. "Where's Julie? Still sleeping off last night?"

Cat leaned against the counter with a smug smile. "I don't know. She sure made a racket last night. I hardly got any sleep."

An uneasy feeling crept over Billie, but she ducked her head and pretended to text on her cell.

Pursing her lips, Ashley whined, "I can't believe Jet would screw her. He promised to come to my room last night."

Billie froze. What did she say? Her senses heightened to red alert.

"You wish. You're just jealous he's been spending so many nights with me."

A high-pitched noise sounded, and Billie realized it came from her. The walls closed in, and she stumbled toward the French doors.

Pealing laughter echoed from inside. She gasped for air and aimed for the walkway.

Approaching from the walk near his studio, Jet smiled, then frowned. "Hey, what's wrong?" He jogged up and grasped her arms.

"No." Flailing from his grip, tears burned her eyes. "Leave me alone."

"Billie. Tell me."

"You slept with them. You've been going to them every night." Of course. That's why he left her earlier without even the pretense of a promise.

He crouched to eye level. "Who said that?"

"Ashley and Cat. And you screwed Julie after we…after we…" Her breaths became shallow. She couldn't lose it in front of him. Wouldn't.

Holding her head, he forced her to look at him. "Listen. They're lying. I think Ashley saw me leaving your place today. Someone stood by the window. I should have been more careful."

With a whimper, she saw the sincerity in his face. His eyes were so blue, like the sky, drawing her up, she wanted to drift out beyond the horizon in that sea of blue. Away from this mess.

His hands along her jaw forced her gaze up. "Listen to me. I have never slept with any of them. They're playing mind games with you, Billie."

Inhaling sharply, she steadied herself. *You knew this day would come.* Just not so soon.

"Don't let them succeed in driving us apart. Please?"

She nodded. Whatever came, she'd have to deal with it.

"Will you come with me? I want you to hear something."

Sniffing, she nodded. Sure, she'd go with the flow. Or drown trying.

* * * *

Man, he couldn't let her out of his sight without something--or someone--trying to come between them.

Kissing the top of her head, he slid his arm around her waist and tugged her toward the studio. "I've been working on something. I want you to hear it." His step lightened as he hurried her to the studio.

Once inside, he locked the door. "Come on, sit down here." Nervously, he positioned the chair in front of the stool where his guitar leaned.

Stiffly, she walked where he guided her and sat where he placed her.

Winding the guitar strap over his head, he sat. "Now this is brand new, so it's a little rough, okay? You ready?" He wished he were.

Sadly, she nodded.

He picked at the strings. Damn. So nervous, his fingers even shook. "No. Wait." Closing his eyes, his fingers moved along the frets, and the lush melody reverberated along the strings.

His gritty, rich voice mixed with the music:

Life's brought me riches
More fame than I can use
But I wander this world empty
Hollow as a noose
Until I met you
I didn't know what I'd been missing
When you're away
I'm nothing without your love

Billie appeared more calm, but more alert. Interested.

The tremor of his voice slid along his nerves, releasing the tension gathered there.

Now nothing's so precious as time
I won't rest until you're mine
I can only be truly free
If I'm bound to you forever
I'm nothing without your love.

He plucked the beautiful melody from the strings, and the final chord echoed through the room. Afraid to ask, he waited for her opinion.

"Oh my God." With wide eyes, she gazed at him.

Shit. She hated it. "Terrible? Because I never claimed to be a poet."

"It's beautiful." Emotion choked her voice.

Excitement gripped him. "Really? Because I already have some ideas about tweaking it. Changing this chord--" He strummed. "--to this, and the lyrics need some work, but..."

"It's perfect. You shouldn't change a thing." Ducking her head, she added, "I'm so glad you're writing new songs."

Then why was she so miserable? "Yeah, well. I've had a lot of inspiration lately."

In a lackluster tone, she said, "It's really exciting. Are you going to record them?"

Why so glum? Wasn't this what she wanted? With a nervous laugh, he shrugged. "We'll see." It must be complete crap, if she reacted so terribly.

At a thump from outside, she turned. "What's that?"

"I don't know." He set down his guitar, went to the window and peered out. "Not Stu, for once." One of the others, though?

"I should let you get back." Shouldering her bag, she went to the door.

He couldn't let her go like this. Sliding his arms around her, he crouched to her eye level. "Are we okay?"

"Yes."

Damn their interferences. He intended to fully enjoy whatever happiness came along. And right now, happiness overwhelmed every other sense. He'd deal with reality later.

* * * *

When *Rock Bottom* aired that week, one segment followed Cat and Ashley at the vanities. After lining her lips with dark red, Cat pressed them together. "I'm getting tired of Jet's lack of interest."

Ashley pulled the straightening rod through her hair. "He has been distracted lately."

"Frankly, I'm bored as hell. I came here to party with the bad boy of rock, and so far, I feel as if I'm a tourist at an old folks' home."

Hair spray formed a cloud around Ashley's head. "He's rehearsing a lot, but that's what I always loved about him. His dedication to his music."

"I don't think anyone needs to rehearse music he's played for years. I wonder if he hasn't gone over to the other side."

Mouth agape, Ashley turned. "What? You can't mean..."

"Playing on the all-boys team. Happens to the best of 'em." The camera zoomed in as she cupped her breasts. "And when he could have all this. Go figure."

"Maybe you turn him off. Some men don't like overly aggressive women." Ashley smirked.

Or completely fake ones. Grabbing the remote, Jet clicked the set off.

Fear shone in Billie's eyes. "They're all suspicious."

He pulled her closer, his nakedness warm against her own. "Why do you bother watching it? It's crap. That's why they air it so late at night."

"All this pressure's going to build up to a nasty explosion."

He loved how he could make a lovely pressure build inside her as his fingers tweaked her nipples. "Cat's gone now. It's just Ashley and Julie left. They're harmless." He slid his hand down her hip.

She curled into him. "No, they're still very interested in winning the prize. You."

"You're not really worried about that, are you?" He nuzzled her neck.

"I'm worried about Stu. He could mean real trouble for you. I don't want you to be hurt."

"I won't. But I don't want you to be hurt, either." Everett could make her life hell. The prick.

"We should…"

"What?" He hovered above her, uncertain of her meaning.

"Stop."

Pausing, he shot a wry smile. "Stop this? Or…"

Rolling away, she sat up and stared out the window. "I don't know."

Shit. She was serious. "Hey, come here." His lips tickled her back as his kisses circled to her side. "Please?" he whispered, tugging her down.

With a sigh, she lay back. "Jet, I--"

"Shh." His mouth silenced her protests, his tongue probing her own. To hell with them. He wasn't about to let anyone ruin it.

Grasping his head, she kissed him with equal force, pushing any worry from his head.

* * * *

Light edged the horizon when Jet's soft kiss interrupted her slumber. In the half-light, she watched through sleepy eyes as he dressed, kissed her again and went downstairs. At the click of the door, she drifted back to sleep, hazy with happiness.

Later, when she powered up her laptop, an email from Everett snapped her fully awake.

What the hell is going on out there? Rock Bottom's falling apart, Jet's mostly a no-show and your posts have been less than impressive recently, although other media are having a field day. Anything you care to share with me, babe?

Babe. He hadn't used that term in months. Not in any meaningful way.

He'd included links to several stories from the usual gossip rags, wild speculation about what Jet had been up to. One accused him of having a secret lover.

Damn. She knew it. Now it was only a matter of time before someone followed Jet, or waited for him to come out of the cottage some night. She wouldn't put it past Stu to have Danny do the dirty work just to drive sagging ratings back up.

Slumping against the sofa, she closed her eyes. Cat's elimination had almost appeared too easy, until Jet told her they'd learned of her live-in boyfriend, rooting for her to win so he could share the hundred grand payoff.

With Cat gone, the atmosphere had eased slightly, but Ashley's sharp glances cut Billie's way more frequently. Julie, strangely, seemed unaffected, but Billie sensed that Ashley would stop at nothing to have Jet.

At that thought, she readied for the shoot. When she entered the house later, Ashley glanced over from where she sat on the sofa. With a sly smile, she flipped through television channels to VH1. "Do you remember that song of Jet's?"

Julie read her magazine. "Which song?"

"I'm trying to remember…it went something like…" Her high-pitched voice wavered through the lyrics:

If you want someone to cook for
If you need someone with you every night
I ain't your man
No, baby, not the one you're looking for.

Frowning, Julie finally glanced up, then uncertainly went back to her article.

Ashley stood, swaying to her off-key song.

If you want someone to bring you flowers
If you need someone to hold you tight
I ain't your man
No, baby, not the one you're looking for.

Billie remembered. The video especially--Jet wearing a sleeveless tee, hips swaying, the muscles in his arms rippling as his fingers danced down the frets with his searing guitar licks. Not a guy in the audience, all the girls swayed along with him, singing along with his gritty lyrics warning them not to reach for him in the night because he'd be gone, already out looking for someone new.

An anthem of sorts for commitment-phobic guys, Jet had written it after breaking up with his fiancée. The hit prompted a lawsuit from Tommy Conwell, whose Young Rumblers had a similar hit, *I'm Not Your Man*. Like Tommy and his band, the lawsuit faded to black, and Jet and his music endured, fueled by dedicated fans.

With a final hip bump in thin air, Ashley gave a whoop. "Ah, that's such a great song. So true for Jet. Until recently. He wrote a new song, you know--just for me." Her gaze met Billie's. "He called it *Nothing Without Your Love*. He said he wrote it because he loves me so much."

With a sigh, Julie turned a page. "Nice."

Closing her eyes, Billie's stomach churned. How did Ashley know about that song? Had Jet really written it for her? His voice came clearly in her head: *She's baiting you.*

Gulping hard, Billie forced her focus to notepad where she doodled nonsense and tried to block out Ashley, still going on about how much Jet loved her. She caught Danny's evil chuckle and glare. When the room seemed to close in, she couldn't stand anymore and stepped outside. Despite the warm evening breeze, she shivered.

Jet rounded the corner. "Hey, I'm glad you're outside. I have to go make an appearance, but maybe we can take off after that, go somewhere." Taking her wrist, he tugged her to the shadows. "What's wrong?"

Other than the fact she couldn't think straight near him? Could anyone really have him? Jet was right there and yet unreachable. *He'll always be out of reach.*

The lie blurted from her without thought. "Everett's being a jerk. If I don't get some work done, he's going to raise hell."

"Okay. How long will that take? A few hours?"

"I don't know. We should just..." With a sigh of frustration, she calculated. Less than a month before the season ended.

"Just what?"

"Everyone knows, Jet. Ashley's..." The pain of Ashley's cutting words returned.

"What's she up to now?"

"I have to work. Please don't come over tonight. It's better for both of us."

"Not for me." He opened his arms to embrace her.

She stepped out of reach. "Yes, it is. You know it is."

"What are you saying?"

What was she saying? She had no idea. "I just need a little space." To breathe. To think. *To remember who I am.*

He cocked his jaw, rubbed it as if she'd sucker-punched him. "That's usually my line." With a humorless chuckle, he headed for the door.

"Jet."

Turning immediately, he searched her face, hope fading when she stood frozen, unable to say any more. Nodding, he slowly continued inside.

Stiff as a corpse, she made her way to the cottage, bolted the door and curled, numb, into the curve of the sofa. It couldn't have been later than seven, but she felt incapable of movement. Light drained away, and darkness seeped inside. She couldn't tell how long she stayed there, or when she'd fallen asleep, but she awoke to the sound of a soft knock, the handle turning. "Billie? Let me in."

Tensing, she rose up on an elbow. Jet. He'd come.

"Billie? Are you in there?" Hearing his voice, it reached so deep inside her, she wanted to cry.

Oh, she had it bad. Worse than she'd ever known. *How could you be so stupid? From the beginning, you knew better.*

The craziness of the past few months rushed at her, weighed her down until she rested her head on the pillow. "I can't," she whispered. Lately, her emotions ranged from dizzy euphoria to sickening lows. A little in-between time, that's all she needed.

* * * *

Whoever said what a difference a day makes had it right. Yesterday, Jet had been dizzy with happiness. Now if someone asked him to imitate Ozzy Osbourne, he'd gladly bite the head off anyone or anything.

Billie dodged him at every turn.

Shit. Why hadn't he forced his way in last night? Standing outside, a sickly feeling had come over him. A whisper nagged him to get to her, not let her believe the crap others fed her. Not let her pull away from him, like he knew she already was.

Today, he'd see her. Convince her. He strode through the kitchen on his way out.

Stu followed him onto the patio. "Whoa, buddy. Let's take a minute here."

"For what?"

"To touch base on a few things." Despite his pleasant tone, his eyes held a hard gleam.

"I'm on board with the schedule. We're good." The sight of Billie stepping outside pricked his senses to high alert.

Nothing short of panic filled her face when she saw him. She fled in the opposite direction.

"What about--"

"Gotta go." He jogged after her. "Hey, can we--"

"No." She glanced back.

His gaze followed hers. Ashley stood behind Stu, watching along with the two camera guys, even Julie. *Shit.*

"No, we definitely can't." She strode away.

From the patio, Stu called to Jet. *Let him wait.* "Billie, come on. Talk to me."

"I can't," she blubbered, and hastened toward the gate where a taxi waited.

What the hell had happened?

* * * *

Billie could hardly speak because of the effort required to restrain her tears. She had the cab driver drop her off at a shopping outlet. Better to get lost in the crowd, anonymous, though she had no interest in shopping. Or anything else in Malibu.

A sudden homesickness overtook her, and she called her mom.

Immediately, her mother picked up the strain in her voice. "What's wrong, honey?"

"I'm confused."

"About?"

Might as well spill. Mom would find out eventually. "A guy. I've never been more miserable. Or happier."

"Sounds like love to me."

That's what she'd been afraid of. Swiping a tear from her cheek, she said, "I miss you, Mom."

"I miss you too. When can you visit?"

Not soon enough. "The season wraps up in a few weeks." The realization struck. Two and a half weeks, to be exact. Then reality would come into play.

She couldn't face going back there tonight. Jet would come to the cottage, and she'd let him in. Instead, she asked a cab driver to take her to whatever hotel was nearest, and cheapest. Once inside her room at the Malibu Motel, she sprawled on the bed and realized how hungry she was. Room service rates were outrageous, but she wasn't venturing out again.

Scanning the menu, the Malibu Winery wine list caught her eye. Oh yeah. Tonight, she'd splurge on that, anyway. And an actual meal.

When it arrived, she dug in like she hadn't eaten in weeks, then settled on the bed to watch television--something else she hadn't done in a long time. Flipping through the channels, she happened across the current *Rock Bottom*. Stu was on screen, telling Jet he'd arranged a few concerts. "So you can't accuse me of not doing my job."

Billie cackled. Right. As if he'd ever done a good job for Jet.

Stu's whine and ingratiating smile grated on her nerves, especially when he said, "But I'm worried about you."

Jet slumped on the sofa in his office, head propped in his hand. "Why's that?" His voice sounded flat, lifeless.

"You're not yourself these days. Where's that old Jet pizzazz? The panache?" Stu swung his hand out like the showman he was.

Jet's deadened gaze turned to Stu. "That Jet's gone. Everything about him died when my brother died."

Stu's nasal giggle sounded. "Then who am I looking at?"

"A ghost."

The camera zoomed in for a closeup, his sad face filling the screen.

Billie cradled the bottle to her chest. "No. You're not a ghost. You have so much to give. Damn you for giving up so easily." Curling into her pillow, she drifted off.

* * * *

The camera cut away, and Jet rose. "We're done now." He'd had enough of letting the world in on his private dramas.

"Not yet," Stu snapped.

The sharpness in his tone drew Jet's bile. Today was the wrong day to mess with him. "Make it quick."

Stu held up his thumb and index finger, nearly touching. "We are this close to being done. Don't fuck it up. All right? As a favor to me?"

"You want me to do you a favor. Too fucking funny." Here he thought he'd been doing Stu a favor for decades. Looked the other way when his manager skimmed a little off the top. Jet didn't care. After he straightened himself out, he'd also straightened out his finances. A neat amount waited in the bank. For what, he had no clue. Sometimes he thought he should start his own recording company. Sometimes he wanted to give it all away.

"Jet." Stu said his name like a reprimand. "Jeff would have--"

Anger sent Jet's fist slamming to the tabletop. "Don't bring my brother into this." By attempting to use Jeff as leverage, Stu had lost any and all leverage.

"I'm just saying--"

"Well, don't. You know better. Or you used to."

"What's that supposed to mean?"

"You know exactly. Neither of us is who we used to be. Keep that in mind." He might not be so understanding of Stu's weaknesses anymore. Not if Stu kept pushing. Yeah, Jeff believed in loyalty. Watching out for each other. So what would Jeff had said about Stu? Convincing Jet to sign up for another season of *Rock Bottom* circus. It padded Stu's pockets, but kept Jet from doing what he loved. Music. Yeah, he'd allowed it to happen.

Well, no more. Too much had slipped from his grasp these past few years. He'd make damn sure nothing else precious got away. Especially Billie.

Starting now, he'd take control.

Striding to Cindy's desk, he asked, "Where can I get a haircut?" Something he'd wanted to do long ago, but Stu convinced him it would ruin his image.

Well, a new image would usher in a new life. None of it captured on camera.

* * * *

If a headache could cause Billie's head to break, her skull would split open like a coconut, milk oozing. Sun glared through the sliding glass doors. Why had she forgotten to close the damn curtains?

A shower provided little help. "Never drinking again," she muttered, gathering her things. She had to return to the cottage. To her laptop. To her little semblance of a measly life.

In the cab, Everett called. "The blog's been dead for two days. What the fuck is going on?"

"I'm not feeling well." Not a lie. Her head could crack open at any time.

"Get me something today, Billie."

"Fine, you'll have something." Powering off the phone, she contemplated pointing the camera out each direction of the cottage, clicking and posting whatever happened to be in the viewfinder.

After climbing out, she paid the driver and dragged herself down the driveway. "Be a professional. First do your job, then go to the cottage and let your head split open."

Cindy would have some painkillers. Maybe even some of the good kind.

She aimed in the general direction of the house and went inside. Cindy's desk sat empty, and she held in a whimper. "Cindy?"

Cindy popped her head out of the office. "Be with you in a sec. Have a seat."

Yes. A seat sounded perfect. Billie slumped into the office chair and held her head, elbows on the desk.

Footsteps approached. "Billie."

She groaned. "No." She couldn't face Jet in this condition.

"Are you sick?"

"Yes." In more ways than one.

Crouching low, he drew back. "You're hung over."

"Okay." She hadn't specified the type of sickness, after all.

"Were you out drinking last night? Is that why you didn't come home?"

Fighting to hold in a laugh at the word *home*, she lifted her gaze to his. "What did you do to your hair?" Inches shorter, dirty blond layers brushed across his forehead, his ears, to his collar but no farther. Damn, he looked better than ever.

Still on his haunches, he eased away. "I cut it. Don't change the subject. Where were you last night?"

Had she forgotten to brush her teeth? God, she couldn't remember. "I stayed at a hotel. Alone. I told you I needed space to clear my head."

"That worked well."

Anger built within as she saw the strength he gained from her weakness. "I'm so glad you find my miserable condition so amusing."

"No. It's a relief that you're as miserable as me." Grasping her hand, he stood. "Come on."

Pulling back, she resisted. "I need to talk to Cindy."

Cindy opened the door. "What's up?"

Billie begged, "Please tell me you have something for headaches."

"Hangover," Jet corrected.

"Both." Billie couldn't let pride stand in the way of pain relief.

"I'll be right back." Cindy disappeared down the hall, returned with a white plastic container and bottled water.

"Bless you." Billie fumbled the cap and downed two pills.

"Keep it. I'll be inside if you need anything else." Cindy went back in the office and closed the door.

Jet strode down the hall. So that was it? He'd given up already?

She laid her head on her arms. Footsteps sounded, and something clunked onto the desk. "Here's some coffee."

"Why the travel mug?"

"Because you're coming with me."

"No. I promised Everett--"

"Fuck Everett. Oops, too late. You already did."

Strength billowed up from her core, straightened her spine. Narrowing her eyes, she said slowly, "I have to work. Why did you cut your hair?" It made it really difficult to concentrate on refusing him when he looked so good.

"Don't you like it?"

"Right, I hate men who look like models." *GQ* would be calling him for a summer menswear spread, she could see it now. Damn him, he'd look even better in classic black-and-white photos.

She rose with the intention of brushing past him, going to find Ashley and Julie, get some quick pics and whatever inane comments for quotes, post it online and go back to bed.

As soon as she stood, he pulled her to him in a kiss.

Breathless, she struggled in his arms, though not convincingly. "I can't think straight. This isn't reality. I don't even know what's real anymore. This place is making me crazy. Crazier than the bimbos." That scary thought should drive him away.

Instead, he slung the strap of her bag over his shoulder, slipped his arm around her and walked her outside.

"Where are we going?" She didn't want to be seen in public with raccoon eyes and unruly hair.

"Away from here." His Wrangler sat in front of the house, and he opened the passenger door. "Get in."

She found it difficult to argue with him when he wore his mirrored aviator sunglasses, which made him look even more like a model. After she climbed in, he set her bag on the floor and fastened her seat belt.

He jogged to the driver's side and she could almost swear his teeth sparkled when he flashed a smile starting the engine. "The seat reclines if you want to rest. The drive's about an hour."

"Drive? Where?" She couldn't piece two words together coherently.

"To reality."

Sure, make a joke of it. Was there a town called Reality in California? Why not? Pennsylvania had Beaver, Lickdale, Butts, Rough and Ready, Blue Ball, Mount Joy, Intercourse, Climax, Paradise...hmm, a definite trend...

The wind rushing through the Jeep lulled her to a haze of semiconsciousness where her headache eased. Jet sang softly as he drove, making her heart ache. They could be any other couple out for a drive. Except they weren't.

They stopped outside a house in the suburbs.

Squinting, she asked, "What time is it?" Her head felt light, a bit airy. Maybe her brains had leached out after all. At least it hurt less. No wonder the bimbos always seemed so happy. Her brother always said, *No brain, no pain.*

Tilting his head, he said, "Come on."

"Where are we?" Why bring her to the suburbs? Did he mean to taunt her with a lifestyle they'd never know?

* * * *

Damn, a hangover never looked so good on anyone. Her mussed hair and drowsy eyes made Jet want to roll her on the ground.

"Come find out." Grinning, he opened her door, then strolled to the front door and rang the bell.

Her eyes widened. "What are you doing? Let's go before someone--"

The door swung open and Sue frowned in confusion. "Jerry? What are you doing here?"

He kissed her cheek. "Hi."

Behind her, the boys ran up. "Uncle Jerry!"

"Hey, when did you grow so tall?" Another inch and the kid would reach his shoulder. Eleven and already checking Billie out. Jet chucked him under the chin.

His younger nephew threw his arms around Jet's waist.

Sue gave Billie the once-over. Twice. "Come on in. The boys just finished their homework before dinner."

Billie glanced at Jet. "No, we can't intrude."

"I always make plenty. I never know who might show up." Sue smiled and inclined her head.

Something registered in Billie. Probably the family resemblance.

Guiding her inside, Jet said, "Sue, this is Billie Prescott. Billie, Sue." Grasping the older boy's shoulder, he added, "This is Jeremy. And Kyle."

"Billie. What an unusual name."

"No more than Jet," she joked.

Laughing, his sister led them through the family room. "I never could call him Jet. It sounds so silly."

Jet slid his hands in his shorts pockets. "Jeff called me that long before the band."

"I don't care. It's just not you." She walked ahead through the dining room toward the kitchen. "Make yourselves comfortable."

Kyle knelt on the sofa. "How come you're here?"

Jeremy stood beside Jet. "Yeah, what happened to *Rock Bottom*?"

Sue's voice carried from the kitchen. "You better not be watching that. I told you not to." She emerged wiping her hands on a towel. "Those reality shows are the furthest thing from reality. Someone should sue them for false advertising."

"Why don't you, Mom?" Jeremy teased.

"Well, I just might." She grinned at Billie. "I have to finish up in the kitchen. Want anything to drink?"

"Sure." Billie paused to take in the scene.

Jet plopped on the sofa beside Kyle. "Hey, what new video games do you have?"

"Guitar Player Four." His voice held a hint of Jet's when he spoke of something he loved.

Jet widened his eyes. "I've been wanting to try that." When both boys clamored to be first, he promised each would have a turn. He winked at Billie before she followed his sister into the kitchen. He silently congratulated himself on such a great idea.

* * * *

Billie wished she'd had time to prepare for this. Meeting his sister and her kids? Why hadn't Jet warned her? No big deal, apparently. To him.

Sue opened the fridge. "So are you a wine drinker, or beer?"

The thought of wine made her stomach churn. "I'd love some milk, actually, if it's not too much bother."

"None at all." Relief sounded in her voice.

When Sue handed her a glass, Billie wondered how many times Sue had to entertain Jet's friends.

His sister poked at a dish in the oven. "It's just chicken casserole, nothing fancy but the boys love it." She wrinkled her nose.

"Sounds great. Like my mom's."

"You're not from around here, are you?" More gray than blue, her eyes held the same sparkle as Jet's.

"No, a little town in Pennsylvania. I miss it." More than she'd realized. She longed to see her mom again.

"I wonder which is worse sometimes, Jersey or California. But I miss home too. We had great times there. Got into some trouble too. Jeff always kept us in line."

"He was your older brother?"

"The oldest. He started the band. Made Jerry focus on the music, always pushing him to make it better and better. When Jeff died, I worried

Jerry might follow in his footsteps." Staring at nothing, she inhaled and seemed to shake it off with an easy grin. "If it weren't for the band, Jerry would've had a very different life."

Billie chuckled. "Normal?"

"No. He had a way of finding trouble. Or it found him. Girls, drugs…" She held up a hand. "I know, those things are everywhere no matter what. But his music's more important to him, you know?"

Billie grinned. She knew. She wanted Jet to remember it too.

A timer dinged, and Sue took a dish from the oven and headed to the dining room. "Let's go round up the boys."

When she called them, all three begged for a few minutes, but she held steadfast. "Pause it and go back to it when we're done." To Billie, she said, "Sit anywhere."

Billie waited for Jet, who wrestled Kyle, giggling, to the table.

Sue set glasses of milk in front of each plate. Sinking to her chair, she scooped helpings. "So Billie, what do you do?"

"I work for *Strung Out*, the music magazine."

Sue froze. "You're a reporter?" Her gaze flew to Jet. "She's *that* reporter? Who writes the blog?"

"Cool." Jeremy's gaze scanned Billie again.

"Yeah." Jet took the spoon from her hand. "That reporter."

A sickly look came over Sue as she glanced at Billie.

"I'm off the clock today. No notepad, no hidden microphones." She hoped that would reassure his sister, who obviously wouldn't have spoken so freely in the kitchen had she known Billie's occupation.

Sue gave a wan smile. "Good."

The boys interrogated Billie throughout dinner--which musicians she'd interviewed, which concerts she'd attended. Sue stayed silent except for reminding her sons to use their napkins and not speak with food in their mouths.

When Billie offered to clean up after the meal, Sue hastily refused. "I'll take care of it. You relax."

She wished Sue would relax. "I promise you, I won't write of anything that occurred today."

Sue nodded. "I'm going to make some tea. Want some?"

Billie glanced at Jet. "No thanks."

Motioning her toward the family room, Sue went to the kitchen.

Billie strolled to the sofa.

Jet nudged the younger boy. "Let Billie sit there."

When he whined, Jet grimaced and jerked his head. Kyle swung to Jet's other side.

Patting the sofa, he said, "Be my good luck charm."

"You do need one." Giggling, she sat.

"I was ahead before dinner."

Billie patted his leg. "I'm sure you were."

He bumped his shoulder into hers. "I suppose you can do better?"

"Anyone can." Jeremy handed her the control.

The boys encouraged her on as she played. Her scores climbed, and she rose from the sofa, putting her body into the moves. The song ended, and she lifted her arms victoriously. Jet clapped and whistled as his nephews whooped.

When she plopped on the sofa next to Jet, he threw his arm around her. "Pretty impressive."

So was this. Reality struck with a vengeance. Her heart ached for what could never be. "We should be getting back." Everett would be pitching a fit by now with no blog post for three days. No way would she share this.

He turned to her. "You sure?" Sadness dimmed his smile.

"You don't want Stu tracking us down, do you?" The thought gave her the willies. She wouldn't put it past him to swoop in, bang on his sister's door.

Sue cackled. "You nailed him. I wish you'd fire the creep."

Jet kissed his sister's cheek. "Nice to see you."

"And it wasn't even a holiday." Winking, she followed them to the door. "Nice to meet you, Billie."

While Jet tousled the boys' hair, Sue surprised Billie with a hug. "He seems happy."

Unsure how to respond, Billie nodded, and was even more surprised when Jet's arms circled her waist from behind. "Time to go."

"When are you coming back?" Kyle tugged on his arm.

"Depends on the tour. Soon, I hope."

Hearing the word *tour*, Billie tensed, glanced back at him in question.

Waving, he pulled her toward the Wrangler. Driving away, they waved to his family.

A million questions swirled through her head. When had he planned a tour? When did he plan on telling her?

She scrunched down in her seat. Probably hadn't because she'd be leaving soon, and out of his life.

He did seem happier than when she met him, she realized. If she had anything to do with it, then she'd cherish their time together. Every expression, every movement she committed to memory. She wanted to remember this day.

* * * *

Smooth, asshole. Way to break the news. Jet's mind raced. How to fix this?

After a few minutes, he turned down the radio. "So Stu's arranging a tour. Did I tell you?" He shot her a tentative smile.

"No, you didn't." Ducking her head, she avoided his gaze. "I'm glad. You need to get out in front of audiences again. It'll feed your creative energy."

Whew. She got it. "Yeah, after the concert that night, I realized how much I missed it." He rubbed her leg.

The tension eased in her leg, and in their conversation. She made small talk, and he reveled in the normalness of it all. Laughter came easily, and he gestured as he spoke, leaning toward her again and again.

When road signs indicated the Pacific Coast Highway ahead, his heart sank. If only they could have stayed longer. They'd already been away most of the day. A few more hours wouldn't have hurt. He wasn't ready to go back yet. To let her go.

He turned onto a small road.

"Where are we going?"she asked.

"I have to make a pit stop." He pulled off into a field along a stand of trees, stopped and unfastened his seat belt in one swift action, unable to wait one more second to kiss her.

"Afraid the paparazzi will--"

His hands along her jaw, his mouth silenced hers. His breath left him, and couldn't catch up to his racing pulse.

Fingers in his hair, she held him like a cyclone raged around them. It might have, for all he knew--all his senses focused on her breath, her warm body against hers, how right she felt.

She pressed toward him but sighed in frustration.

"What's the matter?"

"Your Jeep seems to think I'm in danger." Her hand splayed toward the seat belt, which had tightened, locking her in.

"Maybe you are," he teased.

"It won't let me loose."

"I kind of like it." Angling toward her, he delved his fingers past her buttons and slid his other hand up her skirt while his tongue explored past the edge of her bra.

She clutched his hair. "I'd like it better if I could participate."

"In a little while," he mumbled, moving lower. Right now, he liked that she couldn't move. He eased her panties down her legs.

When he probed, her sighs came faster as his tongue teased, and he worked her like a maestro, building the pressure to its crescendo. She strained against the seat belt, shuddering.

Primal need obliterated all thought. Before he knew it, he was out of the Jeep, opening her door, fumbling her out of the seat belt, pulling her legs around him. He thrust inside her with one deep plunge, his heart beating wildly. She clung to him, rocking against his movements, until explosions circled outward from his core. His shuddering body pressed against hers, arms firmly holding her in place.

When his breaths steadied, his lips took hers in a lazy, lingering kiss. "This is more real to me than anything."

The sky had darkened to indigo, and only distant lights shone. He wished he could see her face better. She was too quiet.

Approaching headlights made him retract his wish. "Uh-oh."

He set her on the seat and zipped up while she hastily straightened her skirt.

The car slowed to a stop. "Everything all right over there?"

Jet held up a hand. "Fine, thanks." Shutting her door, he jogged to the driver's side and climbed in.

Backing out, he burst into laughter. Until he realized she wasn't laughing.

She turned to him. "Did you…"

"What?" He steered onto the main road and grasped her knee.

"It felt a little too…natural."

"Oh. Yeah." *Shit.* He'd been in such a rush. He glanced at her as he drove, hoping she wouldn't hate him.

Her eyes held fear. "You didn't use anything?"

"I didn't have anything with me." Dread stiffened his spine. She hated him.

Her voice sounded small. "Oh."

At least she didn't scream. He could smooth this over. "It's just once, right? And it was so quick…" Hell, what had he done? Blinded by the need to feel himself inside her, he hadn't thought. Not like him at all. *Shit.*

"Right." Pensive, she gazed out the window.

After shifting, he grasped the inside of her leg. Damn, she seemed terrified. "Hey, don't worry. All right? Today was amazing." The truth of those words hit him. It had been a day he'd hold special. And he meant what he told her earlier: the universe threw at you whatever you were ready for. With Billie, he felt ready for anything, no fear.

His warm touch apparently eased her tension. "It was." She rested her hand on his leg.

He laid his atop hers with a squeeze.

The rest of the drive, they talked about everything: his sister and her kids, her mom and brother, how tough Jeff's loss had been on him, how the band fell apart after that.

"But Chalmer seemed like a good addition," she said. "He was no replacement for Jeff, of course, but audiences responded to his antics, though sometimes over the top."

Jet winced. "He couldn't stand anyone else to be in the spotlight. He wanted more special effects to dazzle the audience. I only wanted to dazzle them with our music."

"Did you try compromising with him?"

"I couldn't deal with him."

"He always struck me as being equal parts irritation and inspiration. But you two made a good team, like Lennon and McCartney. He said once he wanted to collaborate on songs more."

"The CD we made together, he put me through hell."

"But the songs turned out great. It went platinum, right?"

"Mmm." How had they gotten on this track? Today of all days?

"It might be worth exploring. You've both mellowed since then."

Near the gate, he slowed. "You're still pushing." Chuckling, he clicked the remote, and it slowly opened.

"Just speaking my mind." Her tone was matter-of-fact.

When he stopped in front of the garage, he heaved a heavy sigh. "I should check in, but maybe afterward, we could--"

The spotlight glared, blinding them. Stu strode toward them. "Where the fuck have you been?"

Damn. Jet yanked the keys from the ignition. "Out." None of his fucking business.

Stu stepped back as he got out. "While you were 'out,' a situation arose. We have a lot to discuss."

Billie got out and stood uncertainly.

"It can wait." Jet pushed past him, wanting to obliterate him from sight.

Stu followed. "No, in fact, it can't. It turns out Ashley lied--she has a kid, and *Entertainment Weekly* showed videos of her pole dancing in some strip club." He slapped his forehead. "Ay-yi-yi. You tell these bitches things like this will show up, but they lie anyway."

"Maybe she needed the money," he ventured. He could care less.

"I don't fucking care. She needed to tell the truth so we don't look like fools." Stu stumbled to a stop when Jet halted and waved to Billie. He couldn't even say a proper goodnight. *Rock Bottom* was ruining his life.

* * * *

Warmth flooded Billie. Returning his wave, she headed for the cottage. Inside, she remembered her cell. She'd switched it off earlier. Four voice mails and six texts.

Everett's impatient tone asked what the hell was going on there, why wasn't she picking up? Next, he asked more loudly why she hadn't posted a blog as promised, even after other media exposed Ashley's past.

The third voice mail sent a shock through her. "You are to get your things together and get the fuck out of there today. Do you hear me? The show's over. I swear to God, Billie, if you... Just do it. I'll call as soon as I book a flight."

Predictably, the next message contained her flight information. "Don't miss it," he'd warned.

Checking the clock, she had just under two hours to get to the airport. She called a cab, threw her things into her suitcase and hastily scanned the room. Leaving her bag by the door, she ran to Cindy. "Where's Jet? I have to see him."

Cindy inclined her head toward the office. "In with Stu. But they can't be disturbed."

A woman's voice mixed with Jet's and Stu's.

"Who's in there?" she wondered aloud.

Before Cindy could answer, Julie said, "Uncle Stu, you promised I'd get maximum exposure. So what if Jet didn't eliminate Ashley? I still win, right?"

"She's Stu's niece?" So the show had been rigged from the start. Billie wasn't sure what to think. All that talk from Jet about finding his soul mate--was that all a ruse? If that was false, what about everything else he said to her? Had the entire thing been a joke to him? Including her?

The buzzer at the gate sounded.

"Oh, damn. My taxi's here."

With a sigh, Cindy buzzed the cab through.

"I have to go. Will you tell him..." Floundering, she backed toward the door.

Outside, the driver sounded the horn.

"Dammit." She grabbed her bag, hurried out and bribed the driver with an extra forty dollars if he broke every speed limit.

As the plane lifted off, the full force of what happened hit worse than the pressure inside the cabin. She'd left Jet without saying goodbye. She had no phone number, no way to reach him. Now that she knew the truth, did she want to?

Chapter 13

For the fifth time that morning, Billie's cell vibrated. Groaning, she looked at the display. Zinta's name appeared. This one, she'd take. "Hello?" she mumbled, muted by her pillow.

"Sweetie? Where are you?"

Billie glanced around the room, familiar and yet not after so many months away. "Home." Sadness welled from deep inside, and her body ached for Jet.

"You are?" Zin sighed in relief. "Thank God. I can tell Everett he's an asshole."

"I'll tell him myself when I get in." She rolled over and rubbed her forehead.

"You'd better prepare yourself. He's in a mood."

Anger forced her to a sitting position. "Well, so am I. He forces me to leave, and I didn't even get to say goodbye."

"To Jet?"

She groaned, remembering. He'd lied about *Rock Bottom*. Maybe everything had been a lie.

"Oh, Billie. You didn't sleep with him again?"

Billie couldn't help but laugh. She'd lost count.

"Twice?" Zinta asked.

"Oh, way more than twice."

Zinta's laugh ended in a squeal. "Outrageous. You can't claim this time it 'just happened.' Not so many times!" Her peals of laughter echoed through the phone.

"I'm so glad you find this amusing." She should tell Zin about yesterday. Screwing in the foothills of California without benefit of protection. The times they'd made love using a condom, she hadn't felt so great about. Yesterday was another matter altogether. How could she have been so stupid?

"Maybe you need a fresh perspective. This has been going on for weeks now. Occurring over and over. Deliberately."

Her head ached. What time was it in California? "So?"

"So you can't claim it's just a one-nighter. That it means nothing. He means something to you, doesn't he?"

"Yes." He did, at least, until last night.

"And let's face it, Bil. He has all those other women. But who does he keep coming back to? Huh?"

"How do I know he didn't go after them too?" *Because he told you, Willamina.*

"Let's review. One: their intense jealousy. Two: their intense jealousy. Three: their *intense* jealousy. Are you seeing a pattern here? Besides, no man has that much goomba to spread around."

Billie felt fairly certain *goomba* wasn't a word, and if it was, Zin hadn't used it in the proper context. Or language. But its meaning clear, she wouldn't argue. "I wonder if it's not his way of escaping from the reality show to reality." The problem was, Billie no longer had any idea which was which. "But I met his sister and her kids." Yesterday seemed forever ago already.

"Okay. Number four: you met his sister."

"But it fits the pattern. I read in a magazine that when you're away from your normal life--say, on vacation or an assignment--that any flings don't count. Because you're not totally you while you're away."

"Who are you then?"

The memory of Jet responding to Stu flashed through her mind: *A ghost.* "I don't know. Not my normal self. I'm *Strung Out* Billie."

"You sure are, sweetie." Zin giggled evilly.

"I was away from my usual life." And it felt great, for a while.

"Getting the real inside scoop." Zin was having too much fun.

Going against every principle she held dear. "Stop."

"You stop reading women's magazines. They're all marketing crap."

Billie knew that. "My point is--"

"Honey, you're avoiding the real point. One time, you can chalk up to an accident. I did, anyway. Twice, poor judgment. Three or more times... you just ran out of excuses, my friend."

Collapsing back atop the bed, she stared at the ceiling, as blank as her brain. "I know. I'm avoiding it. I don't know why."

"No?" Zin's voice hinted at a challenge.

Billie tensed. She hadn't wanted to think why it kept happening. "I have to go. I'll be in soon."

Switching off the phone, she threw herself back onto the pillow. No way could she get back to sleep now, even on a few hours' sleep. She forced herself upright. "Time to face the music, Willamina."

* * * *

Taping the final episode of *Rock Bottom*, Jet kissed Julie's cheek and forced a semblance of a smile. Only after the producer had threatened to sue if they didn't wrap this season up right.

He'd have liked to wrap it up and deep freeze it. Never again would he get sucked into this bullshit.

Going through the motions, the episode fell flat. Even the camera guys appeared bored, their expressions blank as they filmed. Julie finally showed some excitement, but it had little to do with him. She paid as little attention to him as he did to her. No viewer would be fooled by this.

At least it would ensure they'd never invite him back.

The producer called it a wrap. "Let's get the hell out of here."

Jet's thought exactly.

* * * *

The door clicked--too quietly--behind her. Everett paced, thumb to bottom lip. Never a good sign. "You know how I feel about you."

She shifted. "Not exactly." Where was he going with this? Without thinking, she laughed. It caught in her throat when he grabbed her waist and pulled her close.

Pushing him away, revulsion twisted her insides. "What are you doing?"

"You drive me crazy." He curled into her, his lips on her neck.

"Ditto. But not in a good way. Get off me." With one final push, she jerked away.

"Billie," he crooned. "You know why I sent you there. Why I had to."

Had he been taking acting lessons while she was away? Or dropping acid? "I don't recall anyone holding a gun to your head."

Anguish twisted his face, his voice. "Why did you sleep with him?"

Dammit, he had no right to ask. She tucked her tee back into her jeans, but the feel of his hands made her cringe. "Why did you sleep with four other women?"

He dropped his chin to his chest, gave her the look he used when about to seduce her. "I couldn't stop thinking about you. Night and day, work and home. I had to clear my head."

Stepping back, she folded her arms. "You sent me away purposely, so you could screw around? All you had to do was ask for some space." He could have saved her a lot of heartache.

His arms dropped flaccidly at his sides. "I didn't know what I wanted. You confused the hell out of me."

Blowing a breath, the conversation seemed pointless. She simply didn't care. "Don't blame me for your confusion."

With a wolfish gleam in his eye, he stepped toward her. "I didn't know if I was ready for a real relationship. As much as I wanted it."

"God, Everett." He wouldn't recognize a real relationship if everyone around him pointed and screamed: *There it is!*

"I had to send you away to find out how much I missed you. Don't you see?"

She straightened. "Yes, I see very clearly--how pathetic you truly are."

"Fair enough. I'm pathetic. More so since you've been away. It made me realize how much I want you."

Want. Not *love.* Someone else had played with his toy, and now he wanted it back. "When, Everett? Not when I cried and told you I loved you. Not when you were screwing four other women like tomorrow might never come. So tell me--when was I ever your first consideration?"

Moving closer, he spoke to her more lovingly than he ever had. "Billie, we're good together."

"Were, Everett. And I'm not even certain about that any longer." Not since Jet showed her how a guy who truly cares acts toward a woman. "Call Stu. Maybe he can arrange a reality dating show for you. Maybe it will teach you the meaning of real."

Heaving a long sigh, he frowned. "I expected more from you."

She could have said the same thing. Now, it didn't matter what he thought. "Ditto again."

"I never imagined you letting someone like him paw you."

Disgust sizzled along her nerve endings. "Don't take it down to your level, Everett." Jet held her. Spoke with her. Ensured her needs were fulfilled.

"Right. Because Billie Prescott's above screwing around." Chuckling, he sat on the edge of his desk. "Fill me in then. Was it a meeting of the minds? I hardly think so."

Crossing her arms, she made her gaze stony. "You wouldn't understand."

"Look, Billie, this is serious. I need to know." The room temperature dropped considerably.

"It's none of your damn business."

"I'm in a very bad position here." Moving to his desk, he lifted the tabloids one by one. "Each of these, and other media, ran stories implicating you. And by extension, *Strung Out.* The contestants are threatening legal action. Lawsuits against Jet. Against the *Rock Bottom* production company. Against us."

Billie's stomach churned. The show was in ruins.

Everett leaned across the desk. "That's why I have to suspend you."

Suspend? Nothing more? "When can I come back?"

Shifting, he shrugged. "When things settle down."

"Oh. One of *those* suspensions." A bitter laugh escaped. He couldn't just fire her and be done with it. He had to screw even that up.

"Sorry, but it goes to credibility. We have our reputation to consider."

"So do I, Everett. And it's a damned good one." The force of her convictions made her lean toward him, pointing.

Her show of strength had little effect except to calm him, to gather his explosiveness into a condensed ball that he could unleash at will.

Arching a brow, his low voice sounded smooth, belying its restrained voltage. "It *was*."

She bristled. *Bastard.* But she'd match his calm exterior. "No. It *is*. What happened has nothing to do with the quality of my writing."

"No, but--"

"But nothing. If you can't back me up, Everett, then I don't want to be here." Her own words chilled her. She'd played right into his hands.

He strolled behind the desk, sank into his black leather chair and leaned back. "That's your prerogative."

Damn him. He'd known she'd say that. "You're an incredible dick. And I mean that in the worst possible way."

"This doesn't have to get ugly." His eyes held a strange gleam, as if he enjoyed this game.

"If I leave quietly? No worries, Everett. I'd planned to quit, anyway. Just not so soon." She'd done it. For all intents and purposes, she'd just resigned. She strolled to the window and gazed out over the city sprawling below. "I deserve better than you. In every way."

"You always did." His sincerity surprised her.

No. He couldn't worm his way back in now. "I'll need three months' severance."

His counteroffer came quickly. He must've expected it. "Two."

"Three. Or I podcast this conversation online." She slid the digital recorder from her pocket.

The surprise in his face faded. "That's our equipment." He held out his hand.

"Actually, it's personal property. The office recorder broke last month, and I shipped it back for repairs. I bought this with my own credit card. *Strung Out* never reimbursed me."

Something like admiration shone in his face. "California changed you. The old Billie would never have stooped so low as blackmail."

"Right. The old Billie would have kissed your hairy ass and been grateful for the hair in my mouth." From now on, she wouldn't settle for anything less than complete bliss from a willing partner. "Three months, Everett."

"All right. Three months."

Damn. She should have asked for six. "And a written recommendation before I leave. I don't want you trashing my reputation."

"I want nothing but the best for you."

"Then you wouldn't have asked me to take you back." Her stomach churned over on itself, watching, waiting for some sign of hurt or remorse. He gave neither.

Unclipping her photo ID, she tossed it onto his desk. "I'll clear out my desk."

As she opened the door, Francisco and Ryan glanced away and their hurried babble ran together nonsensically.

Halting, she steadied herself. "Don't bother covering. You can hear it from me. I just quit."

Both rushed to her, Ryan squeezed her in a hug and Francisco's hands fluttered around them.

She forced a smile. "We'll keep in touch, right?"

Zinta emerged from the small kitchen and waved her stirrer.

Billie gulped hard. "Hey, I'm leaving. I wanted to say goodbye."

"Where to now?" She rolled her eyes.

"No clue." Tears welled, and she frowned to keep them from falling.

Zinta's jaw dropped. "Not *leaving* leaving. I thought you meant Everett shipped you out on another wacky assignment."

"No. I'm done here." She held out her arms.

Zin set down her mug and pulled her close. "Man. What will I do without you?"

She grinned. "Stay out of trouble?"

"Not likely."

"I'll let you know where I land."

"You better do more than that."

Tears choked her response, and she hugged Zin. Brushing her cheek, she asked, "Anyone have a carton I can haul my stuff in?"

Francisco pulled a plastic bag from his desk. "Does this work?"

Like everything else, she'd make it work. Somehow.

* * * *

Packing up had been a breeze. None of the furniture belonged to Jet, anyway.

He stored some of his things at his sister's, and readied for the upcoming tour.

Shitty timing. He had to talk to Billie. Things had been so crazy, by the time he had a chance, the time difference meant it would be an ungodly hour in Philadelphia.

Why hadn't he gotten her cell number? *Because she wasn't supposed to take off like that.* No goodbye, nothing.

Something had to be very wrong.

He'd make it right again.

* * * *

Lights flashed when she stepped out of the office. Three photographers aimed their digital and video cameras in her direction, and three women in business suits armed with microphones talked at once.

Shielding her face with her arm, she skirted them. "Whoa, you have the wrong girl."

A woman asked, "Aren't you Billie Prescott?" and held the mic in Billie's direction.

"Yes," she said, though she sounded uncertain.

Another said, "Tell us why you left *Rock Bottom*."

Oh, damn. "I was never part of the show." *That's it. Play it cool.*

"But why did you leave so abruptly?"

She stepped to the side, but they swarmed close, worse than pit bulls. "My editor needed me here. Excuse me."

"What about Jet Trently? Weren't you having an affair?" The woman shoved the mic at Billie.

"I said excuse me." She pushed past, but knew her burning cheeks would fuel wild speculation.

Coming home, Billie thought, meant greater freedom. No more being stuck in the cottage, having to trail the bimbos.

But now, paparazzi made her feel imprisoned in her apartment. Each time she opened the door, they sprang to life, boom mics arching over reporters, flashes blinding her. She lay low for a few days, relying on takeout.

Zinta smuggled her other necessities, dodging their questions, but smiling sweetly at the cameras.

Billie hustled her inside. "You're a godsend." Coffee without cream didn't cut it.

"What insanity." She unpacked the bag, then turned, hand to hip. "Any word from Jet?"

Billie's insides tightened. "No. I didn't expect to hear from him." She told herself that every time the phone rang.

Zin clucked her tongue. "He'll call."

False reassurances would only prolong the pain. Everett had taught her that.

Making her tone airy, she set the milk and yogurt in the fridge. "He's moved on. So have I. I have an interview on Friday."

Delight filled Zin's face. "Where?"

"Some new startup alternative." She stirred her yogurt. Too early to get excited. She wasn't even sure she wanted the job.

"A newspaper?" Doubt curdled her creamy tone.

"Yeah. Better brush up on my journalism skills. I'm hoping they'll assign me some entertainment features so I don't stray too far from doing what I love."

"Is that what you want?"

She stabbed the spoon into the yogurt. "I honestly don't know anymore."

"Everything will work out."

Billie nodded. "One way or the other." If fate followed its usual path, it would be the other.

* * * *

Reconnecting with the band reenergized Jet. Despite their differences, he'd missed these guys. At their first gig, he and Chalmer shared the microphone with the camaraderie of brothers. No, Chalmer would never replace Jeff. But Jet's voice mixed with his like they shared DNA.

Kirk whaled on the drums with new passion. Steve's fingers flew across the keyboards, and Marlin's bass helped provide the grounding backbeat.

Yeah, maybe the band had needed a break. Their sound was tight, like they hadn't taken a six-month break.

And the audience ate it up. At every concert, women flung their underwear onstage. Chalmer hung a bra from the fret of his guitar like a flag.

Jet just wished Billie was there. Finally getting the number of *Strung Out*, he called from the road. The dippy receptionist gave him the runaround. After he left his number for the fifth time, he searched for her home number. How many Billie Prescotts could there be in Philadelphia?

None, apparently. Lots of Prescotts, some only listed their first initial. None listed *B*.

He cornered Stu. "What city do we hit next?"

"San Antonio, then we work our way east."

His nerves tightened. "East to where?"

"Memphis, Nashville, a few gigs in Florida.

"Book Philly."

"I looked into it, but--"

"Book something in Pennsylvania. Soon." Even if he played within a few hours of the city, he'd track her down.

* * * *

After the interview, Billie knew she would hate the job if she took it. She'd been with *Strung Out* almost since the beginning, and didn't want to duplicate the experience of another new publication. Always struggling to keep up with the others, outscoop them to build a readership, a reputation. She'd built her own readership, she told herself, and brought a lot to any table. She could afford to take her time.

Being out of the apartment--away from prying zoom lenses--made her hesitant to go back. When a tabloid photo of Jet and Julie, smiling, caught her eye, she lost her giddiness and wanted to retreat.

Ignoring the calls of the reporters, she strode silently inside. Her answering machine blinked, and her stomach clenched. Had she missed Jet's call?

She punched *play*, and her mom said, "Billie? It's Mom. I hope you're all right. I really wish you'd come for a visit. A long one, if you want. I know you quit your job. It would be nice if you'd come home for a while. I love you."

"How did she..." No use asking. Mom always knew. And she was right--Billie needed to go home. To the farm. The one place she could relax, regain her perspective. Take a breather. Remember what was important. Philadelphia no longer felt right. At least for a while, she'd leave the city. That way, she could stop expecting Jet's call.

* * * *

Driving over Peter's Mountain invigorated Billie. Even in rain or snow, she didn't mind the steep climbs and winding curves. They brought her closer to home.

Towns grew more sparse, thinning to farmland, climbing ever higher up. Passing an Amish horse and buggy, she knew she'd come home. Wild orange daylilies lined the long drive. She parked near the barn beside her mother's Cherokee, so old the finish had faded on the hood. The barn too needed a fresh coat of paint.

A spot of yellow moving through the garden caught her eye. Mom stood, a basket of tomatoes in her hand, and waved.

Leaving the car door open, Billie rushed to hug her mom. A rush of emotion choked her words.

With a squeeze, her mom released her. "Let's get you a drink."

Sniffling, Billie followed, scooping up a cat near the fence. "Who's this?"

"Barn cats had a new litter." Mom headed to the side door, the old summer kitchen in the days when people used such things. Another reason Billie loved the old house--its history predated them, and would outlast them.

Setting the basket on the counter, her mom ran the tomatoes under water. "Tom and Amy and the kids are coming over for dinner. I hope you don't mind. It's been so long since we've shared a meal."

"That'll be great." Though inwardly, she groaned. Tom would wag his finger and his tongue would keep time. Amy, who'd rarely ventured outside Berrysburg, would smile, and tend to the kids, who would likely squabble the entire time.

"How old are Jimmy and Alicia now? Five and seven?"

"Six and eight."

"Good thing I checked." Tom would've had another grudge to hold.

Wiping her hands, her mom frowned. "You look tired. Why don't you lie down a while?"

"Maybe for a little while. Must have been all the driving."

"You've been through a lot lately."

Too much. When she climbed the stairs and went down the hall to her bedroom, she bit her lip. The bed linens appeared worn but laundered. Sun spilled in the room, made a dull sheen on the wooden floor. Her white shelves held her boom box and some old CDs she'd left when she went to college. Fingering through them, she found Jet's first recording. The cover photo showed a younger, blonder Jet with Jeff and the other band members, arms locked around each other's shoulders, laughing. Next to that CD stood the second, with a similar photo. The third had been the last Jeff worked on, and he'd died before its release. The black-and-white shots reflected the somber mood of the band after his death.

Studying the young Jet, it all seemed surreal, as if she'd gone back to a high school dream for a few months. She must have been delusional to believe it could last. With a sardonic laugh, she shelved them and curled onto her bed.

The next thing she knew, children's squeals sounded from the yard and the sun had circled behind the house. Stretching, she lay there and listened. Their laughter made her ache with something unnamable.

She rose and went down to the kitchen where Tom stood against the counter drinking a bottle of beer.

"Well, there's Princess Billie." He grinned.

"Hey, Tom. Sorry I slept so long, Mom. I meant to help you."

Mom waved a dish towel to shush Tom. "You needed your rest. But now that she's up, Tom, you bring in her things, will you?"

"Yeah, I don't do much to work up an appetite all day." He took a last swig of his beer and set the bottle on the counter.

A rub already. She knew how hard he worked his farm. "I'll help."

Outside, Amy sat on the stairs watching the kids play tag. "Hey, welcome home."

Billie hugged her. "Nice to see you. Hey, guys." Jimmy and Alicia ran up and threw their arms around her.

Carrying a box, Tom grunted in passing.

She got the hint. "I have to move some things."

Amy enlisted Jimmy and Alicia's help, and soon all the contents of Billie's car sat in piles in her bedroom.

Billie tousled Jimmy's hair. "Great teamwork."

"Dinner," Mom called from the dining room.

The kids scrambled down the steps, Amy calling for them to slow down.

With any luck, Billie thought, they'd have a peaceful meal, no arguments. When she saw the chicken casserole in the center of the table, her throat thickened.

"What's wrong?" Tom plopped onto his chair.

"Nothing." Billie sat and sipped her milk, pushing away thoughts of the last night she'd eaten this casserole. In California.

Mom's shoulders slumped. "I thought you loved this dish."

"I do." Billie loved the person who last shared it with her more. "I can't wait to have some."

Tom smirked. "Probably got too used to that fancy Malibu food."

"How long will you be home?" Amy asked.

"I'm not sure." However long it took to find a job, but she wouldn't open that can of worms for her brother. He had his own lifetime supply of worms with her name on them.

Tom scooped casserole onto his plate. "It's about time you came to your senses."

"I'm taking a break, Tom. Not abandoning civilization." The food tasted too spicy tonight.

"Don't act all hoity-toity. You're lucky to still be alive, living in the fast lane." He swigged his beer.

"My life isn't an Eagles song. I'm not headed for a crash and burn."

"Can't tell by your looks." He shoveled a forkful of food into his mouth.

"Shush. That's enough," Mom scolded.

Her brother shrugged. "I can't help it she looks like hell."

"And I can't help it you have no brains." At least he had a normal name. Not a nightmare name like Willamina. Still, he had the ability to make her feel nine again.

"I said enough. Things will work out, Willamina. They have to. I've decided to sell."

"What?" Not the farm, not her home. Nowhere else on earth did she feel safe. If she still had an income, she'd offer to buy it. Not that she could have afforded hundreds of acres.

Her mom went on. "It's too much for me. I'd love to work here until my dying day, but the township raised taxes again, and I can't find a decent farm worker."

"Oh, Mom. I'm so sorry." Beyond her own sorrow, her mother's had to be triple. She'd lived here for fifty years.

Tom knit his brows. "You could subdivide."

"What about Mr. T?" Billie couldn't let him go to a slaughterhouse, but at twenty-seven, it seemed unlikely anyone else would buy him. Losing the horse would be as hard as losing the farm.

Amy turned to Tom. "We could take him, couldn't we?"

"We'll cross that bridge when we come to it." Glancing pointedly at Billie's plate, her mother asked, "You're not hungry?"

"Sorry. Maybe the news made it a little hard to digest."

"You shouldn't diet," Tom proclaimed. "You could stand to gain a few pounds."

"Tomorrow I'll work up an appetite helping Mom, okay?"

Leaning back, he rubbed his stomach. "Hope you work off some stress too. You're more testy than usual."

Billie shot imaginary daggers in his direction.

Her mother rose. "Who'd like a nice glass of sangria?"

Giggling, Alicia said, "Me!"

Amy tickled her. "No, but I'd love one."

"I'll have another beer, if you don't mind."

"Billie?" Mom paused in the doorway.

"A small one, thanks." She caught her mom's curious frown.

"Let's go out on the porch. It's such a nice evening." Despite her airy tone, Mom moved with the slowness of one who carried too many burdens.

On the porch swing, Billie took in everything: the scent of newly mown grass, birds swooping to their nests to settle for the evening, their song filling the air. The sinking sun's rays painted brilliant gold and orange streaks across the sky behind the outbuildings. The paint on the house was cracked, and a shutter had come loose. With each passing year, her mother kept up with less and less. She needed help. Billie wished she could give Mom whatever she needed. First, she had to find a way to take care of herself.

* * * *

Much as Jet loved touring, the grind worked against his nerves. At least he'd made it to the same time zone as Billie. For the umpteenth time, he dialed *Strung Out*. If the receptionist put him off again, he'd ask for fucking Everett if he had to.

When he asked for Billie, the girl said, "She no longer works here."

Jet's grip tightened on the cell. "What? Where did she go?"

"Sorry," came her response.

"Do you have her home number?"

"We're not allowed to give that out, sir."

This couldn't be happening. "Can't I speak to someone there who can help me?"

"It's company policy, sir. We can't give out personal information."

"But this is urgent." Did he have to pretend to be dying?

Chalmer, Steve and Kirk approached. "We're up, dude."

The crowd in the stadium chanted, "Jet, Jet, Jet."

Fuck. He powered down the cell. Now what?

Passing Stu in the wings, he grasped his shoulder. "What do you have in Pennsylvania?"

"I'm working on it."

Jet pointed before taking the stage. "Work harder."

* * * *

A few days later, Zinta called, breathless. "Billie."

Out for a walk through the pasture, Billie chuckled. "Did you just run the one-minute mile?"

"Listen to me. Jet called again."

"What do you mean again?" Billie laid a hand against her stomach as it flip-flopped.

"He's called about ten times. Didn't that idiot receptionist call you?"

The reception garbled about every third word, so she took long strides up the hill to improve it. "No. Why didn't you call me?" Ten times?

"I just found out."

Reaching the top of a knoll, she sat and pulled up blades of grass."What did he say? Is he angry?" He must hate her. She ruined his show, then dropped off the map.

"He wanted to talk to you. That's all I know."

"Did anyone give him my number?"

"I don't think they had it, sweetie."

"Did he leave his?" Why hadn't she gotten it? *Because all you had to do before was lean out the window and call his name.*

"No. He said he'd try back. I told the others to tell me ASAP if he calls again."

"Good. Thanks." Her heart pounded. Black stars swirled around her head, made her woozy. She lay back against the hill. "God. I'm actually dizzy."

"Deep breaths, hon. And a dose of faith."

She rubbed her forehead. "What should I do?"

"Nothing to do but wait."

Sure, *now* Zin turned Zen. "Right. He won't call again, anyway."

"If he does, should I give him your number?"

"No! Yes. I don't know. Yes."

"I think the yesses won."

Zin's smile sounded through the phone, but she wouldn't chide her for it. Not today.

"Give him my cell. The reception's awful here. He might not even be able to reach me."

"Making excuses for him already?"

She hugged her knee. "Are you sure he called ten times?"

"I didn't count exactly, no. I rounded."

"Up from two?" Her lame joke fell flat as she clutched the grass, waiting to hear.

"No, from nine or eleven. He's been trying to reach you, Bil."

Her heart hung on to those words with all her strength. "Okay. I can't call him, so I have to wait."

"Right."

"I miss you."

"Are you all right? You sound a bit wonky."

"Too much time on my hands." Wasn't that a song? One she didn't particularly like, if she remembered correctly.

Before leaving to interview a new indie band, Zinta asked Billie when she'd come back to Philly.

Billie couldn't say. Whatever her future held, she was pretty sure Philadelphia didn't figure into it. Then again, she had trouble seeing herself anywhere without Jet.

"When did you turn into a hopeless romantic, Willamina?"

The day you met Jet Trently.

* * * *

Farm chores unfortunately required little thought, so Billie had plenty of time to think whether she fed the chickens, collected eggs, weeded the flower beds, mowed the grass, harvested vegetables or mucked old Mr. T's stall. And every thought centered on Jet. Where was he? What was he doing? Why had he called? Ten times!

Nearly a week passed. She'd gone upstairs in late afternoon to lie down for a minute, and the next thing she knew, her cell buzzed. Groggy, she picked it up from the night table and an unknown number showed in the display. "Hello?"

From what seemed the other side of the world, Jet's voice crackled, "Billie?"

"Jet?" she nearly whispered, then repeated it more loudly, scrambling from bed.

The connection scrambled and broke, and only portions of what he said came through. Hurrying to the window, she opened it and pressed against the screen, hoping to strengthen the signal. "I can't hear you. What?"

Going downstairs would risk cutting the connection altogether, so the best she could do was stay put and listen. From the few words that came through, she pieced together "new songs" and "tour," something about Stu and the band. Finally, the words *tickets* and *mail* came through before she lost him.

With a frustrated howl, she glared at the phone. At least she had his number now. If she only had the courage to use it.

Days later, Billie walked to the mailbox. No quick stroll, with their long lane. When she pulled the envelopes from the box, one addressed to her caught her immediate attention. Inside, a ticket for a concert at Hershey Stadium, along with a note from Jet: *Come see me backstage afterward. Show the guard this pass.* In two weeks, he'd open for the band they'd seen in LA. The concert to which he'd given her a lift in the limo. And on the way back, they'd gotten a close-up of the floor of the limo.

Her breaths came too rapidly. He'd be in central Pennsylvania! Her insides lurched, and she had to grab the mailbox while she emptied the contents of her burning stomach.

She could see him--and find out once and for all whether their relationship had been real or a byproduct of a reality show.

* * * *

Man, his nerves rattled. Jet strummed his guitar to calm himself, but nothing worked.

When Stu came in the trailer, he shot upward. "You sent Billie the ticket, right?"

"Of course."

"And the backstage pass?"

"Yes, Jet." His manager's gaze slid left.

Something didn't fit. "If she doesn't show up..." *So help me God...*

Raising his hands, Stu said, "It won't be my fault. She has everything."

Jet let out a breath. "Okay." Maybe lack of sleep made him doubt. The thought of her in the audience made his palms sweat. She'd hear the songs she inspired. The songs the studio would release.

"You're on in fifteen minutes. Don't keep the good people of Hershey waiting."

He wouldn't dream of it.

* * * *

Billie ransacked the closet trying to find something to wear.

Her mother leaned in the doorway, mouth agape at the clothes strewn everywhere. "What on earth is going on?"

"Nothing looks right." She frowned at herself in the mirror. All her hard work these past few weeks had increased her appetite, but the inches should be decreasing, not the opposite.

Her mother frowned. "Maybe you shouldn't go."

"I have to. Even if it's the last time I see him, I have to see him."

Clucking her tongue, her mother sighed. "All right. But don't say I didn't warn you. And you should eat before you go."

"I can't. I'm too excited." The stadium had vendors if her appetite came back, but she couldn't think about food. How would he react when he saw her? He hadn't said he missed her... she didn't think. The connection had been so awful, he might have said he wanted to throttle her and she wouldn't have known. But why hadn't he called again?

Along the way to Hershey, thoughts tortured her. Cars waiting to get in stacked in line far from the booth to pay for parking. All these people to see Jet! Parking and walking in the thick crowd through the immense parking lot toward the stadium, she bit back tears of happiness, and fear. Once his popularity grew to its former fever pitch, he'd forget her. She'd been part of his life for a few months--and most of those, he couldn't stand her.

What am I doing here? Alone? He'd only sent her one ticket, so he hadn't wanted her to bring anyone else. Doom threatened, but she handed her ticket to the gate guard, anyway. Entering the stadium, two-thirds of the seats had already filled.

The ticket gained her access to the front section, with no assigned seats. People generally ignored seating anyway, and crushed as close to the stage as possible.

Scents of hot dogs, popcorn and seafood hung in the humid air. Her stomach churned. She should have eaten a little something. Even if she had, she'd have still felt as shaky, she told herself. Standing alone, others jostled her, jockeying for a good spot. She should have brought someone. Zinta, preferably, but she was two hours away and had plans tonight, anyway.

* * * *

Stage lights brightened and the house music faded. Jet strode onstage with his guitar, and his heart leapt against his ribs. Like some rookie at his first gig.

Taking his place center stage, he unbuttoned his black jacket over his faded blue tee shirt. *Tonight will be great. You'll see Billie.* The tour had dragged on him at first, but his energy level shot up tonight.

The band waited in place, so he took the mic. "How is everyone tonight? In the sweetest place on earth?"

The mass of bodies crowded close, cheering, waving, reaching. Girls squealed and yelled, "We love you!"

With a chuckle, he thanked the band for allowing him to appear. "Kind of last minute. But we wanted to play you a few songs from the new CD, called *Dylan in Reverse*." He announced it clearly to signal Billie. The title was a tribute to her influence.

Squinting against the spotlight, he searched the crowd. No way would he be able to find her in this mass.

Strumming slowly, he launched into the song he'd played for her. His fingers tripped along the frets with skill and ease. Eyes closed, the grittiness in his voice conveyed intense emotion, and hoped it churned up

Billie's own. He sang as if to her alone in his Malibu studio. The only real part of that whole stint.

He hadn't changed any part of it, but it sounded better somehow. Maybe because he took energy from the audience, and gave over every part of himself to his music.

The guitar strings resonated with the last chord, and he stepped back. The stadium roared with cheers and applause, every body in it straining toward him.

Except the one person he needed.

Where was she?

* * * *

The crowd roared, every person reaching toward Jet. Pressing against Billie. Dizzy, she drew back, fighting against the crowd pushing her toward the stage. Body after body bumped against her back, slammed her shoulder. Finally, she made it to the aisle and gripped the rail, inhaling and exhaling until her breathing eased.

Find the way backstage. Wait for him. She located a security guard, who pointed her outside. Jet's music echoed through the tunnel as she walked, and she wished she'd stayed to listen. She wanted to hear every song. Each one sounded better than the last.

After wandering what felt like an entire circuit around the perimeter, she came across two trailers. Security guards kept people behind steel fences, and several girls pleaded for him to let them inside.

Billie waved to get his attention. "Excuse me. I need to go in please."

"Sorry, lady. No one goes in except the band."

"You don't understand. Jet told me to come."

"I'm sure he did, honey," the guard smirked.

"He told me too," said a girl behind her.

Great. Bimbos in Hershey too.

Billie had to make the guard understand. "Listen." She stopped at the sight of Stu approaching. "Stu!"

He scanned the crowd, narrowed his eyes when he saw her and ascended the few steps.

He must not have heard. "Hey, Stu, it's Billie! Can you tell this guard to let me pass?"

Other girls picked up her cry. "Stu, hey, Stu."

Stu held up a hand. "Sorry, Jet's busy. He'll be out later to sign autographs, all right, girls?"

The bastard. He pointedly ignored her. "Will you at least tell him I'm here?"

He gave her his standard sickly smile. "He doesn't want to see you."

"He sent me a ticket. And this note." She waved his handwritten invitation.

Frowning, he asked the security guard to pass it over. After scanning it, he balled it up and tossed it to the ground. "I sent them to all the media outlets. We're building the buzz on his new release."

Gripping the rail, she wanted to scream at him for destroying it. "Then let me interview him."

"Do you have a media pass?"

His sly tone infuriated her. He knew she wouldn't. That she no longer worked for *Strung Out*. "Stu, I have to see him." She bit back the "please" hanging on her tongue.

"Look, do yourself a favor and go home. Forget about Jet. He's forgotten about you. Julie's seen to that."

Her grip faltered as dread chilled her. "But you arranged that." Didn't he?

"I set it up for her to be on the show. I never asked him to choose her." He shrugged, as if helpless to understand it himself.

Now it made sense. Julie had only wanted fame, but Jet must have wanted Julie. He chose her. He must still be seeing her.

Stu stepped inside and slammed the door.

Tears threatening, Billie didn't have the strength to stand her ground against the younger women. One threw her leg over the fence.

The guards pushed the girl back. "Stay behind the line. You'll have to wait for your autograph. You too," he said to Billie.

"I didn't come here for an autograph," she blubbered.

He rolled his eyes. "Whatever."

Stumbling backward, she struggled to make sense of everything Stu said, and everything that had happened. None of it fit.

From the stage, Jet announced the next song, "a little Jamaican flavor for your chocolate." People whistled and clapped, and he strummed the reggae tune and sang, "*I like what I like, ain't no rhyme or reason.*"

"Damn." The song she'd helped him write. Billie half-laughed, half-cried at hearing it. She'd meant something, if only to his music.

What a fool she'd been. Trying to catch his attention in that crush of people, waving like a teeny-bopper. Coming here in the first place.

If only she could go back to that day, back to his house. She should never have left without talking to him, saying goodbye. *Too late now, Willamina.*

Unable to stand any more, she rushed down the path to the parking lot, tears streaming down her face. When she reached her car, she turned up a local radio station to blot out his voice from the concert, from her mind. Her crying subsided after a few miles until the DJ spoke of Jet playing in Hershey. "After a few commercials, we'll play Jet's first CD without interruption."

Groaning loudly, she punched at the radio buttons, settling on a hard rock station. They wouldn't play Jet's songs.

The announcer said, "I'm hearing good buzz about tonight's concert. Jet made a surprise appearance and opened for a new band, then hung around to play a set with them. Incredible. Jet's back with new material, and sounding good. We'll keep you posted on the latest--"

"No." Billie keyed in the next station. "You will not keep me posted." Her head swirled with questions. Someone lied, obviously. But who?

The disc jockey chuckled. "When your girlfriend hints about going ring shopping, I like to play this little ditty. Seems to work for Jet." The speakers blared Jet singing, "*I ain't your man; no, baby, not the one you're looking for.*"

"It's a radio conspiracy!" Anger dissipated her tears. What had he said about the universe giving you things when you're ready for them? "Well, it's giving me a hell of a clue now, isn't it?" She blew her nose and focused on the road ahead--the dark, empty road.

Twenty minutes from home, her cell buzzed.

Zinta said, "I couldn't wait to find out. Are you there? How's it going?"

Going, going, gone. "I'm on my way home."

"No."

"Apparently Stu sent the tickets." Saying it helped harden her heart.

"That doesn't make sense."

"Sure, it does. He wanted maximum coverage, and I happened to be on the list."

"You can't be serious. He sounded so anxious to see you again."

"I'm not surprised. His career's on the upswing. Mine's at rock bottom. Ironic, huh?" Using his words made her break into tears.

"Oh, sweetie, don't cry."

"Sorry. I don't know what's wrong with me. I've been so emotional. My immune system's off. Too much stress, I guess."

Zin faded. "What? I'm losing you."

Zinta wasn't the only one. "I'll call you tomorrow." Billie clicked off her phone, then the radio, and drove the rest of the way in sweet silence.

Arriving home, Mom came out to the kitchen. "You're home early."

"Yeah. I didn't stay." She poured a glass of milk.

"Are you all right?"

"No. I'm exhausted. I think I must have a bug or something."

Her mom eyed her. "You're tired. And emotional. And sick early in the day. Could it be a nine-month bug?"

Billie collapsed onto a chair. "No. I mean, yes, but… God. No."

Mom squeezed her shoulder. "We'll take a trip to the pharmacy tomorrow, hmm? Then go from there."

Go from there? To where?

"Don't stay up too late." Mom trudged to her bedroom at the back of the house.

"Goodnight." Billie went upstairs and lay in bed, fingers tracing her belly. A baby? Excitement and fear made her queasy. She could do it alone, if needed. She'd freelance from home. Writing, editing, blogging. Whatever it took. She'd take care of the baby and herself.

* * * *

What a night. Jet's opening act went so well, the headlining band asked them to return to the stage for a few songs. He nearly burst with the pressure of being forced to wait. What if she left again?

Afterward, he strode to the trailer, intent on leaving.

Stu grabbed his jacket sleeve. "The fans, man. Give them some love." He inclined his head toward the girls leaning over the gate, reaching for him.

Shit. He plastered on a smile and rushed through signing autographs. His smile faded after about the thirtieth photo, the girl snapping gum with her cheek pressed to his. "Sorry folks, gotta go."

Inside the trailer, reporters waited.

"You're kidding." He turned to Stu.

Stu shrugged. "Ride the wave, baby. You're at the top. If you blow them off, you won't stay there long."

Through clenched teeth, he muttered, "Fuck." Stu was right. His life hadn't been his own in too long. He blew a breath and forced a pleasant expression. "Who's first?"

An hour later, he'd had enough. "I need a car."

"We have no car."

No more stumbling blocks. He turned to the crew. "Anyone have a car I can borrow? There's a grand in it for you."

A roadie rushed forth. "You can use mine. It's not fancy or anything, but it'll get you there."

"That's exactly what I need then. Where is it?"

The guy led him out to the parking lot. Jet signed a few more autographs as he walked. When the roadie stopped at a beat-up compact, his hopes fell. "This?"

With a sheepish shrug, the guy ran a loving hand along its door. "Yeah, it's a great car."

Shaking his head, Jet blew out a breath. Maybe he should take a taxi. But this guy looked like he needed the money. Hell, he needed a new car. "Gimme the keys."

Grinning, the roadie dug them from his pocket. "It turns over a little rough but once it's going, it runs great."

The engine chugged to life, and dread washed over Jet. "You're sure it won't leave me stranded?" Bad enough he had no idea where the hell these back roads could end up. No GPS, either.

"I'm tellin' you, it's cherry."

He couldn't help but laugh. *Cherry* wouldn't have been his description. "All right. If you're right, I'll give you two grand. If you promise to put it toward a new car." He rumbled out of the parking lot. At least he'd thought ahead to Google map her address from here. Turning onto Hershey Park Drive, he floored it, and it backfired. "God, help me."

* * * *

Hours passed, drifting in and out of sleep, then birds twittered. Light edged the horizon. Headlights swung up the driveway. A car door slammed, and someone banged on the front door.

Creeping downstairs, she peeked out the window. Her heart fluttered.

Jet stood on the porch. He knocked again.

She yanked open the door. "Jet."

His cheeks appeared flushed, his eyes alight as he looked her over. He spoke in a rush. "I've been driving around this damn countryside all night looking for you. What kind of a place is Berrysburg? There's no town, no landmarks. You should have warned me you lived near a town named Pillow."

She couldn't tell if his words were rushed by excitement, irritation or nervousness. "You came here to yell at me for living in the country?"

"I'd hoped to see you at the concert tonight." His gaze swept over her.

She tugged her tee shirt down over her drawstring pants, conscious of the few pounds she'd gained. Her head swirled, followed by her belly. She couldn't let him lead her on again. "Look, you should leave. Go back to Julie."

Shifting his feet, he moved closer. "Julie? What are you talking about?"

"The girl you want so badly. Is she waiting in the car?" Her mouth puckered. *No. You will not cry in front of him. And where the hell did he get that junker?*

His brows twitched together. "No. She's on her way to New York."

And he thought he'd been lost--if someone asked right now, she couldn't say which direction was up. "Do you have a concert there?"

He let out a sharp breath. "I'm completely confused. I didn't come here to talk about Julie."

"Are all men crazy? Or do you all think women are crazy enough to put up with your crap? First Everett, now you. You make it really difficult to tell the difference between real and unreal."

He glared and stepped closer. "You're back with Everett? Is that why didn't you come tonight?"

"No. I went to the concert." She hugged herself. "I'm sorry to disappoint you, but I won't be writing about it."

"I don't care about that. I wanted to see you. Why do you think I asked you to come backstage?"

A laugh escaped. "To humiliate me?"

"What?"

Had he taken acting lessons? He seemed sincerely surprised. "They wouldn't let me backstage."

His brows furrowed. "Who wouldn't?"

"The guard. And Stu. He said he sent tickets to all the reporters, and I could wait for an autograph if I wanted. He threw away your note. If it was your note, and not some photocopy sent to all the media outlets like he said."

"That son of a bitch." Whipping out his cell, he dialed, strode off the porch into the yard. The conversation lasted less than a minute, building in intensity until he signed off with, "You're fired!"

Walking back, he appeared more relaxed. "I should have done that years ago."

"You fired him? But things are finally going well."

He winced. "No thanks to him."

"What about the tour?"

His voice softened. "Forget the tour."

Had he gone insane? "No. Everything you wanted, all you've worked for, is within reach, and you're willing to throw it all away?" She couldn't let him.

"I don't need Stu. I had to fight him every step of the way."

"Right. Like you fought him about Julie."

"Stop bringing up Julie! If you want to know the truth, yes, I intentionally let Julie stay until the final show."

She threw up her hands. "Finally. The truth."

"I let her stay so I could eliminate the others. I knew Julie didn't care about me. And I care nothing about her."

"Now I'm confused." More than ever.

"Why do you think I drove all night to see you?"

"I…" Why had he?

He took hold of her shoulders. "After I met you, it didn't matter who any of them were. Don't you see?"

She stepped back, afraid to hear whatever he was about to say. Unable to breathe until he said it.

Gathering her in his arms, he said softly, "I want you. No one else. I can't sleep, I can't eat… When I'm not with you, I feel hollow inside. Only you can fill me with what I need." After searching her face, he pressed his lips to hers.

She gave herself over to it, let herself drown in his kiss. She might have heard her mother's footsteps in the hall, but couldn't let go, couldn't risk him disappearing.

His lips brushed along her cheek, to her ear. "I've missed you so much. There's so much I need to tell you."

Stiffening, she remembered. She had a lot to tell him too. He wouldn't want her once he learned her news. "This can't work." If he didn't hate her before, he would after hearing.

* * * *

Rocking her, Jet crouched to her eye level. "Of course it can. It's perfect now." He had her in his arms, and wasn't about to let go.

"No, we're in opposite places."

"Aren't you the one who said: It's not easy but when you care so much, invest so much of yourself, it makes it all worth the effort?" Those had been her words. He'd thought about them every day since hearing them.

He cupped her jaw. "I'm emotionally invested. Completely. I'm crazy about you."

Tears welled, and she sniffed. "Jet--"

No more pretending. "Jerry. Call me Jerry." His real name.

Nodding, she whispered, "Jerry."

"No fair. You never told me yours." He frowned in an attempt to appear serious, but couldn't hold back a grin. He'd wondered for months.

"Willamina." She heaved a dejected sigh.

Somehow, hearing her name filled him with joy. He rocked her in his arms. "That's cute. Jerry and Willamina. A little long for the answering machine, but…"

She clutched his jacket. "I can't… This isn't--"

"Real? It's more real than anything I've ever known, Billie." He kissed her again. "Can we take a walk? So we don't keep your mom awake?"

Nodding, Billie grabbed her jacket and stepped into her flip-flops.

Light rimmed the horizon, red and orange and pink clouds ablaze.

"Red sky at morning…" she let the sentence drift.

"Sailors take warning," he finished. "Gotta expect some rocky seas, babe." Nothing they couldn't weather together.

She shivered, a tear streaked her cheek.

He pulled her to him. "Hey, don't cry. It's going to work out. You'll see."

"I can't," she blubbered.

"What's wrong? You need to stay and feed the chickens?" he joked.

"I wish I could stay. Mom's selling. She can't take care of it all."

Glancing around, he could have whooped. "Perfect." He couldn't have picked a better setting.

"How is that perfect?" Irritation seemed to prick her completely awake.

He linked his arms around her. "I'll buy it."

She blurted, "You don't know how much she wants."

"Doesn't matter. I have some money put away." He knew it would come in handy.

"But she'll hate you for it."

Was she testing him? Or really trying to drive him away? "Nah. I'll let her live here. I'll build a little cabin, maybe an A-frame. How many acres?"

"A few hundred."

He shrugged. "See? She'll never even have to see me. Unless she wants to invite us for pot roast." It really did sound perfect. So why did she look so miserable?

* * * *

"Stop it." Struggling from his embrace, Billie couldn't reconcile Jet with Jerry.

"Why? I want to be with you, Billie. Don't tell me you don't want that too."

"I don't know. It's happening too fast." *Tell him you love him, you idiot!*

His shoulders slumped. "Don't make excuses. If you don't love me, say so. If you're afraid it's too much work, then I'm going to fight you on that. I've been looking for you my whole life. We're good together. Good for each other."

"That's what scares me." She'd never known anyone who understood her way of thinking before she voiced her thoughts.

He ran his hands along her sleeves. "Tell you what. Whenever it scares you, you come to me. I'll hold you until you're not afraid anymore."

After she told him what she needed to say, he might be the frightened one. She had to tell him. No, she'd work up to it. "When I was a little girl, I'd come out here to my tree house whenever the world felt too big and crazy."

"Where was it?"

"Over there."

"I'll build you a new one. Big enough for two. They make them for adults now. Did you know that?"

Oh God. Her litmus test. Had Zinta clued him in? Or did he really read the real Willamina?

Cupping her palm to his cheek, she asked, "Are you sure you're for real?"

"I only feel real when I'm with you."

"I know. Me too." Before she fell into his arms again, she had to tell him. "But I have another reality check for you. A big one."

"Hit me."

Just say it and be done with it. "There's a good chance... I mean, I think I am... pregnant."

His eyes widened, his mouth agape. He stammered, "Are you sure?"

"No. But I'll find out tomorrow. Today, I guess." In a few hours. She gulped hard. "Mom's taking me for a test."

"I'll take you."

Her jaw quivered. He might want her to get an abortion. "If I am, I'm keeping it. No matter what."

He laughed and hugged her. A tear streaked his cheek. "We both will. It's perfect."

"Three 'perfects' in one morning."

"Three. Yeah." He kissed her. "When can we go? Soon?"

She sniffed. "It's probably about six. The pharmacy opens at nine."

"A few hours. In the meantime, we can talk to your mom."

"Or maybe we could sleep." She wanted to nestle into him, feel his arms around him. And he'd been up all night. He needed to rest.

"Yeah."

They walked back to the house, snuck inside. The bed creaked when she climbed in. He slipped off his jacket and shoes and pants, climbed in beside her.

She fell asleep, and awakened next to him. *It wasn't a dream.* Oh, she had to pee, and felt parched. As much as she'd rather lie in his arms, she rose quietly and crept out, and then downstairs.

Her mom sat at the kitchen table. "I didn't know we were expecting a guest."

"Sorry, I didn't know either. I really have to use the bathroom."

"First check the bag on the counter."

A pharmacy bag. "You went to town?" Grabbing the bag, she rushed to the bathroom and ripped open the package. Reading as fast as she could, she followed the instructions.

Holding the meter, she opened the door.

Her mom stiffened, then blinked back tears. Her mom always read her like an open book.

A happy sob escaped. She had to tell Jet. Jerry. She'd have to get used to calling him that.

Snores sounded from the bed. She sat on the edge and watched him. He'd driven all night looking for her. But he'd found more than her. She laid a hand on his arm.

* * * *

At her touch, his eyes fluttered open, and he struggled up to an elbow. "Is it time to go?"

She held up the meter. "It's a plus."

He glanced at it. "Plus? One?" As sure as if all the oxygen had been sucked from the room, his head swirled.

She grinned. "At least."

With a whoop, he hugged her, kissed her, pulled her down to the pillow, smoothed her hair. "I love you, Billie."

"This is too good to be real."

"It's just the start." He pressed his lips to hers in the most perfect kiss he'd ever had.

He'd been right. The universe had waited to give them everything they wanted. And now he was ready for it. All of it.

Chapter 14

The pearl-embroidered satin gown glowed in the late afternoon sunlight filtering through Billie's bedroom curtain. "Do I look all right?"

Zinta's smile contorted as her eyes welled. "You look beautiful."

She held a hand to her stomach. "Not too much?"

"The baby bump's hardly noticeable. It's cute, in fact. You two are so cute, you make me want to puke. If he doted on you any more..." Zin hung out her tongue.

"I know. He's been incredible." Hardly leaving her side for the past month, since he'd arrived. When he left the farm, he brought Billie along. To New York to meet with Rob Hershey, his new manager, a Jersey guy who'd followed Jet's career since the beginning. To Nashville for his first solo gig, playing with Neil Young, Springsteen and John Mellencamp to raise money for troubled American families. And to LA to meet with Chalmer, Kirk, Marlin and Steve to discuss the possibility of touring.

"I take it as a good sign the rest of the boys are here today?" Zin peered over Billie's shoulder, adjusting her pearl headpiece with a short tulle train.

"Their meeting went really well. I'm hoping they'll finally make amends, concentrate on making great music instead of fighting." She pointedly glanced at Zin. "No interviews today. Any other day, but not today."

Zin held up her hands. "I promise. But a full-blown reunion would mean touring for Jet."

"I know. But it's what he loves. And what he does--I'd never stand in the way of that."

"You're lucky. You know he'll rush home as soon as he can."

The door opened, and her mom leaned in. "How's it going? Need anything? Something to drink?" As if anyone could hear, she murmured,

"I make a mean mimosa. Not for you," she said to Billie. "Yours will be plain orange juice."

Zinta's eyes widened. "A mimosa would be wonderful. Thank you."

Halting, Billie's mom gazed at her, then wrapped her arms around her. "Gorgeous, Willamina."

"Thanks, Mom."

"Ooo, wait--there's a keeper." Zin grabbed her digital and captured them cheek to cheek, glowing with happiness.

"I'll be right back." Mom exited.

Zinta fussed with the gown. "I love your mom. She's so cool."

"She's been great. Having Jerry buy her farm and let her stay here made her so happy. And she loves him too. Sometimes I think she loves him more than me."

"Never. I bet she can't wait to be a grandmom, though."

"I hope the house is finished by then. Not an actual tree house--but three stories, and lots of windows and surrounded by trees, so it's like a grown-up playhouse."

Zinta paused to grin. "You're living the dream, kid."

"I know." It still felt surreal. But every day, waking up in bed with Jerry sleeping beside her, reminded her. "Anyway, being near Mom will be helpful when he's on tour too. She offered to keep the baby if I wanted to meet him overnight sometimes."

"You got the fairy-tale package. I'm so happy for you."

A breathy laugh escaped. Billie woke up with that same thought every morning.

Mom returned with mimosas. "You'll have to drink up. They're almost ready for you."

Zinta arched her brows. "Are you ready?"

"Yes." Despite the whirlwind confusion of it all, she couldn't wait. "Are you?"

"Absolutely." Zin kissed Billie's cheek. "See you out there." Humming, she grabbed her champagne glass and floated to the door.

Billie turned. "Zin!"

"What?" Zinta's smile faded, replaced with worry.

"I didn't tell you how beautiful you look."

Arms high, Zin twirled, her short red satin dress clinging to every curve. "Thank you. I do have good taste in bridesmaid dresses." She winked and slipped out the door. Her singsong voice echoed down the stairs. "Don't keep us waiting."

"No." She sat on the bed and gazed around her childhood bedroom. The room she'd shared with Jerry for six weeks. In the haze of early morning, his handsome face on the pillow seemed a dream. But then he'd awaken, see her and smile. Pull her to him. The memory drew her outside. No, she wouldn't keep him waiting. Or herself.

When she went out the kitchen door, Tom hastily straightened from where he leaned on the banister. "You look beautiful, sis." He held out his arm.

She linked her arm in his. "You clean up pretty nice yourself."

Chalmer, Steve, Marlin and Kirk struck up an electrified version of "Here Comes the Bride."

Billie and Tom descended the few steps to the white vinyl path strewn with rose petals. About ninety people rose from their chairs on either side of the carpeting.

At the end of the path, beneath the wide flower-garlanded archway, waited Jerry. Stunning in his tux, his eyes bright as he watched them approach, Adam's apple bobbing when he gulped.

He seemed nervous. A good sign. He also appeared eager. And happy. Great signs.

When he returned her smile, warmth flushed through her. She couldn't wait to begin the rest of her life with him.

* * * *

As she approached, Jet shifted his stance to prevent his legs from giving out. More fucking nervous than he'd been in his life. Meeting her gaze, he calmed. He'd never seen anyone so beautiful, glowing with happiness.

She and Tom passed the final row when the whir of a helicopter sounded beyond the trees. Not one but three approached in a line and circled over.

His euphoria deflated. "No." Never would a camera follow the intimate details of their life. They'd agreed.

She hurried to him. "Oh no! We didn't want any media."

His openmouthed surprise turned to burning anger. "Someone must've found out and leaked it. I'm so sorry."

"It's not your fault." She laid a hand on his chest. "Let's give them a nice shot. Maybe they'll leave. Kiss me."

Could he get any luckier? She knew cameras would follow them everywhere from now on. "Gladly." Encircling his arms around her, he pressed his lips to hers. For a moment, he forgot about the helicopters, and the family and friends who now pointed their cameras, capturing the moment.

Easing away, he murmured, "I love you."

The helicopters hovered lower, long-range lenses pointed out.

"I love you too." Her declaration of love ended in a squeal as her veil lifted, and the whirring blades sent a rush of wind that flattened the flowers, riffled his hair. Too much. It had to end. Now.

He called to his new manager. "Can you do something about them?"

Rob interrupted his cell phone call. "I reached a few people. They're calling the dogs off now."

Zinta leaned over Billie's shoulder. "I really like your new manager, Jerry."

Jerry grinned. "He's a good guy. I hear he likes you too." He'd listened to it all morning.

"Yes. The rehearsal dinner was a blast. I'm looking forward to the reception too."

Rob glanced up and winked at Zinta.

Delight in her eyes, Billie gasped. "You didn't tell me."

Zin smoothed her hair. "You've had your hands full. And I didn't want to jinx it. Do I look all right? Freakin' paparazzi." Zin appeared nervous enough to be serious.

"Beautiful." Billie beamed at her friend.

The helicopters lifted away one by one and disappeared over the tree tops.

Jerry took her hand. "Sorry about that. But it's bound to happen."

She sighed. "Pseudo reality will intrude, I suppose."

He rested his forehead against hers. "Never as good as our reality."

"They'll have to be content with wild speculation."

He ran his hands across her back. "You know what Bonnie Raitt says."

"Oh yeah. We'll give 'em something to talk about." Smiling, she pressed her lips to his.

Aware of every moment, the short ceremony etched in his memory. Jerry slid a platinum band on her ring finger. When she slipped the ring on his, he grasped her hand, eyes sparkling as he drew her close, not waiting for the minister to finish proclaiming them married.

Two long portable canopies shielded the buffet from the late day sun. After dinner, with the blue sky deepening, the band took up their instruments.

Jet joined them for a Rolling Stones song. When he sang about being in love, he finally felt the emotion in the lyrics. Gazing at Billie, he sang, "*Keep me happy.*" He pulled the guitar strap over his head. "Ah, hell. Take over, Chalmer. I have to dance with my wife."

Chalmer picked up the tune and Jerry whisked Billie into his arms. Laughing, she swayed her hips in time with him, in their own rhythm. When the song ended, Billie called to Chalmer. "I have a request."

"Anything."

She smiled at Jet. "It's a Paul McCartney song."

"I think I know which one." Chalmer muttered to the band, and they launched into "Jet." Chalmer jogged over and shoved the cordless mic in her hand. "You should sing this one."

Wide-eyed, Billie watched Chalmer return to the band, then turned to Jerry. "He's right. I need to sing these lyrics."

He sent her off with a kiss. Faking the ones she couldn't remember, she knew the most important lines. Jerry beamed as Billie sang to him about wanting Jet to always love her. He sang along, replacing "Jet" with "Billie."

When she finished, she rushed to him. Catching her in his arms, he kissed her, thinking no one could have scripted it better.

Meet the Author

Cate Masters has made beautiful central Pennsylvania her home for the past 20 years, but she'll always be a Jersey girl at heart. A lover of all great writing, she aspires to entertain and enthrall with her own stories. Music has always had special meaning to Cate, so she loves to incorporate it into her books. Most days, she can be found in her lair, concocting a magical brew of contemporary, historical, fantasy/paranormal stories with her cat Chairman Maiow and dog Lily as company. Look for her at www.catemasters.com, http://catemasters.blogspot.com, and in strange nooks and far-flung corners of the web. Cate loves to hear from readers. Email her at: cate.masters@gmail.com

Cate's Website:
www.catemasters.com
Reader email:
Cate.masters@gmail.com